THE ILLUSIONISTS

LAURE EVE

HOT
KEY
BOOKS

First published in Great Britain in 2014 by Hot Key Books
Northburgh House, 10 Northburgh Street, London EC1V 0AT

A CIP catalogue record for this book is available from the British Library.

ISBN: 978-1-4714-0260-9

1

This book is typeset in 10.5 Berling LT Std using Atomik ePublisher

Printed and bound by Clays Ltd, St Ives Plc

Hot Key Books supports the Forest Stewardship Council (FSC),
the leading international forest certification organisation, and is
committed to printing only on Greenpeace-approved FSC-certified paper.

www.hotkeybooks.com

Hot Key Books is part of the Bonnier Publishing Group
www.bonnierpublishing.com

THE ILLUSIONISTS

For Ioannis
My everything

PART ONE

PART ONE

CHAPTER 1

WORLD

RUE

In her dream, Rue runs.

The dream is a game in a castle, but more than a game; and if Rue loses, she will die. The humming dread that drenches the walls of this place makes her neck clench and she can taste it, like blood on her tongue.

This place is death and the game is that they have to survive it.

The floor is made of cracked, uneven stone slabs, which makes her footfall echo so loudly, each separate noise a cacophony that she is sure will bring every horror this place has to offer right to her, pouncing on her like a ragdoll and tearing her to strips that they can gobble down.

She comes to an enormous king of a door that stretches up into the rafters. When she touches the handle, it opens easily, despite its size. The room beyond is smaller than she expected, its floor made up of uneven slabs that slope steadily down towards a hole in the centre of the room. Like a wound it gapes, coloured in blackness. The floor slabs disappear into it as if they are being sucked inside.

There is only the smallest ledge of slabs up against the walls that don't slope downwards. She has a feeling that if she steps on any one of the sloping slabs, she will slide helplessly towards the crevasse and disappear into it forever.

Rue knows what lives in the crevasse. She can feel it in her bones.

She steps into the room. Her feet slide and slip. She shuffles along. The sense of danger grows so fast she can imagine very strongly that whatever lives in the crevasse is skittering, climbing up the sides of its hole, coming closer to the source of that smell – the smell of her and of human meat. She is halfway across the room. If she doesn't hurry, she will die. Someone enters the room behind her. Rue screams a warning over her shoulder.

Don't come in! Don't come in! Find another way around!

She knows the newcomer has put a foot on the first slab.

She can see it shifting its bulk from side to side as it heaves itself up the sides of the crevasse. The smell of meat is stronger now. Double the strength.

She makes it to the other side and wrenches open the door there. The newcomer is halfway across. Something slithers out from the blackness of the hole in the middle of the ground. Broken pieces of slab tremble and shift. It moves horribly fast, scrabbling upwards in a massive rush.

Don't come in! Rue screams.

The newcomer looks up, her mouth hanging open in terror. She has long, thin, dark hair, which shivers wildly around her shoulders as she looks rapidly between Rue and the hole, again and again.

I told you, Rue says, her voice clipped and gasping. *I TOLD YOU NOT TO CO—*

Rue woke, fighting.

It was too hard to breathe. The screaming had taken away her air.

It took a while to realise that wherever that place had been, she wasn't there any more; she was here, where things were real, and normal, and safe. The overwhelming sense of relief she felt brought tears to her eyes.

Underneath it there was the other emotion that she confessed to no one; the one that made her want to go back into the dream, nightmarish though it had been. A slick, slimy kind of fascination with the place she had visited. A desire to know more about it.

It was the second time recently that she had dreamed of that strange castle, each dream in a different room, but always with that sense of sick-hearted fear to it. The whole place was wrong, so why did she want to go back there? Was it a real place? A dream caused by her Talent? Or was it something she had made up? She wasn't skilled enough to tell.

That girl. She was new this time. Rue didn't know who she was or if she was real – a face that she had seen somewhere before, pulled from the back drawers of her mind and slotted into the dream. Just some girl.

7

Since she was little Rue could remember having dreams of real places she could not possibly know of but visited nightly, through no will of her own. Talent made you travel in your dreams, spy on people and places with your mind – and without them ever knowing you were there.

And if you were freakishly Talented, it also meant you could physically Jump your entire body, stripping away everything between you and somewhere else six feet or even a thousand miles away; treating distance and physics as a second's inconvenience.

Rue couldn't Jump yet, or at least not without help. She couldn't even control where she visited in her dreams; it happened randomly and without her input. She felt helpless, but there was no denying the thrill that rippled through her as she went to bed each night. Where would her mind take her? Would she learn a great, secret truth?

She stretched, feeling her back press satisfyingly into the bed, and turned on her side to switch off the bed comforter, which she managed on the third attempt. Wren had shown her how to do it but she still kept getting it wrong. Although the bed comforter mimicked the warmth and weight of sheets, it wasn't real in the same sense.

Rue lay, thinking.

The small room around her was a dull, metallic grey. The walls were grey. The floor was a soft, fuzzy grey. The bed she lay on was grey. The ceiling was actually white – Wren had told her why it was a different colour, but she couldn't quite remember the reason. Something about how Life worked when you looked upwards. There was a lot from the last few days that she couldn't quite remember. Strangeness upon excitement had taken its toll.

Rue had come to realise that many of her reactions to things were considered, by general people, to be odd. It had taken a while as a child, but eventually she had understood why people pulled faces when she said or did certain things. So finding out that she had a mysterious, rare ability like the Talent had failed to surprise her one bit. Of course she did. It explained everything. It explained the fascinating, frightening dreams she had that were rich and thick as velvet and felt so real it was like living another life while she slept. It explained her constant itch, the craving she had to be away from here, wherever here was. To be doing extraordinary things.

So being recruited to train in the Talent at Angle Tar's premiere university seemed obvious to her. Why have such a skill if it was never to be used? She had gone willingly, leaving her old life of routine and learning and banality behind, the dull ticking of hours and days and weeks.

And everything would have been fine if she hadn't met White.

When she thought about White, her former tutor, she felt a burst of pain, and humiliation, and a horrible, embarrassing, overwhelming desire to be near him. To have him think well of her.

Want her.

But he didn't want her. He probably, all things considered, hated her. He thought she was a rude, stupid girl. Rue knew he was a liar. She had pushed, and she had broken something past repair, and part of her was glad, because if there was one

9

thing guaranteed to make her lose her mind in rage, it was being lied to. It had happened too many times in the recent past. It would not happen again.

So she had left Angle Tar, her home, and come with Wren to World. She hadn't seen it as treason at first, but now she'd had time to think, she knew that Angle Tar probably would. It was illegal for Angle Tarain citizens to travel outside the country. Probably to keep them ignorant of how amazing it was everywhere else, Rue decided. But the point was that she had crossed a very thick, unyielding line.

Maybe, just maybe, that meant she could never go back.

And maybe you'll never see him again, said a small, treacherous voice in her mind.

Rue's reasons for leaving had seemed so clear at the time. The sense of betrayal at discovering the truth about the world outside Angle Tar, and the awful inequality within it, had left her breathless and impulsive. And now she'd left everything she'd ever known behind. No one knew her here in World. No one cared for her here. But she had to make it work. She could leave no space in her head for dwelling on the past. She was already sick of waking up to that chest ache every morning as the memories of what had happened punished her again. She had to put it all away.

When she had come out of the Jump from Angle Tar with Wren that first night, head spinning, she noticed something odd about the light. Wren held her in his arms until the nausea passed and she could stand up straight. They stood on what was clearly a street, though it was starker and cleaner than any in Angle Tar. The buildings were flat and strangely angular, made of smooth, colourless surfaces. The street itself was so wide, a grand and airy stretch of space. Nothing like the tiny, penned cobble mazes of Capital City.

And all the while she looked around for a source of light, but there were no street lamps to be seen. When she glanced up into the sky, she couldn't see the moon, despite the fact that there were no discernible clouds. But she could still *see*. It was dark, like it should be at night, but then it wasn't, somehow.

Wren was smiling. 'It's strange,' he said. 'I know it. But you're not seeing World how everyone else sees World. This is just the platform for World.'

'The what?'

'The platform, the basic "real" version. When you jack into Life, you'll see it very differently. You'll see a sky filled with stars, and a moon. Over there, those long stretches of ground with nothing on them? In Life they're covered in trees. The buildings here, look. To you they're just blank, right? Well in Life, that one is covered in a ten-foot-high mural of a rabbit. And that one, there, it has an advert for *Lost in Time* – it's a Life game. It's got a train exploding on it. I mean, the train is actually exploding, right now.'

He threw his hands wide, and Rue looked around, fascinated. There were no trees anywhere. And there was nothing on those buildings. Nothing at all. But she could almost believe there was, if she watched him.

'I'll be honest with you. Out of Life, it's pretty dull,' said Wren. 'They whine about the sociological problems Life causes, but then they offer us the platform as an alternative. So our choice is trees and beauty and colour and amazing, *amazing*

11

things. Or this grey nothing of the real. Like a dull, blank canvas. It's astonishing that they think that's actually a choice.'

An uneasy frustration crept over her. She couldn't see what he saw. She couldn't understand this place yet. She needed to know how it worked.

'Come, Rue mine,' he said, putting his arm about her shoulders. 'We'll take you home.'

She felt immense relief, and sank into his side as they walked.

'Where am I to stay?' she said.

'With me, of course.'

She stopped in surprise.

'It isn't like Angle Tar, Rue. There's no oddness involved in men and women of age living together without being married. And I live with many people; it won't just be us. You'll see.'

Wren's building looked just like every other building around it – it was a wonder he could pick it out. It was enormous, too; more like the tall houses in Capital City back home, which held twenty or thirty different families inside them.

'It smells funny here,' said Rue, sniffing the outside air.

'No, it doesn't smell of anything. It's a relief after the stench of Capital, right?' said Wren.

She inhaled deeply. That was what had been confusing her. There was no smell.

Wren walked up to what was presumably the main entrance, though the door looked just like any number of the others set into the wall that faced them. He pressed his face close to a flat, black decoration at head height.

'What are you looking at?' said Rue.

There was a series of quick beeps, a little like the noise of droning bees, thought Rue, cut up into slices. Wren leaned back. The door opened smoothly, disappearing into the wall rather than swinging in or outwards.

'It's like a key,' Wren explained. 'Only you use your eye.'

'You use your *eye* as a key?'

'We'll have to get you registered to the building. Until you are, we won't be able to put your eye pattern on the door key.'

Rue was fascinated. Using your eye to open doors! She tried to swallow her nervousness at this strange culture and its magical way of living, tried instead to concentrate on the incredible things she knew it offered her.

'Where's the box? You said you had one,' she said, as they walked through a corridor coloured a uniform grey. He had promised her another world in that box, and she had not forgotten.

'Patience, Rue,' said Wren. 'We'll get to it. It's in my room.'

His room had turned out to be quite ordinary. The box he had shown her before – or one like it – was there, on a thin side table. She'd stared at it, but it was a plain thing and gave up no secrets.

He had insisted she sleep for a while. Though she protested vigorously, it turned out that once she lay down, sleep overtook her almost at once. She didn't remember if he'd stayed with her or not. She hoped that he had, at least for a little while.

She shifted on the bed. She had her own room now, just down the corridor from Wren's, though she hadn't yet stopped feeling like a visitor. It was warm in here, but she was much like a cat – a room couldn't be too hot. She had watched Wren touch the wall to control the temperature but was too nervous to try it herself until she learned the skill of it. Wren called it technology, which was, she supposed, their word for magic.

Magic was so commonplace here that it had infiltrated every part of everyone's lives. They had magic devices set into walls that made food. There was no skill or understanding to it – you asked for and you got. It was so normal that it had become boring for them. Would it become boring for her, the longer she stayed here? Wren thought so, but Rue didn't see how that was possible.

There was a lot she didn't understand, and Wren didn't seem able to tell her how things worked. Where, for example, did the food come from? Was the food device like an ordering service? Were there vast kitchens underground beneath every block of houses in the district they lived in, which received your order and then sent it up by pulley? But how could that be, because the food arrived hot if you wanted it to, and how could they possibly know what you were going to order beforehand, and have it ready to go when you ordered it?

She knew these were stupid, childish questions, so she never voiced them; but when she quizzed Wren about the food devices, he spouted a lot of words that didn't translate into Angle Tarain and then became annoyed with her if she pressed.

That was another thing that had become very clear on coming here. She needed to learn the language they spoke in World, as quickly as she could. Then she could talk to some of the other people who lived in the house with them. They wouldn't seem so strange and distant from her if she could only talk to them. Wren had said there was a quick way for her to learn the language but it took time to set up, so she had held tightly onto her patience and waited, meanwhile spending every day surrounded by people who chatted and talked with him and not her for hours and hours while she sat by his side, bored and trying hard not to show it.

In order to learn World, Rue had to jack in, as Wren kept calling it, to Life – that other world inside the box that teased her with its squat, ordinary presence on his desk. Although he had a box, it was not a common thing to be in possession of one, apparently; everyone else could access Life whenever and wherever they were through an implant – a tiny metallic device that lived inside them. The idea of something hard and cold like that inside her made her shiver, but no one here seemed to give it a second's thought.

She wondered idly if she should get up and try to find Wren. She had no idea what time it was. Would he even be here?

Then she realised she was hungry, and that decided it.

She came out of her room. Much like Red House, her old university living quarters, everyone in this building lived in separate rooms but shared the 'communals' – the kitchen, bathrooms and the social room, where people ate and held parties. But the doors all looked the same, and everything was exact and placed just so; it made her shrink back from imposing herself so much on this place as to dare to move around in it as if she belonged here.

She pressed on a random door, hoping it would open. It did, and beyond it, to her relief, was the social room. Two people looked up as she came in. Neither was Wren, though she recognised them vaguely from the past few days.

Rue stopped, embarrassed. She did her best to smile at them, though it must have come out crooked. One of them, a girl, jumped up and returned the smile and opened her mouth as if to say something, then closed it as she remembered.

Pressing a hand to her chest, she said, 'Sabine.'

Rue understood that well enough. 'Rue,' she said, pointing to herself.

Sabine smiled. She had gleaming caramel-coloured skin, and her hair was rolled into long, swaying tails, the tips of which grazed her elbows when she walked. She looked magnificent, and completely out of place in this dull, grey room. Rue wondered when she herself might be able to learn how to change her appearance like that.

Sabine's friend was a young man (or old, Rue reminded herself, as augmentation made everyone look young) with carefully placed ridges and bumps running the length of his face and neck, and presumably the rest of his body, in various patterns. He had a starburst of little bulbous ridges on his cheek. He looked her up and down quite openly, and inside she rolled her eyes. Wren had warned her of it – every Worlder would find her simple, unaltered appearance strange, but for some it might even border on offensive. Only Technophobes proudly displayed no augmentation, and they stuck out like a sore thumb.

'Oh, not the Technophobes,' Wren had said, when Rue pressed him about the word. 'They're this protest group who think Life is evil, or something of the sort. I think they're religious. They have their implants removed illegally and go off-grid. They attack people for no reason. All kinds of strange things.'

In the meantime, Rue would have to endure the stares. She returned the young man's gaze directly until he dropped

16

his eyes. Let him think she was rude – it was only a mirror of himself.

Sabine spoke. 'Lars,' she said, pointing at the man, who managed a sharp cross between a nod and a shrug.

Rue ventured a little further into the room, then looked around.

In the study at Red House where she was taught in Angle Tar, they had a huge array of books on shelves, a wicker chest stuffed with games, a cupboard full of art materials. But this room was as bare as could be, much like everything she had seen so far in World. She looked around at the walls for the black square shape of a food device, but couldn't see one, and stood uncertainly. Even if she found it she wouldn't know how to work it, but she didn't want to ask these two strangers for help. How would she even get them to understand what she wanted?

Sabine was looking at her, as if trying to work out what she was thinking.

Lars said something, speaking unintelligible World with a bored-sounding voice. Sabine answered him, and they talked for a moment. Rue slid awkwardly onto a seat near the door, not quite knowing what to do with herself.

Being around Worlders was strange – more often than not they seemed elsewhere. She knew this was because they spent most of the time hooked into the invisible, tantalising world of Life, a world she wouldn't be able to see until she'd learned how to use the box.

As Talented, it was easy enough for her to understand that Worlders could see a place inside their head where they didn't

17

physically exist. Rue loved that about World; more than the technology, more than the unfathomable things they did to their bodies, more than the incredible machines they liked so much to create that made their lives an effortless glide.

Sabine kept throwing Rue a glance, as if she was repeatedly considering trying to talk to her. Rue hoped she wouldn't. It was hard enough having to sit and listen without being able to join in, but when mime was resorted to, things became plain strange.

So there they sat.

She wondered if they both had a day off today, and where they worked, and what they did, and whether their parents looked as young as they did with all this augmentation floating around, and whether that bothered them. She was sure it would have bothered her if Fernie, her old hedgewitch mistress, had looked young and pretty. But thinking about Fernie and Angle Tar squashed her heart and gave her pain, so she moved on.

Wren had said he would introduce her to his manager; a woman called Greta Hammond, who sounded like she fulfilled much the same role as Frith had in Angle Tar. Greta was apparently part of a team responsible for the small but steadily growing numbers of Talented who were recruited to World's government programme and put to work using their special gifts. Wren was one of her star acquisitions – a Talented Angle Tarain lured away by the glittering promise of World.

Much like Rue.

She supposed if this Greta Hammond liked the look of her she might be enrolled in a school or training programme here, too, and meet another Talented group she would have to get used to. At least here she would have Wren, and she wouldn't have to make a start in this place all alone.

Just as she was thinking of Wren, he walked into the room. She grinned and ran to him, throwing her arms around his neck.

'Really,' he said with a laugh. His strange silver eyes rested on hers. 'I wasn't gone very long.'

'Wren, I can't wait to learn the language here.'

'Then I have just the thing you need. Want to try it?'

'Yes! Right now.'

Sabine asked him something, her eyes flicking between them. He answered, and they laughed. Wren moved out of Rue's arms and wandered over to the seats.

'What did she say?' Rue said, following him.

'That Angle Tarain sounds like trying to gargle with water when your mouth is filled with glass balls.'

'Oh.'

'Oh, don't take offence – we like to joke with each other. I told her that to us, World sounds like pigs mating.'

'You're mean!' Rue barked a laugh, covering her mouth in mock outrage.

'I am, indeed,' he agreed.

'Where have you been?' she asked.

Wren shrugged evasively. 'Out. Work. You'll understand when you start yourself.'

'You mean when I start training. I can't work yet, I ain't old enough.'

Wren laughed, and draped an arm over her.

'Shall we?' he said.

* * *

19

They sat on his bed together, his little black Life box squatting in between them.

'For you,' said Wren, 'Jacking in is obviously a little harder. You have to have a box to do it, whereas normal Worlders can do it anywhere and anytime they like. They implant you at birth here. Obviously, you don't have an implant, so whenever you want to go into Life, you'll need to use the box.'

The box was black and nondescript. As he worked, his fingers flickering lightly over nothing, it seemed to her, the air popped gently above it and began to glow a faint blue colour.

'Wah!' said Rue in delight. 'A spell!'

'Of course not. This is an interface link.'

'Sounds like a spell to me. Intaface linque.'

'Your accent is atrocious.' He shook his head.

Rue rolled her eyes. She watched him push his hand into the blue shimmer. There were shapes dancing within the colour, but they moved too fast for her to make sense of them.

'And so . . . there,' said Wren, musing. 'Now you have to put your head in it.'

'Put my . . .?'

'Head in it.'

Rue looked at the box, and then the haze above it.

'Then what?'

'Too scared?'

'Shut up.'

'Okay, sorry. Then you'll be in Life. It'll take a moment, and you'll feel like you do when you Jump. There's a bit in between where everything is black and empty and hard to understand, but it only lasts a second. I'll be right behind you.'

'We don't go together?'

'I don't need the box.'

He touched the back of his neck, rubbing a little scar on his skin.

'They put an implant in you?' said Rue, curious, and a little repelled. Somehow, knowing that he had something inserted inside him from this culture made him more of a stranger to her.

'What?' he said, smiling. 'Jealous?'

Rue didn't know what to say to that. She wasn't, quite.

'Don't worry,' Wren continued. 'If you do well here, you'll get implanted, too, I'm sure. It's really hard to live without one, actually.'

How encouraging.

'The box is the oldest form of Life interface, and it's pretty clunky because it isn't portable. But the graphics are just as good, so don't worry about that.'

I'd worry about it if I knew what you were on about, she thought.

'We'll try surface Life, first,' said Wren. 'HI-Life we can tackle once you're used to things. Are you ready?'

Rue felt her stomach roll and flip lazily, like a basking seal.

'But I'll be all alone.'

'You'll still be in this room. Except you'll see it in Life.'

He curled his fingers around the back of her neck and she flinched instinctively. She hated it when he pushed her, but she had to trust him. He was her only guide to this place.

The blue light loomed in her vision.

'Does it hurt?'

'No,' came his voice behind her. 'Just strange, buzzy.'

Her forehead broke the light. It swamped around her skin and sizzled in her ears.

Gods, I forgot to ask whether I can open my eyes.

There was no way she'd risk it – she'd have to keep them shut. She screwed them tighter, afraid.

It was nothing much, at first. Almost as if she had drunk too much, her head slow and thick. Then there was a keening, yammering noise, like fighting cats. She tried to bring her hands up to her ears but couldn't feel them any more, as if the rest of her had somehow become detached, and all that remained of her was a floating head.

The noise faded. Everything faded.

The fear came, the one that told her she could be stuck here like this forever, nothing changing and nothing else happening, just herself all alone; a kind of death. It went on too long.

Then she felt something touching her arm, which was good news, because it meant that she at least still had one.

'Rue, open your eyes.'

She did.

Everything really had come alive.

'It's too much, at first,' said Wren. 'Your eyes need time to adjust to what they see. Like sunlight that's too bright. Give it a moment.'

Rue barely heard him. It hurt a little, yes. But it was too incredible; she couldn't close her eyes again in case she lost it.

The previously bare, grey walls of Wren's room were covered in people. Little, perfectly drawn people in beautiful colours, with flowing hair and dresses so vivid they looked alive. It was hardly a surprise to see they could move. As she watched, a

22

girl near her head on the wall winked at her as she drew water from a well. She was only six inches or so high.

'Grad take me,' she whispered. 'Is she alive?'

'It's only wallpaper,' said Wren, sounding amused. 'From *Old Times*. It's a Life game – we'll play it sometime. Everyone plays it in World, it's very popular.'

Rue looked up further. The people were all moving, two-dimensional creatures going about their business. There was a drunk man who kept falling over, his nose all red. Girls scattering grain for pigs. A boy that in a flash reminded her strongly of Pake – the pleasant but dull farmer's son she had once caught the fancy of back in her old village. He was lying on a wall, looking up at the sky, a smile on his face, until a man next to him walked over and cuffed him about the head. He fell off and rubbed his skull ruefully. Then, as she watched, he moved back to his wall, and the man moved back to his place a little further on. It repeated. The boy lay down, looking dreamily upwards. The man came along and cuffed him, his face twisted in annoyance.

'It's not so different to where I'm from,' said Rue.

'I suppose not.'

'Why do they like it so? They should just visit Angle Tar. T'would be the real thing.'

'Don't be silly. They wouldn't be allowed. And anyway, most people prefer a game to real life.'

'Is it a story?' said Rue.

'Not at all. It's just wallpaper, so it's not as sophisticated as the game. It's a set of pre-programmed clips, repeated. That's all. We'll play later.'

She turned her head, sensing that he wanted to show her more. It was annoying, though. There was so much to see and learn that she felt like she didn't have time to take it in. Wren was always moving forward, onto the next thing. At least she could count on never growing bored.

'How does it work?' she said, looking up. The ceiling had changed, too. It was an endless, textured black, peppered with small dots of light, stars that twinkled and winked. It was just as a night sky in summer would be, a clear one with a still wind.

Wren shook his head. 'I couldn't begin to explain. Some of the mechanics I don't even understand myself. It changes your perceptions of what you see, and hear, and touch. I don't think they've been able to do taste or smell yet. Surface Life overlays everything you see around you with Life. There are trees lining the streets, outside, now, and the buildings will have beautiful paintings on their outside walls. There are gardens that are bare of art outside of Life. A lot of World artists only make art that can be seen in Life, nowadays. The weather in the sky is simulated in Life, and changes with the seasons. Everything in World is more beautiful in Life.'

'But why not make all that real?'

'If it's not real, it can't hurt anyone or cost so much. Do you know how much credit it would cost to run a garden, the people to maintain it, the space? It's so much better for our environment to have the things people want in augmented reality, rather than really existing. So much less damage, so much less cost. And, you'll see, Life is how everyone in World connects. You can meet up with anyone you like in Life, people from three thousand miles away. You can talk to whomever

24

you want, and you don't have to take a ridiculous journey to get to them. You can buy anything, or learn anything, in Life. If you don't know the answer to something? Jack in, find it in Life. All the knowledge of its citizens, everything it's ever achieved, resides in Life. Isn't that incredible? Everyone with access to the same knowledge – no more elitism, no more barriers because of where you live or what family name you have or how much money you have, like in Angle Tar. Everyone with the same advantages, the same choices.'

It was a fairy tale. It was everything that Angle Tar was not.

'Let's turn to languages,' said Wren, lifting his hands and playing them on an invisible piano.

'What are you doing?'

'Looking through my personal account. You won't see what I see because Life recognises my signature and shows some things only to me. I'll show you how to access your account, though it'll be empty at the moment, of course. Ah!'

With a pleased look, Wren lifted his hand up and withdrew, from thin air, a long, blue rod that glowed pleasantly.

'This is the World language. My manager got it a few hours ago and sent it through to me.'

Rue stared at the rod. It looked alive.

'What do you do with that?'

'It's just a data stick,' said Wren, waving it. Its glow left blue trails in the air. 'It only exists in Life. I want you to take it, and push it into your head.'

Rue laughed nervously.

Wren nodded.

'No,' she said. 'That's . . . stupid.'

'I know it sounds it, but trust me. I can't push it into my head to show you – I'd use it up and we'd have to get you another one, which would be impossible anyway. Just . . . take it. And press it against your head. Then slide it in.'

'You do it,' said Rue, feeling a horrible urge to laugh again and swallowing it. She had a feeling Wren wouldn't appreciate it. His face was quite serious.

'All right. If you trust me.'

'I do, of course I do.'

Wren shifted up closer to her and she gazed at the rod.

'It's humming,' she said. 'Is it meant to do that?'

'All data makes a sound in Life, don't worry.'

'It's warm.'

'That's so it feels pleasant when you have to absorb it.'

The sensation of the rod next to her skin was strange because it didn't correspond to what she was seeing. Against her, it felt like a leaf of paper, but when she looked at it, she could see its thickness, its weight.

'It tickles,' she said.

'It will do a lot more than that. Ready?'

'Yes.'

It slid into her head.

The blue glow that gently suffused the room sharpened to a point, and the point was piercing the side of her skull. It was not painful, exactly. It was more as if her brain had been thrown into a jug of bubbling water. The shock shut her down. She couldn't remember with any certainty afterwards whether she had been able to think throughout the whole thing, to wonder at what was happening. It was a shame, somehow.

26

She felt a hand touch the side of her face.

'What?' she said. A part of her was momentarily delighted that she still had the ability to speak.

'That's it.'

Rue looked around. Her head was too slow, as if it had trouble catching up with the rest of her.

'Thassit?' she said.

'It'll take a few hours to integrate properly with your brain. And it'll work a lot better after you've had some sleep.'

'Can we talk World now, then?'

'Not yet, my Rue. But very soon. A few hours.'

'I can sleep now.'

Wren grabbed hold of her arm. Without really being aware of it, she had started to fall sideways towards the bed.

'No, no,' he said. 'You shouldn't sleep yet. It might not sit right. You need to stay awake as long as you can.'

'Sleep,' she insisted without any strength. Her head felt enormously heavy and unbalanced. It was the weight of all that knowledge, she thought, and resisted the urge to giggle. She felt Wren squeeze her to his side.

'No,' she heard him say. 'Come on. Let's take a walk.'

CHAPTER 2

WORLD

CHO

Cho slid into Life, easy as thought.

It began, as always, with a feeling like listening to the opening bars of her favourite song.

A tingle.

A long, wavering note of anticipation.

A sudden, gentle rush.

Underneath, there was relief, crashing waves of warm comfort. And guilt that she had succumbed again.

It took its moment. There was always a boot-up time, a black lag from the surface Life that everyone used; the virtual reality that made trees appear and buildings look beautiful, made a fake sun shine in a fake sky. Surface Life took no time at all – the entire population of World was walking around in it, pretty much all the time.

But full immersion into Life stole a black lag from you. Some people hated that moment of darkness and nothing. Cho loved it. Anticipation.

They called it High Immersion Life, or HI-Life. In HI-Life, you could create and explore entire virtual worlds while your body stayed in reality where you left it, unresponsive, as if you were sleeping. You could hide yourself in a fairy land if you wanted to, or a house made entirely out of cheese. There was a place and a party and a game for everything, somewhere, no matter how strange.

But the one thing you couldn't hide was your identity. It was understandable. How would you know anyone's agenda in a virtual reality if they couldn't be tagged and recognised? There were many, many games and social simulations where you could cloak yourself in an avatar, a representation of you that would look as bizarre or as normal as you desired. But your identity remained the same. Anyone could see who you really were and what you looked like out of Life simply by accessing your profile info. There were no disguises.

Unless you were a hacker, of course.

Cho accessed her Life account. It pulled together around her, manifesting as a small, comfortable room. She had spent a long time buying Life products to decorate her room. It was a sanctuary. No one could access it save her. No one could see it save her.

It was, she liked to think, the absolute opposite of her bedroom in the real.

Spindly tables had tiny jewelled boxes scattered on their tops with nothing in them. Marble figurines of extinct elephants trumpeted at each other across swathes of red-and-gold glittered cloth. Five clocks hung on one wall, of varying sizes. One was completely transparent, so you could see the mechanisms inside it, but there were no cogs, just a series of tiny hammers poised above rounded nodes. On a table sat a group of interconnected glass candle holders, delicate and winding, and an old-fashioned set of scales. In a corner on the floor, eight marble balls clustered together on a little wooden plate, a couple of them as big as a fist. The kind of balls that looked like star systems or planets, with swirls and whirlpools of colour streaking their surfaces. There was a huge Chinese dragon by one wall, a deep mauve colour, carved and intricate and lovely and almost tacky but not in here, surrounded by this oddness, and it came up to the bottom of her ribs when she stood next to it. There was a thick glass jar of sand, and three keys – giant brass things that were heavy when she picked them up and played with them, which she liked to do. A telescope in one corner. To look at what, exactly? Yet she loved it. It didn't matter that neither the room itself, nor anything it contained, was real in a physical sense. It looked real. It felt real. That was the beauty of Life.

Fat icons hung in the air around her head, representations of all the games and social sims she had bought, all the shops she had an account with. They glittered and winked like jewels, enticing. She reached for one and it flew gracefully towards her. Apt because it was a flying game.

Her avatar in this game was a hawk. She had never seen a real one, and she had never met anyone who had. It was hard to imagine the kind of place where it was normal to have hawks roaming, flying about in the sky as if they belonged there. But she knew there was such a place. It was a place her brother had abandoned her for.

Being a hawk in this game was a beautifully physical thing. When you took on the avatar, you *felt* your body shape change. Your torso tilted forward, stomach rounding. Your face elongated, mouth growing hard and sprouting outward. Wings pushed out from your shoulder blades, inch by giant inch. It was a delicate, complex, joyful piece of programming. Cho had contributed some of the code to it. Some people found it off-putting, feeling their bodies change like that. Others, like Cho, couldn't get enough of it.

You could play the flying game in multi mode, in a sky full of other avatars as people in Life from across the world played with you. You could compete for points, collecting small trinkets from hard-to-reach places. But Cho preferred single-player mode. Alone in a sky so big it felt limitless, dipping and swooping, and feeling the wind, and doing nothing but being absolutely free.

She loaded up her avatar, waiting as the code adjusted to her account details. Then she felt herself slowly tipping forward, feet spreading, legs tucking under her. Delicate itching across her back as if tiny mice ran over her skin, their claws skimming her nerve-endings. Sprouting wings and feathers.

When the avatar had loaded, she entered the game space. Her nest was tucked into a hole halfway up a cliff. She had done it deliberately so that the only way she could leave her starting point was by throwing herself into the sky.

She felt the wind ruffle her feathers as she peeked a clawed foot over the edge.

Nothing below.

Her heart was pounding. It didn't matter how many times she'd done it before; it felt as real as ever. That was the brilliance of Life.

She turned slightly, sticking her shoulder out, and rolled downwards into emptiness. She could see a patchwork of vague dark green forest far below. The wind whistled in her ears.

She fell.

Opened her wings, trying to catch an updraft.

For several long, horrible, wonderful seconds, nothing happened.

Then finally, one slammed up past her belly and buffeted her wings, stopping her descent.

She floated into the yawning, empty sky.

FREE! said her mind, ecstatically.

And then she let it shut off, thinking of nothing but wind and blue. And peace, just for a while.

In Life, you could become something else completely. You could live a second, third, fourth, seventh existence. You could play endless games and roam worlds that didn't exist outside of the implant in your head. It was endlessly amazing, endlessly inventive. The most incredible, celebrated artists in World were Life programmers. It was imagination made tangible, shared with millions upon millions of people, all living, working, gaming in it together.

It was better than the real. It was what the real *should* be.

The ultimate in existence.

And it was slowly killing them all.

CHAPTER 3

WORLD

RUE

The box glowed, beckoning to her with flickering blue fingers.

It was surprisingly easy to get used to. A lot of people never switched between reality and Life, preferring to spend most of their waking hours jacked in. For those who didn't, it was as easy as flicking a switch inside your head, wherever you happened to be at that particular moment. But Rue, with no implant, had to content herself with being holed up in Wren's room, chained to the box, whenever she wanted to go into Life.

Wren was gone a lot. It was his job, he said. He never told her exactly where he went, though she asked all the time. Occasionally, he came home very late at night and went immediately to bed. Sometimes he even looked a little bit ill. Once, he'd come home and locked himself in the bathroom for an hour. She'd heard the unmistakable sound of retching.

When she banged on the door, he didn't answer, so she talked to him incessantly through it, threatening to break it down if he didn't tell her whether he was all right. All she'd got for her trouble was an irritable plea for her to stop banging and that he'd be out in a minute. And when he finally emerged he just shrugged it off, saying he'd eaten something bad at work.

She wanted to help him, to comfort him. But he wouldn't allow it, fobbing off her attempts with a small smile and insisting nothing was wrong. He was just busy. And what could she do? She had no way of finding out what was wrong without him telling her.

Her day currently consisted of this: when Wren left in the mornings, she could use his box and go into Life. When she was hungry, she could go into the social room and order food. He seemed to think that those two things should be enough for her.

They weren't.

He'd told her not to go wandering outside the apartments. Her appearance might get her into trouble. People would automatically think she was a Technophobe. He'd said there wasn't much to see, anyway, without an implant. She had pressed him as hard as she could, stoically enduring his shutdowns until he'd finally given in and programmed what he called her 'retinal scan' into the outside door key, just to 'stop her incessant questioning'.

So she went out, exploring the city.

On leaving for the first time alone, she'd stood outside the building, wrapped up in World clothes that sat funny on her, bunching in places they shouldn't bunch and stretching in places they really shouldn't stretch. She had breathed in, nervous and excited. The air was flat.

She promised herself she wouldn't go far, in case she got lost. Just wander for a few minutes at a time, checking that she knew how to get back. And then she set out, her eyes widened to catch all the incredible sights that she would undoubtedly see.

But the thing that really irked Rue was that Wren had been right.

Without Life, the city was dull. All the buildings were made of the same shade of grey-coloured materials. She didn't see why exactly that had to be, but Wren just shrugged and said it was necessary as the platform for Life. The streets were uniform and wide, much wider than Capital City streets, but there was nothing much else to say about them. It was hard to remember any detail at all. Everything was so . . . neat.

She had money, or credits, as they called money here. Wren's mysterious employers, whom she was increasingly anxious to meet, had given her enough in her account to last months. She could spend them on whatever she wanted – once she got the hang of spending something that didn't physically exist in her hand.

But in Wren's city, there were no shops to visit, because everything you could ever wish to buy you bought through virtual Life shops. As fun as that was, it didn't have that tangible thing of going into a store, running your fingers lightly over cotton dresses and silk shirts. Desiring, because you could see and touch and smell those exquisite things.

Shopping alone was no fun, either. Clothes shopping made her mind inevitably slide towards the trips that Lea used to drag her on, to expensive boutiques and evenings filled with trying things on and giggling while Lea spent more money on a brooch than Rue would see in a month. It was . . . flamboyant and wasteful, she supposed, to do that. Worlders certainly seemed to think so. Clothes were unbelievably cheap here, and for a while she had been enamoured at the thought of all the new things she could own with just a handful of credits. All the brand-new versions of her she could make.

There were little eat places dotted about the city streets, where people could meet and order food and drink from the food units there. But all anyone in those places ever seemed to do, once they sat down with their food, was jack into surface Life and talk to each other there. Still, plenty of people went to eat places on their own, so she didn't feel strange about sitting at a table by herself, even though those solitary people were never really alone – they were surrounded by people in Life.

All in all there was hardly anywhere outside of Life to socialise, but that apparently didn't bother anyone because socialising, in World, was arranged.

According to Wren, everyone went to regular parties at other people's houses, and held parties themselves in their own houses. You would be messaged the time and place for your next obligatory party, and attend or host you most certainly did; if you missed any, a black mark was put against your Life account. What having a black mark on your account meant Rue didn't know exactly, but she understood that it wasn't good.

The great thing about the system, apparently, was that you got to regularly go to parties for free and, until you yourself were hosting, you didn't have to organise a thing – your local government team did everything for you. They chose who went to which house and when. They chose who hosted and who didn't. They chose everything, it seemed, very carefully. Rue thought this bizarre. No one else seemed to, though, so she filed it away as another custom she would have to get used to.

Wren had promised her that today, finally, something would happen. He had been trying to arrange a meeting between Rue and his manager, Greta Hammond, for weeks. A meeting, at last. Something, anything, to stop the slow, spidery sensation of listlessness that often seemed to creep over her nowadays.

Sat at Wren's little desk, the box in front of her, Rue flicked through her Life account. There was a letter sat in her message box, and she waved one hand over it. Wren had shown her how to open her mail, but she still couldn't get past the sensation that she was performing magic. The letter unfolded without her having touched it. She knew if she jacked out of Life, the letter would disappear. Everything she now saw would disappear, because it wasn't real. But because enough people had decided that what they saw in one reality wasn't necessarily more important than what they saw in another, the letter *was* real. It simply wasn't real everywhere.

The letter read:

Vela Rue –
I invite you to a meet. Wren has spoken so much of you and I am keen to see you for myself. Would today at fifteen hours be too short notice? Wren will show you to my office.
Greta Hammond

She had been told to expect as much from Wren, who had seemed a little short about the whole thing when he had mentioned it to her last night. Quizzing him never helped when he wasn't in a mood to talk, she had learned. Nevertheless, fifteen hours was the time he had told her to be ready, so here she was.

She followed the room link at the bottom of the letter. The link would take her to Greta Hammond's location in Life. Touching it with her finger, she waited as the console flickered.

There was that blackness again while she dropped into full immersion, and her body in the real went a little limp in its chair, her eyes peacefully closed. Funny how similar descending to full immersion felt to the place in between places, that space of nothing and creeping strangeness that she used to find herself in when she practised throwing her mind in lessons with White.

It took a moment, but then the blackness passed, and there was Wren's avatar, standing in Life, waiting for her in front of an ordinary-looking door.

Wren was out on assignment and away from the house, and had only paused in his day to meet her in Life and introduce her to this Greta Hammond. Rue smiled at him, feeling her pulse skip in excitement.

'I told you fifteen,' he said. He seemed anxious.

'I know it. I'm not late, am I?'

'Come on, come on.'

He took her arm and led her to the door. In a sudden flash of irritation she shrugged him off, and walked through before him.

The room beyond was the best-looking completely virtual place she had seen yet. Some of the places she'd encountered in Life were often a little flat, as if depth couldn't quite make the grade. But this looked and felt the part. This was someone's room, not just a manufactured space.

The woman before her was petite and lovely, her golden hair done up into a bouffant kind of style and with a little too much paint on her eyes. Her cheeks were patterned with a trace of dark green scales, which set off her colouring handsomely. Wren had told her that Greta was middle-aged – it didn't show, but then again it rarely did in World.

Rue shook off her nerves and opened her mouth to say hello.

'You didn't knock.'

'I wasn't told to,' said Rue.

Greta smiled. The smile didn't reach her eyes. Her gaze flickered briefly over Rue's shoulder to Wren, who had come in behind her. She gestured with her hand, something that presumably meant sit. Rue did so, taking one of the hard metal chairs in front of Greta's desk. Wren took the other beside her. The chair squeaked when he sat on it. It was a perplexing thing, to create a virtual chair that squeaked, but fitted nicely with what Rue had seen of Greta's personality so far. I'm in charge, said Greta, with everything she had.

You're a bit of a sot, aren't you, Greta? thought Rue, relishing the chance to use a slang word going about Wren's friends at the moment.

The World language had settled within her like a blanket. It took an effort to switch between Angle Tarain and World, but she hadn't spoken a word of her native language for days, so didn't see this as much of a problem. She still couldn't quite keep up with the constantly shifting nature of World speak, but could at last talk to people and understand them, even if

39

the data stick had given her a kind of stiff and formal version of the language.

'So. Wren tells me you're an orphan,' said Greta, folding her hands together. 'How can that be?'

'I suppose it can be when your parents leave you on a farm doorstep with no explanation,' said Rue.

'Orphans are a rare phenomenon in World. I'm curious as to how it happens.'

'So am I.'

'Do you have any other family you are aware of?'

'No.'

'Good. Hopefully that will have made the transition easier. It's one of the reasons Wren picked you, and I'm pleased he hasn't faulted in that area.'

Rue frowned, picking over Greta's words.

'Why are you telling me this?' she said.

'Because a little bit of truth never did anyone any harm. I want you to be under no illusions, Rue. You were hand-picked, so you can feel proud of that, if you wish. But the rest of your Angle Tar group was also tested. In most cases, they would have found the transition too difficult.'

'Because they have families?' said Rue, incredulous.

'That's only a part of it. There were other factors.' Greta looked at Wren. 'You can leave now. You have projects to finish.'

Wren stood up and bowed. 'My lady,' he said, with the merest touch of playful insolence, and moved out of the room.

Rue felt her heart sink. She didn't want to be left alone here. She needed Wren; she couldn't navigate this strange culture without him.

'So, Rue,' Greta began, but Rue cut her short.

'Wait a minute,' she said. 'Just . . . please.'

She had barely begun to process the revelation that the rest of her group had also been approached, and presumably by Wren; the thought of him seducing them with his strangeness and loveliness and promise of an incredible adventure made her cheeks flush. So she wasn't the only one he had done *that* with, then.

Did she care? *Should* she care?

'What is it?' said Greta.

Rue searched for the right questions. 'So Wren picked me because I'm an orphan? How did he know anything about me in the first place?'

'I'm sorry, I can't tell you that, much as I'd like to. It's a part of a larger operational issue.'

'What does that mean?'

Greta raised a brow. 'It means I can't tell you.'

Rue wanted to press it, but kept silent instead.

'Do you find him handsome?' said Greta, with a smile.

'What?'

'It's an easy question, I'd have thought. Do you find Wren handsome?'

Rue watched her, but those constructed green eyes gave nothing away.

Was this some sort of test? What was the right answer?

'Yes,' she said, cautiously.

'Naturally. You know he didn't used to look like that, don't you? When I first met him, he was a podgy, rather drab-looking boy. He knows how to disguise himself, that one. He's good at

41

showing you what you want to see. That's why he's so useful to us. That and his Talent.'

Rue felt herself diagnosed under that gaze, but Greta's expression was warm and pleasant.

'Which brings me to you,' she continued. 'In many ways, you're quite different to Wren. His Talent is obvious, ridiculously so. He likes to flaunt it. You don't. You're shyer, and sweeter, than him. A less complex nature.'

Rue couldn't help it. Her eyes narrowed.

Greta laughed. 'Oh, don't take it as an insult, I meant it in quite the opposite way. That's an attractive quality. And you're naturally pretty, which is another point of difference to Wren.' A little smile spread across her lips. 'Very pretty, actually.'

Now what was *this* all about? What was she supposed to do with such twisty sentences that seemed to have more than one meaning, none of which she could fathom? She was supposed to blush, she supposed, and be coy. Or say something equally twisty back.

So she didn't.

'What are you doing?' she said, instead.

Greta's smile stiffened. 'What am I doing?' she repeated.

'Yes. It's weird. I don't like it. Why don't you speak straight?'

There was a pause.

Then Greta laughed. 'Oh dear. You don't take compliments well, do you? You might want to work on that.'

She was supposed to feel stupid now, she knew; out of line and clumsy. But Greta's face had an edge to it that wasn't there before, and she knew she'd upset something.

42

Begun well, haven't we? she thought. *Oh, Rue. Perhaps you should learn to play games better.*

But she couldn't see much of a point in that.

'So,' said Greta. 'I'm sure you'd like to know a little bit more about how things work here.' She leaned back. Her avatar's eyes were a lovely old velveteen kind of green, like plush upholstery. The kind that made you feel rich and beautiful when you sat on it. 'Much like in Angle Tar, we source Talented people and take them under our care. I run the research division of this programme, where we try to determine what Talent is and what it can do. I work directly under Alasdair Snearing, so you can imagine how seriously we take our Talented programme here.'

She raised a brow when Rue didn't react.

'Alasdair Snearing?' she said.

Rue shrugged. 'I don't know who that is.'

'He's a rather famous politician. Haven't you been familiarising yourself with the culture here?'

'Yes.'

'I see. Well, that is what I do.'

'And what do *I* do?' said Rue. 'I mean . . . why did you pick me? Why am I here?'

'Why *are* you here?' Greta replied.

'I don't understand.'

Greta spread a hand. 'Why *are* you here?' she repeated. 'I've told you that we picked you out based on compatibility. I've told you that we sought you and others like you. But *you* were the one who said yes. You were the one who responded to Wren. And *you* made the choice to leave. We would never have forced you, but you were eager to go. I'd be very interested to know why.'

43

Rue was silent, a war raging inside her. White's face surfaced in her mind, inevitable.

Why did you run away, Rue? Because right now, you can't think of a good reason. Not one.

No one wanted me there, she argued back silently. *I bet they don't even miss me, not a bit. And they lied about the rest of the world; they kept us from it! It shouldn't be illegal to know the truth. They all lied to me, even Fernie. Sat there for years while I told her I saw the world in my dreams, and she said it was nothing. Lied to my face.*

Oh, said her other self, amused. *But here they'll tell you the truth. Won't they?*

'I'll let you think about it, shall I?' came Greta's voice. 'In the meantime, why don't you go home and brush up on current events? I'd like you to integrate yourself here, Rue. Go to parties, socialise. In time, we'll begin a few studies on you to help us further our research. Wren will look after you. Rely on him. Trust him. Eventually we'll get you an implant. I think you'd like that, wouldn't you, instead of having to use that decrepit old box all the time?' Greta smiled. 'We're here to help you become a Worlder, Rue. And if you work hard to do so, you'll be one in no time.'

Rue felt a strange twisting chill down her back.

That was what she was supposed to want, wasn't it?

She came out of Greta's room and made her way back to her Life account, pushing carefully up from HI-Life to surface Life, until she opened her eyes and saw the now-familiar shifting and dancing wallpaper of Wren's bedroom once more, watched those *Old Times* characters go about their repetitive business.

Well.

That had not gone the way she had expected it to one bit.

What did you want? More people telling you how special you are? Stop being a child. You're a grown-up now.

Brush up on current events. Integrate into World.

Might as well start now.

She remained in Surface Life, scrolling aimlessly through news feeds until one heading caught her eye. It was about a suspected Technophobe accused of hacking into a major World city's power grid with the intention of shutting it down.

Rue read it through, then lifted a finger and pressed on the word 'Technophobe'. The new search brought reams of images and words scrolling past her curious gaze.

The Technophobes had started out as a moral protest group. Such things were common here, apparently. Rue couldn't conceive of such a notion. If you were unhappy about something in Angle Tar, you spoke to your mayor's representative about it, who would do something if the price was right or if he felt like it, but more often than not had no power to change anything. Here, protesting appeared to be something of a national pastime.

The group was small at first, and easily ignored. But no one had predicted how big their voice would get. In only a few years they started to become something of a concern to authorities, as they never appeared to go away or grow tired of their protests, and they liked extremes.

Images rolled past her eyes, of words and paintings daubed on walls and street pavements. People screaming and roaring into a row of silent police with guns and face shields. Like

45

watching the sea crash against a cliff.

Interviews with Technophobe sympathisers, or haters. Opinions, opinions everywhere. Faces expanded in her vision. Images of people attending rally meetings, surging crowds. Such ordinary looking people, to her. Some of them looked like children, they were so young.

White.

Her heart leapt straight into her mouth.

She stared at the image that had just played.

That was *him*.

She paused the screen and expanded his face until it filled her vision.

He was younger, but it was him. He had the same sharp edges, the same eyes. His skin wasn't yet as luminous as she remembered it to be, but it was as pale.

A peculiar feeling came over her, one she couldn't immediately place. The pit of her belly was squeezing, knotting her up. She looked at the details flashing beside his face. He'd had a different name, before Angle Tar. It was Jacob Yun.

Jacob.

She put her finger on his face.

The image opened up in a rush towards her. Information poured out. Images of an older White, thinner and hollow. She saw the word 'interrogation'.

More words, one in particular. 'Prison'.

He had been in prison.

She shouldn't be looking at this. It was his private pain, a past he would never want her or any other Angle Tarain knowing about.

46

Current whereabouts: Angle Tar was listed. Capital City was listed.

An image of him standing next to Frith, taken from afar.

So it was true. That particular rumour she'd heard about him really was true, and he had betrayed his country by leaving it.

Just like you did, said a voice in her head.

But unlike Rue, White had been imprisoned first. Tortured. Humiliated and ripped to pieces. The most pain Rue had ever endured was rejection; nothing compared to this.

Did this change something? Now that she understood him a little better, was she supposed to forgive him for the way he was? Should it matter?

She gestured, pulling the information away from her field of vision as if she could sweep him from her mind, too. Sweep him away and forget him, because it was all too late for that.

A soft bleep sounded in Rue's ear. She switched to the view of her Life account, and saw the bouncing icon of a new message. She opened it up.

It was a party invitation from their area team. She looked at the list of invitees included in the message. Wren was on there, too.

Her first party. She supposed she should be excited by that, but instead all she felt was a churning nervous sickness.

You'll get used to it, she told herself. *You need to give it time.* She sighed.

When Wren wasn't around and she didn't feel like leaving the house, Rue spent her time alone jacked into Life, playing games, endless varieties of games. Some games let you become another person for a while, let you keep a pet or build a house,

47

or go to strange places where people danced to the most bizarre noise Rue had ever heard and had long, involved conversations with each other. Other environments she had stumbled upon in Life were too odd to mention or make much sense of, and she had left those places quickly.

Old Times was rapidly becoming her favourite game. It really did seem the most popular game in World – at any one time, it told her that millions of people were playing it. All it seemed to consist of was chores and tasks, a hundred different things she had done every day of her life as a young girl. Milking, feeding, cooking, making beds, sweeping out stalls, washing. Male players spent their time farming out in virtual fields, made tools, reaped and sowed.

She supposed, from a Worlder point of view, that she could see the fascination of it, of such an extraordinarily different way of living. No one here seemed quite able to believe that there was a place in the world where people really did still live like that, even when she told them about it. For herself it was like being a child again, working on the farm back in her old village. It reminded her very strongly of Angle Tar, and it was confusing, and irritating, to know that she couldn't let go of her old life as easily as she would have liked.

The virtual world of Life was becoming everything that she knew. There was something about that feeling that appalled her, but her choice was limited.

It was that, or nothing.

CHAPTER 4

WORLD

WREN

Heart screaming in terror, legs like paper and crumpling treacherously underneath him, Wren ran for his life.

The thin rustle-buzz of its wings filled the corridor, filled his ears. It sounded like it was right on top of him, but he knew it wasn't. He knew he was outrunning it. He had to know that and to believe it or he was dead.

He turned a corner. The corridor before him was completely different. A carpeted floor instead of flagstones, flimsy blowing curtains lining the creamy walls and skirting the ground. He slowed.

The buzzing had been cut off.

He risked a quick look behind him, his insides churning in dread, but the thing had gone. He was all alone.

He put his back against the nearest wall. The chill pressed

up against his palms. His heart still smashed painfully in his chest, but it had begun to slow, calming. It took a while. There was no noise, he told himself, over and over.

It had gone.

He started to walk along the corridor, eyes wide for anything lurking.

A little further along sat a massive chest, pushed back into an alcove. It had thick black hinges and gold scrollwork etched across its lid. Closer to Wren another alcove held a tall, spidery lamp, made of some material he couldn't even begin to guess at – like smoked glass, but with curling tendrils peeling away from its stem that were too thin to be anything he could fathom. Hanging from one of the tendrils was a little brass key on a chain.

The lamp was closest. He inched towards it. The key glinted, tantalising him. It opened something. It had to *mean* something. He was obviously meant to find it. There would be doors around here, hundreds of them. There always were in the Castle. The key would open one of them, and behind the door would be a clue to the power this place held. A way for him to get it.

Or maybe it opened that chest over there.

The lamp was really very strange, up close. Smoked glass was a poor way to describe what it was made of – like calling the sea a big puddle of water. The material was impregnated with tiny figures, creatures that resembled nothing he'd ever seen before. The stuff looked solid, but when he touched it, it felt like gel, and his fingers, when he pulled them away, were smeared with it. And it seemed thin from far away, but up close he realised that it was actually huge. Thicker than his arm. No, thicker than a bed. No, even thicker than that. Maybe as wide as a house, or a garden, or maybe even a whole town.

'You should stop that,' said a voice behind him.

The lamp's spell was shattered. He didn't bother turning around. The voice was all too familiar.

'Why?' he said.

'It's one of those "the more you examine it, the stranger it gets" things,' said the voice. 'You'll get lost in it. It's really easy to get lost, here. You shouldn't have run away from me.'

'I'm fine.'

'That thing nearly ate you. I rescued you.'

Wren turned, finally, amazed. '*Rescued* me?' he sneered.

'I pulled you to another part of the Castle, far away from it.'

The Ghost Girl tilted her head to one side, her scribbly eyes examining him.

'What were you trying to do?' she said.

Wren considered. Lying was extremely difficult here. He didn't know why. He always fudged it when he tried. It was just easier not to speak at all, but he wasn't very good at that.

'I was trying to talk to one of them,' he replied.

'You'll probably need to stop being so afraid of them first, then.'

He looked down, before his eyes could give away the rage he felt.

'You can't just run away from me every time I call you here,' she said. 'You'll get lost. You'll die. I told you not to try and open the Castle. Not to talk to them. I told you what would happen if anyone did. Don't you understand?'

'Oh, shut up,' said Wren wearily.

51

But she was edgy. Sometimes he could push it, but not this time. Too fast to feel it before it happened, and he was on the floor as if he'd been smacked off his feet. She stood where she had been, a little statue. She hadn't moved.

He felt a spasm of pure, beautiful rage. It propelled him up, but she held him down. And he couldn't fight her.

You'll pay for that, he thought, because he couldn't seem to speak. *The day I'm more powerful than you, I'll come looking for you.*

'And how will you find me?' said the Ghost Girl, as if he had spoken aloud. 'You can't even come here by yourself. You can only come when I let you.'

SCREW YOU, screamed his mind.

'I wish you weren't so angry, Wren,' she said, eventually. 'I wish that for you.'

He managed a wheezy laugh. 'I like being angry,' he said.

'Because you think it gives you power. And I'm sorry about that. I'm really sorry.'

'I don't need your pity.'

She said nothing.

He pulled himself upwards grimly, building himself back into a whole piece until he could stand again.

'You're unhappy,' she said, her voice soft.

He scoffed. 'I'm fine.'

'You're unhappy,' she said again. 'I thought going to World would make you happy.'

'It does. I just love my life here. It's perfect. I love being tested and prodded and poked and made to feel like an incomprehensible little pet. I love being told what to do all the time, where to go, who to see and not. I'm like a rat that knows it's in a cage.'

She watched him. 'I didn't make you go.'

'You were the one who *told* me to go!' he shouted. 'You were the one who said World was so special! It's the place for me, you said!'

She fluttered. Her whole body was willowing, shifting before his eyes. Her hair grew sleek and long, her limp little dress turned into a winter cloak, trimmed with black rabbit fur around the hood and those little emerald-coloured buttons – the fashion before he'd left. Her face filled in, took on edges, cheekbones high and proud, eyes dark and secretive. It happened over seconds, until it was no longer the Ghost Girl standing before him but an extremely convincing replica of White.

Wren turned his head away, feeling sick and empty, his heart pumping erratically as if it would break.

'I only told you that near the end, when you were unhappy,' said the Ghost Girl, in White's voice. 'You had already wanted to go to World for years, Wren, and you know it. It's been your dearest, most secret wish since you were a child and you watched those foreign ships come in behind the dock fences.'

She paused.

'You said you couldn't stay in Angle Tar around White. That you'd kill him if you stayed. And World is the most logical place for you. I told them to take care of you, yes. I arranged it. And if they're treating you badly then I'm sorry. But you have to fit in somewhere, Wren, don't you see? You have to bend a little or you'll never be happy.'

'The only place I fit into is here.'

53

That seemed to shock her into silence.

Eventually, White's voice came again. 'No one belongs here.'

'You belong here.'

'I don't have a choice.'

'Why not?'

She was silent. She never got angry about his questions, or told him to shut up, or ever did anything other than be silent. It was like trying to talk round a chest of drawers. She simply shut down.

He could understand that. You were supposed to guard your secrets. The game was trying to break down those walls so that you could get at the secrets, spill them out into the open, collect them as weapons, stored away for future battles. Everyone had a crack in their walls, eventually.

But what could you do with silence? Her strange scribble eyes gave nothing away, and her ghost frame was too odd to read, almost like she was deliberately designed to be completely unfamiliar. Even when she took on another form, as she had done in the past once or twice, it was the same. White stood before him, but it was an approximation of him, like seeing him created through another's eyes. It was his voice, but it was her words and manner of speech. It wasn't White.

'What about the girl they've given you?'

He looked up. 'Rue?' he said, coldly. 'What about her?'

'Is she useful?'

'Hardly. She can't even Jump yet. Why do you want to know about her?'

The White approximation watched him. 'I'm interested in all Talented.'

Of course she was. But she seemed more interested in some than others. He didn't know whom else she compelled to visit her here at night, but it seemed obvious that it was the more gifted ones that held her special regard. Why else would she know how to look like White?

'She's naïve, and irritating,' he said.

'Have you noticed anything special about her?'

'No.' He rubbed his arms. You never got used to the cold, here. The Ghost Girl had said that some parts of the Castle were warm, even hot, but she'd never taken him there. He'd find those places on his own.

Somehow, *somehow*, he'd find a way to come here without her.

'I've been told that she and White were involved.'

Wren snorted. 'That's old news.'

'Is that why you picked her, Wren?'

He stared hard at the wall.

'Is it because you miss him?' she said.

'It's because he needed to be taught a lesson.'

'What lesson is that?'

'That you can't just treat people like toys you grow out of.'

'I see,' came her voice, and it was her voice this time. When he looked back at her, she was herself again.

'No, you don't,' he said. 'You see nothing, holed up in here. You have no idea what it's like to wake up every day in the real, with the weight of all the crap of your life pulling you down. You float around the Castle, judging all of us. Holding this place back from us. Taunting us with it. "Don't open the Castle. Don't talk to them. Don't do anything. Just come here when I want you to, so I can stand there and tell you everything that's wrong with your life."'

He actually saw her flinch.

'You pull me here whenever you feel like it. It's been months since the last time I came here. What, did you just forget about me? Don't you care?'

'I do. You're something to me, Wren.'

'Well, you', he said, 'are *nothing* to me.' He spread his arms. 'I don't care what you want from me any more. I don't care about your secret little agenda. Are you hearing me? Just leave me alone. Stop pulling me here. Don't talk to me. Find someone else to play with. Just let me go.'

She said nothing.

'Let me go.'

Still she stood, watching him silently.

'You LET ME GO. NOW.'

He took a step towards her, with no thought in his head of what he would do.

She took a step back, mirroring him.

'You can leave, if you want,' she said. 'I'm not stopping you.'

But she sounded strangled and sad.

He couldn't look at her any more, or stand to hear that tone in her voice. So he pushed, and she was telling the truth – for once, there was nothing stopping him from leaving. She wasn't controlling him. He was free.

He almost fell into awake, dropping with a slam back into his body, his mind buzzing from the shock of it.

His room was dim. He jacked in to check the time – 3:34 a.m. No more sleep tonight. He never could relax after a Castle dream.

Wren's mind turned back to the Ghost Girl.

He had never been able to fathom what her agenda was. Most of the time, all she'd seemed to want to do was talk. Talk talk talk, when his whole being itched to explore. But she wouldn't let him. Why pull him to the Castle, then, if he wasn't even allowed to see everything it held?

She was probably lonely. No one to talk to there except for monsters. Well, how tragic for her. Everyone was lonely; it was the state of the damn world. Stupid, condescending prig of a girl. Whoever she was, whatever she was, she could go hang.

Then there was Rue. Wren often stared at her when her attention was elsewhere, trying to divine from her face and her body what it was about her that had so captured White. Trying to see her secrets.

But he couldn't. She was just this country girl, soft and guileless. There was nothing extraordinary about her at all. He hated her, suddenly. She'd caught White in a way that Wren could never compete with. It was monstrously unfair. It made him feel on the outside again, looking in, that same gnawing belly isolation he'd had his entire life.

Well, maybe he'd visit Sabine again tonight, and see if he couldn't chase some of that away.

CHAPTER 5

WORLD

RUE

Rue's first World party was in full swing.

It was at a house much like Wren's, but at the end of a half-hour walk. Wren had complained the entire way of how far they had to go, and how unfair it was that they had been forced to attend a so-called local party that wasn't even local. Rue had found this both amusing and stupid. But then, World had almost no way to travel around except your own feet, and Worlders never needed to consciously stay healthy; their doctors did that for them. Life gave them everything else. It was surprising, perhaps even alarming, how acclimatised Wren seemed to have become to World.

Rue looked around the room. The Worlders surrounding them, that cocktail of strange hair and clothes shapes she was slowly getting used to, were laughing and kissing and waving their hands in the air. There were a number of different drugs on offer, spread across the table in the middle of the room like a child's banquet, in the form of tiny cakes, sweets and pastries. A list of holographic instructions shimmered at one end of the table, listing what could be mixed with what and what should be kept separate if you wanted to make sure all your fluids remained inside your body for the duration.

So people here liked to sit in a house together, carefully unscrewing their awareness with various different methods and seeing what happened. She knew quite a lot about plant drugs and their effects from her witching lessons with Fernie, way back when. At first the thought of it was much like sitting around and taking medicine when you weren't ill. She had been drunk before; but drinking was for celebrating. Wren told her that drug parties celebrated being alive. It was a pretty thing to say, and she couldn't really argue with it. She wanted to be one of these wild Worlders, and learn their love of losing control, didn't she?

She leaned against a wall with Wren. 'What do you have?' she said, looking at the little cream puff he held in his hand.

'It's an old favourite,' he said airily. 'It's a higher-than-sky. It makes you feel like you're flying, like everybody is flying. It's pretty good. You should try it.'

'One thing at a time, jack,' she said, and Wren laughed. She liked to make him laugh; he thought her attempts at slang hilarious.

'You're getting used to the language fast,' he said, through a mouthful of cake.

'I still sound like I'm stumbling about,' Rue said, swirling the drink Wren had procured for her.

'Not at all. Sabine said only yesterday how much better your conversation had become. She said you're starting to lose your accent, now.'

'Good.'

They were interrupted by a statuesque girl with short white hair and neon green paint around her eyes. 'WREN!' she bellowed, taking his arm. 'Where have you BEEN?'

Rue watched as he was pulled away into a small crowd. No one took any notice of her. She clutched her drink, feeling suddenly exposed, and looked out across the room, her eyes skidding along the backs and faces of the party goers. Such exotic faces, so many colours. It was almost too much, especially when set against the bland background of the room.

One girl in particular caught her eye. Her skin was a lovely lily-white colour, which reminded Rue inevitably of White, and brought a sharp pain to her stomach. But thankfully there the comparisons ended. The girl was round of face with large, soft lips, and had a small number of silver dapples painted on her cheeks. Her eyes were a sharp, startling shade of purple and her ears were encased in silver-coloured cuffs.

Her gaze shifted, catching Rue's, who looked away.

But not before Rue's heart had started to thrum. Realisation ran cold, prickling fingers over her.

I've seen her before.

Stone walls. Humming dread. Things that ate.

The girl who had come into the room with the hole in the floor.

No.

There was no possible way she'd dreamed a girl first, and then seen her in real life. She'd made it up somehow. Remembered it wrong. That had to be it.

Because the alternative was just too much, even for a Talented.

The girl was stood at the far end of the room, talking to a man wearing trousers so brightly, cheerily orange it looked like his legs were on fire. The girl was playing with her hair as she chatted. She was sweet and delicate looking.

'Hi,' said someone close to Rue's ear.

A man had appeared, leaning against the wall. He had reptilian eyes, and was bulky and wide in the fashion that some people seemed to like to augment, projecting an imposing, almost ugly kind of air, rather than a beautiful one.

'Hi,' she said.

'That's odd. I can't access your name.'

Wren had warned her about this. Worlders would automatically try to sync with her Life account to look up her name and details. It was their way of greeting.

'I don't have an implant,' Rue said.

'Oh, really? How extraordinary.'

She shrugged.

'No augmentation. No implant. Bit of an accent,' mused the man. 'You must be from Angle Tar.'

Rue looked at him. 'How did you know that?'

He laughed. 'Well, it must happen all the time, Angle Tarain coming here seeking citizenship. I mean, it's hardly surprising, given the conditions you have to live in over in that tiny place.'

Rue bristled at this.

'It works the other way, too,' she said.

61

'How do you mean?'

'Worlders come to Angle Tar.'

The man laughed again – the kind of laugh that seemed specifically designed to irritate.

'I don't think so,' he said, with an indulgent smile. 'Why on earth would they, for a start. Secondly . . . in all practical terms, they wouldn't be able to live unconnected from Life. The idea is . . . horrible, and just ridiculous. Who would voluntarily want that kind of existence?'

'I knew someone from World,' said Rue. 'Quite well, actually. He seemed to manage it just fine.'

'He was obviously deranged,' said the main airily. 'Worlders don't go to Angle Tar. But Angle Tarain apparently come here in droves, you know. I think World is a little too generous, sometimes. It's a wonder we haven't accepted half the population of Angle Tar into World – I'm sure they've tried.'

'What a big bag of jack,' said a voice behind Rue.

She turned. The girl that had caught Rue's eye stood next to them both, her face full of scorn.

'You don't know what you're talking about,' she said. 'As usual. A Worlder giving opinions that aren't even their own, just something they've found in the news feeds. You don't even know if what they tell you is true, and you just accept it. Typical.' She said a word then, something that the World language data stick obviously hadn't included, because Rue didn't understand it at all. It sounded like *mudak*.

'You're quite aggressive . . .' the man paused, '. . . Cho, aren't you? But I suppose I should expect nothing less from someone with *your* interests.'

62

'Whatever that means,' said the girl called Cho, 'coming from a man who likes to spend his time at the animal pits.'

The man snorted and walked off.

'The animal pits?' said Rue, fascinated with everything that had just been said, and picking that one subject randomly.

'Making artificial animals fight each other for entertainment. It's stupid, and so of course everyone loves it.'

'Do you know him?'

'Of course not. It's on his personal profile, that's all.'

'Oh. What was that word you said to him at the end?'

'It was just a word in another language.'

'What language?'

'*Ehkitay*. It was the language of URCI, back when we were independent. It's sort of this insane mix of two old languages, Russian and Chinese.'

'Aren't you from World?'

Cho shrugged. 'Sure. But we were all separate countries before World happened. URCI was one of the last to join World, only a few decades ago. That's why a lot of us can still speak our original language.' She leaned back against the wall, her eyes darting over the crowd. 'What's your name, then, implantless girl?'

'Rue.'

'Short and sweet, like mine.' Cho paused. 'What? You're staring.'

'Sorry. It's nothing. Um. Have you met as many Angle Tarain as he seems to think he has?'

'Tuh. It's all jack, like I said. These pitying images of poor Angle Tarain flocking to World like refugees. You could give a perspective. Does that seem true?'

'In honesty,' said Rue, 'I was taught that there was nothing much outside of Angle Tar except backward countries and wastelands. And unless things have changed much in the time I've been gone, I expect most of the population is still under that impression.'

Cho smiled properly – a wry smile, but one nonetheless – and it transformed her face. 'That's what I keep saying, but no one believes it. No one ever wants to know stuff unless it suits what they already think.'

Rue felt Cho had got it somewhat backwards, but kept silent.

'I heard you say you knew a Worlder in Angle Tar.'

'Yes,' said Rue, hoping her face hadn't betrayed the sudden spike in her heartbeat.

'What was this Worlder like? Had they come to escape?'

'I believe so,' said Rue, thinking of the old news feeds she'd found on White.

'That's usually the case,' Cho replied. Her voice was both bitter and smug. 'I had a brother, you see. He left because of what World is, and went to Angle Tar. He couldn't stand it here any more. But I decided to stay and work from the inside. That's braver than just leaving.'

'What do you mean, work from the inside?'

'I'm a hacker.'

'What's a hacker?'

Cho raised a brow. 'Seriously? Sorry, I forgot where you're from for a moment there. It's just another word for a coder. If you can change anything in Life, you can code, and if you can code, you can hack. It's really not hard. And it's just stupid stuff, you know – breaking into someone's Life account and changing their avatar to a pig's head, or something. There are hacking *championships*, for jack's sake. It's practically a sport. And all the most famous artists are hackers. It's just that hacking can sometimes lead to, you know . . . more nefarious activities.' A tiny smile hovered on her lips. 'Like being able to access information the government doesn't want you to see.'

'It sounds dangerous.'

Cho shrugged, turning to the food unit in the wall next to them. The hosts had unlocked it for the guests, and Cho took her time procuring something multicoloured and sparkling for them both that she called rainbow water. Then she dragged Rue over to a corner of the room where no one was sitting. They sat down together.

Cho took a sip of her drink, staring out across the room.

'I was told about you,' she said, suddenly.

Rue stared at her. 'By who?'

'Oh, you've been doing the rounds on the local chat feeds. Most people have never met an Angle Tarain, there was bound to be talk. Anyway, then I got the invite for this party and I saw your name on the list, and, well . . . I couldn't really pass up the opportunity to talk to you.'

'Why?' said Rue cautiously.

Cho grinned. 'You don't have to look so worried. It's just, being Angle Tarain, you're sort of naturally Technophobic. I find that interesting.'

'Should we be talking about this?'

'Oh, don't worry. You can't get in trouble just for talking about Technophobes. You should never hide your opinions, anyway.'

'So are you saying you are one?'

'Not necessarily. But maybe I know some.'

Rue took a big gulp of her rainbow water. It was like drinking liquid cherries.

'How much do you know about the Technophobes?' said Cho.

'Not a lot. I've seen some stuff in the news feeds.'

Cho leaned back. 'Well, you might have heard the rumours of a whole network of them, all spread across World. One group for each major city, living off-grid. Unconnected from Life, outside of civilisation, totally cut off from everything technological. It sounds like fantasy to me, but it's a nice idea. And people say it's impossible to live off-grid.' Cho grinned. 'But then I've never really believed anything people say.'

Rue resisted the urge to point out that everyone in Angle Tar lived without technology just fine, but she supposed if you were such a creature of it like those in World, living without it might very well seem near mythical.

They spent the next couple of hours talking together, Cho exclaiming at all that Rue didn't know about World and talking animatedly, her agile mind jumping from one thing to the next.

Rue began to realise how much she liked this girl. Cho was brash and confident, awkward at times, but she didn't hide anything. Everything else fell away for the time that they shared, and Rue found herself lost in the pleasure of such a back and forth with someone – a simple, vibrant connection.

Eventually, Wren came to find her and take her home. Cho sent her a Life message with her details so they could meet up again. Wren seemed pleased that she'd made a friend, but other than that was uninterested in talking. It didn't annoy her for once, though, because Cho occupied her thoughts now.

She really was the girl from Rue's dream. Same hair, same eyes. The more they had talked, the more certain Rue had become. Part of her tried to quash the feeling, insisting that she'd confused the whole thing. No one could foretell the future with their dreams – even White, the most Talented man in the world, had never been able to do that.

But a voice inside urged her to keep Cho close, because it felt like something deeply strange was flexing its wings.

Starting to take shape.

CHAPTER 6

ANGLE TAR

WHITE

For everyone else, life went on.

For White, there was an interrogation masked as a friendly chat in a small room. Questions barked at him by unsmiling government men about how he had allowed a rogue Talented to infiltrate campus and steal away one of his students.

About the exact nature of his relationship with that student.

There were rumours whispered, and looks thrown at him, but they might as well have been trying to cut ice with cotton for all he could rouse himself to care. Shutting everything off in such a fashion was his best refuge from pain, and it was almost fine.

Somewhere in the back of his head, he knew he would have to surface eventually. But for now, the disconnection helped him get through the day. If he didn't think, he couldn't care. So it went.

And then it all changed.

He was with Tulsent in a Talent lesson. The smallest and most nervous of his students this year – a mouse of a boy. White went through the mechanics of the lesson bit by bit, working on automatic. This step. The next. Thinking of nothing more than curling up in bed in his rooms as soon as this was over and losing himself to some blank, undemanding sleep. He'd had no Talent dreams since Rue had left. In fact, he hadn't had any kind of dream at all. The last one he remembered had been the night of her departure, and it had been a particularly horrible nightmare. He'd been in a castle, with an awful monster big enough to end worlds, and a girl who looked like a ghost. An echo of it slithered in his head in unguarded moments, but he hadn't dreamed of that place again.

Tulsent was talking through his recent dreams. There weren't many – the boy had a particularly bad memory for them. But this one had obviously stayed with him, because he said, '. . . And he had silver eyes, which I thought was weird.'

It took a few seconds.

Silver eyes.

White stirred. Tulsent must have sensed his sudden shift, because he blinked rapidly.

'Who had silver eyes?' said White.

'The boy in my dream. Silver eyes. No pupils, you know? Just . . . Just all shiny in the middle.'

White felt like someone was pouring scalding coffee into his veins. He strained, suddenly, his neck so stiff it could snap.

'What was his name?' he said.

* * *

69

Two days later, he risked a quick glance with his mind into the dining room of Red House, home to his Talent students. Tulsent had said they would all be there tonight, with no plans of going out on the town.

And there they were. Sat together, chirping to each other sleepily and cleaning the last of the sauce from their plates.

This was it.

He pushed his body there.

A black moment.

Then he squirmed his way out into brilliant light and heat, into the dining room, and appeared two feet from the end of the table where they lounged.

The popping air from his entrance knocked Lufe's glass over. Liquid splattered across the table and dripped over the edge. No one noticed.

'Threya take us!' Lea squealed.

The boys were silent, their mouths round.

He was gratified to see their shock. It powered him.

He said, 'I have a question for you, if you please. How many of you have been dreaming about a boy with silver eyes?'

'I didn't know you could do that,' said Lufe accusingly.

'What you do not know would fill Capital City,' said White. 'I interest myself in what you do know. Put up your hand if you have ever had a dream about a boy with silver eyes.'

No one moved.

White spread his arms wide.

'Here is what will happen,' he said. 'If you do not tell me what I want to know, I am going to follow you. I am going to follow you and spy on you, and you will never even know I am there.'

He sucked in a breath.

'I will choose a moment when you are asleep to Jump next to you,' he said. 'I will take you to a room. I will lock you in the room. It is a small room. I will keep you there until you tell me what you know. You have very little idea of what I am capable, but I am sure you may begin to understand. You will tell me about this boy. He has been coming to you in dreams. Put up your hand if you have seen him. *Now.*'

Lufe put his hand up first. Admirable. Lea followed shortly afterwards. Marches stared at them both. Tulsent had his eyes on the table.

White looked at Lufe. 'You – self-elected group leader. You will tell me everything about your dreams of the boy.'

Lufe looked around. Seeing no help from anyone, he licked his lips.

'It's nothing, syer. Really. Just a boy. I thought he was just someone I'd made up, at first. Then I thought he could be a Talent dream. But we were always just in my bedroom, so it didn't seem like Talent. I didn't know about anyone else dreaming of him.'

'How long?'

'Not long. Only a couple of visits. No more often than that, otherwise I would have found it odd.'

'You will now tell me why you have never once mentioned him before this,' said White.

Lufe swallowed audibly.

'There was no need for it, syer,' he said.

'An integral part of your lessons with me involves speaking to me of every dream you have, so that I may determine if they are of importance or not. Why did you not mention all the dreams you had involving the boy?'

'Not all, just one or two,' said Lufe.

'Why?'

'It was just two!' Lufe protested.

'You will tell me everything that happened in each one of these, with detail.'

'But nothing happened in them!'

White put out his hand to touch Lufe's shoulder. His speech had evidently worked, because Lufe shrank back from him.

'Fine,' he said crossly, to cover his fear. 'You told us not to mention anything that was just sex, right? You said sex dreams were to do with physical responses and weren't important!'

White took his hand away. 'It was that kind of dream?'

Lufe crossed his arms, his face a mask of furious, embarrassed thunder. Lea was looking at the table top, her cheeks flushed. So was Tulsent. Marches was staring at everyone with an expression of utter shock.

'Is this true for all of you?' said White.

No one spoke or moved.

It was small wonder none of them had told him about Wren. That manipulative bastard had made sure they never would. And he was the one who had told Wren about disregarding those kinds of dreams, hadn't he? Wren had laughed at him for it at the time.

And now he'd used it against him.

'That's enough,' said a soft voice behind White's shoulder.

He turned.

Frith had appeared without a sound and was lounging against the wall.

'How long have you been there?' said White.

'Long enough to see what an idiot you're making of yourself.'

'Then you heard them. You will not let him have this. You will not let him meddle like this. You will not let him ruin *everything* again!'

His voice had risen to a shout. Frith appeared not to have noticed, for he merely waited for the noise to subside, and then spoke in the same quiet voice as before.

'I'll have no more idle talk of punishment. You would be imprisoned for less and you know this.'

'I am never idle,' said White. 'I mean every word.'

'You may feel like you do now,' said Frith, detaching himself from the wall and coming closer. 'Of course you do. But you must think on the consequences. I cannot, and will not, allow you to harm these students. Do you want to test that? Their parents will scream for your blood if you so much as smack any of them across the ear. Do you want to test that, too? I'm trying to protect you.'

Protect, thought White, *with white-hot bile. Yes. Protect your little turncoat Talent pet.*

But Frith had deflated him. He was too tired to keep this up.

You win again.

One day, I'll win.

He looked at the group. They were slouched miserably in their chairs. Tulsent was actually trembling. He felt his wrath fade. They hadn't understood what Wren was. Sometimes they were sweet, and clever. Sometimes they were arrogant and stupid. But they were not treacherous, and they had never meant to cause harm.

73

They were not like White.

Frith moved in front of him, blocking his eyesight. White could hear him speaking to the group gently, herding them up towards the door.

'Is that what happened to Rue, then?' came Lea's voice.

White stared hard at the wall opposite.

'No one told us why she left,' said Lea again, nervous, defiant. 'She was my friend. No one even bothered to tell me. Was it . . . Was it because of this boy?'

'I am sorry,' White said. It was all he could manage.

He heard Frith talking to her quietly, but not what was said.

Together they slunk out of the room. He watched Frith turn towards him. Incredibly, Frith had a wary expression on his face.

'You need to eat. And sleep,' he said. 'You don't look good.'

'Why were they not interrogated, like me? If you had done so, we would have found out about this sooner. He was trying to *recruit* them!'

Frith took a moment.

'I'm sorry about the questioning,' he said, eventually. 'But you have to understand, after I reported that Rue had gone, there were some concerns from my superiors. Concerns only you could address. It hasn't escaped anyone's notice that it is you in particular who Wren seems to enjoy attacking.'

White folded his arms, trying to hold himself in.

'Did you know he could do that? Infiltrate people's dreams.'

'No,' said White, exasperated. 'I told them in the interrogation, no. I had no idea. He never told me about it.'

'So I take it that it's not something you can do.'

'No. I did not even know it was possible.'

Silence fell for a moment.

'You are not attempting to find Rue, are you?' said White. 'Despite her treason?'

Frith regarded him. His face was a careful, inscrutable mask.

'All you need to know', he said at last, 'is that she won't be coming back to Angle Tar. Ever. Which I think is for the best, don't you? Considering your recent history with her.'

'You do not even *care* that she has betrayed everyone?' White said, his voice rising, rising without any way of pulling back. 'You will just let her go? Just like that? You JUST –'

He stopped. The world swayed, and he swayed with it.

'Sit down, White.'

He felt his back slap against the wall. His thighs bunched, trying to stop him from falling, and he managed a half-slide to the ground.

Frith was watching him. Frith was thinking how pathetic he was. But it was impossible to stop. Thinking of something else didn't help. He bit the inside of his cheek, took hold of a pinch of rib flesh between his fingers and squeezed as hard as he could. It hurt. He could feel it. But the pain was just a flash, just an instant, and the more he did it, the less it helped, until all it did was bruise his skin.

And then he felt a hand on his arm. And then Frith was pulling him, and he felt himself slide into Frith's arms. Frith held him in silence.

It was very strange to feel him. Head resting on his chest, casually, as if it was supposed to be there. Frith's breathing was regular and soft, and it helped. He was a small man, but his arms were tight and unyielding – it was like being wrapped in iron bars instead of flesh.

75

White calmed. Slowed.

A sudden memory flashed into his mind, of the day Frith had told him about his past, and a boy named Oaker. He stiffened. He had a head-pounding urge to rip those arms away and run, but the arms had felt him change and let him go, carefully.

Frith was gazing out over the dining hall when he spoke.

'You need to forget her, White. She chose Wren.'

That round, passionate face of Wren's, laughing with him. Ready to change the world. Then twisted with violent hate. White had often punched that face to nothing in his head. Pounded it until it disappeared.

'Do you think he will come back?' he said.

'He won't Jump here again. I've upped security. He won't be able to try his little dream trick again, now we know. And he sticks out, of course, so he can't go roaming. The only thing we should worry about is whether he can mind spy on us.'

White had thought about this. It was easy enough to tell when a Talented was spying on him with their mind. An insistent tickling at the back of his head, like someone running their fingers lightly through his hair. And the feel of it was always particular to each person. He knew Wren's feel very well; they used to try and mind spy on each other all the time, as a kind of game, though Wren had only got any good at it just before he'd left. Wren's mind was a kind of sharp, tangy lemon-coloured haze, spray-painted into the air. He couldn't explain it better than that.

'I would know if he was here,' said White.

'You didn't know he was visiting Rue.'

'That is different! I cannot just smell where he has been,

like a dog. The only way I would have known about him is if she had told me. Which she did not. But I would know if he was anywhere near *me*. I would feel him.'

Frith would know, as well. He had asked White for training, once, to see if he could tell whether someone was mind-spying on him – but he hadn't needed it. Even without Talent, Frith's senses were freakishly tuned. White's own tests had shown that a lot of un-Talented could feel it too; they normally attributed it to an air draft, or even a ghost.

Frith sighed. 'All right,' he said.

'What are you doing about Wren?'

Frith was silent.

White turned his head to look at him.

'What are you doing about him?'

'Not a lot.'

'What?' said White. 'Why not?'

'He didn't do this by himself, White. He's just a boy, and he's a coward. He was put up to it by his Worlder superiors. They're trying to poach from us. It's a compliment, in a way.'

'They cannot do that!'

'Yes, they can,' said Frith. 'This is politics. We hurt them, they hurt us. We won't do as they say, so they try to screw us. That's the game.'

'So this is just . . . the end of it, then?'

'I'm protecting you. Just as I always have. That's all you need to know.'

Frith's voice had an edge.

It was useless for White to argue. It got him nowhere. He'd get a sunny smile, hiding the 'don't push it' darkness underneath. Then Frith would shut down, and leave.

And what could White do in the face of that?

A big fat nothing, that was what.

A big, fat, useless nothing.

If he were determined, courageous, reckless, and all those other words that heroes were made up of, he would just leave, wouldn't he?

He'd go find Wren, somehow, with no real idea of where he was, just that he was somewhere in the world, an insistent tangy yellow ache in the back of White's head. He'd find a way, though, because that was what determined heroes did.

He'd find Wren, and they would face off with each other. They would fight.

It would be brutal. Nasty. Near misses and crunching bone. Maybe they'd fight with their minds, forcing each other into the nothing blackness that existed between Jumps. They would fight there in the empty places, alone and desperate. It wouldn't even echo with their shouts. The energy and noise and flesh colour they painted onto it with their presence would be sucked away. Because everything there was sucked away.

They would fight an exhausted, raging fight. White would win but be left battered and bloody. He would crawl out of the nothing and fall to Rue, who would hold him in her arms and tell him how incredibly brave he had been. He would bring her back here.

She would be here.

If he were a hero.

But the idea was ridiculous and embarrassingly stupid and never made it out past his daydreams. So he stayed here, and told himself she wanted Wren, and that she hated him. He stayed and he let Frith in a little more, because Frith gave him a purpose. The purpose made him feel better about his life, as if he had a right and a reason to be here, and didn't just exist for existing's sake. It made him forget all his shame. All the stupid things he had done that taunted him now and had led him here. So he would content himself with childish fantasies, and he would play Frith's games and jump through Frith's hoops, because in the end he would be allowed to be part of something.

And there's one more reason, a small voice inside reminded him.

You have nowhere else to go.

CHAPTER 7

WORLD

RUE

Rue was dreaming.

She was back at the party the other night, sat on a little couch watching dim shapes dance and laugh before her, a mass of humanity that she was no part of.

She felt alone, but not. One person in a string of people, going all the way backwards and forwards to forever. She felt like she could travel along her own line, move backwards to a past she had forgotten, move forwards to a future her with grey hair and wrinkled skin. Move further forward to a future without her in it.

She was thinking about this, and how natural it all felt. How she should be scared by it but could only be calm about it. About how it would be to sit like this forever, in the dark and the nothing. She was thinking all this when she felt someone by her side and turned, assuming it would be Wren.

But it wasn't.

It was White.

Rue felt herself go stiff and prickling.

Her heart started to pound, pound, pound against her ribs.

He was sat next to her, looking bewildered. She'd never seen him look bewildered.

Yes, you have, said a voice in her mind's ear. *The last time you spoke to each other. He looked pretty damn bewildered when you told him –*

Rue gave the voice an angry shove. It stopped.

'Where's this?' said White. He was gazing around the dark.

'Some party,' she said. 'What are you doing here?'

He didn't reply.

White. It was White. So it was only a dream, but it felt real enough.

He was prettier than she remembered. Not so imposing. Slim and compact and hesitant. But then this was her ideal dream version of him, she supposed, not him as he really was.

He glanced at her.

'You look good,' he said, awkwardly. 'I guess World suits you.'

Rue frowned. 'Your Angle Tarain is a lot better. You used to have more of an accent.'

'We're speaking in World.'

'Oh. I didn't even notice.'

'How did you learn it so fast?' said White.

'Data stick.'

He looked surprised. 'Those things are expensive.'

Rue shrugged, unwilling to say how she got it, and that she was beholden to someone.

81

Silence, then.

White sighed, leaning forward, resting his arms on his thighs. She noticed how his back strained underneath his shirt. He was past pretty and well into beautiful, she realised. Odd looking. But maybe that was what made him beautiful.

It was funny how much simpler everything felt in a dream. Around him in real life, she had never been able to think clearly. She could only dance around what she had wanted to say.

She could feel the warmth of his thigh against hers. He shifted away from her slightly, and their legs lost contact. She was heartbroken.

'I don't know what to say to you,' White said, staring out across the darkness. 'I've thought about it often enough. Even in a dream, nothing comes out the way it should.'

'I don't know what you should say, either,' said Rue. 'But you don't have to say anything.'

White seemed to take this to heart, and they sat together for a while.

'How's the rest of the group?' said Rue, trying not to sound forced.

'They progress. Some more than most.'

'Let me guess. Lufe is the best, Lea the worst. He's fiercely proud of himself, she doesn't care too much. Marches would be better if he wasn't so lazy, and Tulsent is too afraid to try harder.'

White laughed. Rue was delighted with the sound. Would he laugh like that in reality, or had she made that sound up?

'You know them so well,' he said.

'I suppose,' said Rue. 'I miss them. Even though sometimes

82

I hated them. I think we all knew each other well, even after the first week or two. It's strange, right?'

'I wouldn't know. I've never felt that close with anyone.' He opened his mouth as if to say more, but then fell silent.

Rue saw, for the first time, the edge of an opening into him. The word 'prison' flashed through her mind. 'Not even when you were younger?' she said.

White leaned back. His shoulder brushed her own briefly, before he re-positioned himself. They were sat extremely close together. He didn't move further up the seat from her, but neither did he seem to want to touch her. It was just these sorts of confusing messages, thought Rue, that had made her so nervous around him in the first place.

'I was lonely as a child,' he said. 'There was no Talent programme I could join. No others that could help me understand why I was so different to everyone else. Only my mother. But even she never knew all the things I could do. And we had to be careful. You weren't allowed to talk about Talent back then.'

'Why?' said Rue.

White smiled a hard smile. 'They were afraid of us.'

He talked. Rue listened, passionately caught. She wanted every word he could give her about himself, every little thing that made up every piece of him. Nothing he could say would be too small, too strange or too dull.

She watched his mouth move as he spoke.

She wanted to run her fingers over his mouth, and him to let her.

I'm sorry, she wanted to say. *I'll make it better. I'll take it from you.*

White stopped.

'I've upset you,' he said.

'No, no.'

'I didn't mean to speak about those things to you. I never meant to tell anyone. I don't want –' He stopped, took a breath. 'This is not about self-pity.'

'No,' Rue said firmly. 'Why would you think that?'

'I'll leave you alone.'

He stood up. She did the unthinkable, then – reached her hand up, stretching it far enough to lift herself off the seat, taking his arm, clutching onto his sleeve.

'Stop,' she said. 'Sit down.'

He did, meek as a child. She smiled, enjoying her version of him – enjoying the pretence of it. She could make him do things the real him never would, and wasn't it fun?

'Sit with me,' she said. 'And tell me more.'

He looked at her.

There was something, then.

There was that moment when someone is close enough to kiss.

You watch the thought pass across each other's eyes, and wonder if either of you will lean forward. You wonder as the seconds peel off, and then it's been too long, and it's too late, and that's it.

It was like that, except the thing that broke it was not him dropping his eyes, but someone else calling her name.

'Rue. Rue!'

It was Wren.

Rue woke to find him crouched next to her bed, one hand on her arm.

'You spoiled my dream,' she said crossly.

'I came to check on you, and you were completely out,' Wren exclaimed. 'I didn't know if you were all right.'

'Why wouldn't I be?' she muttered, rubbing her eyes.

'My dear, it's past lunchtime.'

Rue sat up. 'What?'

Wren sat back on his heels, looking amused. 'Tired, were we?' he said.

CHAPTER 8

ANGLE TAR

WHITE

White woke, reluctantly.

Rue was all around him, beside him and hanging in the air like a scent. The dream had been sweet, and too short.

They had been in a place he didn't know, a dark room filled with the feel of other people, but with Rue he'd made an island in the midst of the crowd. It had been just him and her sat together, close like lovers, talking. She'd looked at him in a way that lit his skin on fire.

He wondered briefly what it meant, and then dismissed it. It meant that he was still obsessed with her. That was all.

It was easier to forget about it during the day, buried amongst a thousand distractions – smells and people and buildings, talking and concentration and teaching and eating. But it was much harder here in the velveteen darkness, all alone with hushed silence and that night-time feeling of delicious strangeness, a feeling that anything could happen, that you could look outside your window and see centaurs roaming the streets under a sky lit by three moons. The night was a different world he used to love to visit, but not any more.

He sat up in bed, resigned to spending the next hour or two awake and feeling sorry for himself. As he moved, he heard something hiss sharply beside his ear, and then came a small, dull thunk.

He froze.

As a multitude of things marched briefly across his mind – *some sort of rat. Something fell. The bed collapsed. I imagined it. I'm still dreaming* – he saw a dark shape drop soundlessly from his ceiling.

Open-mouthed, he watched it come towards him.

A cat. A dog. An animal. Some kind of bird. Very big bird.

'Hello?' he said, his voice blurred with sleep. The word swam into the silence of his room and was swallowed up whole.

'Is anyone there?'

The shape had melted into the gloom.

For a long, agonising moment he sat, straining, flickering silently between assuring himself he'd been imagining it and shouting that there was still something there. It went on so long that he had almost decided on the former, but trying to sleep now without being sure was unthinkable.

Just when he was about to force himself to reach over to his bedside table and light the lamp, just to be safe, there was a little something.

A sheen of a whisper out of the dark. And then the dark moved.

He really should just get up.

He really should just get out of bed.

He should do something. Don't just sit there – *do something*.

Then there was a click from his bedroom door, as if it had been opened. A second of nothing. The shape gliding towards him was pushed sharply off course, crumpling downwards. He could hear scuffling. His bed shook suddenly – something had smacked the side of it and set the whole frame trembling.

A low groan from the floor.

The scuffling stopped.

'White,' said a voice. 'Put a lamp on.'

He reached over unthinkingly, fingers outstretched, feeling for a match from the dish on his bedside table and setting his hands to work. Warm, thick light rolled out from the table lamp and he slid out of bed, peering towards the end of it.

There was a man lying on the floor, and there was Frith crouched over him. He looked up as light flooded across his face.

'It's fine,' said Frith, his voice cheery. 'He's just out, not dead. He was sneaking around your room with a blow dart.'

White looked down at the motionless shape. He could just see the side of the man's face, pale and unmarked. His eyes were closed.

'He is Angle Tarain,' said White, his voice steady. Perhaps hysteria would come later, when he was alone and could show it.

'It appears so. But he'll have been recruited by World.'

'To do what?' said White, though he already knew.

Frith didn't bother answering but finished his inspection and stood up.

'Are you all right?' he said.

White shrugged, heart pounding. 'Perfectly fine. I just – Yes. Fine.'

'Sit down,' said Frith. 'Please. Sit.'

White did so, perching on the side of the bed.

'Why now?' he said.

'Things are moving faster. They know how important you are to our Talent programme. I suppose they decided now was a good time.'

After a moment, he felt the bed sink down as Frith sat next to him.

'Are you sure you're all right? You look a little sick.'

'I am fine,' snapped White. 'For a very nearly dead man.'

'He was a poor shot, I'll grant you. But I don't think they want to kill you, White. I think we'll find his dart was dipped in some sort of knockout drug. They probably planned to kidnap you, drag you back to World.'

White remembered the hiss and the thunk. The dart had missed him by inches.

'I sat up,' he said, realising. 'I sat up because I woke, and so he missed.'

Frith was quiet. The bed creaked as he shifted.

It dawned on White how closely they were sat together and he tried surreptitiously to move away.

'What are you going to do with him?' he said. He looked down at the man by Frith's feet. He tried not to start imagining that the man was only pretending to be unconscious. That in a moment he would be up, the surprise knocking Frith off balance. Giving him time to slit Frith's throat with a handily concealed knife. Turning to White. Plunging the knife into his chest like slicing butter – that gentle resistance. White feeling the man's breath on his face as he died.

'Oh, just ask him some questions. I don't need to know who sent him. But I imagine, shortly, the rest of his team will know he's been caught and will decide to quietly disperse. I'd quite like to talk to all of them,' said Frith.

White watched Frith poke his foot carefully into the man's side.

'Where were you?' said White.

Frith glanced at him.

'Where were you?' White repeated. 'You stopped him. How did you know he was here?'

Frith was silent for a second. When his voice came, it was contemptuously amused. 'White, you didn't expect me to leave you alone and unguarded while all this is going on, did you? I said, when you first came to me, that I had ways and means of protecting you. I didn't tell you what those ways were. I'm not going to tell you now.'

It was good. It was very good, in fact. Just the right amount of impatience and disappointment, as if White should be cleverer than that. As if he should have worked that out by himself.

But something was off. It was categorically impossible that Frith could have known that there was someone in this room and then arrived in time to stop it.

There could only be two explanations.

One. Frith had Talent, had somehow seen the danger and Jumped into White's bedroom in time to prevent it. This meant that Frith had been lying to him all this time.

It was wildly unlikely. White knew that he would have felt

it if Frith was Talented – especially as ridiculously Talented as to be able to do *that*. There would have been signs, even from someone as hard to read as him. It was an extremely difficult thing to hide.

So that left two. Two was that Frith had been somewhere nearby; somewhere so nearby that it might very well be next door. And that he had the means to watch the inside of White's rooms whenever he chose.

No. Frith was Frith, but that was just ridiculous. He couldn't camp out next door every night just in case something happened, and he couldn't watch White for hours on end in secret, invading his privacy in such a horrible way.

Could he?

A suspicion began to twitch its legs.

It was stupid, the suspicion, and ridiculous, and a million other things. But it was also awfully, awfully possible. In the deepest, darkest part of White's heart, there was that something that he had begun to suspect of Frith but never thought could really, absolutely be true.

He could feel Frith's eyes on him. The room's thick silence buzzed heavily in his ears. If he said it out loud. If he just confronted him.

'How did you know he was here? How could you possibly have known?' he said again.

Frith tutted. 'I'm not going to tell you, White, so this is the last time you should ask.'

He sounded annoyed. But his gaze was steady on White's face. Steady and calm.

He wants me to know. He wants me to work it out.

White looked away.

'I hate this game,' he muttered, out loud and barely conscious of it.

'It's nearly over,' said Frith. 'One way or another.'

White's heart spiked in fear.

An image of a golden-skinned boy, dappled by sunlight and laughing as he disappeared, flashed into his mind.

More scenes came to him from Frith's drunken confession that night a few months ago. A crowd of children, a young Frith in the middle, small and sweet-looking, gazing at the golden boy's proud face. Ruining his life, and doing it because he couldn't get what he wanted. Because of love.

A knock came from outside the bedroom door. After a moment, Frith got up from the bed.

'Come in,' he called.

The door opened inwards and an older face peered around the edge of it.

'Syer?'

'Take this, would you?' said Frith, pointing at the man crumpled on the floor. 'See that he's secure. I'd like to talk to him when he wakes up.'

Two men came in. They must have been well trained – neither of them showed the slightest hint of surprise at the man. They took hold of him and dragged him out. He still hadn't woken, or moved. Whatever Frith did in those short seconds had been effective.

And just how had Frith called them in, anyway? White hadn't seen him do it. They had simply shown up.

'Well,' said Frith brightly, when they had left the room. 'I think your sleep has been disturbed enough for one night. I'm going to go and see what we can find out from him. I'll come and find you between classes in the morning. Try not to worry. It won't happen again, I can assure you.'

White nodded. He felt like a child, and a pet, and a prisoner, and something else darker that he couldn't even name.

He watched Frith leave, and then waited as long as he dared.

He had to be sure, even if there was a chance they were still watching.

He started with the bed. He ran his fingers across every surface of it, checking the headboard, and the sides, and underneath the mattress. He stood on it, skirting over the lamp bracket on the wall above his head.

He moved to the bedside table, feeling its smooth insides.

He checked every wall for bumps and holes, sketching his fingers lightly across the wallpaper.

He started to think that he had been completely, utterly and embarrassingly wrong, when he found it. Nestled in the wooden bracket of a wall lamp and about as big as a fingernail. It looked fairly innocuous. Even in daylight it could be mistaken for an imperfection in the wood. But buried in the hole at the edge that pointed towards his bed and the rest of his room was a tiny, tiny lens.

Frith had a camera in his bedroom.

Frith had a *camera*.

In his bedroom.

Frith could see everything. Frith watched him. He watched him in his own private space. He might sit there for hours, watching him sleep. Who knew what he did in his sleep?

Frith had been watching him sleep tonight.

World technology in Angle Tar. It utterly failed to surprise him that Angle Tar would possess such a thing at the same time as it was illegal to even know about technology like that. It would be bought on the black market, but only those little things that would aid the government in protecting its citizens. Of course. Cameras would fit in nicely with that.

He sat on the edge of his bed, his hands clasped tightly together on his lap. His stomach rolled, and for a moment he thought he would be sick on the rug, right there. The urge passed, but the nausea remained.

He felt very small, and very alone.

Are you going to do something about this, finally?

His thoughts turned fierce and snapping, like a cornered dog, but just as quickly they fled. They came occasionally, these angry waves of rebellion, and he had no choice but to let them pass. They didn't help him.

He remembered Frith's words. 'It's nearly over, one way or another.'

He was afraid. Truly and completely.

CHAPTER 9

WORLD

WREN

Greta Hammond's avatar was beautiful, even by World standards.

Today her gold hair was artfully pinned to look precarious, as if it would spill down her neck at any moment, and she wore a loose, open-necked shirt that hugged her tiny frame perfectly. She was lovely.

She was also the most devious bitch Wren had ever known.

He watched her lean forward on the screen stuck up on the opposite wall. A loose hair curl brushed lazily against her neck.

'How's our latest recruit?' she said.

Wren shifted uncomfortably on the test bed. He hated pleasing her. He'd never really liked pleasing anyone, truth be told – but there was something in her, a god-awful knowing, manipulative core, that made him automatically want to do the opposite of anything she said.

'Adjusting,' he answered, eventually.

'And the language pack is working out?'

'Yes, which is a relief. It's really quite irritating having to talk to her in Angle Tarain.'

She smiled. 'It's your native language, Wren. Surely you're used to the sensation.'

'I prefer World. It's . . . less restrictive. Talking in Angle Tarain is like having to dance with a stick up your backside.'

Greta laughed. The laugh was careful, like the rest of her.

'You are eager to shed the old Wren, aren't you?' she said. 'I can understand that, after all you've been through.'

Everything she said seemed to have several meanings at once. It was easier to keep quiet, but she didn't like that. She liked to provoke until he talked. And he wasn't very good at quiet, anyway.

'There'll be no problems from their end,' she was saying. 'Frith will keep his part of the bargain – no attempts on their side to get Rue back.'

Wren snorted. 'So we'll just bow to their wishes like good little children and hide away over here? There's a couple more I think I could get, if you let me try again.'

'Our end of the deal was to leave White alone, not the rest of them.'

He sat up straighter. 'So I can go back?'

'Patience. We have more pressing priorities right now.'

Tests. Always tests.

He felt sick, and suddenly violent about the whole thing. Greta was head of Talent research here – he had been handed over to her almost as soon as he'd arrived in World. Most people didn't seem to care exactly how the Talented worked – especially not in Angle Tar. But Greta wanted to poke around inside, peeling back his layers until he spilled his guts out for her to root around in. Needles and drugs were commonplace to him now.

He needed to be useful again. He needed to *do*. Poaching Rue from the Angle Tarain group for Greta had been the most fun he'd had in months. Surely they should be training him up as a spy? That was what Frith had been doing with his Talented – everyone knew it. But here they didn't seem to trust the Talented. They saw them less like normal human beings and more like exotic creatures that had to be caged and understood.

How dare they violate him. How dare they try to chain him. He should refuse. Today should be the day when he told her where to shove her tests.

She saw it. 'You're going to have to make your peace with this, Wren,' she said, a gentle warning note creeping into her voice. 'If you want to stay. You'd like eventually to get permanent citizenship; I know you would.'

More fool you, he thought savagely. *I'm not your citizen. I don't belong anywhere.*

But let her think that, if she liked. A practised grumpy expression flittered across his face. She saw it and seemed satisfied.

He knew better than to ask; she didn't enjoy his questions. But that had never stopped him before, so he asked.

'What are you going to do with Rue?'

He had begun to suspect something for a while now. Greta had never told him exactly why she'd wanted to poach from Angle Tar, or why she'd encouraged him to go for Rue in particular. But he thought that it might have been the same reason that *he* had wanted to take Rue.

Because of White.

Greta raised a brow.

'I'm just curious why you wanted her so much,' he said, with a light smile. 'It's not like she's amazingly Talented. She can't even Jump without help.'

'As I recall, you were rather eager yourself to go after Rue when we found out what she was to White.' Greta smiled indulgently. 'Your little feud.'

He hadn't bothered to hide it; that was true.

'It's not a feud,' he said, affecting nonchalance. 'Because it's over. I don't care any more. I won.'

'And what if he ever came after you for revenge? He tried to kill you, didn't he?'

Wren felt his chest tighten – the memory of that gun pointed at his face, and White on the other end of it, his eyes freezing cold and black.

But in front of Greta he yawned, passing his hand lazily over his mouth.

'Well, I admire your confidence,' she said.

'You doubt my Talent?'

'Not at all. You're the most Talented boy I've seen. Apart from him.'

Bile flooded his throat, but he choked it down with an easy laugh.

'Now you're trying to make me angry.'

'No, Wren. Just reining in that cockiness of yours. I think you've been too long used to power. People like you need people like him to remind you of your own mortality. You keep each other in check.'

Greta laughed, the noise like a fluting bird. Venomous snake. Inside his head he thrashed and raged. He crossed his arms but said no more. He'd lost this round. She was a hard one to play the game with. Some opponents were more formidable than others. But everyone did it, manipulating where they could, all out for what they could get. If he faltered, he would lose. Only the weak lost.

'Shall we begin today's set?' she said, nodding at the two technicians standing patiently in the corner of the room. They came forward and began to fiddle with a small set of machines on a table next to Wren's test bed. He'd stopped watching them prepare by now – he couldn't even begin to fathom how any of their equipment worked.

'Begin procedure one,' said the fatter technician, and he waved his hand in a curt gesture, activating something in Life that only he could see.

The air over Wren's body felt suddenly heavy and strange.

It was like being stroked, at first.

Such a light touch as to just raise the hairs on his skin and brush them, gently, gently.

Then the touch grew a little heavier, more pressing than stroking. Something like pens being rolled down his arms.

Then it started to pinch.

Then it started to hurt.

However much Wren tried not to give the two men watching him the satisfaction of listening to him whimper, those pathetic little noises always managed to escape between his clenched teeth.

They talked in quiet tones above his head, as if he wasn't there. They didn't need to ask him questions about how he felt – all they did was toss brief glances to the side, eyes glazed as they checked the readouts in Life: his heart rate, body temperature, nerve responses, brain patterns. And he knew that each bit of data was being recorded, so they could look through it in more detail later. All they were really there for was to make sure that it didn't go too far. That he didn't become permanently damaged, or die.

He knew this because they had explained as much to him the first time.

He was supposed to take the pain. He was supposed to be strong, so they could measure how far he could go before buckling. They tinkered with his thresholds, adjusting carefully, testing and prodding. They did it as if he wasn't even real.

When he got home later and Rue caught sight of him, she would be all eyebrows up and looking at him with her stupidly open face, each emotion on display for everyone to see. Because he'd look awful. He always did, on a test day. She'd ask questions. The girl was one giant, irritating, relentless question mark. It was hard to keep smiling, keep telling her not to worry, when all he really wanted to do was crawl into bed and not exist for a while. Why didn't she just accept things? Why did she have to know about *everything*?

Complaining to Greta got him nothing; she didn't care

about him or Rue. All she wanted him to do was obey. Well, he had, hadn't he, as long as it suited him?

It was really beginning not to suit him any more.

No choice there, though – not right now, at least. He had to bide his time. Biding his time was not something he was very good at.

It's not forever, Wren.

Just keep playing the game until you can figure out your next move.

The pain stopped, all at once.

'How was that?' said Greta, peering out from the holographic screen.

'Fine,' said Wren. But his voice came out broken, and he struggled with a sudden flare of temper.

Never let them see your weakness!

'No worse than childbirth,' she replied. He didn't know whether she was making a joke, or expecting him to reply in some fashion. He doubted anyone in World knew what childbirth felt like, let alone Greta. Sabine had told him a while ago about safe Cs – people had an appointment at the medical hall on a nice convenient date and a doctor removed their baby while they were unconscious. This culture didn't understand pain. They'd carefully circumvented almost all circumstances in which you could be in it. It was an admirable thing to have done. Who the hell wanted to feel pain?

Of course, they seemed to have no issue with inflicting it.

'Tee eye two zero one,' said one of the technicians over Wren's head. The other nodded.

'What?' said Wren.

No one replied.

He watched them fiddle with a tiny bottle of colourless liquid, plunging a needle into its sealed top and filling the syringe.

'What is that?'

'It's a new version of the inducer,' said Greta.

'No.'

Greta raised a brow.

'No, what?'

'I don't want you putting that shit in me again.'

There was a silence while everyone in the room tried to work out how to respond. He could see each option run through their faces. Restrain him? How? He was here by choice. If he wanted, he could simply Jump out of here.

All right, 'choice' was a strong word. If he had *choice*, he wouldn't be here at all.

'It's been improved, Wren,' said Greta finally. 'It shouldn't have such unpleasant side effects this time.'

'Oh good! That's a weight off my mind.'

'Wren –'

'You didn't have to endure those side effects, did you? No. I did. I'm not doing it again. Besides, it doesn't even work.'

'Think for a moment. This is an important step towards progress. If we can get this drug working, we can use it on the Talented who don't have control over their abilities the same way you do. They can take the drug and induce the Talent, and we won't have to waste precious time waiting around for them to learn how to do it themselves!'

Her voice had become forceful. He couldn't tell whether she really was impassioned or just faking to get him to do it.

Either way, she'd misjudged him. He didn't want hordes of drugged-up Talented running around. The only Talented he wanted running around was him.

'No,' he said flatly. 'And get that needle away from me before I start feeling violent.'

The technician who had been surreptitiously hovering by his arm froze.

Greta sighed.

Her eyes slid to the other technician, who walked around the back of Wren. He tried to twist around but before he could move, arms came down around his neck and pressed into his chest, locking him into place.

The pain from the previous test had made him weak. He struggled, but it was a pathetic attempt, all slow and trembling. The arms around him didn't even shift. He felt his arm gripped tightly against the chair rest. A sharp little pain on the skin as the needle punctured its way in.

Nothing, for a moment.

Then his heart slammed into his ribcage and every hair on his body stood on end and he felt *charged*, like he could run screaming headfirst into the ceiling. His mind was tumbling over and over, a slot machine spinning past choices and thoughts too fast for him to pick. He couldn't think or decide and there was no path, there was just spinning, and he gasped to keep up but there was no keeping up with that. The drug pounded inside him, forcing him on, and he couldn't fight.

The Castle flashed briefly into his mind.

And then the pain was gone, the lights were gone, the arms around him were gone.

He wasn't in the test room any more. He wasn't anywhere in World.

He was in the Castle.

The cold prickled his skin.

He stood up, carefully. The weight of the air here was heavier, somehow, lying like a coat over his frame. Closing in.

He felt an enormous thrill run through him. Terrified and elated in equal measure. Here again, and so soon.

He couldn't believe it. He'd never once been able to come here without the Ghost Girl before, try as he might. She had always, always pulled him here. He looked around for her, but she was nowhere in sight.

Jesus, Greta, he thought. *Your drug.*

It works.

A shuffling noise to his right made him whip around, heart pounding. It was the technician who had held him down. He was on the floor, his eyes wide and staring, his expression wild.

'Ha,' said Wren. His voice echoed around the room. The technician jerked.

'Let me guess. You're Talented.'

The technician looked like he might be sick.

'What?' he whispered eventually.

'We're in the Castle. I've no idea how, but somehow I've pulled you here with me. I doubt I'd be able to do that with a Talentless.'

Wren stalked up to the technician's prone figure on the flagstones. Power over someone felt good here. In the Castle you were nearly always powerless.

He crouched, and stared into the technician's face.

'So the whole time you've been sticking needles in me and electrocuting me and forcing drug cocktails into me, you were a hypocritical, lying little bastard,' he said brightly. 'And I'm supposing Greta doesn't know about this. I'm supposing no one knows about this.'

'Please,' whispered the technician. 'I'm not. It's just funny dreams, sometimes. That's all. I can't do all the weird jackstuff you can do. It's just dreams! I just ignore them! I'm fine! I'm normal!'

Wren was mystified. 'Ignore them? How can you ignore them? It's like ignoring the fact that you have arms.'

'I don't care! I just want to be normal!'

'Well, you're not. And I hope you're happy taking my place as test bunny, because that's all you have to look forward to now.'

The technician sucked in a deep, shuddering breath.

'They won't,' he said. 'I'm a Worlder. I'm a *citizen*. I love World.'

'You might want to think about alternate plans,' said Wren, not unsympathetically.

The technician glared at him. 'We're not a nation of torturers, all right? Look, you agreed to those tests! We didn't force you, did we?'

'If by "force" you mean "offered no other choice" – yes, you did. If I want to stay in World, I have to do it. So what kind of choice is that?'

'If you hate it so much, why don't you just leave?'

Wren was silent.

'You stay because you like it,' he said. 'And because it's convenient.'

Wren looked at him sharply. 'What would you know about it?'

'I know plenty. You're all the same. Expecting to be handed everything on a plate just because you can do something other people can't.'

The technician sneered. He had small eyes and a tired, puffy face.

'You should all be locked up,' he said. 'You're not worth the trouble.'

From outside the room they were in came a noise. A far-off roar, wafting in between the stones.

That was fast. They weren't normally so fast.

The technician's eyes went wide.

'What was that?' he whispered.

Wren tried to smile a nasty smile, but his breath had grown short – an instant response to that sound. You never got used to it. You were never unafraid here.

One day you'll stand in front of one of them and talk to it. And it will listen.

Wren straightened. 'Something you don't ever want to meet.'

'Wait! Where are you going?'

'Back,' he said, as if it were obvious.

'You can't leave me here!'

He shrugged. 'You're Talented, you can get back by yourself.'

'Wait!'

Wren ignored him. The prick had made his feelings clear. This was only what he deserved.

'I can help you!'

'Of course you can,' he said soothingly, searching for that feeling behind his shoulder blades – the tug that meant 'normal', the path out of here that would lead him back to the life he hated.

'I can! Whatever you want! I can get it! Information! Or . . .' The technician searched wildly. 'A way out of the city?'

Wren sighed. 'I'm not a criminal, idiot. I don't want to live off-grid like some jacking Technophobe.'

But then an idea came to him. Perfect. Fated, almost. He turned.

'I'll make you a deal, though,' he said, striving for calm.

'Please! Whatever you want!'

Wren smiled. It was almost too easy.

'You're going to get me access to the inducer drug you just pumped me full of. You're going to get it for me whenever I want it. And when we get back in front of Greta, you're going to lie and say it doesn't work. Clear?'

The technician looked astonished. To his credit, he thought fast.

'What do I get out of this?' he said.

'You get me not telling Greta that you're a lying Talented sack of shit. The rest is up to you. See if you can wriggle out of it. I promise I won't say anything. I'll back you up. Deal?'

'What if I can't get you access to the drug?'

'Then you have a problem.'

The technician glanced around the room in a panic, as if something in it could help him decide. But there was just stone, reeking of fear, and the noises outside. They were getting louder.

'Decide fast,' said Wren, impatient. 'That thing will be here soon. Do we have a deal?'

The technician licked his lips nervously.

* * *

'What happened? Wren! WREN!'

He stirred in the test chair. His head had lolled to one side and the inside of his cheek throbbed alarmingly from where he'd apparently bitten it. The metal tang of blood glossed his tongue and he swallowed, grimacing.

There was a groan from the floor. The technician.

The other was busy scanning Wren's Life implant readouts, from the glazed look in his eyes.

'Wren, answer me,' came Greta's sharp voice.

Just SHUT UP a minute, would you?

'Heart rate elevated, but nothing to worry about,' said the other technician, a little frown on his thin face. 'No other abnormal readings.'

'Oh good,' Wren managed, his words thick and clotted.

'What happened?'

'I obviously passed out,' he said, trying to sit up.

'Obviously,' said Greta.

'How long was I unconscious?'

'Twenty seconds, perhaps.'

'What?' said Wren. He couldn't hide his astonishment. It had felt a lot longer. It had *been* a lot longer, surely.

'Why are you surprised?'

'I feel like crap,' he said, forcing irritation into his voice. 'It seemed longer than that.'

'What happened?'

He took a deliberate moment. 'Nothing,' he said at last, with a puzzled air. 'Just unconscious. I don't remember anything.'

'You didn't Jump?' Greta said.

'Obviously not.'

'Not even a little mind Jump?'

'I don't think being knocked out can be counted as a mind Jump, no.'

'So what happened to him?' She pointed to the technician he'd inadvertently dragged with him.

Wren shrugged. Offering an explanation would sound rehearsed. 'No idea. What did happen to him?'

'He fell unconscious at the same time as you.'

'Oh. That's odd. Maybe I've developed a superpower that makes people touching me faint.'

'Wren.'

'What?' he said, irritated. 'I've no idea. I was unconscious at the time. Why don't you ask him your questions?'

Greta glanced at the technician. 'Dr Cheever will answer them in time.'

The technician looked terrified at the prospect.

Well, I did the best I could for you, thought Wren. *They suspect, but they don't know for sure. The rest depends on how good a liar you are.*

'I don't know what happened,' said Dr Cheever. 'I really don't. It must have been something he did.'

Wren laughed. Greta shifted her eyes to him, and he stopped laughing.

'Well, not on purpose, I can assure you,' he said.

Greta watched him. He made a show of coughing.

'So the inducer didn't work?'

'It didn't work. So sorry. Maybe next time.'

'Yes. Because there will be a next time, Wren.'

He rolled his eyes, but his insides curled miserably, and his hatred snapped its jaws.

They made him lie back down as they buzzed some more, monitoring, checking, feeling, administering. Poking and prodding while he lay, passive. But now he had something to comfort him: the knowledge that for the first time since coming here, he had what he so desperately needed.

An advantage.

Sometimes he wished that the version of World he'd sold to Rue was the version he actually lived in. It had seemed so perfect, once. Once felt like a long time ago. Now he understood that ideals and realities never matched. Humans were flawed. No system worked. No culture had it right.

But it didn't matter, because he had the Castle, the centre of everything – the place that was all places and all times. No country on earth could ever come close to that. When he was there, he felt it plucking at every tiny piece of him, promising power. The kind of power that people like Greta couldn't even begin to stand against.

With that power, no one would ever be able to tell him what to do, ever again. With that power maybe he could even remake the world, change things for the better. Politicians wouldn't do it. The Talented couldn't be trusted to do it – White had proved that. He was on his own.

That was fine. He'd always been on his own.

If he could open it, he knew that everywhere would become the Castle. It would be like living permanently in a dream, barriers down, the laws of reality as substantial as smoke. It would be incredible. Better than Life, which only gave you the scope of human imagination.

The Castle was something else.

He would stop all the pain, and the misery, and the banality of human existence. Nothing would ever be dull again. No one would worry about money, or disease, or poverty. Those things seemed so far away in the Castle.

Now that he had the drug to get him there, he would find a way to open it and share it with the world.

It would be the best gift he could ever give.

CHAPTER 10

WORLD

RUE

So it turned out that Wren was a bit of an ass.

One minute he was grinning at her and calling her sweet little names. The next minute he was losing his temper with her and stalking out of the house for hours at a time. Rue didn't understand how to deal with him, or what she was supposed to do. So she lost her temper too, and they fell out often over stupid things. She wanted him to trust her, to open up to her. Just once or twice she'd caught sight of a vulnerability in him, an edge that made her wonder what he could be like if he would only stop isolating himself from everything as if he were better than it all. He had heart and passion. That had drawn her to him, in the beginning. Now it just made her want to scratch at him until he bled his secrets – but he was having none of it.

At least there was Cho. Spiky, fiery Cho, her face flushed with delight as they sat in her room and she showed Rue the code she'd created, the games and worlds she'd helped make. She was a Life coder, a creator of alternate realities – a power at least as impressive as being Talented, to Rue. When she'd told Cho that, the girl had seemed embarrassed and delighted at the description.

They had grown close fast. Cho's edges were sharp and she was all off balance. She fascinated Rue because of it. But the closer they became, the more Rue worried about her. Because Cho had a dark side, too, alternating swiftly between cagey and far too intimate, telling Rue things about her hacker friends, the strange and addictive lifestyle of it. It was obvious that it was the danger that attracted her. She said she needed it to feel alive. To give her existence shape and meaning.

That sort of thing could really get you into trouble.

So it was Cho who occupied Rue's days – but her nights had slowly, inexorably been given over to White.

Rue had seen him again last night.

She knew what she was doing – conjuring him up in her mind as a substitute for being with the real him. They had been in a dim room, similar to the party room she'd been in when she'd first dreamed of him. Or maybe it was the same room – it was too dark to tell. She was perched on a little couch.

He emerged from nothing, a thick and solid shadow. She watched him come to her.

The air was still and the light dark. Comforting.

He stood in front of her, silent.

'Hi,' she said.

'Hi,' he replied. It was strange to hear such a word, so casually spoken, come out of his mouth.

113

'Do you want to sit?'

He was still for a moment, as if debating. Then he moved forward and sat himself next to her. They looked out together across the darkness, but there was nothing to see, save each other.

'Tell me something,' said Rue.

She felt White shift beside her, gently.

'What is it you want to know?'

'Something more of you. You told me of your childhood last time. But I want to know about something else.'

'Why?'

'To piece you together. I want to make you real.'

There was a silence. She watched him watch the dark.

'Aren't you afraid you won't like what you find, in the end?' he said. Listening to him speak in World was something else. His voice was no longer stiff and spiked and hesitant. Words rolled off his tongue like oil, his voice a piano being played.

'I suppose that's always the risk,' said Rue.

'So ask me a question.'

Rue thought. It had to be something of the utmost importance, something that would give her, in one answer, such an enormous key to solving him that she would understand him completely and all at once.

'What's your favourite food?' she said.

White looked at her, and laughed. It was rich and lovely. She basked in its warmth.

'Why are you laughing?' she said with a smile. 'It's a serious question.'

'There are a few. I couldn't possibly pick a favourite.'

'Name some.'

'It's too hard. I like extremes. Caramel cakes and saltfish pies.'

'Me too. Another.'

'An old URCI dish called char siu pork.'

'I don't know it, but you should introduce me to it sometime. Another?'

'Potato Roise.'

'That's an Angle Tarain dish, from the country,' she said, delighted. 'You're lying to please me.'

'Not at all. It was the first proper meal I ate when I came to Angle Tar.'

'Were you alone?'

'I was with Frith.'

His face had fallen.

Rue looked down.

'I suppose he must hate me,' she said. 'For leaving.'

'I'm sure he doesn't.' White sat forward, his arms locking, hands clasped together. Rue watched him for a while, but he wouldn't look round at her.

'I've always wondered why you danced with me at the midwinter ball back in Angle Tar,' she said eventually. 'Will you say?'

'It wasn't planned. I just needed to be near you.'

Rue felt a delightful shiver creep along her skin. 'I wish you would have told me then.'

'So do I.'

His hair was loose this time. Some of it was wrapped, twining around itself, and it draped like a rope over his shoulder.

'I hope –' he stopped. 'I hope you're happy, where you are.

I hope you're finding what you wanted to find.'

What she wanted to find. No. Not yet. She wanted truth, but all anybody gave her here were more secrets. She wanted to tell White that she often thought about what she'd given up. About how she belonged nowhere any more.

She couldn't bring herself to say such things to him, though. She couldn't bear to be so disappointing.

He was watching her. She felt it on her face, like sunlight. She wanted to turn into it, bask in it, but it was too hot and bright. He was too much for her, but she chased that feeling. Half of her hoped that it would never feel normal between them. She didn't want to lose the glamour of him. Better to never know him so well that he became just another person, with toes and bad judgement and maybe even stupid jokes that made her roll her eyes.

But the other half wondered what it would be like.

To be with him like that, all up close, fierce and stupid. The fantasy him was removed from her, keeping them both at arm's length, which was nerve-wracking, exciting – but maybe, in the end, it wouldn't be enough.

'I'm sorry,' said Rue. She caught his surprised glance. 'For the things I said to you before I left.'

'You were right. I knew about the tunnels, and I know about many other things. I've done things that would make you hate me.'

'Maybe. I don't know. I don't think I left because of the tunnels. I think I left because I can't face anything real,' said Rue, willing her voice to come out wobble-free. 'When it gets real, I just run away. Like a coward.'

116

'I know what you mean.'

Silence, then. It crowded in, thick and dark.

'I waited,' said White. 'I know it's stupid, but I've been waiting for you to come back. Just appear in my rooms. Or in my classroom. I wanted you to come back and be angry at me, if you wanted. You could shout. I would have taken it. I would have told you.'

He swallowed, and fell silent.

Rue watched him.

'Told me what?' she said.

But he couldn't, or wouldn't, say it.

'Why did you never say those kinds of things to me back then?' she said, curious.

'I thought you'd find them repulsive.' He took a breath. 'I thought you found me repulsive.'

Rue laughed. 'You're very clever, but you don't know girls very well,' she said, amused.

He smiled. 'You're right. But now it's your turn. It's only fair.'

Rue slotted her legs underneath her. It felt good, this dream; it felt good that they were in the middle of it, and they had a while to go, maybe. But it would still be over too soon.

'What's my turn?' she said.

'You curl yourself up like a cat.'

'It's comfortable. What's my turn?'

'Well, I should know more about you this time.'

Rue grimaced.

'None of that,' said White. 'You have a lot of me; I have nothing of you.'

'Frith must have told you some things.'

White laughed in derision. 'Frith told me only what I needed to know, and he didn't think I needed to know much about my students in order to teach them.'

He looked at her properly now. He seemed urgent, his face sharp. It made her uneasy, and excited, and she tried to position her body casually, as if that would calm everything down.

'All right,' she said. 'I'm from Kernow. Bretagnine, to posh people.'

'I know *that*.'

'Fine,' she snapped, growing mock cross. 'What do you want to know?'

'What do you want?'

'What?'

'Out of this life,' said White. 'What do you want?'

Rue thought.

She thought of all the things she had wanted. To be the best at something. To be desired. To have power. Little, petty, common dreams. The most common dreams of all.

'I want what everyone wants,' she said, surprised at how sad and empty she sounded. 'I'm just like everyone else, actually. And I tried so hard not to be. I don't know what I'm supposed to do.'

'No one does,' said White. 'It's what we all have in common.'

'I think I just want to be with you.'

White looked away.

Rue felt her heart thrum anxiously. 'Is that . . .? It's too small, isn't it? It's boring.'

'No,' said White. 'It's the best thing anyone has ever said to me.'

118

'You mean it?' she said, delighted.

He only smiled in reply, and wouldn't look back at her.

'I read in Life that nothing means anything, because we all die,' she said. 'And since everyone will always be dying, even people that haven't been born yet, all you ever do will never mean anything to anyone, eventually. So what's the point of anything?'

'That's true.'

Rue looked at White in surprise. 'You agree?'

'Well, yes. Because it's true. It's also true that if you believe that, you might as well kill yourself right now. I suppose the beauty of being human is that we can choose which things we want to believe. The one I prefer is: do something that has a long-lasting ripple out into life. Do something that affects someone else, even if it's just one person. Even if the thing you do is only to love them. I suppose that's the only way we can be happy. And if we're not happy, there's not much point in just existing until we die.'

'I think that's right,' said Rue. 'And I'd like to change things. I'd like to mean something.'

'You already do.'

Silence.

'Jacob,' she said. 'That's your real name.'

Silence from him.

Then, 'Yes, it is. How do you know that?'

'I know a lot of things about you now,' she said, teasing.

Her knee was pressed gently against his leg.

'Rue,' he said, under his breath.

'Yes.'

119

He was watching her, as if hypnotised.

There was no one to interrupt this. It was terrifying.

'I feel like my heart's stopped,' she said.

'Why?'

'Because you're looking at me.'

She uncurled her legs on the seat, and as her thigh dropped into place it touched his. She felt him move towards her. His hair slid forward over his shoulder. He smelled of male – a strong smell, hard to define.

'Rue,' he said again, in her ear. Hearing her name from him made her insides twist. Then his cheek brushed against her nose as he turned his face, and caught her mouth with his.

He was warm. She didn't know why she was surprised by this. His marble skin had life underneath it. He kissed her like he was starving for her. Almost the way she had thought about him kissing her in her head, only that had been long and languorous, and in control.

This didn't feel in control. Her heart was thundering in her chest. The more he kissed her, the faster everything got, until she felt like she was stumbling to keep up. His hands were on her shoulders, and then the back of her neck, underneath her hair, gripping there. She felt like she couldn't breathe.

It was the best moment of her life.

She could feel the muscles in his back slide and shift underneath her hands as she pressed him against her. She felt completely helpless, and safe.

Please, don't let it end.

It felt real.

Gods, it felt real.

CHAPTER 11

WORLD

WREN

It was time to try again.

He didn't care what Greta would say if she ever found out. He didn't care because he couldn't stop himself.

He had to know.

He'd always struggled with mind Jumps. Dream visiting White's little Talented group had required him to body Jump back to Red House; he'd always found it much easier to slide into people's minds if he was physically close to them. He'd only managed a mind spy once or twice with White in the past, and after leaving Angle Tar he hadn't dared try it again.

But just a little risk, now he was on top. It couldn't hurt. Maybe White wouldn't feel him this time. The Wren that had left Angle Tar was a weaker creature. He'd come a long way since then.

He didn't know what he wanted to see, exactly. He told himself it was to make sure that White wasn't coming after him in some way. He told himself that he just wanted to see how he was. If he was still a cold, miserable bastard or whether he was happy now.

He wouldn't be. White had never known how to be happy. It was almost like he held the power he had as some sort of awful curse, rather than the extraordinary gift it was. Too bad for him. Wren had no time for cowards. Taking Rue away had seemed perfect at the time – the most sublime punishment. White had thought Wren beneath him. Well, he didn't any more.

Did he?

It was an anxious, grubby kind of thought, lingering and dancing in the back of Wren's head.

What if he's fine?

What if he doesn't think you're powerful?

What if he doesn't even think about you?

Just a little look, then. Using White as the anchor, rather than a place on campus, was the key. Thinking about his face, his voice, the shape that he left in the world. The stiff coats he wore, and the shirts cuffed at his wrist bones. His stupid, prim clothes.

There – a faint glimmer of it. Don't think. Just let it grow bigger. Don't get excited.

In this way, he skirted around the edges of the shape of White. He knew it was taking a while, but he had no concept of time in this state. Closer and closer he grew to it – then a little ebb.

And then, all of a sudden, like a sneeze, he was there.

White was in a parlour. The bedroom door behind him was open just a little, showing a sliver of rumpled sheets. He sat at a table, poking his food listlessly with a fork and leafing through the papers scattered in front of him.

That smooth, pale skin. Liquid black eyes, creased in thought. His hair pulled back into its customary plait. He never let his hair out. Sometimes it escaped, tendrils sliding out from its bonds to dance and stick on his shoulders, but this time it was all in place.

One half of his face was in the dark. His nose was thrown into relief, cheekbones shadowed, angles that Wren had often found himself staring at when they had been friends. He was chewing delicately on his top lip. His eyes were cast down. He was reading.

Calm. You'll lose the control if you don't keep calm.

Wren circled, invisible and fascinated. He tried to catch sight of what was on the papers, craning as if White would feel his breath, tensing his muscles to move as softly as he could, and had to remind himself that there was no need. There was only his mind here. So he moved to the papers and drank them in.

There were bits of beautiful, half-hidden pencil drawings. Diagrams and rendered sculptures of human bodies. Notes, all written in White's alarmingly messy spider writing. He'd always found writing hard. It wasn't a necessary skill in World, learning to write longhand. Wren had laughed at him back then, but he could appreciate it now.

The notes were incomprehensible, though. If he had time to sit down and go through them, maybe – but White's idea of taking notes was to write a list of numbers and dates, and then break off in the middle of it all to sketch a hand, writing a paragraph across the palm on the early characteristics of Talent, and then cover every bit of white space around his scribbled words with ever-growing geometric doodles.

No drawings of Rue. Or not that Wren could see.

Somehow he'd expected some sort of sign that White was visibly affected by her departure. But maybe he'd miscalculated. Maybe White had just had a minor thing for her. He seemed to be getting on with things just fine here.

No. He'd seen the look on White's face that evening, after he'd taken Rue. It was a look he'd craved to see for such a long time – unguarded, defences utterly gone. White's defences were hard to crack, but he'd done it. He'd caused the misery in those eyes.

He watched White put down his fork, drinking in his face, unhindered by propriety. It was so freeing, watching someone who didn't know you were there. White turned a piece of paper over, turned it back again, and then, without any kind of warning, slammed his closed fist down on the table. His fork rattled and the plate jumped.

The noise it made was deafening in the quiet.

'Get out,' said White. He spoke in World instead of Angle Tarain, addressing the tabletop. 'I know you're there.'

Silence.

'You think you can mind spy on me, and I wouldn't know? I can *feel* you, you fucking prick.'

Wren felt his heart give a panicky leap. He watched, struggling with the idea that he wasn't there, not really. So White couldn't hurt him. White couldn't do anything.

124

'You can hear me, too. I know you can,' said White. 'So hear this. If I ever find you, I will kill you.'

Wren wanted to laugh. He wanted to taunt, and show that he wasn't afraid. But he couldn't do any of that. He was powerless.

'I'll kill you, Wren. And I'll enjoy it.'

He still stared at the tabletop, his face perfectly, calmly set.

Wren started to lose his grip. *No*, he thought, but his heart was racing too much, and something *pushed* at him.

'Get out,' said White.

Something *pushed* at him again, like a gale, buffeting him back with invisible hands.

'Get out,' White repeated.

The push became a shove. And another. The room lost focus, blurring.

'GET OUT.'

The shove became a punch.

It was fast and awful and Wren didn't even understand what had happened until after it had. When he knew anything more, he was slumped in his room, slicked in sweat, and his hands were trembling.

Holy. Shit.

It was not fear. He was not afraid. Simply surprised.

How had White done that? How had he *known* how to do that? What else could he do that he kept to himself? It wasn't fair. Power should be given to people who had the guts to use it. It shouldn't languish within a coward.

If you were still friends, his mind posited, *maybe you'd know about what he could do. He would have taught you.*

I don't want to be his student, he snapped back. *Just because*

125

he has more raw ability than me, doesn't mean he's better than me.

He leaned his head back against the wall, trying to calm down.

Somewhere, buried under the shock and the jealousy and the shame, he felt the tiniest bit relieved. Because at least White still thought about him.

He risked a look down at his hands.

After a long moment, they stopped trembling.

CHAPTER 12

WORLD

RUE

Cho had disappeared.

No more calls. No wry messages in Rue's Life account with links to strange music and even stranger art videos. No meet-ups in energetic, fractured Life cafés that were art gallery, restaurant and dance hall rolled into one. Cho drank a lot, Rue had come to realise, and took drugs almost absent-mindedly. But then everyone seemed to do that, here. They took what they called supplements for everything – to feel less tired, to feel happier, or calmer, more revitalised, or sleepy. They liked to change moods as quick as changing clothes. It was normal to them.

It had been a precarious kind of fun, at first – making friends with hackers, hanging out in strange, luminous places, as if she were trying to become the kind of fire that Cho was – but no more. Cho was far too indiscreet. What if she'd got into trouble?

Rue had only found out that Cho was going to a party this evening when one of her friends sent a message about it to a whole group of people, accidentally including Rue. So she'd go, too. All casual. Just to check on her. She didn't care much for the stupid system that said she couldn't. Who was to stop her, anyway?

Rue stared, checked the address she'd written down again. It was definitely the right place. But instead of grey, listless walls, the entire building was elegantly carved out of what looked like white marble, though when she examined it she could see it was a kind of strange, light stone that she couldn't place. It was set off the main street in a private cul-de-sac. Colonnades clustered around the front entrance – there was most definitely a front entrance. Curved steps like stacked smiles led up to a large, imposing door. It was the most familiar-looking place Rue had seen since coming to World. It seemed that Worlders were not quite as equal as they first appeared to be.

Her feet crunched on the gravel driveway. She took the steps, forcing confidence into her posture, and rang the door alarm.

A moment, and then it was flung open. The girl standing in the doorway was a curvaceous thing with chocolate-coloured skin and a mass of dark hair like a cloud around her head. She looked Rue up and down.

'Yes?' she said. 'I can't access you. Aren't you jacked in?'

'Oh, I don't have an implant,' said Rue brightly. 'I'm from Angle Tar, and I only moved here recently. They haven't given me one yet.'

'They haven't . . .' the girl paused, confused. Rue saw her advantage and pressed.

'I'm here with Cho. Cho Peven. She might already be inside – I'm a bit late, sorry.'

The girl's eyes glazed. 'You're not on the list,' she said. 'Everyone's already here. What's your name?'

Rue hesitated. They swapped their names around, here. She still hadn't gotten used to it. 'Rue Vela,' she said.

'Um . . .'

'Maybe you could get Cho to vouch for me?'

'Well . . .'

Rue smiled sweetly. 'It'd be quicker.'

The girl's mouth twisted, and she closed the door.

Rue stared at it for a moment.

Well, she'd just keep ringing, was all.

As she raised her hand, the door opened again. The girl was back, and this time she had Cho with her.

Rue couldn't help it; she broke into a smile at the sight of her. 'You're okay!' she said.

'What?'

'I've been trying to get hold of you.'

Cho shrugged, looking uncomfortable.

'So, you do know her?' said the first girl, with a raised brow. She looked amused.

'Look, it's not like that,' Cho snapped. 'She's just a friend.'

'Oh, so I am your friend, am I?' said Rue. 'Why have you been ignoring me, then? I was worried, you idiot.'

Cho glanced at the first girl, whose smirk grew as she walked off.

Rue watched her curiously. She'd been all prepared to get angry, but there was something about Cho's behaviour. She was almost dancing in the doorway, her body anxious, eyes tired and tight-looking.

'What's wrong?' said Rue.

'Nothing. Look, what are you doing here? You weren't invited. You're crashing. They don't let people crash.'

'So what?' said Rue. Cho's eyes snapped to her, surprised, and she shrugged. 'I wanted to see you. You disappeared on me.'

Cho was now practically jiggling on the spot.

'Oh, just come in,' she said at last. 'Just . . . come in off the street.'

Rue followed her inside, down into the mouth of a pale, airy corridor.

'So where have you been?' she said to Cho's back.

'You never stop asking questions, do you?'

'Well, excuse me for caring.'

They moved into the main room. It was dark and stuffy. People murmured and laughed around them.

Cho rounded on her. 'Why *do* you care?' she demanded.

'What do you mean?' said Rue, taken aback.

'Why do you even give a shit? You barely know me.'

That stung. Rue knew it had only been a couple of weeks, but it had begun to feel like they were close. 'I . . . just do. Why does anyone care about anyone?'

Cho watched her for a long, long moment.

'You shouldn't have come,' she said at last.

Rue had had enough. 'Cho,' she said, her anger and worry blooming, '*what is going on?*'

'Nothing. I can't . . . Nothing. I've just been really busy, okay?'

'Stop it. Something's wrong. You're jumping out of your skin. Tell me.'

Cho opened her mouth, her eyes hard and angry. This was turning into an argument, and Rue had no idea how they'd got there. But she wasn't going to back down. She'd have the truth.

She saw it in Cho's eyes first. They changed, her gaze fell, glazed over, as if distracted.

Then Rue heard it, too.

The noise was low, really low, and it seemed to come from her feet. She hoped it wasn't the Vibe music that everyone seemed to be obsessed with at the moment. Some of the music in World was a revelation, a whole new way of hearing beauty. Music that could encapsulate an emotion so precisely, your heart ached when you listened to it. Infinite varieties that triumphed over staid Angle Tar music so completely she wondered how she could have ever thought it was anything but dullness itself.

Vibe wasn't like that. From what she had heard so far, it either sounded like people dying, or was so incomprehensible she couldn't say where the melody, voice or beat was, or what they were supposed to be doing.

But the noise they were hearing wasn't music.

Everyone in the room had puzzled frowns on their faces, their mouths open in the midst of words.

The noise was growing, rolling, moving. A growling, booming note, a steady far-away tiger roar that went on without end.

It was something from beyond the walls.

Cho muttered a sharp word under her breath. She took something small out from her shirt and pushed it into her ear. Rue watched her in astonishment.

'What are you doing?' said Rue.

131

'They're early.'

Cho turned and slid through the small crowd towards the door.

'Wait,' said Rue, puzzled.

Thunder rolled through the room from outside. You couldn't hear it exactly. It was more that you felt every cell of your body vibrate with it. The room held nothing but statues, silent.

A voice spoke into the quiet. 'Shit, I think it's –'

The walls shook. The low roar from the ground climbed higher into a scream.

People had their mouths open, crying out, but Rue could hear nothing over the noise, the colossal wave of sound that pushed over everything else and smothered senses. She clapped her hands to her ears, but it did nothing.

Everyone around her was dropping, falling hard, their hands clutching their heads, screaming silently, voices unheard.

Rue looked around in amazement. She was the only one left standing.

Everything told her to run. She stood, fingers in ears, fighting hard, fighting to stay, to think.

I've dreamed this, she thought, filled with horror.

I've seen this before. People dropping. Only me left standing. In a grey place. Gods. A grey, empty place. I dreamed it. Months ago.

What in seven hells is happening to me?

She dropped to her knees, crawled to the nearest figure.

'Are you all right?' she screamed at him. 'What's wrong with you?'

He was moaning. She pressed her ear to his mouth.

'MyheadmyheadmyheadHURTS' was all she could hear, over and over.

She stood up, panic bucking at her, a terrified horse.

Why was she unaffected? What was different about her? Immediately, the answer came.

You don't have an implant.

Bodies pressed into themselves, curled on the ground like beetles.

She searched for Cho, but couldn't see her in the dimness. Just still bodies. Some with their mouths open and their eyes screwed shut, moaning soundlessly.

The rumbling went on.

Rue ran to a window, her heart pounding at what she would see outside. A face appeared, and Rue felt her heart stop.

It was Cho. She jerked her head impatiently. *Come outside.*

Rue ran to the door, hauling at it.

The noise was so loud.

She pressed her hands to her ears, tears streaming from her eyes.

Cho appeared, her face urgent. She gripped Rue's arm, tugging her out of the driveway and along the grey streets.

Others were running, too, but not many. Most, supposed Rue, were still curled on floors, trying to process the shock of whatever had been done to them.

Pounding feet. Cho's back just ahead. Rue focused on it. Cho's determined back and small shoulders would get her through this.

There were two, three, four booms then. More felt than heard.

Cho sped up. So did Rue.

They came to a building that had the distinction of a

startlingly blue segmented globe symbol set into the door, overlaid with a curly, three-pronged design. Rue had never seen anything like it before.

The door opened. A man stepped out, moving his hand frantically at them to hurry. Rue could see running people swerving from the street into the open door, relief on their faces. The relief spurred her forward.

She passed through the door, Cho just ahead. They shuffled through a brightly lit hallway that sloped gently downwards. She could hear the frantic chatter of people ahead of them.

'He just dropped. I mean dropped, like his legs had been cut out from under him. I've never seen anything like it.'

'On the floor and in so much pain and I didn't want to leave her but –'

'I was just about to jack in. JUST about to.'

'I'd only just jacked out, and that's only because Evelina was shouting at me to eat dinner in the real as usual.'

They trooped ever downwards, voices like panicked birds around them.

Rue reached forward and tapped Cho on the shoulder.

Cho turned her head. She was fiddling with her ear. The hallway was wide enough for two. Rue squeezed in beside Cho as she slipped a little disc out from her ear and put it back in her shirt.

'Cho. What is going on?!'

'Don't worry, it's over. We'll be okay down here anyway.'

'Cho.'

But she didn't reply. Someone behind them piped up.

'Do you know what's happening?'

Rue looked over her shoulder. A well-groomed woman with her hair striped like a tiger cat was peering at them both, her face shifting desperately between a patina of calm and frightened misery.

'No,' said Rue. Cho was silent.

'Oh my. Oh my,' said the tiger woman, muttering. 'Oh, it was nearly me. I was nearly – I mean – oh. What if he's dead?'

Her voice had risen.

'He's not dead,' said Cho. 'No one's dead, okay? Stop panicking.'

The tiger woman looked at her, caught by the anger in her voice.

'But what if . . .?' she said, lamely, and trailed off. 'I just left him there.'

'You did the right thing. You remembered the training and came to a safety hall. He'll be fine. Don't worry.'

'But what happened?' said the tiger woman. 'What happened? Why aren't they telling us what happened?'

'It was Technophobes,' said someone else behind her. 'Isn't it blindingly obvious?'

'No, it isn't,' said a third. 'That's everyone's hysterical fallback to everything, that is.' The stranger's voice took on a whiny, sneery tone. 'It's the *Technophobes*. Your Life account loads slower than usual – it's the Technophobes. Your dinner comes out warm instead of hot – Technophobes. Don't you think they have better things to do with their time?'

'What, other than disrupt technology?' said the second man's voice, sharply. 'Which is basically what they exist to do?'

'But they've never done anything like this before,' said the

135

tiger woman, bewildered. 'All that happened before was that they'd manage to shut off Life for a few minutes. You just couldn't jack in, that was all. This was . . . this was horrible.'

Rue glanced at Cho. Her face was carefully rigid.

After several minutes of walking downwards, they came out into a medium-sized hall. It was a white and austere tiled blankness, with a vaguely concrete floor. Dotted about were angular tables and chairs. A few people were milling about or sat down, talking. The atmosphere seemed shockingly, positively relaxed. Rue looked at the thin crowd. Some people were even smiling and laughing.

'Why is everyone so happy?' said Rue.

Cho muttered something under her breath. 'Because they're stupid,' she said out loud. 'And probably because they've taken calmers. Look, you can see a drug-dispensing machine over there. These halls are always filled with them. It's mandatory, in case people turn hysterical. Wouldn't want that, would we?'

She sat at an empty table, and Rue slid into the seat next to her. The chair was hard and cold against her back.

'But,' said Rue, trying to understand and feeling once again forever lost, behind, somewhere back *there*, 'what is this place?'

'See the segmented globe image on the door? It's the symbol for World, right?'

'I didn't know that.'

'Well, these halls, they started building them after the first few signal bombs. Safe houses. They're filled with signal dampeners. Means no one can be hurt through their implant. Also means the implants are completely useless. Can't track anyone, can't jack into Life, can't find anything out. It's horrible to find yourself alone, where you can't just . . . shift your focus and find out anything you want. You're totally helpless, unable to connect to anyone else.'

'You can connect to someone else,' said Rue. 'It's called talking.'

'Look, I know, okay? I'm the first to admit we're too reliant on Life. But when it's taken away, everything stops. It wasn't just pain that stopped the jacked-in people from doing anything except lying there. It's the body shock of silence. It's never silent in World. You're never alone with your own voice in your head and nothing else – not unless you want to be. And most people don't.'

'You're confusing,' said Rue. 'You talk one way and then the opposite, and you're angry about both of them. So which one do you believe more?'

Cho sighed. For a moment, Rue thought she wouldn't speak. Then she twisted in her seat to look at Rue directly.

'What do *you* believe? Really.'

'I don't know,' said Rue, taken aback. 'I just . . . with this ability, I suppose I see things a different way to most other people.'

'Ability?'

'We call it Talent, in Angle Tar. I can do things. With dreams. And some people can Jump to different places.'

Cho just stared at her.

'It doesn't matter,' said Rue, giving up. 'I think I'm still working out what I believe.'

They sat in silence for a while. The crowd in the hall had grown considerably. It was calm, conversations rustling like paper around them.

137

'How long will we be here?' said Rue.

'Several hours. Or only a couple. Depends how quickly they can get everything up and running again. Sometimes they keep everyone locked down here to make sure it's all over. They never learn. The attacks don't last more than minutes, and there's never another one for months. But they can't have people walking around with malfunctioning implants, trying endlessly to jack in. Down here it's all blocked. No signals. No World. No Life.'

Rue tried to imagine what it would be like to lose Life, all that instant wealth of knowledge, all those voices, all that everything. It would be like losing most of your brain, she supposed. Suddenly you wouldn't know the answer to anything. You wouldn't be able to know what was going on anywhere but the area within your sightline. You wouldn't know how to think or what to believe, because there would be nothing authoritative to tell you. Your sister, or your father, or your children – you wouldn't be able to talk to them if you weren't in the same room. You wouldn't be able to play a game to pass the time – you wouldn't know how games worked outside of Life. You wouldn't be able to read anything, watch anything except the people around you. There would be nothing there, nothing at all, to distract you from yourself.

It would be awful. Rue could never understand how awful, because to her Life was a toy, fascinating and occasional. She had not yet learned to incorporate it into her existence. It was quite a terrible thing for someone to do to someone else.

She thought about the little disc Cho had slipped into her ear.

'You knew,' said Rue.

Cho said nothing.

'All those people out there. Did you have something to do with it?'

'Don't be ridiculous. I was just warned about it, that's all.'

'Well, that's all right, then.'

Cho sighed, her voice low. 'Just . . . relax. It was only a couple of cities.'

'A couple of *cities*?'

'Keep your voice down.'

'Was it the Technophobes?'

'Depends on which theory you believe today. Tomorrow there'll be another one. I think the current favourite to blame is Ifranland, or maybe China because of what's happening with trade agreements at the moment. It's all over the news. People latch onto the news.'

'Who's China?'

Cho looked at Rue, the ghost of amusement in her face. 'It's another country. They're more advanced than World in some ways. They like to express their disapproval with World's lack of cooperation on certain things by financing groups like the Technophobes to drop disruptor bombs and wipe out the Life signal. It's nothing.'

'But it's the Technophobes who actually do it. Isn't it?'

'You're not seeing the big picture. Who actually calls the shots? That's more important.'

'No,' said Rue, her voice rising, 'It's really not. One person's actions are more important than a hundred people's wishes. So why don't they just own up to it?'

Cho hissed. 'Rue, just please keep your voice down!'

Cities. Cities, plural. Hundreds of thousands of people. Millions?

'It's a cruel thing to do,' she said.

'Oh, what do you know about it?' Cho sneered. 'You've never even lived here. You're here for a couple of months and you think you can pass judgement on everything that goes on. You have no idea, none at all. You go on back to your quaint little island paradise and laugh at us.'

'It's not a paradise,' said Rue, angry. 'That's why I left.'

'You haven't seen what Life can do,' Cho said. 'People can only cope with one reality at a time. They'd like to think they're cleverer than that, but they're not. Give them a choice and they'll kill themselves trying to live three lives at once, when only one is worth it. No one really believes there's anything after death, because no one can prove it. People only believe in gods when things get really bad, because what else will stop forces you can't control? So everyone tries to cram everything into this existence, and they should. But Life is a drug, and people get addicted, and they stop caring about anything else. They don't want to live in reality any more.'

'I don't understand your way of thinking at all,' said Rue. 'The Life system is as real as this hall. Who says you can't live both?'

Cho just shook her head.

'It's people like you,' she said at length, 'that came up with ideas like Life in the first place, and screwed us all. You're just like my brother. He lived inside his head so much he stopped caring about anything outside of it. Couldn't appreciate what he had because he was always looking for what he didn't bloody well have.'

Rue crossed her arms and pressed her mouth into a line to stop it from opening and saying very stupid, very pointless things. No one could argue with someone like Cho. It was almost a trait to be admired, except of course when you were on the receiving end of it.

Cho took a tiny box out of her pocket and popped it open. Inside was a pile of little gold stars. She picked up three with the tip of her finger and laid them on her tongue.

Rue watched this, wary. 'What are they for?'

'Go away,' said Cho. She closed her mouth and swallowed.

Rue didn't go away, though. She stayed, even when Cho began to sway on the spot from the drug in those little stars and nearly fell off her chair.

Rue sat beside her and had Cho lean against her side. Her eyes were closed but she wasn't asleep. Occasionally she would jerk.

The sadness and fragility Cho had running through her blood was obvious when she became angry, and she seemed to be angry most of the time. It was easy to be offended by her, but just as easy to let go of it. Rue didn't want to leave her alone in this state.

Besides, there was no one else to go to. Just another room full of people she couldn't connect with, or didn't want to connect with. Did that make her small minded, or mean? She wasn't sure.

Rue knew she didn't really care about Wren. She had been angry when he had seduced her, with all his silver-eyed charm, away from Angle Tar and White. He'd acted as though she was a special thing, as though he hadn't been able to stand her staying in Angle Tar. As though he had wanted her for himself.

141

So he'd come to take her away to World, a fantasy place that seemed to fulfil every desire she'd ever had.

How pathetic that seemed now.

How childish.

If she kept chasing dreams, she'd only end up being more and more disappointed, until she withered and dwindled and drew into herself.

It was time to face reality.

She looked around the hall, wondering how long they'd be stuck here for. Wondering if they'd bring food round. It reminded her of the tunnels underneath Capital City that had so shocked her. The tunnels reminded her of White, and the last words she had ever spoken to him. The dreams she'd been having of him recently, and how they had opened up the beautiful pain of him in her chest, turning her thoughts to him, again and again.

Nothing happened for what seemed like slow, agonising hours, until she was drooping, and Cho was practically asleep.

Then movement caught her eye, and she turned to see a clutch of uniformed men she assumed were police, wearing darkened plastic wraps over their faces that hid their eyes and noses, spill into the hall. They drew the eager crowd to them just with their presence. Rue stayed where she was, mistrustful.

The men told everyone they could go home, and that a list would soon be circulated on Life of people who had been taken to nearby medical halls, and that they should check that list if they got home to find someone they lived with was missing, and someone in the crowd started crying loudly, and everyone else just stood watching with dumb faces until the men herded them up out of the hall like geese and broke them back out into the wide world, and gods it was so dark outside.

Cho pushed away from her on the way back out, suddenly, and Rue lost her. She tried to see which way Cho was walking, at least memorise a street name, a general direction, but there were too many people in the way, and then that was it. Cho had gone.

Well, you have her address, she thought. *Just go round there and make her talk to you. Don't let her slip away again.*

Out on the street, people streamed back to their houses, panic in their eyes. Would they find someone missing? Alone, Rue walked home, mirroring the way she had come.

There was a strange quiet. No one around. An alarm or two in the distance. She could only guess that they were the sound of medical teams. She walked and rubbed her arms, cold. What if she got in and found Sabine on the floor, her eyes blank? Or Lars?

She reached her building. The key spell scanned her eye and the front door slid open.

She stepped into the hallway.

It was dim and cool.

'Hello?' she called.

Gods, that had sounded loud. Like no one was home. She checked every room and all the shared areas, just in case. But she was all alone.

Rue felt a hot unease start in her chest.

She should never have thought what she'd thought about Wren earlier. She should never have been so ungrateful to him. She should never. Because what if?

She slid into Wren's bedroom. For a split second, she wondered if the box would be missing, or maybe even exploded into messy pieces from the attack, unusable.

But it was there.

She switched it on, the familiar hum trilling into a whine. The blue glow crept upwards, a screen of light. Rue put her head into it.

Then nothing, for one heart-stopping moment.

Then her account gathered around her.

And there. The bouncing icon of an unread message, waiting. She opened it.

Rue – am all right.

Apparently we got warned it was happening, but endlessly stupid government said it was a joke and ignored it. Keep that to yourself. Anyway, wasn't jacked in.

Home soon.

Rue read it twice through, then began a third time before stopping suddenly, irritated.

Yes, okay. She'd been worried about him. But hadn't he been even slightly worried about her? A 'how are you?', though a bit trivial, would have been better than nothing.

Rue – am all right.

As if that was her first concern. Of course. As if she had nothing else to worry about. Nothing else like –

Just what the hell happened to everyone?

Or *I think I dreamed about this, and then it came true.*

Or *I'm friends with a girl who might be linked to actual*

144

terrorists, and oh yes, I dreamed about her before I met her, even though that's completely impossible.

According to him, all she had to think about was *Is Wren all right?*

No caring about her in that message. Not even a bit.

Rue dumped the message in her account bin and sat, hugging her knees, watching the wallpaper across from her play its little stories. The girl at the well. The Pake lookalike as he rubbed his head. She sat, and she watched, and she thought of everything that she had done in her life that had brought her to this place. All those turns, all those decisions. All the moments that had built, brick by brick, into a prison, hemming her into the here and the now.

She thought of the undeniable fact – a fact she now woke up to every morning with a burning sickness – that she'd made the wrong choice.

CHAPTER 13

ANGLE TAR

WHITE

White had found three more cameras in his rooms.

A quick search of his classroom revealed five, tucked into shadowed corners.

People followed him. It was discreet, and almost invisible. Now that he saw Worlder kidnappers in every corner, he could also see his shadowers. Had they always been there? Maybe they had. Who would trust him enough to let him loose without being able to put him down any time they wanted?

Every second of his life here was already mapped out for him. He couldn't decide he suddenly wanted to be a farmer, or a shopkeeper, instead of a tutor. He couldn't leave the city, or even the boundaries of the university. The only thing that he still had of his own, that they couldn't find a way to control, were his dreams.

His head was full of Rue, and of Frith. Where was Rue, and what was happening to her? Did she still hate him? What the hell would Frith do next, and just what was he going to do about it? He chased questions around and around again, but had no answers. It was driving him mad.

Everything was driving him mad.

There was a knock on his door.

He stood. His heart crashed and pounded in his chest. It was Frith. Had to be.

The knock came again.

'Mussyer White? Syer? It's Lufe. Are you there?'

Lufe.

White stood for a moment.

'Syer?'

The knock came a third time.

'Come,' he called out. Their lesson wasn't until tomorrow. Why would he be visiting now, this late at night?

The door opened and Lufe craned his head around it.

'Apologies,' he said. 'I know that you weren't expecting me.'

'Please, enter.'

Lufe slinked into the room. He had changed considerably since White had first met him. He had the distinction of being one of the most Talented students White had taught so far. He could now Jump fairly accurately, though his dreaming skills were less disciplined. So it came as little surprise to see the telltale golden sparkle of a brooch pinned to his lapel in the shape of oak leaves spraying from a single branch. The sign of a student being groomed for a government department.

Lufe hovered. 'May I sit? I'll be quick.'

'Please.'

Lufe looked around the room. 'It's odd,' he said eventually. 'Having the authority to call on you in your private rooms now. I feel like I'm being rude.'

'Not at all. You are a government man, and may do as you wish.'

Lufe touched his brooch self-consciously. 'Yes. It's all happened rather fast.'

'You are very Talented,' said White. 'This makes you extremely useful.'

'Well, when you put it like that,' said Lufe, and gave an awkward laugh. 'But we will still have lessons, right?'

'Of course. I teach many older Talented who already work in government. Not only students.'

'Yes, I forgot.'

White offered him a drink, wondering at his strangely shy behaviour. What was he here for?

They sat together in silence. Lufe took a long pull from his glass.

'Lea and I are getting married,' he said, in a rush.

'Ah, I see. Felicitations,' said White.

'Thank you. I can't stay long; her parents are waiting on me. We are all to dinner this evening.'

'What are they like?' said White. It was comforting, sometimes, to hear of others' personal matters.

'The mother is Lea but older, and much less attractive,' said Lufe. His face had taken on a peculiar mix of happy thunder. 'The two of them together are unbearable. The father is convinced I'm not high born enough, as if he doesn't even

148

know my family name. He glares at me when I kiss her. Because kissing in public is so incredible nowadays!'

Lufe ranted. White listened, watching the young man's face. It was a sweet thing to see him pretend to detest them so. They were the parents of his beloved and he would do nothing to deter them from him. He seemed to enjoy the head butting, as if it presented a challenge to be overcome. He and Lea would have a life. It would be many things, both good and bad, but it would be together.

'So things are going well for you,' said White.

'Yes, they are.'

Then Lufe was silent, looking into his drink.

'Lea's aiming to teach here, eventually,' he said after a pause. 'Her Talent has never been up to much. She's gifted in other areas.'

'Will you have children?' said White. It was the kind of conversation where he should say the right things about all the possible bright futures ahead.

'Lea wants them. I don't know. It seems selfish, doesn't it? Bringing them into a world like this. All the secrets and spying.'

'People have been bringing children into worlds like these since the beginning of humanity. Life never changes. People never change. You must make your happiness while you can and enjoy every second of it.'

Lufe was watching him, his expression carefully constructed.

'Lea wants to know where Rue is,' he said in a rush.

White crossed his arms. He was annoyed at himself – his heart still stopped briefly whenever her name came up.

'I've asked around. But I keep getting shot down. I've been told in no uncertain terms to drop it.'

149

'Then you should,' said White sharply, but his tone didn't seem to bother Lufe.

'It's not just Lea,' Lufe continued. 'We all want to know. I mean, she can't just leave like that without anyone even bothering to try to get her back.'

White was silent.

'So,' Lufe hesitated. 'I said I'd ask you.'

'I have no idea where she is,' White said.

'Haven't you tried to find her?'

'No.'

'But . . . I thought you . . .'

White watched him. 'You thought what?'

'You were, you know . . . involved.' Lufe blushed scarlet. 'Weren't you?'

White was silent, his jaw clenched tight.

'No,' he managed, finally. 'We were not.'

Lufe had a deeply confused expression on his face. 'Look, I understand why you might not want to confirm it to someone like me, but I think I should tell you that we all know about you and Rue. We've known ever since the moment she fell for you. It was like a match being struck.'

There was a part of White that couldn't bear to listen to this. In a violent rush, he remembered that feeling that he'd had when she had danced with him; that she could like him, that there was a chance. He tried to push it away.

'What are you doing?' he said. His voice was snappish. 'Are you playing some sort of idiotic trick?'

Lufe held a hand up, his face shocked. 'God, no. Honestly. I mean it.'

White looked away.

'Didn't . . . you realise?' came Lufe's voice, his tone curious. 'Didn't you see it? We all thought you were having an affair. She practically smelled of you. A couple of times, we shared her dreams. Did we ever tell you that? We didn't mean it, though in Marches' case I think he tried his hardest to do it all the time. I think it only happened twice, but –'

Lufe paused, searching.

'But it didn't start happening until Rue got here,' he said finally, firmly. 'It never happened before that. It was Rue. That was her Talent. I've never been able to pull people into my dreams; I didn't even know you could *do* that. And I know none of the others can.'

White stared at him, astounded.

Lufe carried on, oblivious. 'One time we all got pulled into Rue's dream. It wasn't that long after she first got here. It was you and her in a room together. You were talking about something or other. Psychology, or art, or something. She was asking you how you saw her. And then she told you that she didn't think of you as a teacher, and she was blushing. And then you . . .'

Lufe stopped, his mouth spreading into a sly smile. There was no mistaking what he meant.

No. No, not possible.

Kill me now. Earth, swallow me whole.

'That was *my* dream,' said White, his voice a horrified croak. 'That was *mine*.'

'I don't think so. I think she pulled you into hers. Because she was definitely dreaming it. I felt it from her point of view, not yours. It was very . . . You understand? Very powerful. And

151

that was the moment that I knew she'd fallen for you – and you for her. I was jealous, actually. You were the one we wanted to impress the most, but it was Rue who had all your attention. We fell out with her about it. Well . . . we never told her why. I feel bad about not telling her.'

White was still and silent with shock. That had never happened with anyone before. Never, he was sure of it. He'd never shared his dreams with anyone, had he? How could he know, without asking everyone he had ever dreamed about?

What did it mean? He remembered her pressing into him from the floor. Her little teeth on his neck. Had she really done that?

What about the last few dreams he had had of them together in a dark room? He'd thought it was his own longing that produced those embarrassing, secret scenes.

Now Lufe was telling him that it was really *her*.

'Perhaps I shouldn't have said anything,' said Lufe, with the cheery demeanour of someone who meant exactly the opposite. 'But if I've made you want to go and find her, then it's for the good, and Lea will be happy.'

White felt his bewilderment sour into anger. 'Why would I wish to find her? She left. She betrayed and left everyone behind her, like they meant nothing.'

'I don't know', said Lufe quietly, 'if it's Rue you're really talking about there.'

White didn't reply. Inside his head, he had punched Lufe in the face for that. Because it was true, and because it hurt.

Silence fell like a heavy blanket.

After a moment more, Lufe stood, and made a short bow.

'I'm sorry, Mussyer,' he said in a careful, formal tone. 'I spoke out of turn. I must go to Lea. I hope that you won't think badly of me, and that we'll see each other tomorrow with no ill will.'

White said nothing at first, his throat too tight to speak.

'Give Lea my best wishes,' he managed.

'I shall.' Lufe hesitated at the door. 'If you do try to find her, and you succeed . . . will you tell us? Please?'

White managed a stiff nod.

The bottom of Lufe's coat frisked grandly as he left, shutting the door behind him. White watched him go. And as soon as the door clicked closed, he stood up, agitated.

There was no point trying to prove it the next time he dreamed of her. His dream version of her would say yes if he asked whether she was dreaming this too, somewhere in World. Dream Rue would say yes and he wouldn't know whether it was the truth, or whether it was because he wanted her to say it.

And it was no good thinking about anything, or planning, because Lufe had opened the gates again with his casual remarks, and it was all decided the moment White realised that the life he had when he was asleep could be the life he had when he was awake, too.

There. He had made the decision, and it had only taken a moment. One innocent conversation.

Everything has been coming to this, he told himself. It would have happened anyway. You know it. Don't think about it. Don't argue it.

It was Rue that filled his vision, Rue the reason, the excuse he needed to cross a line he had never dared cross, until now.

He knew what he had to do to escape.

He had to kill Frith.

CHAPTER 14

WORLD

RUE

Rue woke.

The dream ran its fingers through her once more, soft and wet, before fading.

That one had been about Wren. But not a Wren she knew. This Wren had been fake, a puppet being made to dance. Something else was living behind his eyes. Something that made her want to be sick.

Wren was an idiot, but he was also the only Talented she knew here, and she needed to talk to him about these dreams she kept having. Either, she decided, she had somehow developed the ability to see the future, or she was just dreaming. Something like that had never even been mentioned in connection with the Talent. It had always been about trying to see the now, elsewhere. About moving across, not forward. Surely White would have told them about so monumental a skill if he had known of it?

No. No one could see the future. This was beyond ridiculous.

And not all of her dreams were of the future, were they? She couldn't exactly see herself going to that nightmare castle with Cho, with awful things that slithered in the black spaces. She certainly hadn't been dreaming of a future time with White, had she, in the last two dreams she'd had of him? There was no way she was ever going to see him again. And a Wren that wasn't Wren, with something crawling inside him? Just how possible was that?

But she remembered Cho's face so clearly in that castle dream. And then a few weeks later there Cho had been, suddenly, a stranger at a party they both happened to be invited to. Wasn't that too much for coincidence?

And the Life signal attack. That horrible, vague night. She had dreamed that too, hadn't she, way back in her old home with Fernie? People falling down around her like rain, nothing in their eyes, their mouths stretched open.

Maybe she was connecting dots that weren't there. Maybe she was making her dreams fit future things to suit her. Maybe she could drive herself mad with trying to reason it on her own.

She would find Wren and talk to him about it. He would take it seriously. He'd help her know what to think.

Rue waited all day, until it was way past the time he was usually home, and Wren still hadn't materialised. She hadn't seen him since last night. She checked his room, but he wasn't there.

She began to feel the first chest-burning itch of anxiousness.

Her dream of him still lingered in her mind, its taste tainting everything.

Maybe he wasn't all right.

She switched on the Life box and jacked in, descending to Surface Life. Cho had given her a little trick piece of code, a game hackers played where one would try to hide their Life signal and the other would try to find them. She rifled through her messages, and then opened up the code that Cho had sent her.

When the search box came up, she painstakingly tapped out Wren's Life signal code. He'd given it to her when she'd first arrived, in case she needed to prove to anyone who asked that she was living with a World citizen. At the time she'd dismissed the incomprehensible string of symbols and numbers as something she would never be able to understand. Now she was learning to stop underestimating herself so much.

To her surprise, the search indicated that he was in the building. But where? She looked at the little blip of his signal, and then, suddenly, she knew.

It was only two doors down.

Rue slipped out into the corridor and to the room Wren was in. She pushed on the open button on the wall outside, thinking it would be locked, and then she'd have to knock, and what if she was just ignored? Would she stand there looking like an idiot for a while, and then slope away?

But it wasn't locked. The door slid open.

Sabine had her lights set to dim, so the room was lit well enough to see them both outlined in her bed.

'Who's that?' a voice came, half whispered. 'Wren, there's someone there.'

She watched them disentangle themselves.

'Rue?' said Wren, peering up at her, his eyes in slits. 'What are you – ? What are you doing?'

'I need to talk to you,' she said.

'What . . . now?'

'Yes, now. It's important.'

Wren flopped back on the bed. 'Go away,' he said tiredly.

'Wren, you can do whatever you're doing later,' Rue snapped. 'This is Talent stuff. Come on.'

'And it really can't wait until the morning.'

'If it could, do you think I'd be standing here now?'

Gods, Wren. Some things were more important than lounging around in bed with a girl in the middle of the afternoon.

'Just tell me what it's about.'

Rue glanced at Sabine, who was looking between them with an impatient expression on her face.

'It's Talent stuff,' she repeated stubbornly.

'We can talk about that in front of Sabine, it's fine. She won't know what we're on about, anyway.'

Sabine's eyes flickered.

'Charming,' said Rue acidly.

'Will you just get on with it? I'm tired. You woke me up.'

Rue gasped. 'You weren't *asleep*,' she tossed at him, suddenly furious.

Why did you think he'd listen? Her mind's voice was amused. *Why keep giving him chances? He just doesn't want to take them.*

Truths tasted sort of sour, she decided, exploring the sensation she had in her mouth. Here was another truth, more bitter than the last: that she was bored of this.

157

Really, really bored.

It came like a shock of ice water, dumped on her. She remembered the river behind Fernie's house, how it would make her squeal when she washed in it, even in the summer. How it would clear everything away with its sudden, all-encompassing *now*, because there was no room for anything other than it.

That was how she felt. Clear as ice.

Gods, what had she been *on* this whole time? It was obvious now. Maybe her dreams weren't the future. Maybe they were just telling her that she needed to go.

She would listen to her dreams.

She turned and started back down the corridor. She heard Wren call her name but ignored it.

Cho would help her. She would go to Cho. They hadn't spoken in the last few days, not since the Life signal attack, but there was no time for that now. She needed to get out of this place, and away from Wren.

A hand closed on her arm.

He only had his trousers on, undone, and his hair was ruffled. He looked truly lovely, like a wild creature. But that was all it was — a look. It didn't match the vain selfishness that lay underneath his beauty.

'You're angry with me,' said Wren. 'About Sabine.'

'Not really.'

She watched his forehead twitch in a frown.

'Honestly,' she said. She meant it. 'I'm not angry. You should be with someone you really like. Everyone should.'

'Well, I wouldn't go that far,' he said. 'I mean, Sabine and I, we're having a good time. Everyone has a good time here. It's kind of understood. So I just wanted to say that, in case you thought it meant something. Because it really doesn't. It's just fun. That's how it is, you know, with adults here.'

It was hard to know which part of that speech was supposed to rile her the most. She smiled, instead.

'It's fine,' she said. She tried to tug out of his grip. He didn't let go.

'Where are you going?' he said.

'I'm leaving.'

'Leaving?'

Inside, Rue snapped at herself. Why in seven hells had she said that?

'Yes,' she said, trying to sound normal. 'On assignment. You know Greta has me on assignment right now? I'm going away in the morning.'

Wren watched her.

'Where?' he said.

'Well, I can't tell you where, can I?' she said, forcing irritation into her voice. 'It's secret.'

Those stupid, horrible silver eyes. They gave her nothing but a shining blankness.

Gods, she was such a bad liar.

'She hasn't said anything to me.'

'Why would she? It's my assignment, not yours.'

Wren searched her face.

'What's the problem, Wren?' she said. 'Are you worried that you're not her special little boy any more?'

His expression grew dark.

'I know more than you ever will,' he said.

'How mature. Is this a game of one-up, two-up?'

Wren lost his temper.

'Oh, yes, Rue the innocent. Mustn't sully her sweet little vision of the world, must we? Do you have any idea how irritating it's been for me having to babysit you? You're barely Talented. You can't even Jump. What are you *good* for?'

She called him a word. He laughed out loud, delighted.

'Where did you pick that up from?' he said. 'Some divey Life café? Don't you know I know everywhere you've been and everything you've looked at in Life? It's been part of my job to monitor you. Of course. Because I certainly couldn't be doing anything more important than that. And you know what, Rue? Spying on you is really dull.'

'At least I'm not a stuck-up pretty boy who fucks everyone he meets to make himself feel special!'

His hand tightened on her arm until it hurt.

'Ow,' she said. 'Get off me!'

She aimed a knee at his balls.

He buckled back out of reach and his smile curdled. 'Didn't you say you weren't angry with me?' he said.

'I will be if you don't let go of me!'

Her body had started to squeeze, as if she was trapped under a bed and couldn't get out.

She knew what that meant. He was pulling her into a Jump.

'Wait, wait!' she said, hating how panicked she sounded. She'd never be able to leave this place if he Jumped her somewhere she couldn't get back from.

She tried to shove him away, but he had his arms around her, and gods it was too hard to fight that feeling of thinning,

160

half of her pouring like sand through a hole to an elsewhere. She had nothing to move with.

Everything went dark.

Her head was spinning, spinning. How she hated that part.

She waited until she could feel life seeping back into her bones, then tried, weakly, to wrench out of the arms encircling her. She felt them let go, and Wren stand away from her.

'Where are we?' she managed.

'An empty bedroom upstairs. The door's broken, so no one can get in or out until an engineer comes to fix it. And they won't send an engineer until someone is assigned to this room, which hasn't happened for weeks. But everything works, the heating, the lights, the bed. You'll be fine.'

Rue turned her head. He was standing behind her, his arms folded.

'You're locking me up? You can't do that!' she said.

He shrugged. 'Of course I can. I'm responsible for you. I can't have you leaving to go to some mysterious place you won't tell me about. Greta would kill me. I'd get in a lot of trouble, Rue. Do you even care about that?'

'Frankly,' said Rue, 'I don't give a shit.'

Wren just laughed.

'You've picked up a real dirty mouth since you've been here, haven't you?'

Rue scrambled up and ran to the door. It was definitely broken. The lock panel light was dark. Nothing she pressed or thumped did a thing.

Bastard.

Bastard.

She turned, her back against the broken door.

Wren was watching her, amused.

'Look . . .' she said. 'I just want you to leave me alone. I'll stay here.' She swallowed in the lie. 'But no more of your sneaking around. I don't care about any of your silly games. Do what you like.'

'Oh, really? I thought you liked truths,' said Wren. 'I've got a good one for you: the truth about Sabine. About why I sleep with her.'

Rue felt disgust creep up her spine. 'I don't want to know, you pig.'

'Yes, but I'm going to tell you anyway. She knows a hacker, you see. And just a couple of days ago this hacker managed to get me copies of the files Greta has on White.'

'Gods, Wren, I don't want to know!'

'AND,' he said over her, 'AND I saw Cho's file, okay? Your friend Cho. Do you know who she is?'

'I don't –'

'She's White's sister.'

Rue felt her stomach flip and then drop, falling down, down. He stared at her eagerly.

She wavered, her thoughts tangled and wild.

'I don't believe you. You're lying for some stupid, hateful reason of your own.'

'Rue!' Wren said, losing his temper. 'Think. White is the most powerful Talented you've ever met, right? So what would they want with you, or even me? It's all about getting *him* back to World. I just knew it, ever since Greta asked me to poach you. She wanted me to get *you*, Rue. Not anyone else. You. Because of

162

White. They're making coming back here as attractive as possible to him. They're taking away everyone that means anything to him, so he feels like he *has* to come back. Now they have his girlfriend here, cosying up to his sister. Don't you see?'

'I'm not his girlfriend,' Rue said faintly. Wren didn't bother to reply.

It was all too much. Too much, too fast. No time to think or understand. No time for anything except the most ardent desire she'd ever felt, bursting into flame inside her, to be away from here. Away from all of it.

Cho is White's sister.

'They don't even have the same family name,' she said, uncertain.

'Because that matters in World? Names don't mean a thing. Your only identity is your Life signal code. Everything else is changeable. You know that.'

'Why are you telling me this?'

Wren sighed, irritated. 'Do I have to spell it out? You've been lied to!'

Rue lost her temper.

'Don't patronise me,' she hissed, slipping back into Angle Tarain. 'Yes, I've been lied to. By *you* most of all, you insufferable cock! So Cho is his sister. So *what*? There's no game if you're playing by yourself, Wren. Because I don't *care*.'

She felt herself start to choke on thick, rich disdain.

'You're not worth dirt to anyone,' she said. 'Things are happening to me. Things I would've talked to you about if you weren't so bloody up yourself. I needed you. But you'd rather go to parties and sleep with Sabine and keep all your

163

little secrets. Well, you're not the only Talented around here, even though you act like you are.'

He just stared at her.

She snorted in disgust and turned back to the door. She'd tear it down if she had to. She'd bite bits off him if she had to.

'And where exactly are you going?' he said behind her, his voice low and taut. 'There's nowhere for you to run to.'

'Fuck off.'

'You child. What do you have to be angry about? What have I done to you, except be your friend? And more than that. I took you away from the life you hated. Are you just going to *forget* all of that?'

'Yes,' she said sharply, examining the door panel, her fingers scrabbling in desperation. 'Because I didn't hate my life. You just made me think I hated it. You're just a big fat liar, Wren. You've no honour.'

He laughed. He'd come up behind her. She flinched and turned around, her skin crawling between her shoulder blades.

'Honour,' he echoed, his voice a sneer. 'Jesus. You think your precious friend Cho is honourable? She's friends with terrorists, Rue. That practically makes *her* a terrorist. Do you know the kinds of things they do? And god, her brother is worse, much worse. People with so much power can never be good people. You think your White is so high and mighty, but he's broken a few rules in his time. Done a few nasty things. How do you know he hasn't been watching you? He can do that, you know. He could have been watching you all this time without you knowing. Those moments when you thought you were alone. You know. The secret, embarrassing ones –'

She hit him. She'd meant to just clip his face, just – gods! – to shut him up, but she caught his cheekbone with the edge of her hand, and it buzzed in pain. She rubbed it, watching him.

'You're the child,' she said softly. 'And that's all you are. I don't ever want to see you again.'

He was clutching at the side of his face.

'And how about this for you? I like the idea of him watching me. I *like* it.' She looked at him distastefully. 'If I ever found out *you'd* been watching me like that, I'd hit you again. Then I'd throw up.'

His eyes flickered. For a moment, he actually looked hurt. *It's just an act.*

'Fine,' he said. 'So what are you going to do now? Run straight to Cho? You've got nowhere else to go.'

'Shows all you know, doesn't it?' she said sharply. 'Let me out. Now.'

He made a sudden grab for her, but she'd seen it in his face and dodged out of the way, her heart kicking in fear. She turned to the door but he was on her again, pulling, and she fell. He crawled over her, using his body weight to pin her down, and she bucked and she bucked but she couldn't get him off – GODS more than anything she just wanted him off if he didn't get OFF she would die from white hot anger she opened her mouth to SCREAM in his face but he pressed his mouth to hers. It was a painful kiss but it wasn't about a kiss, it was about power, it was about shutting her up, and control. More than anything else this seemed to break something free in her. Snapping like rotten wood, she rose up inside, her whole being bent towards escape, escape, escape.

Wren's face was sucked into black. The room blurred and poured into her, dimming. A kick in the middle of her chest told her this was a panic Jump, no thought or direction.

Cho filled her, Cho with her silky blunt-cut hair, her purple eyes and pale skin. Cho filled the black, dominating it until there was her instead of nothingness.

Cho

She thought, and suddenly, she was there.

She was in Cho's bedroom, and Cho was in front of her, clutching a T-shirt in one hand. Looking straight at her.

Cho opened her mouth and screamed.

CHAPTER 15

ANGLE TAR

WHITE

The whisper had gone round.

Frith was back.

It was long into the fourth day of his return before the knock came on White's door, though. He steeled himself.

You can do this. See it through.

'Come,' he called. His door opened and Frith's familiar head appeared around it. He slid his way in and closed the door behind him.

They watched each other.

'You are returned from your trip,' said White.

'Indeed.'

'Was it all right?'

'Fine. Just fine.'

There were no specifics. There hadn't been for a long time.

The trust was all gone. Frith told him nothing any more.

There was a pause.

'You're looking tired, White,' said Frith, eventually.

White shrugged, trying to make light. 'Too many dreams.'

'Dreams you should report to me?'

'No.'

Silence.

Frith lingered just inside the closed door.

It was such a delicate game. How to get him closer?

'I wonder', said Frith, moving off to the side of the room, 'if you ever dream about me.'

White's heart lurched.

Frith walked, his feet noiseless on the rugs. Moving in a wide circle towards the fireplace, never within arm's reach.

He knows. He won't come close, so he knows.

'No,' said White. 'Never.'

'You dream about a lot of people. What they're doing, where they're going. You must know some of my secrets, mustn't you?'

'I don't,' said White. 'The dreams are random, even for me. I cannot force them to a subject. You know this. I have tried.'

'But you could be there without me knowing, while you're awake, couldn't you? Watching me.'

The way you watch me?

'No,' he said out loud, stubborn. 'You would know I was there.'

'I'm not Talented. I wouldn't feel you.'

'Yes, you would.'

'Sometimes I think you are there,' said Frith, his voice dangerously quiet. 'But perhaps that's more my imagination.'

White said nothing. He would not be drawn into this. Whichever way he took, it would be wrong. All roads led to the centre of Frith's web.

'You'll need to be investigated in the next couple of days,' Frith continued, effortlessly changing tack. 'Routine questions. Just a follow-up after the Wren and Rue debacle.'

White stared at him.

'You suspect me of treachery?'

'No. I'm the only one who doesn't. The Spymaster's dogs have been itching for an excuse to take you in.'

'Wren. It was all Wren. You know this!'

'The dogs see a different truth. The dogs see you conspiring with the only other Talented remotely equal to you – your former best friend. How former, though? They think perhaps you're still working for World. You and I know that isn't true, but truth isn't always defined just by its participants. Is it?'

White felt his fear surge. Is this how Frith would ruin him, after all this time? Would he die in a prison cell somewhere in the bowels of Capital, alone and skeletal?

'Frith,' White said finally. It was his only card. He prayed it would work.

Frith watched him.

'Frith,' he repeated. It was not hard to sound weak. He *was* weak, and tired, and scared. All he needed to do was to let go a little, let it sink through his voice. 'I would never leave. Do you understand?'

He swallowed.

'I will never leave you,' he managed. The words sounded forced, but then they would, even if he meant them.

Frith was stood by the fireplace and hadn't moved.

'And how am I to know that?' he said finally, his smile pleasant.

'I cannot lie to you. No one can lie to you,' White pleaded. *Just come a little closer!*

Frith was silent.

White took a risk. He made his way to the fireplace, carefully, as if Frith were a bird and quick movement would startle him away. He stood in front of him, close enough to touch, but he didn't reach out, not yet. Too soon and it would ruin everything.

'We seem to be bound to each other, you and I,' said Frith.

White's blood ran cold.

'Yes,' he said. 'We are.' It was an awful truth.

Frith half turned, his eyes flickering briefly over White's face. White dreaded what Frith saw but tried not to hide it, which would only be too obvious. Instead he let everything show – a confusion of emotion. Too many signals.

Then, there it was.

There.

It was the moment he had been waiting for, when Frith held his gaze. Inviting him. White moved his hand forward and clasped his wrist. Frith did not push him away.

It would take just a moment.

He wormed his way into Frith's unguarded mind.

He thought of green, dim coolness. Wheeling bird song. He thought of love and hurt, and cruel laughter. He thought of Oaker's downy brown skin, dappled with sunlight. He found Frith's tail, the line inside that tracked Frith's everything, stretching all the way back and all the way forward along his life. He could hear Oaker's voice, if he listened hard. He could see Oaker's presence on Frith's line, bending it like a rock balanced on a piece of stretched ribbon, distorting everything around it, drawing everything to it.

White felt the wrist in his grip move as a vague feeling back there, somewhere. He pushed forward, holding on as tightly as he could to every sensation of the place he was trying to get to – the smell of damp earth, the tiny scratches of claws on bark, the way the grass would spring back against his hand if he pressed his palm against it.

And then the grass was there, tickling his fingers.

Frith was beside him in the clearing. He sprang apart from White like a startled dog, looking about him.

'What the fuck did you do?' he screamed.

White stared at a Frith unmanned, too grey and sick to wonder at the sight of it. Frith out of control was embarrassing, and horrifying.

'Where the fuck is this?' came another scream.

White only shook his head. He watched Frith stalk closer, knowing he didn't have the strength to move.

'Tell me now, or I'll slit your throat,' said Frith.

White felt a panicky laugh rising, and the end of him if he should let it escape. He forced out the words.

'Woods in Tregenna,' he managed. 'From your childhood.'

Frith looked around again. 'You can't Jump someone without Talent,' he said, eventually.

'We haven't Jumped. Not . . . in that way.'

'You're making no sense. Make some.'

'We are in your memory.'

Frith laughed. 'Don't be absurd.'

'We are in your memory,' said White again, levering himself up to a sitting position. Would this greyness ever dissipate? He had never felt so tired; it had sucked everything out of him. Cho had always loved it when he'd done this trick with her. It never used to be so hard to do, as a child. It used to be as easy as thought. Perhaps because children's lines and memories were so simple, made up of such easy colours and smells and tastes. They hadn't yet learned to complicate things.

'So you're saying that physically we're still in your room, by the fireplace?' said Frith.

'Yes.'

'But that somehow we're now in a memory? That this . . .' he indicated the trees. 'This isn't real?'

'No.'

Frith laughed, threw up his hands. 'How many other things can you do that you've been keeping from me?'

'A few,' said White. Frith watched him speculatively. White hated that look. It was an experimental look, the look of an engineer itching to take a machine apart to find all its secret workings.

'You still do not believe me.'

'I believe you,' said Frith. 'You wouldn't claim such an incredible thing that you couldn't prove. So prove it.'

'If you go to the riverbank,' said White, 'you will find yourself there, and Oaker, at age fifteen. I do not know which moment it will be. Perhaps the moment he disappears. Perhaps in one of the hours you spend waiting for him to come back afterwards. I think it is dependent on which moment affects you most.'

172

'Why did you do this?'

'Because I want to hurt you,' said White. He hesitated. 'And I thought about killing you. But I cannot. I cannot do it. I am not built that way.'

Frith laughed. 'I see. Why now?'

White was silent. He was reluctant to say her name, but Frith saw it anyway. His face darkened like a sky pregnant with storm.

White said, simply, 'You took Rue from me. When you knew how I felt about her, you took her away from me.'

He wanted Frith to deny it. He wanted that very badly. But it was so wearily unsurprising to see that he had no intention of that.

Frith sat himself back down beside White in an imitation of companionship.

'Very well,' he said. 'If you want to know what happened, I made a deal with the Worlders. I said that if they promised to leave you alone, they could have any of the new students. They just had to choose. So they sent Wren off to see which of them he thought was most Talented. I may have told them of your thing with Rue.'

Thing was said with the utmost venom. White recoiled from the sound of it. Why did it still surprise him when Frith showed him the depth of emotion he hid so successfully from the world?

'I met with Wren's manager,' said Frith. 'He had apparently begged her to have the chance to take Rue, when he learned that you felt something for her. He really does hate you. Do you know why?'

White sighed. He ached. Everything ached.

'It's because you're far more gifted than he is. You were the first person he ever met whose Talent absolutely outstripped his own. I wonder if you'll ever experience that in your lifetime.'

'I have wondered myself.'

'I doubt it,' said Frith. 'And that's a dangerous thing.' His composure was back, wrapped around him like a cloak.

'Perhaps.'

Frith was looking out across the clearing they were sat in.

'Are we going to fight?' he said. 'I have a knife with me, memory or no. I can still feel it in my boot. I have several ways to kill you on my person. Can you die here?'

'I do not know,' said White. He collapsed as Frith leapt on him. The ground smacked against his back and shook his bones. He could feel the muscles in Frith's thighs twisting and bunching as he was squeezed close. He could feel the prickling of the knifepoint at his belly. Frith was over him, on him, fingers pressing on his throat. He wheezed. He looked up into Frith's eyes.

'I don't know what to do about you,' said Frith, his face inches from White's, his eyes carefully searching, as if he could find the answer he wanted. 'You're too unpredictable but too valuable. I argue and counter argue, I weigh the pros and cons of keeping you alive. I have done ever since I first met you. I'm good at decision making, but you fog me somehow. Do you see?'

'I see,' said White, his voice raspy. 'Will you try to make *me* love you, too?'

Frith recoiled. It was enough. White punched him in the face, as hard as he could.

He couldn't Jump about in the space of someone else's memory – it wasn't his to manipulate. He could only move into it and out of it, and right now was far too soon for out. He hoped that Frith would not realise in time what power he had here in his own mind.

Frith was sat back, shaking his head. He would be up in a second. White dragged himself to his feet and leaned back against a tree, watching him. His hand was buzzing in shock. Soon enough it would hurt, even in a memory. The mind replicated whatever it could.

Frith stood up slowly. He touched a finger to his nose and it came away smeared in blood.

'Why are you throwing *everything* away for her? What the hell is so special about her?' he said. The words were muffled and numbed.

White just shook his head, too weary to try to explain.

'She tried to sleep with me,' said Frith, his voice thick and cold. 'She came to me just before she left and she tried to sleep with me. She cares nothing for you.'

White could see the child Frith used to be, so clearly. Frith's weapons were leaving him. He had only child cards to play. Maybe, trapped in a memory from his childhood, he couldn't help but revert backwards, growing smaller and less controlled.

'No, she didn't,' said White.

'How do you know?'

'I know.'

Frith paused.

'She'll never understand you, White,' he said, finally. 'You're something else, a creature apart. She's just an ordinary girl with a bit of Talent. You'll grow out of her. You'll leave her behind. You'll cause her pain. Do you really want that?'

White closed his eyes, trying to will that poison voice silent.

'What do you think will happen now?' said Frith, after a moment.

'I just want you to leave me alone. I want everything to do with you to go away.'

'Will you go back to World?'

'Perhaps.'

'You'll go back to prison.'

'Perhaps.'

Frith stared out past White's shoulder.

'This place is exactly how I remember it,' he said softly.

White heard the breeze setting branches far above them dancing, the noise like the sound of the sea.

He asked the question before he could stop himself.

'What happened to that boy? The hedgewitch's son?'

'He's dead,' Frith said, and laughed. It was a sharp, tangled noise. 'He got run out of the village, eventually. His mother tried to hold the other villagers back, but it didn't work for long. They said he was a demon, and that he'd use his gift for spying on them and reporting back to her. So he went up North. Used his talents to turn thief, and sold himself to buy food. He lasted a few months. There was a brawl one night between local criminal gangs. He got caught in the crossfire. He died. I don't know why he didn't just Jump out of there and save himself. Perhaps he didn't see it coming.'

Birdsong dipped and spun overhead.

'Do you feel something?' said White, curious.

'I didn't sob into my handkerchief when I found out, if that's what you mean.'

'No, Frith. I am asking you now, do you feel something?'

Frith shrugged. 'He was just . . . someone. He was much less than he persuaded me he was. But then, we are easily persuadable when we're young.'

'But you think about this place, and him, often.'

'Occasionally, perhaps.'

'No,' said White. 'It is always there. I saw it. It influences everything you do. Why do you let it?'

Frith sighed shortly. 'Believe what you will.'

They fell silent. The noise of the wood washed over them. White felt an enormous tug of weariness. It was the memory's power. The longer he stayed here, the harder it would be to leave. Frith's mind would not let him. The grass looked invitingly soft. It was warm. Calm.

'I am so tired,' he said softly.

'Stay with me,' came Frith's voice. 'I'll protect you. Just as I've always done.'

He felt eyes on him, inviting.

'You will hurt me.'

'No. Not if you stay.'

White hesitated a moment. Was he going to see it through? Was he going to live with it?

Yes. He would live with it. At the end of it all, if someone stood in judgement on the things he had done, he would be okay about that. He would take whatever punishment was given him, and he would have to be okay.

He walked towards Frith, who stood waiting, a small smile on his face.

He started to let it go.

Let it all go.

The feel of Frith, the sound of this place. The hate that had begun to eat at him, the hate that smelled and felt like Frith.

He was halfway there when Frith noticed what was happening.

White pushed, hard. He had very little time.

The last image he had as he left was of Frith giving a scream of fury and pulling his knife. But it was too late. He'd gone, leaving Frith stuck in his own memory, alone.

When he woke, it was to find himself standing by the fireplace as before. Frith was beside him. White let go of his wrist and took an alarmed step backwards, stumbling on legs that felt like a stranger's.

Frith didn't move.

White reached out a hand. It was a bad idea, but he had to make sure. He pushed Frith on the shoulder. His body gave under the push, but nothing more happened.

'Frith,' he said.

Frith was silent. He blinked, once, but his gaze stayed on the grate.

'Frith,' said White again.

This was worse, much worse, than he had thought it would be. He had been expecting something like sleep, peaceful and unaware. But Frith's eyes were wide open, and he stood as he would at any other moment. He had not collapsed, moved or done anything. He just wasn't there any more.

He was trapped in a memory.

White backed up to the door, in case. There was a part of him that was convinced Frith was pretending, that he would start to move, stir to life, and look around for him. He couldn't stop watching. If he took his eyes away, Frith would come back.

But then, Frith wasn't Talented. White knew what a horrible, relentless pull that memory would have on him. He might never get out.

And even if he did, White would be well away from him.

You're supposed to kill him now. Kill him so you never have to worry about him again.

But White couldn't do that. He saw that now, as clear as anything in his life. He saw himself as a murderer and laughed at the idea of it. Take a knife, walk up to Frith and stab him with it? Feel it forever after, echoing in his arm at bad moments when his mind wanted to punish him?

No, and never. The thought made him sick to his soul.

So this, instead. A temporary death.

Maybe it was worse than killing him. White had never left anyone trapped inside themselves before. He had no idea what would happen to Frith, over time. It was a horrible thing to do. A disgusting, despicable thing.

I'm sorry, thought White. *I'm sorry, Frith. I've done this to you. I've done it and there's no going back.*

But there wasn't any other way.

You'd have had me killed soon. I know it. Every time you looked at me, I could see it. You'd have destroyed me the way you destroyed Oaker, and I won't let you. You took Rue from me. You'll take away everything I've ever wanted and you'll leave me with nothing but you.

I don't want you.

White pulled the message bell, then leaned against the wall

179

next to it for a moment. He couldn't bring himself to leave Frith there alone, uncared for. Even if there were cameras on them right now, it might be a while before anyone realised there was something wrong.

Frith stared into the grate.

White took a breath, feeling sick, and Jumped.

CHAPTER 16

WORLD

CHO

A faint popping noise made Cho turn her head, unthinking.

There behind her was a face.

She screamed.

It's the police. They've come for you. They've got you and you're going to prison. You're going away just like your brother did, but this time no one's going to help because no one cares about you.

'Fuck!' she said hoarsely, when she realised who it was.

Rue stared up from her crouched position in the corner of the room. She looked panicked.

'I'm sorry!' she said. 'I didn't mean to! I didn't. I'm sorry! I –'

Rue stopped, looking around wildly.

Cho threw the T-shirt she was clutching at Rue's head.

'Don't DO THAT!' she shouted, her heart galloping.

Rue seemed puzzled. 'You're not bothered?' she said.

'Bothered? Yes, I bloody am! You can't just come barging in here whenever you feel like it!'

'No, I mean . . . you seem okay with what I just did,' said Rue, looking more confused than ever.

'Well, you're Talented, aren't you? That's what you told me last time.'

'But . . . I didn't think you knew what I was talking about.'

Cho snorted. 'Oh please. I grew up with one. You lot are all the same. My brother hadn't the faintest idea about privacy. Nosy sot.'

This seemed to shock Rue into silence. She opened her mouth, her face urgent, but Cho cut her off.

'What are you doing here, anyway?' she said. Inside her head she winced at her own rudeness. Why did she have a pathological inability to just be nice?

Rue didn't seem the least bit affronted, though. She straightened, hugging her arms to her body. She was squirmy and furtive.

'Hiding from someone?' said Cho, wry.

Rue seemed to struggle to answer this, turning it over and over before answering with a defiant, 'Maybe.'

'Then go away,' said Cho.

'I just need to talk to you,' said Rue. 'It's important.'

Cho sighed, her gaze on Rue's face.

She'd be called plain by a lot of people. Chestnut hair, but not even highlighted to bring out the red. Soft brown eyes, but no gold rings or colour flecks to make them interesting. Nothing fantastical about her at all. But there was something gorgeous, there, if you looked at her for a while. She was touchable. The kind of girl you wanted to curl up against and grip.

Rue shifted her gaze to Cho, forcing her to drop her eyes. Harder to have thoughts like that out in the real, where blushes couldn't be controlled. She cleared her throat.

'So come on, then. Talk. What's so important?' she said.

'I need help,' replied Rue, simply.

'You don't mess about, do you? What kind of help?'

'I need . . . I need somewhere to stay. Not here. But maybe you have a friend.'

Cho snorted. 'Huh. What makes you think I'd help you, jack?'

Rue looked about, as if she didn't know what to say. Then her face hardened.

'Because I know about the kind of people you're friends with.'

Cho laughed, a jagged sound. 'Oh, lovely. Blackmail. I respond really well to that kind of thing.'

'Please, just listen!' Rue cried. She pushed her hair back from her face, her slim wrist flickering in and out of her sleeve. 'I'm sorry about that. I didn't mean it. You're my friend, Cho. You're my only friend here.'

Cho raised a brow, trying to look unimpressed.

'Maybe if I tell you everything I know, then you might – you might believe me,' said Rue.

The poor girl looked miserable, and confused, and a thousand other things. She seemed so unbalanced. This was wild Rue, all flying hands and darting eyes. It was unnerving.

Something bad had happened.

Cho shrugged, cautious. 'So tell me.'

Rue sat, plaiting her fingers, rubbing the nails together in an anxious gesture.

'I first saw you in a dream,' she said.

'A dream.'

'Yes. It was before I ever met you. In the dream, we were in a castle. Big stone rooms.'

Rue swallowed. It didn't look like it had been a good dream, by the expression on her face.

'Then, weeks later, I . . . I met you at that party.'

'Okay, well . . .' said Cho. 'So what?'

'What?' said Rue, astonished. 'Weren't you listening? I had a dream about you. *Then* I met you. I dreamed of your face, your name, before I ever knew of either.'

Cho shrugged. 'Well, you're Talented; I get that. My brother was too, okay, so I know all about it. I mean, he could do things that would terrify most people. What you're saying is that you had a dream of the future. Well, I've never heard of anyone being able to do that, but fine. Say I believe you. What then? What do you want me to do about it?'

Rue looked away.

'Can I ask you something?' she said, staring at the floor.

'What?'

'What was your brother's name?'

Cho bit back her irritation. 'What's this got to do with anything?'

'You told me that he left World to go to Angle Tar,' said Rue, slowly. 'And that he was Talented. Right? So what was his name?'

Her face was carefully constructed, waiting for a response she was obviously looking for.

Cho gave it to her.

184

'His name was Jacob,' she said.

'Jacob Yun?'

'Well . . . yeah.'

'But your last name isn't Yun.'

'We had our family name changed a few years ago.' Cho fixed her with her best stony stare. 'That *is* allowed here, by the way.'

Rue stood up so fast that Cho flinched back, her hands automatically flashing out behind her to stop herself falling.

The girl was trembling. She was actually trembling. She turned away from Cho and stared at the door.

'What the jack is the matter?' said Cho, feeling a curious, nervous burning start in her chest.

She wondered afterwards if some part of her knew, before it all fell out of Rue's mouth.

'What?' she said again. 'Come on!'

Rue spoke to the door. 'I know him,' she said. 'I know your brother. Only he didn't call himself Jacob when I met him. He called himself White.'

There was a deafening pause.

White. That stupid nickname he had always insisted on using.

'You know my brother,' said Cho, her voice flat with disbelief.

'He was my tutor. In Angle Tar.'

'Your tutor.'

'Yes,' Rue snapped, glancing at her. 'Are you just going to echo everything I say?'

'Jacob. Tall. Pale skin. Dark hair. Cold, condescending prig.'

Rue managed a laugh. 'That's him.'

Though the girl looked shaken, Cho couldn't be absolutely

certain this wasn't a trick. Her natural inclination was always to distrust, even though her instinct told her that Rue was telling the truth. Still. She had to be sure.

'Tell me something about him.'

'What?'

Cho spread her hands. 'For all I know, you're lying,' she said. 'So tell me something you could only know if you'd met him.'

Rue looked wild. 'Like what?'

'Something personal.'

'He never talked about himself! Ever! I didn't even know he had a sister!'

Well, that sounded about right. It still hurt, though.

'Wait,' said Rue, suddenly. 'I know about your mother. Her . . . Her disability.'

Cho scoffed. 'You can get that crap from my Life files. Medical files, social files. That information is everywhere.'

'White was . . . he was in prison for a while, before he came to Angle Tar.'

'Files, Rue. You can get that from files.'

Rue stared hard at the floor.

Cho shook her head.

Rue looked up. She looked straight into Cho's eyes.

'When he talks,' she said, 'you absolutely believe him. He could make fairies sound so real, they'd almost seem boring. He sometimes wears his hair back in a plait, but bits of it always escape. He hates social things. He must have hated the parties here. He makes you feel stupid, almost as an afterthought, as if no one he's ever met could possibly understand him. But then when you've got his attention, you feel like you could

186

drown in it. When he opens himself up, it's overwhelming.'

Cho looked away. Underneath her folded arms, she took a pinch of rib flesh in between two fingers and squeezed, until her eyes were dry again.

'Fine,' she managed. 'So you know him.' She laughed.

Rue turned and leaned against the door, arms folded tightly to herself.

'You're his sister,' she said, soft. 'I really didn't believe it until now.'

Rue looked at Cho, and Cho looked at Rue, and the longer it went on, the harder it was to break. No one really looked at each other. Not truly. It must be because of how much was revealed through a gaze, and how disturbing it was to have someone see you, really see you.

'You do look like him,' said Rue, finally.

Cho tried to laugh, but it came out as a strangled little cry.

'I'm sorry,' said Rue. 'I didn't know. I would have – I don't know – said something.'

Cho picked at her trousers, trying to straighten her face out. It felt crumpled.

'This is screwed up,' she said, eventually. 'Do you know what the chances are?'

She was about to break, and ask her how Jacob was. If he looked different now. What Rue thought of him. A million things.

'Gods,' said Rue to herself. 'Wren was right. It is all about him. It's all been planned, somehow.'

'What are you talking about?'

'Nothing.' But there was something in her eyes. Something she held back.

'Rue. You tell me what's going on, right now. Or you go.'

'I don't know what's going on. Truly.'

Silence fell.

Rue came and sat on the bed beside her. Cho felt her heart flutter. Their eyes locked.

Cho dropped hers first. 'Just because you know Jacob, you think I trust you now?'

'No. But you should. I just need . . . I need some time. I need to stay somewhere tonight. Please. Is there anyone you know?'

Cho fidgeted.

'Fine,' she said, finally. 'There's someone. But you'd better tell me everything before I let you anywhere near her house.'

Rue nodded tightly.

Cho surfaced from HI-Life beside her with a little sigh. It looked so easy, as if she'd just taken a little nap.

'Okay,' she said. 'I've got someone. Livie – you've met her before. She'll let you stay tonight. In the morning you'll probably have to go. We'll see.'

Rue breathed out. 'Thank you. Thank you so much.'

Wren would never find her. She had no implant to track, and he couldn't Jump straight to a stranger's house.

Now she just had to get there.

They left Cho's apartment building together a few minutes later, and began to walk down the road. Rue glanced around anxiously, raking her gaze across the streets, expecting at any moment to see Wren stepping out of thin air, come to drag her back and lock her up again. She didn't know if she could panic Jump twice.

'Okay,' she said after a while, feeling the other girl's stare burning a hole into her cheek as they walked. 'What do you want to know?'

Cho's first question took her by surprise.

'Tell me,' she said, strangely uncertain. 'Was it – I mean, you said you were Jacob's student . . .'

'Yes,' said Rue. 'For a while.'

'And he taught you the Talent. That's what he does there, is it? Teach.'

Rue's shoulders moved uncomfortably. 'Yes,' she managed.

'What's he like? I haven't seen him in so long. I want to know how the Angle Tarain see him.'

It was astonishing, considering she had been the one to bring him up, how little Rue actually wanted to talk about him. The dream him and her memories of the real him had merged somewhat, forming a strange and divided picture of the White she remembered.

'When I first met him, I hated him,' said Rue.

She felt Cho's eyes on her.

'He was cold and pompous. He made me feel stupid, so I made fun of him. He didn't like that. We argued.'

Cho was silent, swallowing it up.

'I was told that I had to give him a second chance; that White was the only one who could unlock my Talent. So we continued our lessons. He was annoying, and I disliked him. And I thought about him all the time. And, I don't know . . . Something happened.' Rue sighed. 'I had this . . . dream about him. I just forgot about it, afterwards. I've had dreams about a lot of things. But then he took my hand at the ball, and he danced with me.'

189

Silence.

'Were you sleeping with him, Rue?' came Cho's voice eventually, hard and hot and accusatory.

'No!' Rue squirmed. 'I'm not really sure. Maybe a part of me did.'

'What on earth is that supposed to mean?'

She stared at Cho, helpless in the face of her. 'I don't know. It's complicated. I thought he liked me, just me. And I got angry – someone told me things about him. And I believed them. Now I'm not sure they're true. Even if they are, I don't care any more. I wouldn't mind about any of it, if he . . . if he liked me.'

'But he's a complete bastard,' said Cho. 'How can you talk like that about him?'

'He's not!'

'You haven't had the benefit of years of experience, so it's no good getting snippy with me. Sisters and lovers will never see someone the same way.'

'I'm *not* his lover,' said Rue, growing hot. 'Well –'

She faltered, remembering the last dream she had had of him.

'He doesn't think of me like that. I'm sure I'm just an idiot to him.'

The words were sour in her mouth.

'Did he say that?' said Cho.

Rue was silent.

'I mean, did you ever ask him how he felt?'

'It's none of your business,' said Rue, glaring at the scenery.

'You didn't, did you?'

'What would you know about it?'

'I know my brother. He might be a Talented genius, but his ability to interact with people on a normal level has always been crap. I'm positive it'll only have become worse since he left.'

'I wish I could see him again,' said Rue, softly. 'Just to be sure.'

Cho didn't reply.

An image of White, his hair sliding forward across his shoulders, flittered across Rue's mind. Saying her name, low in her ear. His thigh, pressed and straining against hers.

'Oh gods,' she blurted in Angle Tarain, her face hot. 'Go away.'

'What?'

'Nothing,' Rue said. She cast about desperately for something to say, something to distract her and dislodge the very clear memory of the way his nose had touched hers as he had tilted his head to kiss her mouth. 'Tell me more about the outside, where your Technophobes live. You call it off-grid, don't you?'

'They don't all live there.'

'Okay, some of them. Some of them live outside. What's it like?'

'It's like . . . outside, you know? It's hard to describe. Our cities have their own power grids, environmental controls. Everything's regulated. My dad used to say that the first environmental controls caused mental problems, because people were used to seasons, and the weather inside a city was always the same all year round. So they made it colder in the winter and warmer in the summer, with more light, but never, you know, extreme. And of course the Life signal only works inside a city. Once you're out of it, you're away from the signal and the environmental controls, in the filthy open air, weather throwing everything it has at you, the place crawling with insects and stuff.'

Rue's heart fluttered, hardly daring to believe.

'You mean . . . there are trees outside?' she said. 'Real trees? Birds? Animals?'

'And real sun to give you skin cancer, and airborne disease, and all that crap,' Cho replied.

'Gods,' Rue breathed. 'I've missed it.'

Cho glanced at her in surprise.

'There's no environmental controls in Angle Tar,' Rue said. 'Nothing like that.'

'You mean you all live in the open air? I always thought that was kind of a joke. What about disease?'

'There's disease. There's always disease, everywhere. It's natural.'

'No, it isn't,' said Cho. 'Oh, gross. Jacob's probably riddled with viruses. He's probably halfway dead by now.'

'Not when I saw him.'

'He wasn't, you know, ill, or sickly, or anything?'

Rue couldn't help it. She laughed, a robust snort of contempt.

'Don't be ridiculous,' she said. 'He was fine. Everyone's fine.'

'Maybe,' Cho replied, moodily. 'I've heard stories. We've got weak immunities in the cities. I've heard about people going off-grid only to die within three days in the outside air. I've met people who said it was all fine, but what do they know, really? None of them were doctors.'

That struck Rue as an extraordinarily similar story to the one she had always been told about everything outside of Angle Tar being nothing but dangerous wastelands.

They walked. Cho seemed lost in thought. Rue's mind swam back to poisonous waters. To Greta. Had she really orchestrated all this, just to get Rue and Cho together? To get White back to World? But Rue had met Cho by chance, at some party. You couldn't orchestrate that.

Could you?

Except the parties were controlled by civil government teams. They chose who went to which parties. It wouldn't too hard for someone like Greta to make sure two people were at the same one, would it?

Everything fell out of her head when they arrived at the house. She had been here before – the beautiful mansion with the gravel driveway.

Cho hopped up the steps and waited. Rue looked for a bell or a knocker, or even a retinal scan panel, but there was nothing she could see.

The door opened, and the same striking girl from last time with the chocolate skin and cloudy hair appeared. She looked Rue up and down.

'This is Livie,' said Cho. 'You met before.'

'Not really,' Livie sniffed. 'You never even introduced us properly. Come in, then. My parents are away seeing my grandmother for a few days, so you're lucky, otherwise they'd be all about the questions.'

Rue followed them both inside.

'So,' said Livie over her shoulder, 'Cho says you're hiding from someone, which frankly sounds fascinating.'

Haltingly, as best she could, Rue began to explain.

193

CHAPTER 17

ANGLE TAR

WHITE

It took all his courage to raise his hand and knock on the door.

It was raining. He had come through the woods, and the trees had kept the worst of it off, but he was still soaked. He hadn't minded at first. There was something cleansing about it. But now the cold crept in, lying on his skin. He hated being cold.

He stood on the doorstep, his shoulders jerking in a shiver now and then, and waited.

She wasn't in.

He looked about, wondering if it would be too dangerous to go around the back and find some shelter. But then the door opened, and his heart stopped, just for a moment.

The woman who peered back at him was exactly the way he'd pictured her from Rue's descriptions. The cottage seemed to bend around her frame, rolling your gaze towards her. She was round, draped in a shawl, and in her hand she clutched a lantern. Her hair was mussed and she looked like she'd been sleeping – except for her eyes. They were bright and piercing.

When she saw his face, she inhaled sharply.

'Zelle Penhallow?' said White, trying not to shiver.

She looked at him for a long, long moment; too long to be comfortable. Her eyes roved over him, unreadable. He opened his mouth to speak, do anything to stop her stare.

'You look like a ghost,' she said, soft.

White was taken aback. He struggled. 'I wished to speak with you for just a moment.'

She didn't reply. Just gazed at him.

'My name is White,' he tried.

She sighed. It was a strange, sad little sound.

'Come on, then,' she said, and stepped back, motioning him inside.

The door shut behind him.

He stood in the hallway, dripping gently onto the floor.

'I am sorry it is so late,' he said, trying to sound contrite.

'Never mind that.' She turned, walking off down the hallway and elbowing a door open.

'Zelle Penhallow,' he called.

'Fernie, please.'

'Don't you wish to know . . . who I am, why I am here?'

'Oh, don't worry about that stuff.'

White tried to puzzle this out.

Fernie was peering back at him from the doorway. 'You'll explain soon enough, I'm sure,' she added, as if it were an afterthought. 'Come on in here, then. The fire ain't sleeping

195

yet, and I'll give you some tea, and you can tell me all about it.'

The promise of warmth did it. He moved forward, grateful.

She was in the kitchen, bustling at the stove. He trudged to a chair next to a giant oak table and huddled on it, staring in dismay at the wet mud footprints he'd left on her floor.

At first it was awkward. She took her time about the tea while he watched her, trying to pull the soft warmth of the fire into himself. But she didn't quiz him and he didn't want to stop her rhythm, and gradually it became a companionable kind of quiet. He felt safe here. Absurd, really. They didn't know each other. She could turn him in. Or back out, into the cold. But from her bustling form he felt only a forthright kind of welcome. An understanding. It wasn't long before he thought that he might be able to tell her anything.

Rue had once said that Fernie was magical. He'd scoffed, at the time. Now he wasn't so sure.

She put a heavy teapot in front of him, and a cup already filled. Steam curled towards his face. He leaned in. Fernie eased herself onto the chair opposite and looked him over with the same assessing, somehow knowing gaze.

'Why don't you start at the beginning?' she said.

So he did.

And he ended up telling her everything.

It was deep into early morning by the time she commanded him to go to bed. She put him in the spare bedroom, she said, though White suspected the little cottage only had two bedrooms, all told. Which meant he was in Rue's old room.

It didn't smell of her, or look how he'd thought it might.

It was plain, and clean, and fresh. He crawled into the bed, cocooning himself in the blankets, and let himself be enveloped by thoughts of her. Later, things would feel clearer. He could plan then. He could plan.

But for now . . .

When sleep came, almost at once, he didn't dream. It was a black and comforting velvet sleep, the first of its kind he'd had in weeks. The sleep of safety.

He didn't wake until well into the afternoon, when the cold winter sun was streaming full through the flimsy curtains.

Not long after White woke up, so did Frith.

CHAPTER 18

WORLD

RUE

She didn't even quite realise she was dreaming at first.

She was walking along a corridor. It was dark and felt like the pit of a night, hushed and small. The flagstones under her feet were big, and cracked in places. Every few feet the wall bit off into a neat little sconce, and the further down the corridor she looked, she saw that each sconce was lit with a different kind of lamp.

Beside her, the elegant gas lamps with their slender glass bottles that she remembered from the corridors of Red House. Farther off and on the right, the squat square metal ones that Fernie used to have dotted around the cottage. She passed a whole row of the giant storm lamps that were shored up in the cellar of the farmhouse she grew up in – silent sentries, waiting for their chance to shine in a crisis.

There wasn't a moment where Rue thought, *Oh, I'm in the Castle again*. She just was. The air she walked through was old, and cold.

She passed doors, so many doors. They were plain, wooden things, and blurred into each other, until she came across one that jumped out.

She stopped.

It was a slide door, like the ones they used in World. Grey and smooth and blank. Without thinking, she moved to it and touched its surface.

It opened, noiseless.

Beyond it was a plain World room, as somehow she had known there would be. In it was Cho, sat in lifeless surroundings, her back pressed against the bed there.

She was crying.

Not in a pretty girl way, either. This was the kind of crying you did when no one could see you. Shuddering hiccup wails.

It hurt Rue's heart to see her so. Her eyes started to fill in unconscious response. It wasn't fair that the world gave such pain without thought. Nothing was fair. Fair was a fantasy people had made, to get themselves through life without just giving up.

Cho's voice dwindled and whimpered like a wounded foxdog.

Rue had liked foxdogs. She wondered, suddenly, where all the animals were in World. She missed animals. Plants. The sky – the real sky – in all its unpredictable glory. Weather. Rain. She missed the real world, painfully, heartbreakingly. She missed it so much it felt like dying inside. Fantasy only fed you for so long.

She stepped back, unable to take the whimpering noises that Cho was making.

The door closed swiftly.

She moved on.

Further down the corridor was a thick slab of a door, hinged with wide black metal strips. It felt more than the other doors she passed, just like the slide door had. She couldn't describe it better than that. It was *more*.

She turned the door handle.

This room was Fernie's kitchen.

And there her old hedgewitchmistress was, bustling at the kitchen table, making soap. Rue could tell by the clouds of citrus smell that puffed out at her when the door opened. Fernie was surrounded by pots of different sizes, measuring tubes and ladles laid out neatly. Her hands were covered in gloves.

Her quick, thick-knuckled hands. Rue remembered the shape and texture perfectly.

When she looked up again, the room wasn't Fernie's kitchen any more, it was Til's bakery. Til himself was right there, the quiet and beautiful man she had coveted back in her old village. That was odd, because of course he lived in the city now – he and the woman he'd had an affair with. There were a handful of people in line, and him serving warm loaves wrapped in paper with a nod and barely a word. Strands of his hair were coated in flour, and his nails were dirty with work.

Now it was Beads. She stood close to the door, by the bead sacks. Damm was nowhere to be seen, but her two harpies were chatting comfortably by the counter, their pecking hands sorting through a basket of mismatched lace.

They wouldn't see. She'd be quick. She leaned to her side and plunged her hand into the nearest sack. She felt the beads shift against her flesh, and pushed her arm further in, up to the elbow.

Now it was the village square. She stood, breathing in the smells. Gods, how she had missed smells. Til's famous tomato and walnut bread, still warm from the oven, wafting out of the open door of the bakery. Grass, clean and sharp after a bout of rain. Pig manure.

It was all there, but somehow removed. Like she had to step further in to really be there, even though it felt like she saw and smelled and breathed it.

Like a memory, maybe. Like the past.

She backed up, letting the door close, and walked on.

There were doors she didn't recognise, further on, but they jumped out at her the same way the previous ones had. One was huge, made of glass, with a long metal handle that had once been coloured gold, now obscured with black patches and tarnish spots. When she looked through it, she saw nothing, as if it only worked one way. So she grasped the handle and pushed.

Inside was White.

He looked like he was in pain. He sat, his back braced against the wall, eyes closed. A vein in his forehead throbbed. The hollow of his throat, exposed by the open shirt he wore, glistened with a little pool of collected sweat.

Someone else came into view, their back to Rue. She couldn't tell who it was – they wore a long overcoat that brushed the ground, and had short, nondescript hair.

Until he spoke, that was.

'Well?' he said. 'What's happening?'

It was Wren.

White gasped. 'Close that time,' he managed, his breathing ragged. 'Closer. I almost talked to it.'

Rue felt her mouth open in sheer puzzlement.

White and Wren? Since when were they on speaking terms?

This was no memory of hers. She looked around the room, trying to place it, and that was when she noticed a third person, sat cross-legged against the furthest wall, watching.

It was a thin girl who looked very much like a ghost.

She seemed familiar, as if she'd walked across Rue's mind before now. It took a moment, but then Rue had it. She'd dreamed about her before. This ghostly girl and White, in this very Castle, she screaming warnings at him while something shuddered and howled outside the room, and Rue could only look on in horror.

But there was something . . . off about her. Like she wasn't with White and Wren in that room at all. Outside of it, even though she sat inside.

As Rue gazed at her, trying to work it out, the Ghost Girl sighed suddenly, and rubbed her nose.

And looked up, straight at Rue.

Her expression dropped.

'What are you doing here?' she said, in a loud, indignant tone.

She looked utterly shocked.

Rue took a step back. The girl flowed to standing and was at the door in an instant.

'You can't be here!' she said.

Neither White nor Wren had stirred. They were talking to

each other; White whisper-soft with exhaustion, Wren nervous and twitch-filled.

The girl closed the door behind her, blocking off Rue's view.

'What did that mean?' said Rue. 'Those two together like that? What were they doing?'

The girl was silent. Her black hole eyes were wide, and fixed on Rue's face.

'This is impossible,' she said at last, a murmur to herself. '*Impossible.*'

'Who are you?' said Rue.

She started to grow unnerved at the way the girl was studying her face. 'Look. I understood the rooms before. Memories, right? Memories of mine? They felt like they'd . . . gone, already. Somewhere behind me, like paintings of the past.'

The girl looked up and down the corridor, shifting, guarded.

'Yes,' she said eventually.

'But that room was different. It felt like . . . something unfinished. Like lines were only half drawn, or . . .' Rue twisted a hand absently, trying to express it in a way that fitted. 'The future?'

'Perhaps. No. One of them. LOOK,' the girl shouted, suddenly. 'What are you doing here? How did you get here?'

'You mean the Castle? I've been coming for a while.'

'No. No, you haven't. I've never pulled you here, not once. How did you *come* here?'

Rue searched. 'I just . . . wake up here.'

The girl stared intently into her eyes. She was a strange construct, all limbs and strange sepia tones. She didn't look right at all. Like someone's drawing of a ghost.

Rue started to feel bolder, more in control of herself. It helped that she wasn't afraid. The things that lived in the Castle terrified her, but the girl didn't. She looked like she'd break in two if you touched her.

'Why are you staring at me like that?' Rue said, cocking her head and staring right back.

The girl broke off her gaze and swept the walls with it, restlessly.

'You're prettier than I thought,' she said.

'Than you thought, what? And what's this about pulling me here? And what exactly is this place, anyway, since you seem to know so much about it?' said Rue, and then she sucked in a breath to steady herself, in case she choked right there on all the questions forcing their way out. 'And who', she concluded, 'are you?'

The girl said nothing for a moment.

'Come on,' said Rue, firm. 'I'm not going anywhere until you tell me.'

The girl fidgeted, looking for all the world as if she would run right away.

Rue did something without thinking, then. She just did, as fast as she could. She reached and took the girl's arm. It was like taking hold of a thin, whippy sapling branch. The girl gave a cry and shrank back, then looked down, unbelieving, at the hand on her.

'Holy shit,' she said. 'You can touch me.'

Then suddenly, she began to laugh.

It was a strange, gasping laugh, as if she couldn't draw enough breath to make it. But it grew, gradually, until it shook her whole body. Almost a shrieking. Rue let go.

'Stop it!' she said, astonished.

'I'm sorry,' the girl managed, in between torn-up breaths. 'It's just that . . . you can touch me. And I have *no idea* what that means.'

This statement seemed to bring on a fresh wave of hysteria. But it didn't last long. The laughing hiccupped and stuttered, until she made no more noise. She seemed even smaller, if possible, than before. Small and fragile, and alone.

'Um. Maybe we could sit down,' said Rue.

She moved over to the wall and sat with her back to it, looking up expectantly.

After a moment, the girl joined her. She looked solid enough, and felt solid enough, if strangely thin and rigid. Rue watched her slide carefully downwards and rest her arms on her knees.

'You want some answers, now, I suppose,' she said.

Rue said nothing, giving her a moment.

The girl rubbed her face. Then a peculiar, wavy little smile stretched her mouth, as if she were bitter and delighted and frightened and resigned, all at once.

'All right,' she said. 'It's probably a good thing you're sitting down. First question.'

'What is this place?' said Rue. She felt her whole body start to tighten.

Answers.

Truth.

'The Castle? Too hard to explain,' the girl replied. 'Let's just say it's the place in between all the other places that have ever existed, and will ever exist. Let's just say it's the

205

everywhere and the everywhen that glues everything together. You'll have to be satisfied with that, for now. The more you come here, the more you will know what it is. It's the only way that seems to work.'

Rue felt the edge of understanding worm into her mind and begin to flower.

'All right,' she said. 'For now.'

The girl shrugged, as if it were all the same to her.

'Second question,' said Rue.

She watched those thin shoulders twitch.

'Who are you?'

The girl sighed, a sharp sound, as if the breath had been slapped out of her.

'This one might be more of a struggle.'

She played her fingers together, rubbing the nails against each other.

'All right,' she said, suddenly. 'So, my name is Rue. I live in a part of the world called Kowloon. I'm a couple of years older than you, but I am you.'

Rue looked at her.

'I mean,' said the girl, her eyes searching. 'I'm you from the future.'

Rue began to laugh.

PART TWO

CHAPTER 19

ANGLE TAR

FRITH

He came out of it fighting.

He kicked, and the pressure on his arm eased. A thump and a rattle of metal on metal in his ears.

'He's awake!' called a voice.

'Oh, really?' said a second voice from the floor, with a wheezy note. 'I couldn't tell.'

The trunk of someone came into his sightline, but at a strange angle.

I'm lying down, he thought. *Why?*

He made to get up, but it was a struggle. Everything felt weak and pliant, as if he'd been drugged.

Kidnapping?

'Mussyer de Forde?' said the first voice, above him. He managed to lever himself up to sitting. His hands gripped smooth, thick sheets.

209

It was a hospital room.

Unadorned, spartan. But expensive. The furnishings were heavy, well made. A man in a blue doctor's robe peered at him, looking anxious. Frith didn't know his face.

A second doctor appeared from the direction of the floor. He had a thin hand pressed to his side.

'I kicked you. I'm sorry.'

'It's quite all right,' the second doctor replied, his voice still a little frayed. 'Reflexes.'

'Where am I, please?'

'You're in Laennec Medicale, in Vaucresson.'

'Which Vaucresson?'

The doctors exchanged glances. 'Sorry,' said the first. 'I'm not sure what you –?'

'Am I in Angle Tar?'

'Well . . . of course. Vaucresson. Just outside Parisette.'

He felt a very peculiar sensation begin to pick its way delicately through every bit of him. It danced as it went, leaving in its wake nothing but an awful, empty blank.

Parisette meant something. Parisette rearranged itself to Capital City in his mind. Vaucresson, too – vaguely, though he didn't think he'd ever been there.

But he didn't know what to think of next.

What would place things for him? Remembering what had happened to land him in a hospital. But he didn't remember. Okay, so before that. What did he do?

He was a . . . he worked for a company. Some sort of company that went overseas a lot.

Wasn't it?

Where did he live?

Somewhere. Somewhere . . . in Capital. Or . . . outside it?

What was his name?

'Syer?' said the doctor, his voice a careful, balanced note. 'How do you feel?'

'What happened?' he said. A peculiar sensation trickled down the crease in his back. He tried to ignore its spread.

'We're not entirely sure. You've been . . . unconscious for three days, almost. You were found in your rooms on campus.'

The sensation reached his thighs, blossoming. He felt a surging in his veins.

Panic, he thought. *This is panic.*

'I don't remember,' he said. His voice was beautifully calm.

'Perhaps it will come back to you in time. For now we need –'

'No. You don't understand.'

He looked at the doctor.

'I don't remember anything,' he said. 'I don't know who I am.'

The panic blossomed like a fire, covering him.

'You can't,' said the Spymaster.

'Can't I?'

'It's all nonsense. I can have you detained, and you know it. You have amnesia, Frith. You're ill.'

The Spymaster regarded him. He always seemed as though he was looking at you with his moustache. It bristled with the slightest movement of his face, alive.

Frith remembered him, but not well. He knew, now, that he worked for the Spymaster. He knew that he lived in Capital. He knew his own name. He knew certain things. But there was no detail, no whole. It was like trying to see through fog. He strained and peered, but glimpsed only the ghosts of memories, vague shapes. And there were still whole chunks of his life, of *himself*, that were missing, as if hidden behind a locked door.

He needed a key.

He thought, perhaps, he had a key.

'Penhallow,' he said. 'It's a name. One of the few things I can remember clearly. Did you find anything?'

'It's rather hard to simply conjure up information from so little to go on.'

But Frith hadn't lost everything of himself, it seemed. Some things were like muscle reflex, close to the surface and automatic. He knew the Spymaster was lying.

'Just tell me,' he said, sharp. 'My reports. You said that I'm a meticulous notekeeper. Did you find the name Penhallow in them?'

The Spymaster looked at him. The look said that normal Frith wasn't so expressive, so emotional. That he was behaving unusually. It maddened him. Everyone around him knew more about Frith than Frith did.

'Yes,' he said shortly.

'Well?' said Frith, after a pause.

'You really don't remember, do you?'

Frith wanted to scream.

Do you think I'm making this up, you ridiculous idiot? Do you think this is fun for me? What possible motive could I have?

'As my doctors have already attested to you,' he said out loud, his voice clipped with anger.

'It was only a few months ago.'

'Time apparently means nothing in my case. There are whole swathes of my childhood that have gone. Neither can I remember anything that happened just a week ago. So, please, enlighten me.'

The Spymaster shifted on his chair, and took a look around the room. His distaste for hospitals was clear. In another life where he was a whole person, Frith might have wondered why. In another life, he might have *known* why.

'Very well,' said the Spymaster. 'Penhallow is the name of a hedgewitch you recruited a girl from. Her apprentice, Rue – she came up here with you a few months ago for the Talent programme.'

'Recruited?'

'Good gods, Frith. Your programme. Your obsession, I might add,' he said, with a puckering of the lips. He clearly didn't like Frith's programme, whatever it was. 'The Talent. You can't have forgotten the Talent.'

That was it. The last straw.

'Well, I have, haven't I?' Frith said, his voice rising. 'I obviously have, otherwise I wouldn't have to keep asking you what the hell you're talking about. Will you please just assume that I've forgotten everything pertinent and get to the damn point?'

The Spymaster's expression was one of pure shock.

I don't normally lose my temper, thought Frith.

'Calm down, or I'll have the doctor back in here with a sedative,' said the Spymaster.

Frith closed his eyes.

Just hang on. Press down on the constant waves of fear that you ride, up and down and up and down until you feel permanently sick, your stomach full of poison balls.

Press down on that voice that screams at you, tells you you'll never get your memories back. That this half-person is all you can ever be now.

Ignore that feeling of vertigo like you're falling over, again and again, even though you're perfectly still. Press it all down. Press it away.

He opened his eyes.

'I apologise,' he said. His voice was even. 'This situation has been a bit of a strain. I just . . . I need to know. I think you can understand that. Some piece of the mystery. A lead to follow. I just need something. Anything.'

He watched the moustache in front of him twitch and huff.

'Penhallow,' the Spymaster repeated eventually, and Frith silently rejoiced. 'It's the only thing you remember?'

'No, not the only thing,' said Frith. 'But the name is very clear to me, when everything else feels grey. The name . . . and a forest. A forest by a riverbank.'

And a horrible, sick feeling when he thought about that riverbank. Something had happened there.

'Well, she does live in a rather rural area. The two might be connected.'

Frith leaned forward. 'Where?'

'Why? So you can go there?'

'Yes.'

'And you think I'd let you?'

Frith looked at him for a long moment. He may have had the appearance of a benevolent walrus, but he hadn't got to Spymaster without being extraordinarily clever and determinedly ruthless.

'I think you'd let me have a sabbatical,' said Frith at last. 'For my health. Considering what state I'm currently in, I can hardly go back to work at the moment. I think you'd want me to try any means necessary to restore my full faculties.'

'In which case, I think the best course of action would be to keep you here and let the doctors have a good look at you, Frith.'

'The doctors don't even know what happened to get me in this state. They can't even tell me why I was unconscious. The doctors haven't a clue and you know it, because undoubtedly that is the exact same thing they've reported to you, albeit probably in somewhat less truthful language.'

'That doesn't mean they won't.'

'Then give me two weeks. Two weeks to get there and see what I can unlock. If I come up with nothing, you can send whomever you like after me. You can come yourself to drag me all the way back.'

It was an interesting way to test just how important an asset he was. Evidently very, because the Spymaster seemed to be contemplating his offer quite seriously.

'Fine,' he said abruptly. 'I don't have the time or the energy to argue with you. I have to get back to Capital before it all falls apart without me.'

He levered himself off the chair and stood, looking over Frith. 'But if anything goes wrong down there, just know that no one will be coming to rescue you. A hedgewitch is not a doctor. You'll get no proper medical care. When the two weeks is up, if I haven't heard from you, I'll start sending people, Frith.'

'Fine,' said Frith. 'The address?'

The Spymaster's moustache twitched sluggishly. 'A village called Tregenna, on the west coast of Bretagnine. Ask anyone you like for the hedgewitch Penhallow once you get there. They'll all know their local hedgewitch. You can get down to the Bretagnine border by public train, then hire a private carriage to Tregenna.'

'Do I have money?' said Frith.

The Spymaster seemed about to laugh, but checked himself. 'Do you have money?' he repeated. 'Yes. You do. But you won't even need that. Just tell the public train staff your name. You're a de Forde. They'll fall over themselves to give you credit.'

He nodded stiffly, then moved to the door.

'You weren't unconscious, you know,' he said.

'What?'

The Spymaster lingered in the doorway. 'When they found you. I don't know what they've been telling you, but you haven't been unconscious this entire time. You've been awake. But gone. Vacant. The way people look when they're daydreaming, only it was impossible to snap you out of yours. They tried everything.'

Frith felt a feather touch of sickness in the pit of his belly.

'I'm telling you this because I don't believe it's a medical condition. I believe it's something else. And my advice to you is to brush up on the Talent on your way down there. It's something to do with that godsdamned Talent. Read your notes. You have extensive research on it from your prized possession, White.'

The Spymaster regarded him carefully, as if expecting to see his face change.

216

Frith just looked back at him.

'White,' the Spymaster repeated, raising a brow. 'Who mysteriously vanished around the time this happened to you. No one's been able to find him yet.'

'I don't know what you want me to say,' Frith replied, annoyed. 'I don't remember who that is. Why is he so important?'

'It doesn't matter. Let me worry about that. I have people out on the hunt.'

The Spymaster watched him for a moment more, his gaze calculating something. But what?

Then he left, mercifully closing the door behind him.

Frith settled back against his pillows, his mind working furiously.

The Talent.

Penhallow.

A key.

Tregenna looked positively dreary in the rain.

Vaucresson had been bad enough. This was backwater hell. The roads weren't even gravelled properly. The private coach was a ramshackle thing, its horses plodding and bowed. Still, his name had got him all the way down here without a hitch, and the bank in Vaucresson had been only too happy to loan him enough to live on like a king for a month or more. Because if he didn't have the answers he needed in two weeks' time, he wasn't coming back. As long as it took.

The private coach dropped him off in the village square, and the driver, who was local, had given him directions to the river.

He had no idea which spot of the river it would be, but it made sense to head for the nearest bank to the village and go from there until the picture in his head matched the view in his eyes.

His bags stored safely at the best room in the local inn, he set off, walking briskly under his shade while the rain tried to batter him into submission.

It only took about half an hour to find it, a little way down from an obviously popular spot where the grass was worn thin. It was a scrubby bit of the bank, well hidden with wild tangles of vegetation and tall sentry trees. It looked lost and forgotten. This was it. The place he could remember so well when all else was locked away.

Frith stood on the bank, hugging the handle of his shade to his chest, watching the rain chop at the surface of the river. He turned in a slow circle, taking everything in. Each part of the scenery he let his eyes rest on for a few moments. He didn't force anything, allowing it to sink into him. Releasing him.

But it didn't come.

The fog didn't lift. Not even a little bit.

Desperation reared its head. He felt it crash through him. He screamed in pure frustration and threw his shade at the nearest tree. It bounced off and fell onto the mulching leaves, and he let himself stand in the rain, welcoming the way it soaked him and made his shoulders shiver miserably.

'What in seven hells are you doing here?' came a voice.

Frith turned, heart pounding.

In between two trees stood a woman. He guessed in her sixties or seventies, round of body, with masses of dark hair caught up in a fat messy bun and a cutting gaze. From one

218

arm dangled a lidded basket and her cloak was fastened tight around her neck. She was obviously wet through and should have looked bedraggled, but somehow she didn't.

There was something about her eyes.

'I know you,' he said. But his voice wavered with uncertainty. He was pretty sure he'd never been the uncertain sort before his memory loss, which was probably why he hated the feeling so very much.

The woman said nothing, but her face changed.

She's surprised. Now she's suspicious.

She knows me, too.

'What are you doing here?' she repeated. 'Has something happened to Rue?'

Rue. The Penhallow hedgewitch's apprentice girl that he'd apparently recruited for this Talent programme he was supposed to be running.

'Are you . . . Are you Zelle Penhallow?' he said, not quite daring to believe his luck.

'What's wrong with you?'

He held up his hands. 'This may sound strange, but I've lost my memory. Something happened to me, and I have selective amnesia. Please . . . you're her, aren't you?'

The woman watched him. 'I don't like lies,' she said flatly. 'And I don't like games. And you was always so very good at both, Mussyer Frith. What's this game you're playing now?'

And she doesn't like me.

Frith held himself back. This had to be carefully played.

'I need to talk to you,' he said. 'If you're her. Just a minute or two of your time.'

'The last time you took a minute or two of my time I lost Rue to you,' she said. 'And the time before that I lost my son. So you'll forgive me if I ain't happy about doing it again.'

Frith shook his head, desperate. 'I don't know what to say. I don't remember those things. I really don't. I'm sorry if I've hurt you in the past. But I need your help. Please.'

The woman gazed at him for a long moment as the rain pattered around them. He felt speared to the tree behind him, opened up and examined like a frog under those eyes.

'Sorry, Mussyer Frith,' she said, finally. 'But I don't want to help you.'

She turned and walked away, squelching over the forest floor.

CHAPTER 20

ANGLE TAR

WHITE

'I need something removed,' said White into the keyhole.

'What?'

He hesitated, glancing around. It was early evening and the Border City street this grand little townhouse sat on was quiet enough, but this was not a normal request he was making, and the man on the other side of the door not quite a normal doctor.

'An implant,' he said.

Silence.

He had left Fernie over a day ago – it had taken that long to travel up to Border City, first by several different trains, and then coach. He'd never been this far north before, and couldn't Jump somewhere he'd never visited, or at least not consciously. Not yet. It had only served to remind him how lucky he was that he could Jump at all. Having to use public transport was risky, if people were looking for him – but more than that, it was just so tediously godsdamned slow.

'How did you find me, please?' said the voice through the door.

'Someone gave me your name and address a long time ago.'

'You will give me the name of this person, please.'

'De Forde Say Frith.' As White said his name, his stomach dropped to the ground. If the man needed him to be vouched for by Frith somehow, he was screwed.

But then the door clicked as the key was turned on the other side, and then White was shuffling into a narrow hallway.

The man before him scrutinised White keenly. He was short and round, with a balding head and pleasant features.

'If they come from Frith, I do them for free,' he said.

White was silent. Frith had said as much when he'd given White the doctor's name, not that long after recruiting him.

So much had happened since then.

'Come into the office and let's have a chat.'

He led White down the corridor and into the room at the end. It was small, the walls violently decorated with a mishmash of paintings and words and impossible colours.

The doctor sat behind a polished trewsey wood desk. He noticed White staring at the walls and smiled. 'One of my eccentricities,' he said. 'I do miss it still, you see.'

'Miss what?'

'Life.'

White studied him. 'You are a Worlder.'

'Not any more. Got my Angle Tarain citizenship a few years ago. Now,' he said, and steepled his fingers, 'you wish to have your implant removed.'

222

'Yes,' said White, but maybe there had been something in his voice, because the doctor raised a brow.

'You understand what you're doing, don't you? I apologise if I seem patronising, but if you change your mind afterwards and want another implant, there are places in World – illegal, rather unwholesome places – but it will be much more painful an operation and the new implant will never be as fully immersive as the one you have now.'

'I understand.'

'Well, I don't know what you've heard about it already, but it's actually a fairly simple procedure. Have you been living without Life for a year yet? I generally say a year before I'll even consider removal.'

'Longer,' said White. 'I have been in Angle Tar a while. I was given your name when I first arrived here, but I did not think –' He paused, trying to understand it. 'I suppose a small part of me thought, somehow, that it was too far a step to take.'

'Of course,' said the doctor, with some sympathy. 'So now you've decided to remain in Angle Tar permanently?'

'No,' said White. Rue flashed in his mind. 'I wish to have my implant removed because I am going back to World.'

CHAPTER 21

WORLD

RUE

Rue sat on Livie's spare bed, hugging her knees, and stared at the wall opposite.

Now, in the night, when everything was dark and still, and everyone else was asleep. When it was all so real. Morning brought light and clatter and breakfast and music, and things that pushed the dark away. In the morning she might not understand any more.

Now. Now to think about what it all meant.

I'm you from the future.

The voice echoed in her head.

The things the Ghost Girl had shown her. Her memories, played out in Castle rooms, room after room, her secrets, watching her own body and voice act out a play she remembered from inside her head. So many things that no one else could possibly know about her. Little things she barely remembered. Big things she couldn't forget. But then other things, too – memories that had never happened to her, but had clearly happened to the Ghost Girl.

At some point, the girl said, they had begun to diverge. Lead different lives. It was on purpose, she said. She had come back, through the Castle, to change their past.

'But,' said Rue, still struggling with the enormity of the truth. 'But I don't . . . If you're me, what happened in *your* future? And how could you possibly change the future? That's not . . . You can't do that.'

'Through the Castle you can,' said the girl as she looked out across the corridor they sat in. 'I can pull people here from my past. Only ever people I know, though. It's like the Castle is a mirror of your mind; you can only find things in it that relate to you. You've seen the rooms. If you can find the right room with the right person in, you can pull the real person right here, through their dreams, at the point in their life that the room shows you. And, hopefully, I can get them to do things differently. I just have to persuade them. I have to make them see.'

'See what?'

'What's going to happen if they don't change things.'

'So what's going to happen?'

The girl was silent. Rue began to be afraid that she wouldn't say.

But then the girl looked at her. The scribbly eyes searched her face. 'You don't want to hear this,' she said. 'Just remember that I said that. That I warned you.'

'But you'll tell me anyway.'

The girl's mouth twisted, a bitter line. 'I'm you. You're me. We might have different pasts now, but I know you. You won't ever stop wanting to know the truth.'

Rue was silent.

'Things were different for me,' said the girl. 'For a start, Wren never went away from White. When I started at the university, they were already great friends. Best friends. Everyone knew of Wren and White – they were inseparable. And that was the problem.'

The girl looked down at her hands as she talked.

'But I knew if they fell out, it would give me a chance to separate them. So I started to pull Wren here, when he was younger. Maybe . . . a year or two ago, now, in your time. We just talked, the first couple of times. He told me things about himself. He was curious about World. He longed for it. I think that's what binds the Talented more than anything else. We all want to explore. We want it so much we've somehow managed to make it so we can, without the inconvenience of physics.'

Gods, that's right, thought Rue. *That's it exactly.*

'So I told him I could get him to World. I could find people to look after him. All he had to do was leave. But he was reluctant, at first. Because of . . . because of White. It didn't take much, though.'

Rue narrowed her eyes. 'What does that mean? What did you do?'

'Just . . . pushed him a bit. Told him some things about White.'

'What kind of things?'

'Bad things, okay?' she snapped. 'It's not like it took much. Wren was already jealous and paranoid. Look, they needed to be separated! It all goes wrong from there, in my version. Their friendship. That's where it starts.'

She leaned back against the corridor wall. Rue saw her visibly swallow.

'You have no idea how powerful they are together,' she said. 'And then I came along. I tried to stop them, in the end. I really did. I started to realise what it would all mean. They were the two most Talented people in the world. No one else could have done it. I'm not even sure they could have managed it separately. But *together* . . .'

'What did they do?' said Rue.

'They worked out how to open the Castle.'

Rue felt her skin fur as her hair stood on end, delicately rising. *You don't want to ask, but you have to. You have to, Rue.*

'What happens when the Castle is opened?' she said.

The Ghost Girl sat for a long time. Then, finally, her mouth opened and the words fell out like heavy stones.

'Monsters,' she said. 'Monsters come. The ones that live here. They break out into the real world. And everyone dies.'

Rue stared at her. 'How?' she said at last.

'They use us as vehicles. Once the Castle is opened, anyone who comes here through their dreams, consciously or not, can be possessed by one of them. And so they come flooding out. Taking hold of us. What they like most of all is to kill things. We thought people were going mad, at first. People who'd never harmed a thing in their lives suddenly turning into murderers. But it's them, inside us. And you can imagine what starts to happen once people in positions of power are taken over.'

'Is that . . . Is that what's happening to you right now? In your future?'

'It's already happened. There aren't . . . There aren't many of us left. I tried to stop it. I tried.'

Her voice had faded to a scratching whisper.

'What happened to White and Wren?' said Rue. A horrible suspicion began to grow.

The girl shook her head.

Rue stared at her in horror.

'No,' she said. 'He dies? White. Tell me. *Does he die?*'

The girl said nothing.

Rue felt her heart try and crawl its way up her throat.

'That's what you're trying to do,' she said. 'You're trying to make it so he never died.'

'I'm trying to make it so no one has to die.'

'Yes. But most of all you're trying to make it so *he* doesn't.'

The girl didn't correct her. How hard it was to keep the truth from yourself, when yourself was telling it to you. There was no escape from that.

Selfish, thought Rue. *She's so selfish.*

That means I am, too.

'So, what?' said Rue out loud, her voice colder. 'You've been pulling people here, manipulating them. Telling them things that aren't true. Messing with them. What have you done to try and get him back?'

The girl scoffed. 'You make me sound like I'm some sort of master controller, everyone dancing to my tune.'

'Aren't they?'

'Do you know how hard it is in this place? Do you think I can just easily find a room that gives me the *right* person, in the *right* time I need? Do you know what it's like to hold different futures

228

and pasts in your head at once, and try to decide which one will give you the outcome you want? And then work out a way to get to a room that will give you a point in the right person's timeline, and pull them here to try to make them do something that *might*, just *might*, affect the future? All the while knowing that each visit you can't take too long, you have to hurry hurry *hurry*, that you're forever under a ticking clock, because it's only a matter of time before the monsters come and find you?'

Tears had started to slip from her eyes. She didn't even seem to notice.

'I set up the Talent programme. I visited people in World and persuaded them to do it. I visited Frith in Angle Tar and persuaded him, too. I did it to find White and Wren. How could I make sure they were separated if I didn't even know where they were? Because I can't *do* anything from here. I can't change anything myself. All I can do is sit in the Castle, pulling people in, talking at them, hoping they might believe me, they might do something *for* me. Pulling random strings every so often, hoping against hope that the string I'm pulling is doing something useful and not just – oh, I don't know – killing everyone in the world or screwing up my past so much that I don't even know which version of me is me any more. I'm terrified of changing things so much that maybe White stops existing any more, or maybe even me. Or maybe we never meet. Do you understand how carefully I have to tread at the same time as having no idea what I'm doing? Do you know what that feels like?'

She subsided, staring into nothing. 'The only way I know if I'm having any effect at all is by going back into the real world, your future real world, to see if everyone's still dead or not.'

Rue shook her head rapidly. 'I can't –' she faltered. 'Oh gods. This is impossible. What you're trying to do is impossible.'

'Yes.'

'And you've been trying to do it alone all this time.'

Her thin shoulders shrugged, but there was a whole wealth of emotion behind that shrug.

'I could have helped you,' said Rue. 'You could have come to me earlier.'

'I had no idea what would happen if I pulled myself here. Can you imagine? I didn't realise you could come here too without both of us . . . dying or exploding or never existing or something. I had to concentrate on finding White and Wren. There's just not enough time each visit.'

She laughed. 'Not that time means anything here,' she said.

She didn't look like Rue. There was nothing about her that felt like gazing into a mirror. But would anyone recognise themselves if they met another them in disguise? Everyone had the version of themselves they carried around. Was it the true one? Was there such a thing?

'How long have you been coming here? I mean, to try to change the past?' said Rue.

'I told you. Time doesn't really have meaning here.'

'But how long for you, in the real?'

She shrugged. 'A few weeks.'

Only weeks. Yet she had affected years' worth of Rue's time. Getting Frith to set up the programme. Having a young White recruited, and a young Wren. Then a few years later, persuading Wren to leave Angle Tar. All those little nudges and shifts.

230

What would weeks' worth of wandering around the Castle's hallways and rooms do to someone?

'How can you spend so long here?' said Rue. 'Those things. They come for you, don't they?'

'Every time, eventually.'

'What are they?' she half whispered.

'I don't know. But I think we give them shape. I told you that the Castle is a reflection of our own minds, well . . . I think they are, too. Who knows what they look like when we're not here? I'm not sure they have a true form. They're in-between creatures, just like the Castle is an in-between place.'

'What are you saying? They exist because of us?'

'Maybe. We're like beacons to them. They like to eat us, but what they want most of all is to leave the Castle. Become flesh. They desire the real world. You should see them, out there right now.' Her shoulders twitched in a shudder. 'They love it. Running around, killing. They don't get much chance to do that penned up in here, but when we opened the Castle we gave them a whole world to eat.'

Rue felt her skin crawl.

The girl was gazing out across the corridor.

'One day I just won't be fast enough, you know?' she said. 'The more time you spend here, the more you'll understand. You start to . . . want it, somehow. You just stand there and wait for them to come. You have a tiny thought in the back of your mind that wonders what it would be like to just . . . let it happen.'

Rue stared at her. 'That's called suicide.'

The girl didn't reply.

An awful thought struck Rue.

'If you died,' she said, 'would I stop existing, too?'

'Yes. But . . . I don't really know.'

'But can the past me exist without the future me? I mean, there's two of us, right here, right now . . .'

'The more you try to understand,' said the Ghost Girl, 'the less sense it makes. All I know, all I let myself think about, is that I can change the past from here. One decision at a time. I change my past to change my present. You being able to come here . . . you talking to me like this . . .' She laughed, a shocked little pant. 'I had no idea it was even possible. Even now I feel like I've made it up. I'm at the end of my rope. I've got no options left. I don't know what else to do. So maybe my mind has made you up to comfort me. Maybe I'm sitting here, talking to myself.'

'Well . . . you are.'

The Ghost Girl snorted.

'But', said Rue, 'you *have* changed your past, haven't you? I mean. You separated White and Wren. So they can't open the Castle now.'

She shook her head. 'It's still open. Every time I go back into the real, I mean . . . Some things have changed, a little. But not much. Everyone's still dead. I haven't stopped it. Somehow, they'll still open the Castle.'

'Can't you find a way to close it?'

'Aren't you listening? It's too late for that. Closing it now still means they're dead. I have to change the past so they're still alive. So that it was *never opened*.'

Rue tried to think.

'What if we make it so they can definitely never meet again?'

232

'And how would we manage that?'

Rue swallowed. 'I s'pose you've thought of the obvious.'

The Ghost Girl raised her eyes to Rue's and her voice was calm.

'Kill one of them?' she said.

'No!' said Rue. 'Just . . . just Wren.'

'Oh. So he's more deserving of death than White?'

Rue was silent. The girl reached out and took her hand.

'I know Wren is more . . . difficult . . . in the version I've made,' came her voice. 'I carry that guilt with me. I try to help him. Because I'm responsible for screwing up his life.'

'No, you're not. People make their own choices.'

'Yes. But sometimes their choices are limited by their situation. And I changed his situation. More than once.' She sighed. 'Would it surprise you if I told you that I loved the Wren I knew?'

Rue met her eyes, taken aback. She smiled.

'Like a brother. Like an annoying, bratty, brilliant, selfish brother. He was so Talented, Rue. He was like White. You could feel it oozing out of every part of him. He was passionate. They were like fire and ice together. So different but so similar. I loved him.' She dropped her eyes. 'You couldn't take a life. Not if you were really faced with it.'

'Not even to save everyone?' said Rue.

'Would you kill White to save everyone?'

Rue stared hard at the ground.

Would I?

If I knew it could stop something awful happening?

'No,' said the Ghost Girl, whisper soft. 'You wouldn't. You'd

233

try to find any other way to change it. You'd keep coming to the Castle, spending your whole life here while your body slowly fell apart in the real – keep trying, keep tweaking, keep doing anything rather than that. Separating them was the last chance I had left. Everything else had failed.'

She snatched her hand back, violent. 'And it's still failed. I haven't changed anything. The Castle will still open. Everyone will still die. I don't . . . I don't know what to do any more.'

She didn't even seem upset. Simply hollow, like everything had been scraped out of her and there was nothing left.

Rue knew. She knew.

'It's on me now,' she said.

I can save it all. I can save him.

'Rue . . . don't.'

'I'm not going to kill Wren,' she snapped. 'Look, you were right. He's a git, but I'm not *that*, am I?'

'Then what?'

'The truth,' said Rue. As soon as she said it, it felt right. It felt good. 'The truth. No one else has ever told the truth to each other. We'll talk. We'll make it right.'

'You can't bring them together. Don't bring them together.'

'I won't. I'll do it separately.' She turned to the Ghost Girl. 'Don't you see? I've got more time than you. Out there in my world, there are no monsters coming for us. I can find them. I can make them *see*.'

'I don't know . . .' said the Ghost Girl, reluctantly.

'Have you got a better plan, then?' Rue replied.

They looked at each other.

234

CHAPTER 22

WORLD

WREN

Rue's disappearance was a complete and utter disaster.

That sneaky little country rat. Pretending to be all high and mighty about the truth when she'd been keeping secrets of her own from him. She'd never been able to Jump by herself before. Had she been practising all this time?

She was almost certainly with Cho. He'd never been to Cho's apartment building so he couldn't Jump straight there; instead he had to walk all the way. Not even Rue would be so stupid as to stay there where she could easily be found, but he had to make sure. And maybe he could pick up a lead on where she might be now.

But there was nothing. Cho's house friends were vague and unhelpful, even after he'd ramped up the charm. He'd managed to get a date with one of them later on that evening, but not one hint as to where Cho might be now, or even if she'd had a visit that day from a girl who looked like Rue. No one noticed anything any more. A fucking herd of elephants could go rampaging past, but as long as people were in Life, they wouldn't bat an eyelid.

He could order a location trace on Cho's implant. But that would have to go through Greta, and she could not know about this.

Stupid, stupid Greta. Why hadn't she implanted Rue the moment she'd stepped onto World ground? What was the hold-up? Bureaucracy, she'd probably say if he asked. Bloody useless network of office drones, people who weren't out in the field, people who wouldn't know a Talented from a rock. That was one thing about Frith he did miss. The man got things done.

Wren sat on his bed, rolling the little bottle in his fingers.

He should be panicking. He should be planning on what the hell to tell Greta once she worked out that Rue was gone.

But the bottle made everything else so far away, so overwhelmingly insignificant. So Rue was galloping around somewhere. They didn't really need her. They'd find another way to get White back, if Greta had anything to do with it. And Rue would probably come back to him in a couple of days, anyway, all contrite and embarrassed.

So Greta would be angry with him. It wasn't the first time. It wouldn't be the last. But what could she do, really?

Nothing mattered now that he had this.

He brought the bottle close to his face.

It was filled with little pill capsules. Colourless. Dull. The most powerful things often looked like nothing much. Dr

Cheever had come through for him. One bottle was all he had managed to get for Wren, but it held enough pills for several trips, if he was modest with the dose. In turn, still riding on shocked ecstasy that it had been so easy, Wren had assured Greta that the technician had not a whiff of Talent about him. Whether she believed him or not would come out in time, he guessed, but it didn't matter, it didn't matter. Because he had the upper hand now.

Just give me time enough to use them properly, he thought silently. *Then you'll see.*

There was no use in delaying. Planning had always seemed pointless to him. People of consequence, of history, took action. So he opened the bottle, upending two little pills onto his palm. The technician had warned him never to take more than two at a time – they hadn't tested beyond that.

Wren stared at them, as befitted the moment. It should be marked, the next phase of his life. Pity there was no one to mark it for him, but it couldn't be helped. He couldn't trust anyone with this but himself. It was selfish to want an audience, and dangerous, too. He knew that now. Show-offs were not the people that really changed things.

He swallowed the pills.

It seemed to take a while – it was not like the first time at the test facility. He waited for the surge, but when it came it was more like a rising, slow and graceful, his heart speeding up, his body kicking smoothly into overdrive.

He closed his eyes, thinking of nothing but the Castle.

The drug did the rest.

A moment more, and he was there.

The corridor he found himself in was squat and the walls were papered with flower designs. The cold ruffled across his arms, setting his shoulders in a shiver twist.

He stared at the nearest door. Where to go? He didn't even know what he was looking for.

Explore, said a voice inside. *Find its secrets.*

But he'd barely had time to put his hand on the smooth glass handle when he heard a long, animal cry that froze his blood.

No.

No.

How could one of them be here so soon? He hadn't even been able to scratch the surface of this place. He needed a weapon, or something that told him what they were and how they worked. *Something.* He needed more *time.*

The wailing filled the corridor, clouds and clouds of sound threatening to drown him. God, it sounded like it was just around the corner. His legs kicked into gear without him and he started to run.

Doors flashed by as he ran – so many doors – and objects that he couldn't examine, pieces of furniture, things that might have helped him, but the wailing never got any quieter. At times it seemed to get louder so his whole body buzzed with it and he could think or feel nothing but wordless, sick terror. He must get away, he must, he must.

Listen to me, said a voice in his head.

He screamed in reply. It might have been a scream of 'shut up I can't think right now'. But the voice insisted.

Listen! It wants you to run. It wants to chase you. Can't you feel that? It feeds on your fear. So what if you stopped feeding it?

238

Not even possible. His hindbrain was in control now, instincts driving him.

Let me take control, said the voice. He knew the voice of old. It was the one that pushed him on when he wanted to give up, the one that urged him to gain the upper hand on everyone, that won the game for him sometimes when he just couldn't face it any more. The one that stopped him from being weak. He relied on that voice. That voice would help him to climb out of the pits of obscurity. That voice would help him become great.

I don't understand, he managed.

Just let me take control. Stop running.

He did.

He stopped. He wasn't out of breath, and though he sucked in air in heavy, dragging pants, he didn't know if it was actually air he was breathing. Did the Castle even exist in that way?

The wailing grew louder. Wren trembled on the spot, every nerve in his body, every physical part of him screaming to go. He clamped down.

He turned, facing the thing as it came.

I'm going to see one of them for the first time. Actually see it.

There was nothing, at first.

Then there was something.

They were black, and they crept across the walls and the ceiling like long, thick sticks, jointed so they could crook and beckon. Beyond them was some kind of mass.

The mass filled the whole corridor. Top to bottom, side to side.

The black sticks crept closer. They weren't far from him

239

now. He felt himself start to give, his vision cloudy. Was the drug running out?

No, you just want out of here, said the voice. *You're forcing yourself out and back to the real.*

I won't, he thought fiercely.

I WON'T.

And he held on with everything he had until the feeling passed.

The mass was closer now. He started to make sense of it – you just had to know how to look. It was something like a giant cockroach, an insect with too many feelers and whiskers and pincing, brittle arms.

Wren held fast.

I'm going to die, he thought, now calm in the face of it.

Maybe not, said the voice.

The black stick feelers were inches away from his face. And then, incredibly, the wailing died. The mass stopped scraping itself through the corridor.

He couldn't see any eyes, but felt himself scrutinised.

Wren opened his mouth.

'Hello,' he said. His voice sounded sickly, trembling. But at least he could still speak.

The thing didn't reply. Who even knew what language it spoke? If it couldn't understand him, this might end up badly after all.

'My name is Wren,' he said into the dark, his voice barely carrying over whispery scraping as the mass retracted its feelers.

Silence.

Then a voice vibrating through his skull, so loud that he sank to his knees.

WHAT IS IT

Wren moaned, bringing his hands to his ears and gripping the sides of his head tight, even though he knew that could do nothing.

WHAT IS IT

The thing repeated.

Wren had his eyes clamped shut. 'What do you mean?' he shouted.

WHAT IS IT THAT IT DOES NOT RUN

IT IS AFRAID BUT IT DOES NOT RUN

'I'm Wren,' he yelled. 'Wren. I'm . . . I'm a human.'

IT IS AFRAID

He hesitated. What if it knew when he lied?

'Yes!'

IT DOES NOT RUN

'No!'

God, the scraping, the horrible scraping of that voice on his brain.

WHAT DOES IT DO

'I wanted to talk to you,' he forced out.

DON'T TALK

EAT

'If you eat me, you'll never know why!'

The mass shifted.

WHY

'Why? I want to talk to you! I came here to talk to you! To find out about the Castle!'

WHY

'Because . . . I . . . because I want to open it!'

241

He still had his eyes screwed closed. It occurred to him how bad a move this was. He couldn't see what it was doing. But maybe it was better not to see it coming. He felt himself drop inside, a sickening lurch.

And then there was a curious feeling of vacuum, as if the world had clicked into a different setting while he wasn't looking.

Open your eyes, urged the voice. *You have to know*.

So he did.

'No!' he screamed, when he saw his bedroom. His ordinary, ordinary, so-dull-it-physically-hurt bedroom.

He was back. Either the drug had run out, or he'd lost control of himself and had kicked back into the real.

I've got to go back. I was so goddamn close. I was talking to it.

But the memory of that voice and those black jointed sticks surged inside him, such a feeling of wrongness that his stomach clenched into a pulsing fist and he threw up on his floor. He threw up and threw up until his skin was covered in a blanket of sweat and he could barely sit up without feeling like he would collapse.

He heard his door open. He opened his mouth to say something to the intruder, but his voice wouldn't come out.

'Wren? I heard . . . I heard weird noises . . .' came Sabine's voice. And then, 'Oh. My. Wren!'

'M'okay,' he muttered. But he wasn't. He really, really wasn't. He'd never been so decayed and limp. He felt her hands on him.

'I'm calling the nearest medical hall,' she said, and he didn't have the strength to protest.

CHAPTER 23

WORLD

RUE

Rue blinked. The bedroom had taken on full light. It was mid-morning, at least. If they hadn't checked on her yet, they would soon. Maybe Livie would even be asking her to leave already, and she couldn't – she hadn't found White yet.

No more thinking.

It was time.

She straightened up, gathered the bedclothes around her protectively, quietened her breathing. She started to concentrate on Red House, letting her sense memories of it fill her mind. It was the most likely place to start looking for him.

But it wouldn't come.

It had worked with Cho, hadn't it?

You were threatened. Panicking.

I can't exactly threaten myself right now, can I? I have to learn to do this like any other Talented, not just when I'm terrified!

She tried to calm down. Try again.

Half an hour later she was covered in sweat and no closer. She buried her face in her hands.

No, said a voice in her head sharply. *Don't be a baby. Don't give up. Don't get all tantrums because it's hard. Calm down and try again. And again. And again. Until it works. Just. Keep. Going.*

It was gods knew how long later, and her concentration was broken by movement downstairs. Maybe Livie, or Cho, coming to check on her.

They can't come in here, she thought. *It's got to be now before I lose it.*

Her heart rate had reared up a notch. She felt the difference immediately.

Calm doesn't work with you, you drama queen, she thought to herself with a grin. She would have to tell White that when she saw him. He had always insisted that the calmer you were, the easier it was to Jump.

Voices at the bottom of the stairs.

Come on, come on.

'Rue?' called a voice. It sounded like Cho. 'You awake?'

If she didn't say something, Cho might come in to check on her.

'Give me another hour,' she called. 'I just need a bit more sleep.'

A long pause.

Her pulse pounded. She had time to register Cho's movement back down the stairs. The blackness rushed at her, sudden, easy to feel now she was anxious. Here it was, unending. It waited for her, inviting her in. She was careful not to rush into it.

Red House. There. The dusky brick, the old furniture. The smell of lamp oil and books, polish and mud on boots and fireplaces, coal lumps and ashes.

She pushed her way through.

She was in a room. Her old room. A fire burned cheerfully in the grate. In front of it lounged a girl, her skin lit by the flames. She looked up as Rue arrived, one hand spread on top of an open book.

They stared at each other.

'Hi, Rue,' said the girl, at last.

'Hi, Lea,' said Rue.

Lea got up from the floor and walked carefully over. Before Rue could decide what she was up to, she'd encircled her arms around Rue's neck and hugged her close.

'I missed you,' she said into Rue's hair.

'Don't squeeze. I'm still a bit strange from the Jump.'

'Oh, sorry.'

Rue hugged her back. It was nice to talk in Angle Tarain again.

'Where did you go?' Lea demanded when she pulled away. 'I mean, they said you defected to World, but I never believed it.'

Rue looked down at the carpet.

'Oh, *Rue*.'

Lea sank back down next to the fire. Rue joined her, hesitant.

'I'm sorry,' she said. 'I really am. I should never have left. I see that now.'

'Why *did* you? Was it that boy, Wren?'

Rue glanced up, astonished.

'He came to the rest of us, too,' said Lea. 'He was . . . well, you know.'

'Well, at least you weren't stupid enough to fall for it.'

'Was it all lies, then? The things he said?'

Rue opened her mouth, but something stopped her. 'Yes and no,' she said. 'Well . . . mostly no, to be honest. The things he told me about World were true. But he made it sound perfect.' She made a face. 'Nothing's perfect. Nothing, ever. You got to be really addled to think you could ever find any place that's right in every way.'

'You should come back, then.'

Rue smiled. 'I don't think they'll be letting me back, do you?'

'We'd make them.'

Lea was all ferocity. Rue found herself missing this, a sudden desperate ache in her heart.

'Maybe,' she said, pushing it out of her mind. They'd probably never let her back. But she had no time to cry over that. 'In the meantime, I got to go speak to someone.'

'Who?'

Now it came to it, how ludicrous to voice it out loud. But hadn't she said to her future self that truth was the way? No more hiding.

'White,' she said. 'I need to see him.'

Lea's hand flew to her mouth and her eyes went round.

'Oh gods, you don't know,' she said. 'Well, of course not, how could you? I just thought maybe, after what Lufe said, that you'd be talking to each other somehow, maybe White had even been visiting you, or you him, or something –'

'Lea. What?'

Lea rubbed her bare arms with her hands, as if she were suddenly cold. 'White's gone,' she said. 'He's gone. I'm sorry.'

The nausea reared. Rue resisted the urge to hold her stomach. 'Gone where?'

'No one knows. They're looking for him.'

'That's ridiculous. He could have Jumped anywhere.'

'I know, but you know what they're like. Most people barely even believe in the Talent. Anyway, he can't go back to World, can he? So it's either here or nowhere.'

'There are other countries,' Rue said, thinking madly. 'He could have gone somewhere new.'

'Maybe, but how would you ever find him?'

Rue looked up at her. 'What happened?'

Lea shook her head. 'No one really knows. For a while they were saying that he attacked Frith and disappeared, tried to kill him or something. But apparently Frith's fine, only he's gone somewhere, too. Presumably to look for White.'

'Frith's not here, either?' said Rue, her voice thin with despair. Now what would she do? How would she ever find White?

'No. I'm sorry. But . . .' Lea broke off.

'But what? Tell me. Please.'

The older girl looked into the grate for a moment, her shoulders stiff.

'I shouldn't know this, maybe,' she said.

Since when had Lea been shy about knowing anything?

Rue stayed silent, encouraging.

Lea cleared her throat. Mercifully she still couldn't stop talking for long, it seemed. 'Well . . . Lufe said he went to see White, not long before he disappeared. We haven't told anyone else this, mind you.' Her voice became sharp. 'In case they thought Lufe had anything to do with it. But he said that White didn't know about what you could do with your dreams, and he acted really funny when Lufe told him. To be honest, when he disappeared we thought he'd gone back to World to find you.'

'What? What can I do with my dreams?' said Rue, puzzled.

'You pull people into them, Rue. You dreamshare.'

Rue stared at her.

Lea blinked. 'But . . . we all thought you knew.'

It made sense.

It clicked beautifully into place.

She'd been pulling White into her dreams. No wonder he never acted the way she'd thought he should in them. No wonder it had always felt like it was really him there, instead of her made-up version of him.

'I know how to find him,' she said.

Lea smiled. 'Took you long enough.'

Rue looked at her. 'You seem different. Is it 'cos I missed you, or are you really different?'

'You seem different, too.' Lea put her head on one side. 'Older. Like you know things.'

Rue thought of the Ghost Girl. The Castle. Wren. Cho.

'I know things,' she agreed. 'Listen. I have to go. But I need one thing from you before I do. And in return, I'll make a promise to you.'

'Promise first, then.'

'All right. The promise is that I'll come back. I'll tell you . . . I'll tell you everything. I'll explain. No more secrets. It can't be now. But I promise I'll come back.'

'There's something else going on, isn't there?' said Lea.

'Yeh.'

'Can we help?'

Rue looked at her seriously. 'Maybe,' she said. 'But for now, it's got to be just me. D'you trust me?'

'Yes.'

Rue felt a rush of complete affection for her. She hadn't even hesitated.

Lea hugged her knees comfortably. 'What's the thing you need?'

'Sleeping powder,' said Rue. 'Got any?'

CHAPTER 24

ANGLE TAR

FRITH

Six days until people began arriving to herd him home, if the Spymaster was to be believed.

Six days left.

He'd launched a campaign. He'd told the owner of The Four Cocks, the inn he was staying at, about his memory loss. The owner had thought this far too fine a story to keep to himself, and now most of the village knew. He'd been spending his days going from shop to shop, business to business, buying a 'souvenir or two' and making friends with the owners, having cups of tea and passing the time while he shyly expanded on the rumours they'd heard. They all greeted him by name, now, inviting him round to their houses of an evening, for drinks and supper. Crossing the village square earned him at least one or two hellos. He'd bought bread almost every morning from the bakery, to be seen. The baker's wife, gorgeous and heavily pregnant, had taken an especial shine to him and often gave him a free saffron bun. Even the baker himself, a monosyllabic brooder, had time enough to spare him a hello and a nod.

There was no time for subtlety.

Several villagers recalled seeing him here before, a while ago, but other than that they couldn't tell him much more. He'd been a rather elusive figure back then, and had consequently caused a lot of gossip. They knew he was a recruiter of some kind for the university, and that he'd taken Rue off with him to a life of newfangled learning, but that was all they'd known. Some of them had asked about Rue, too, and how she was getting on, but he could give them no answers. He just didn't remember her.

Oh, but if he wanted help in getting his memory back, they knew what he had to do – go see their hedgewitch, Zelle Penhallow. She was marvellous. Not one to be crossed, mind. But if there was anyone who could help him, it was her.

Did she have any good friends in the village, asked Frith. Someone who could perhaps put in a good word for him with her?

Oh no. No good friends, said the villagers, with little laughs or uneasy looks. I mean, everyone was *friendly* with her. They respected her no end. But you couldn't be proper friends with a witch. They knew too much about you. They knew your secrets.

Frith saw her around a lot. He'd even hailed her on passing her in the square, and once in the bakery when they'd been there together. She'd nodded to him and nothing more.

So one morning he'd sat in his cramped little inn room at the rickety desk underneath the window and written her a letter. He'd made sure that it was short, without platitudes or flowery presentation. He got the impression she didn't like that kind of thing. She liked direct, truthful types. So he would be one.

He tried, as best he could, to summarise what had happened to him. The things he could remember, what precious few things there were. And then he tried to describe what it was like to walk around feeling only half alive because you had no idea who you were supposed to be or how you were supposed to act. That horrible feeling that you were constantly on the verge of falling apart. That maybe you'd never get your whole mind back and you'd be fractured like this forever.

He'd thought it was a good letter. He'd taken care over it. He'd paid a messenger boy to take it to her house that same day. And he'd waited.

But nothing came back. Not that evening, not the next day, not the day after that.

Frith sat brooding in his little room, turning over options, wondering what means he would have to employ to get her to help him. Violence didn't seem right. And god help him if word got around that he'd threatened her – the whole village would turn against him. Entreaties hadn't worked, either. He was out of options.

So he did a potentially stupid thing, and went to her house.

There was no plan. He simply couldn't think of what else to do. He had no idea what he would say once he got there. He had no cards to play. No memories and no identity meant no cards. He had no angle on her, no grip on anything. But sitting around waiting was killing him slowly, one hour at a time.

There was no point in going during the day – she'd have visitors, or she'd be out herself at people's houses. Evening was best, so he waited until dusk before setting out. It was a good three miles from the village square to her cottage, but the rain had eased in the last few days, and it ended up being a pleasant walk.

Her house was set back from the footpath, with the forest edging up silently behind it. It was small and thatched like almost everything else around here – the comté still seemed to be about a hundred years behind Capital. Frith opened the front gate and it gave a little squeal. Well, she'd know he was coming, at least.

He thumped the door knocker. It was heavy and dark, shaped like the head of a foxdog.

'Zelle Penhallow?'

It was a minute too long and he began to worry that she wasn't home. But something told him she was.

He knocked twice more.

Eventually, the door opened. She looked him up and down but said nothing.

'I'm sorry,' said Frith. 'I know you said you didn't want to help me, but I'm desperate. So I'm going to keep trying.'

'That's called harassment,' she said. But she didn't seem afraid, or even angry. She just said it.

'I think you probably have ways of dealing with people who harass you,' said Frith.

''Cos I'm a witch?'

'No. More because you're you. But I don't know what witches are capable of. I always thought they were healers.'

'They are,' she said, brow raised. 'And more besides. Come in, then.'

Frith watched, astonished, as she turned and went back inside, leaving the door open for him.

'Shut the door,' she called, as she disappeared into a room on the right.

He did so, turning his back to the hallway, and then he felt a gust of air and something cold slide against his throat.

Idiot, said a voice inside his head coldly. *Why did you not see this coming?*

'This is a knife, just in case you were wondering,' came her voice behind him.

'How did you move that fast?'

'That's the question, ain't it? D'you know the answer?'

'No.'

'I don't believe you.'

Frith laughed. 'You seem content to convince yourself that I'm lying and I've no idea why. You obviously don't like me, but I've no idea why. I can't *remember why*.'

'Do you know the name Oaker?'

He thought about saying no. He should say no. But he'd done his research.

'Your son,' he said.

'And you don't remember him, either.'

'No.'

'But you've asked around about him.'

'Yes.'

'And what do they say?'

'They say he left here a long time ago. He was trouble for

you. They say that he died somewhere up North.'

'Did they tell you why he left here? Why exactly?'

'They wouldn't say.'

'Prolly thought I'd hex 'em or something,' she said behind him, faintly amused. 'Well, it was because of you.'

Frith stiffened.

'Are you saying you don't remember that, either?' came the witch's voice.

'I don't. I don't know what I did. I'm sorry for it. But I didn't even remember that you had a son.'

He could feel her hesitation. In that moment, his instincts snatched the reins. His hand came up and grabbed her wrist –

For god's sake don't break any bones!

– and he snapped it to the side, making her gasp and drop the knife. Frith turned, quick as lightning, and faced the witch.

Zelle Penhallow's eyes were fixed on his, her wrist cradled to her chest.

'I don't like being threatened,' he said shortly.

'I can see that.'

'Did I hurt you?'

'Yes.'

'It might swell a bit, but it should be fine.'

She nodded. She didn't even look angry.

Frith felt his curiosity unfurl.

'How did you do that?' he said.

'Do what?'

'Get back here so fast. You were in another room.'

'Oh that,' she said dismissively, and offered nothing more, still studying him.

He knew it was some sort of test, but had no idea what would make him pass it. He stood still, returning her gaze.

'It's the Talent, isn't it?' he said. 'You're Talented.'

'You say that like you don't believe in it.'

'I know what it is.'

Zelle Penhallow watched him.

'You're easy to read,' she said eventually, with a sniff. 'You've got emotions walking all across you. You've never been easy to read before.'

'Does that mean you believe me?'

She shrugged. 'No,' she said shortly. 'Not yet.'

And with that, she moved out of the hallway and disappeared into the same room as before.

'Are you coming, then?' her voice drifted back.

Frith breathed out, and followed.

She was in the kitchen. It was messy, pots and pans hanging from the ceiling or lying on the surfaces, used bowls and cups and smears of powder everywhere. A strange mix of smells. A solid table was set off to one side underneath the window, which looked out onto a garden. He could see the tops of what appeared to be tomato vines in the clear starlight outside.

I know what tomato vines are, he thought. *I know that table is made of oak. I can smell lemon, and lavender, and biscuits baked not long ago. I know these things.*

But I don't know myself.

'Sit at the table,' she said. She was rubbing a spicy-smelling salve onto her wrist. Frith watched as she wrapped a cloth around it and tied it up.

He felt a little guilt. But then he remembered the knife.

She hung a kettle over the fire. 'I'm going to make you some tea. Fair warning, it ain't ordinary tea.'

Frith slid onto a chair, watching her. 'What kind of tea is it?'

'Truth tea,' she said, as she bustled. 'And mark me, it works. The Frith I know would never agree to this, 'cos dear me, the things I could ask. The things I could know. He'd find some way to get out of it, convince me otherwise. He's always had too many secrets, and a weakness of his is that he'd do anything to keep 'em from you. So I've got you in a bit of a bind, wouldn't you say?'

He saw exactly what she meant. If he refused, she'd think he was lying about his memory loss. But if he drank it, she could peel him apart. She could dig up things the Spymaster would throw him in jail for letting loose. Or worse.

It didn't matter. Strange how nothing did when you were only half a man. He couldn't remember anything to be afraid of revealing. So he wasn't afraid.

'I don't care,' he said. 'I can't tell you secrets I don't remember.'

Zelle Penhallow smiled, and set a cup before him.

'Give it a minute to brew,' she said. 'Then drink.'

She seated herself opposite him with a sigh. Frith waved the thick steam away and peered dubiously into the cup. It was a faint yellow.

'What will it do?'

'Nothing horrible. Just put you in a mind to answer any question I might have. Puts you in a place where it just never occurs to you to lie. There's no reason for it, see. Drink a bit.'

You're in a stranger's house, about to drink some potion, probably

257

made of bird shit or something awful. Think about this, Frith.

There's nothing to think about, he argued back. *There's no choice, is there?*

This woman hates you. She might be trying to kill you.

Frith sighed. It felt painful, the sigh, like something trying to crawl out of his chest.

Zelle Penhallow was watching him, that curious look back on her face.

'If I wanted to hurt you, I've already had my chances,' she said, as if she could read his mind.

Frith curled his fingers around the cup. It was warm and comforting against his skin. He drew it to his lips and drank.

'What now?' he said.

'Give it a minute. Keep drinking.'

So he did. But after a moment, he felt like something was off. Like he was kicking his way up from a deep, dark dream. He shook his head.

'Er . . . sorry,' he said. 'Did I just nod off, there?'

He blinked, trying to focus his eyes. His head was starting to throb.

Zelle Penhallow was slumped back in her seat. She had a plate before her, a crumb or two on its surface. Where had that come from?

'You've got a headache, I expect,' she said. 'It helps if you eat something. I'll get you something. What do you fancy?'

'Wait,' said Frith. His hand was still around the teacup. But it was empty, and stone cold. 'Don't you want to ask me questions?'

'It's done, dear,' she said, as she hauled herself up.

'What?'

'Have a look at the clock on the wall there.'

She pointed, and he followed her finger.

Three hours.

Three hours since he'd set off from The Four Cocks. It had taken an hour, at most, to get here.

'I don't . . .' Frith stumbled. 'Ow.'

'Yes, it does give you a blinder of a headache, truth tea. Sorry. You'll be all right, though. Here.'

A plate of crumbly cake appeared in his line of vision. 'The sugar'll help,' said Zelle Penhallow.

'What happened?'

'I asked you some questions.'

'What did I say?'

'It's what you didn't say. Eat the cake.'

Frith broke off a piece and put it in his mouth. 'What didn't I say?' he echoed, his words muffled with cake.

'Most things. You couldn't tell me how old you are.'

Frith paused. He'd spent a long time staring at himself in the mirror. He recognised his face, of course. There was a certain familiarity. But with most of his childhood and teenage years missing, and his recent adulthood a murky mess, actually knowing what exact age he was supposed to be had been a challenge.

'You don't even know what the Talent is,' she continued. 'Well, you do, but you sounded like you'd read about it in a report. Which is interesting, Mussyer Frith, because it's your obsession. But you don't sound like a man who's obsessed.'

'So you believe me?' he said.

Please say yes.

She was gazing into nothing, her chin on her hand. 'You're different every time we meet,' said the witch. 'I can never keep up with you. But then none of it's in the right order.' She smiled a peculiar little smile, but he had absolutely no idea what she was talking about and was in no mood to quiz her further with this pounding headache.

'Will you help me, Zelle Penhallow?' he said.

'It's Fernie,' she replied absently, and he knew then that she would.

Frith finished the rest of the cake. It was incredibly good, dense and lemony sweet.

'We'll get started in the morning,' she said. 'You can come back about ten.'

His heart sank. Walk back three miles, now?

She was looking at him archly. 'I'm not a fan of gossip,' she said. 'And I ain't sure you are, too. So you best get on back to the inn.'

But there was something more playful about her tone.

Fernie handed him a wrapped bundle. 'Take the rest of the cake,' she said. 'You'll probably want more when you wake up.'

He felt better than he had in days, despite the headache. 'It's very good cake,' he said.

'I know.'

A walk actually sounded good right now.

Frith left the kitchen, the cake under his arm.

CHAPTER 25

WORLD

RUE

She curled up on the bed.

Livie had let her stay one more day. Tomorrow morning, Cho said, she'd have to start thinking about what she was going to do next. Rue had nodded along, her thoughts only of White. It had to be tonight, then, didn't it?

It took a while for the sleeping powder to pull her under. Every minute of that she spent concentrating fiercely on White. If he was still in Angle Tar, it was late enough there for him to be asleep. If he wasn't asleep, well . . . she'd keep trying.

White, she said his name in her head, as her eyes closed. *White, White, White*. Like a chant, a call out into the dark. *Please come to me. Please.*

There was no wait. If time passed, she didn't feel it. There was falling asleep, and then there was him, in the black. He was waiting for her on the same little couch as always. He sat, his elbows resting on his knees, looking up expectantly.

Her desperation, her fear, it all melted away when she caught sight of him.

'You're here!' she said.

'Because of you. You pulled me here.'

Her face changed, and he saw it.

'You know about that?' she said.

'I do now.'

Rue looked away. 'So this is real,' she said, at last. 'I mean . . . we're sharing a dream right now. My dream. You're somewhere and I'm somewhere, but here . . . we're together.'

'I think so.'

She stood, uncertain for a moment of what she wanted to do now she had him. She hadn't thought further than this.

'I've been trying to find you,' he said. He stood up, holding his hands loosely at his sides, awkward. 'In the real. But it's impossible. I don't know where you are.'

'I've been trying to find *you*. But they said you left Capital and I didn't know where else to look.'

'I'm moving around a lot. What about you?'

'I could tell you exactly where I am. Would that work?'

He shook his head. 'Not unless I'd been there before.'

There was nothing else for it, then.

Rue held out her hand. He looked at it strangely. She could see him more clearly now, clearer every time. It wasn't arrogance. It was nerves. He didn't seem to know how to behave around her.

'What if I tried to pull you out?' she said. 'If you followed me.'

He looked at the ground, his face blank. 'Through a dream?' he said at last. 'I've no idea. I didn't even know *this* was possible.'

Rue raised her eyebrows, swallowing the smile that threatened to curl her mouth. He was always so serious.

'What's there to lose?' she said lightly.

'Our minds? Our lives?'

'Well. There's a risk of that with everything we do, isn't there?'

He looked at her. Assessing.

'This seems to be the only way,' she said. 'I want to see you in the real again. I want to *see* you.'

He hesitated a moment, then took her hand.

How to leave a dream.

Don't think about it. If you think it might all fall apart.

Just go.

She turned and put her back to him, gripping his fingers tight.

Wake up, she thought. *Wake up now.*

She closed her eyes. Calm wasn't the way, was it? Not for her. Stress did it. She willed her heartbeat to go faster.

Put it this way, said a voice inside her head. *If you can't do this, you may never see him again. Remember what the Ghost Girl said?*

If you can't do this . . . he dies.

Her pulse skipped manically.

WAKE UP. I WANT TO WAKE UP NOW.

She opened her eyes.

Light. Bed, underneath. Good. Still curled up.

Rustling from the floor. She sat up carefully and looked over the side, her heart hammering.

White was bent over on all fours, his head hanging down. Hair loose, draped and pooled on the carpet, hiding his face.

Rue slid off the bed, crouching in front of him. She meant to touch him, to pull him up, but couldn't quite.

'White?' she said anxiously.

A small grunting sound came from the bent shape.

'White? Look up. Tell me you're okay.'

His pale face tilted up to her. 'That was . . . strange,' he said.

'Are you okay?' Rue repeated.

'I think so.' He uncurled carefully and leaned his back against the side of the bed. His long legs were a jumble. He stretched one out and bent the other, using it to prop up his elbow and lean his head on his hand. All this Rue watched, each movement so odd to her now that they were so close and she could see him. After all this time, he was here and real and right, *right* here.

'I feel fine,' she ventured.

He managed a small laugh. 'Something you can do better than me. I've finally met my match.'

Rue hugged her knees close, wrapping her arms around them. 'Is this really real, then?' she said. 'We're not still dreaming?'

'It's hard to tell when I'm with you. But I don't usually feel so sick in dreams.'

He rolled his head towards her. His black eyes landed on her face, and she felt her belly roll.

'It's so strange to hear you speak in World,' said Rue, soft.

'And you.'

'In a bad way?'

'Not at all.'

Rue felt the change, then, all of a sudden.

'We're different,' she said.

'Things have happened.'

'Yes.'

He contemplated her for a moment.

'Would you rather it was how it used to be?' he said. 'At the beginning?'

She made a disgusted sound. 'No,' she said, firmly. 'I was an idiot.'

He smiled. And he smiled in the real. His smile in the real was worth a thousand in a dream, because it was his face really doing it. His muscles and his will.

'You're very beautiful,' he said in a rush, and then cleared his throat. 'I didn't do that very well. Sorry.'

She wanted to hide away. Her blush was radioactive. The room would melt down.

Don't sit there and squirm, Rue. Say something back!

'I . . .' she tried. 'Um. You make me feel sick.'

His eyes widened.

THREYA TAKE US, screamed her mind. *YOU ARE THE STUPIDEST GIRL IN ALL THE WORLD.*

'I mean,' she said hurriedly, 'since the beginning, whenever I see you, I feel sick. Really low down inside. I've never felt sick over anyone before. And after I've seen you, I can't think about anything but you, not for hours. It wasn't always good thoughts. You annoyed me a lot.'

OH MY GODS. WHY DO YOU HAVE TO KEEP OPENING YOUR MOUTH?

'You annoyed me, too,' he said, and she looked up, surprised.

265

'It was because I couldn't work you out at all. I tend to hate things that take me by surprise.'

Rue smiled. 'And I hate things that I don't know the truth of. You're such a mystery.'

'Not to you. You always seemed to know just what I was about. I couldn't hide anything.'

'I didn't know you liked me,' she said simply.

White looked away. 'I should have said something.'

'I should have, too. Maybe I wouldn't have left. Maybe . . .'

But she didn't need to say any more.

They were both sorry, and it was done. She had made him think about Wren. She could see it in his face. Wren made her think of the Ghost Girl, and what she had promised to do.

But it could wait, couldn't it? He was ill, and tired. He was here, and Wren was not. It was all fine.

'Get into bed,' she said. 'Maybe you'll feel better if you lie down for a minute.'

'Where are we?' he said, as he levered himself up from the floor.

'A friend's house. No one you know.'

Rue watched him stretch out carefully on the bed. He hadn't undressed. A whole level of awkward neither of them had the ability to face right now. She slid in beside him, careful to keep a slice of mattress between them.

He had his eyes closed. 'What time is it here?' he muttered.

'Late. Sleep.'

Silence.

She had never been in bed with a boy before. The bed was not the same. The room was not the same. His weight there drew everything to him.

She shifted, trying to arrange the comforter so that it covered them both.

'Don't go,' he said, suddenly, his eyes still closed. 'Don't go anywhere, please. Stay there until I wake up.'

'Okay,' said Rue. 'Promise.'

It was very warm.

Something had woken her. Maybe it was the fact that at some point she didn't remember she had pressed herself to his side, one leg draped over his thigh. She could feel his arm under her neck, and his fingers tangled in her hair. She felt them pull as she raised her head.

Rue looked at her hand in surprise. It was on his chest. His bare chest. Bare and pale, because his shirt was no longer in the way. He must have taken it off. His skin was warm.

She looked across to his face, worried for a moment that he was already awake and wondering why she was staring so much, but his eyes were still closed.

Then a noise came from outside the door. A knock.

'Rue,' said a voice. 'Come on. You've been sleeping forever again, and it's late. You're starting to worry me.'

It was Cho.

Rue stared at the door, frozen.

Cho had not even entered her head. White had driven everything else out of it.

She had not one single idea what to do.

'Rue.'

She opened her mouth to say something. Anything. 'I'm fine. I'll be up in a minute.' That was what she should have said. But in the time it took for nothing to come out, she had glanced back at White's face, catching his open eyes. And Cho had opened the door and come into the room.

She stopped dead. Her gaze went from White to Rue, and back to White again.

Well, at least now I know he's definitely here and I'm not dreaming, thought Rue.

She watched Cho's mouth open. Her own did the same, an unconscious response. But nothing came out. Again.

The three of them were silent. Rue glanced at White. His eyes were on Cho.

Cho turned and walked out of the room, closing the door behind her.

Rue felt White's chest contract as he struggled up, suddenly galvanised. She pushed herself back from him. He was staring at the opposite wall.

'That was . . . my sister,' he said, his voice still thick with sleep.

'Yes.'

He turned to her. His eyes were blank.

'You know my sister,' he said.

Rue watched him nervously. 'It's a long story. Yes.'

'How?'

'Um. Maybe later. Maybe now we go and find her. I think that's a good idea.'

'Okay,' he said, still blank.

Shock, Rue decided.

She could have wrung her own neck. Why hadn't she told him? Why hadn't it even crossed her mind to mention it? Why hadn't she even thought about Cho in all this?

She watched him slide out of bed. He bent down, his hair slipping forward over his bare shoulders, and retrieved his shirt from the floor. Rue got up, relieved to find that she hadn't disrobed in the middle of the night.

Cho, she thought miserably.

She went out into the hallway, thrumming with nerves.

'Cho!' she called.

She took the stairs two at a time. What if Cho had run out of the house or something? Well, she couldn't Jump, so she couldn't have gone far. Rue looked in every room. All empty. The last place was the social room.

She won't be there, thought Rue. *She's gone.*

But she was. She was at the food unit, stabbing at buttons with her fingers.

'Cho.'

Cho turned. Her face was thunderous.

Rue stopped. 'I'm really sorry. I should have said something. I just . . . I didn't think.'

Silence.

'It only happened a few hours ago,' she said. 'I pulled him here. It was me, not him. I've been trying to find him, you see. And he said he's been trying to find me.'

'It's fine,' said Cho.

It was so clearly not fine.

'Though I don't expect Livie will be too happy about it when she hears. She's still thinking you should go today.'

'Okay,' said Rue, though her heart sank. Well, if she had to go, then she would.

'Okay?' said Cho incredulously. 'Okay?! So you're just going to sod off with him and leave me behind? My own brother?'

Rue blinked. 'What? But you said –'

Cho's gaze shifted, and Rue knew that White had come into the social room behind her. The chilly silence had gone. This was explosive Cho.

'Three years!' she screamed, her eyes fixed on White. 'Three years, and not one fucking message! Not one little jack into Life just to tell me that you were okay!'

White was taken aback. 'There's no signal in Angle Tar –' he began.

'You selfish bastard! I hate you! You left and you never looked back! I hate your guts! I wrote you letters, and I *know* you got them, because they disappeared out of our hiding place! I can't believe I wasted my time trying to talk to you. What was I even thinking?! You couldn't care less about me, or the rest of your family!'

'I got your letters,' said White.

'You never answered! You must have used your stupid Talent to come back to World to get those letters! You could have written me something back and put it in the hiding place, or sent me a Life message, even if you couldn't *bear* to come and see me!'

'I was too afraid to jack in. And I was too afraid to come and see you. They would have found me. You would have been in troub—'

'Oh please! They'd never have found you! No one could ever find you! You can just go dancing off into the sunset whenever you feel like it! That's your problem, Jacob! Why didn't you care?' Cho stopped. The anger had mutated to hurt, written plainly across her face. 'Why didn't you care about me?'

'I'm sorry,' said White. He stumbled over his words. 'I'm sorry.'

Rue had edged out of the firing line. She dared to glance at White. His face was shocking. He looked utterly miserable.

Cho had fallen into silence.

White was statue still. He was staring at her.

'I read all your letters,' he said again. 'Every single one. I was terrified to come back, do you understand? Out-of-my-mind terrified. But I did it. I didn't even mean to do it the first time – I was just thinking about you. I was drunk. I lose control when I'm drunk. And I just . . . Jumped there. To our hiding place. I was thinking about that time when we were just kids and we were hiding from Jospen, and we were in hysterics, we couldn't stop laughing. Do you remember? And suddenly I was just . . . there. I started to panic when I realised what I'd done, but then I saw this bunch of papers, wrapped up into a roll. And I took it, and I Jumped. I was too afraid to stay. I thought they'd know I was back. They said they could track my implant. I thought they would know.'

His voice had grown quieter.

'I read them. They were . . . I loved them. But they were painful, too. Because you talked about what you were doing, and what was happening. Because they had you all over them. They hurt . . . They hurt a lot. And I wanted to forget everything here, because it was easier than remembering. I pretended I didn't have a past, except for one night every few months; one night when I Jumped back and got your next letter and brought it with me, and read it for one night. And that was it.'

271

Cho was crying.

'I'm sorry,' said White. 'I never meant to cause you pain. I thought by going away I'd stop doing it.'

'You idiot,' Cho wobbled, still managing to sound irritated through her tears. 'You're such an idiot. You don't know *anything*.'

She crossed to him and threw her arms around his neck. He stood for a moment, seemingly unsure. Then he put his arms around her and held her close.

Cho stayed there a moment more and then let go, suddenly awkward. She stepped back. 'I don't get it,' she said, her voice blurry. 'You're here now. Can't they still track your implant?'

White went still.

Grad take us, thought Rue. *They could come after him. They could be coming right now.*

But Cho was faster. 'No,' she said. 'No. Way. You had it removed.'

White said nothing.

'When?' Cho whispered. Her mouth was slack with shock.

'A couple of days ago.'

'Did it hurt?'

'A little.'

'But . . . *how*?'

White shifted, uneasy. 'There's a doctor,' he said. 'In Angle Tar. I was given his name when I first went there. He's a Worlder, originally. He was good. Quick and clean. He's done it before. Many times before.'

'It's really . . . it's really gone? No more Life?'

'No more Life.'

They looked at each other then. Rue watched them both. Something that she couldn't be a part of was passing between them.

'But . . . if you got the name of this doctor ages ago, why did you wait until now to get it done?' Cho demanded.

White looked away, at the wall. 'Because, until recently, I never thought I'd be coming back here.'

A heavy silence descended.

Then Cho glazed over. 'Shit, Livie's on her way back,' she said. 'She just pinged me a message.' She looked at Rue. 'You're going to have to explain this.' She jerked her head towards White.

'He's *your* brother,' Rue said.

Cho snorted. 'Yes, but *you're* the one who brought him into her house.'

They grinned at each other.

Rue's grin faded. Well, she'd done it. She had White here. It was time to tell him, wasn't it?

Time to tell them all, maybe. Because she didn't think she could do this by herself. The Ghost Girl had tried to – had *had* to. She'd been alone. But Rue wasn't alone.

'Does Livie want to know what's going on, too?' said Rue.

Cho raised an eyebrow.

CHAPTER 26

WORLD

WREN

He woke up in a medical bed. He could tell it was a medical bed because it was uncomfortable. That and the tubing coming out of his arms.

Wren tried to move.

'I wouldn't,' came a voice. 'You're still weak.'

It had come from the end of his bed. There, stuck onto the far wall, was a screen. And there on the screen was Greta's face.

Wren fell back onto his pillows, too empty and tired to hide himself from her.

'It's no good looking upset,' she said. 'You brought this on yourself.'

Her voice had lost its usual playful quality. Warning bells began to ring.

'Brought what on myself?'

His voice was a horrible croak.

Greta sighed. 'You're in trouble, Wren. You've kept from me just how much. I thought I could turn it around for you. I knew when I first got assigned to you that you were damaged. But we thought, with my intervention, you could become useful. We thought you *wanted* to come here. You seemed to like it so much at the beginning.'

An old spark of the game flared. 'I do like it,' he protested. But his heart wasn't in it, perhaps, or Greta had decided to stop believing one word that he said. Her expression was stone cold.

'Really? Then why do you jeopardise your life here at every turn? Hacking files. Disobeying me as much as you dare. Losing the asset that *you* recruited. Oh yes, I know about that. Don't you worry your selfish little head about it, I'll find her. I'll clean up your mess. You just stay there and rest, Wren.'

He wanted to be angry, righteously angry. But it was actually a relief that it was out in the open now. Such a relief that he began to laugh. It hurt his throat.

'What exactly are you laughing at?' said Greta, her voice rising.

He shook his head, still laughing.

'You find your situation funny? Look around you. They're finally tired of your antics and they've ordered me to incapacitate you. You're no longer useful to us, you see. You're a liability.'

Wren snorted, curling onto his side to prop himself up. The movement took everything he had. He was weaker than a newborn, a curious sensation. The tubing tugged gently in his veins. 'You can't lock me up.'

'Wren, dear. I think if you tried to Jump right now, you'd find it quite hard.'

She was just playing the game, trying to scare him. Later, when he didn't feel so weak . . . Later, when she had her back turned, he would get the hell out of here.

'I'm assuming you expect to feel stronger soon, yes?' said Greta. Her skin was so smooth on the screen. Was she that smooth in real life? 'You're thinking that we're trying to get you better?'

Wren froze.

'Oh dear. Perhaps I should tell you that the drips attached to your arms are feeding you a cocktail of drugs. The drugs keep you weak and your mind confused. Just confused enough, we've found, to prevent any kind of Talented activity. Not our most sophisticated method, but it's proven effective. Sort of our fallback, you might say.'

Greta paused, letting it sink in.

He felt himself tremble. Was it the drugs, or was he afraid? *You're afraid*, said the voice.

Greta's face was mild, her way of expressing extreme smugness. He wanted to crush her. He wanted to obliterate her from existence. She was everything that was wrong with this world. Everything he could fix, if only she didn't exist.

His hand went down the inside pocket of his trousers, and there, lying against his inner thigh – relief. He still had it. They hadn't taken it. Maybe they didn't know about the pocket. If they'd kept up with the latest fashion, they would have.

He fished the bottle out and gripped it in his fist.

'Do you have an itch?' came Greta's annoying grate.

He popped the cap open and shook out two.

Three.

Four.

Five pills.

'What's that?' she said, her voice suddenly sharp.

'Something you missed,' he whispered, and swallowed the pills.

His eyes went up to the screen. She was looking at him in complete, naked shock. The sight would sustain him for a long time to come. She knew what the pills were. She knew he'd lied about the technician. She knew everything, suddenly. It was all over her face.

'What have you done?' she said.

He lay back.

'You'll overdose!'

The door opened, and a technician came running in. He went straight to the drip, his eyes glazed with Life.

It was all over, and there was only one place left to go.

'Stupid boy,' he heard Greta say. She sounded strange. Almost sad.

The drug kicked in. It was like being slammed full-body against a wall. He shot across the universe, racing the stars. It seemed a long time before he reached the Castle, arriving out of breath, everything moving too slowly for him, as if he were galloping far ahead and time and space were behind, shouting at his back to wait for them.

He had no idea how long he had. If four times the drug would give him four times the length of stay, or if he would simply burn out four times as quick. Or if any of that stuff even mattered here. He came out of the room he found himself in, a room that was a parody of the hospital room he'd just left, complete with a ghostly shadow technician, like a sentry made of smoke next to his bed.

The corridors were endless, but he would search them all.

He set off, calling hello as he went in the loudest voice he could. He realised it wasn't sound he was making. He was calling with his mind, and his mind echoed off the walls of this place, carrying through the stone, or the paper, or the wood, or whatever the walls were made of. He suspected they weren't made of anything he would know. The wood and the stone were what he saw. Other visitors would see whatever made sense to *them*.

He wondered what the monsters saw.

It didn't take long, or it did – he wasn't sure which. But after a time, he knew he was being followed.

He stopped.

Whatever it was stopped with him.

He turned around, insides lurching.

It was a mirror.

No.

It was him.

He'd expected black sticks creeping across the walls again, or wet jelly eyes bigger than his head, or something with tentacles. He'd never liked tentacles. But what stood in their place was a very ordinary looking human figure. His height. His face. His body.

Wren stared at himself.

His copy stared back.

He felt an awful sinking feeling, a cold wash of realisation swim behind his eyes.

'You're the Ghost Girl,' he said, his voice savage. She just loved to change her look, didn't she? She'd never turned into him before, but there was a first time for everything.

The Wren copy tilted its head.

'What?' it said, in his voice. 'Oh. No, this isn't her. She's a visitor here, like you.'

Wren stared at it, untrusting.

The Wren copy looked back.

'But you can change shape, like she can,' he said, accusingly.

'Everything can change shape here. You can change shape here.'

'What? I can?'

'Yes. You've never tried? No. You've never tried.' It answered its own question, as if suddenly receiving it from some invisible source.

It's copied your memories, said his voice. *It can see you've never tried by looking through your memories.*

'The shape you wear here is just a habit,' said the Wren copy. 'You adopt it unthinkingly. But you could change it if you wanted.'

Wren couldn't stop looking at it. Was that really how pointy his chin was?

'But . . . then I wouldn't be me,' he said, still cautious.

It looked human. It even seemed like it had the weight and texture of a human. He could feel his fear draining away rapidly, now he was faced with something he understood.

That was dangerous, wasn't it? Because underneath, it was still a monster.

'Of course you would,' said the Wren copy, impatient. It sounded *impatient.* Presumably the same way he did. 'You are you. Shape means too much to you, when it should mean nothing.'

'Why did you choose to look like me, then?'

'So we can understand each other better. It's easier to talk to you in a shape you recognise.'

'Why have you never done this before?'

What kind of thing chooses to look like a monster?

The Wren copy put its head on one side, as if it was considering what to say.

'Well . . . I wanted to eat you before,' it said. 'Can't eat you in this kind of shape.'

Wren took a step backwards.

'What do you want?' he faltered.

'What do *you* want?' it shot back. God, it was . . . it was really him. It was the strangest feeling, to stare into yourself. Watch yourself talk and gesture, watch emotion cross your own face. 'Last time you were here you said you wanted to open the Castle.'

'Yes.'

It smiled.

'That's easy,' it said. 'Do you know how?'

'No,' he said, while inside he skipped with excitement. 'Can you teach me?'

It laughed.

Did he really laugh like that? What a strange, fake sound.

'There's nothing to teach,' it said. 'I can simply show you.'

Wren tried not to crow into the ceiling. Nothing could stop this now. Just, please, let the drug keep working. Keep him here. Everything was riding on it. *Hurry hurry hurry* said his voice. *Before Greta pumps your body full of some other drug she hasn't told you about, some neutraliser designed to drag you back screaming into the real world.*

If you pull this off, you'll never have to face the real world again.

But still, there was something that pulled him back. A voice he mostly ignored that told him to think about this for a minute. Just think about what this might mean. Think about the fact that it was a monster in front of him, a monster that wanted to eat him.

It seemed so laughable now, though. Now it looked like him, it just seemed like a joke they'd shared. No one ate humans. They were the top of the food chain.

Monsters weren't real. Well, okay, they were real here, but not really real. This wasn't a real place. It wouldn't be real until it was opened.

The copy must have sensed his hesitation.

'It's really easy,' it said. 'It doesn't hurt.'

His copy's body looked like it was straining towards him, pulling at a leash that he couldn't see. But it didn't move forward an inch.

It's trying not to scare you away.

It looks like you so you'll trust it and you won't run and disappear like last time. It thinks you're afraid.

'What happens?' said Wren. 'When the Castle is opened. What happens?'

'Everything you want. Everything you've always wanted. Everything normal stops. Everyone can explore. All the things you hate will go away.'

'Just like that?'

'Just like that.'

It was practically vibrating.

'Why can't you open it?' said Wren.

'It needs someone from outside it to open it. And you need to *want* to open it. Everything always runs. But you stopped running. You're different. You're special.'

Why is it flattering you so much?

Because it wants something, Wren snapped back. *It wants the same thing I do.*

'What do I have to do?' he said.

'Just stay still. That's all you have to do. Stay still and let yourself open.'

'Let myself open?' Wren echoed. 'How do I do that?'

It paused. Maybe trawling through his memories again.

'The way you feel when you're in the blackness,' it said, at last. 'The feeling of possibility – the endless, boundless possibility of blackness and of nothing. You feel nothing there. It's only when you think of where you want to go that you start to feel something. The weight of the real place that drags you back.'

Wren found himself nodding along. That was it. That was it, just so.

'Think of the nothingness,' it said. 'Think of it now. And that's it.'

'That's it.'

'Do it now,' it said. 'What are you waiting for?'

The drug might stop working, urged the voice. *And then you'll go back to a world that has nothing for you, nothing except people like Greta who try to cage you and dissect you and don't give one tiny little crap about you. People like White who cast you off like an old jacket with holes in, not a second goddamn thought.*

Stupid, stupid people everywhere, just screwing up the world,

282

not because they can, but because they're nothing more than thoughtless, mindless animals. They're born, they eat, they work, they churn out more copies of themselves who will do exactly the same thing, and then they die.

There's nothing for you back there.

Be something. Show them. Change it all.

Don't back out now, you fucking coward.

Wren closed his eyes. It was easy to think of nothing here, in this strange nothing place that tried to be everything at once. He let go.

And then he felt something touch his head. It was touching his head.

He flinched automatically, but the touch didn't go away. He tried to twist and turn, a fish on the end of a hook. He couldn't see what it was. The pressure grew, gripping his skull, surrounding his head. No . . . it was *in* his head. He screwed his eyes shut, the pain throbbing into him, too much to think or do anything about.

Then came a horrible, awful sucking sensation.

It was sucking on his head.

Maybe he was screaming. He could no longer tell. Nothing was everything. He felt like his mind was being peeled back, layer by layer, every discarded layer allowing more of everything in until it flooded him, *everything*. He could see and feel it all.

Everything is everything, he thought, incoherent. *I am everything.*

It's all over.

The last thing he thought of was White's face.

His long, shining hair.

CHAPTER 27

WORLD

RUE

They sat in a circle in Rue's bedroom.

Livie was there. Cho said she trusted her with anything. Hackers traded in secrets, secrets were currency, and they were making Livie rich. Livie, rather than feel annoyed at all this disruption to her life, seemed eager.

White sat quietly, his hair pulled back into its customary plait. Rue was painfully aware of him. Every shift his body made, the sounds of him up close.

She paused a moment, trying to ignore their eyes on her face, trying to order her thoughts. For a while, she'd thought about how much to tell them. How much to explain and how much to keep to herself. Not lie – she couldn't do that. Just not say everything.

But that was all wrong, wasn't it? Truth was their only way

out now. If people just told the truth from the beginning, things might be so different. If they thought her mad, then that was something she would have to deal with. But she had to try first. She had to give them that.

Rue looked up.

'I'm going to say something that will make you think I'm insane,' she began, picking her way slowly across the words. 'Some things for you, Cho and Livie, that might make you wonder what's wrong with me. But there are some things that even *you* will have trouble believing.' On the *you* she looked at White. He was gazing at her steadily.

'Livie's a gullible jack, she'll believe anything,' said Cho, and laughed. Livie shoved her. They were nervous. It showed in their shoulders, the way they set their mouths.

You should be, she thought.

'There's a place we call the Castle,' she said out loud.

Her eyes flickered to White. He nodded.

'White and I, we've both been there. But I think you can get there even if you're not Talented. You just need to be pulled there by someone who is.' She glanced at Livie.

'S'okay,' said Cho. 'She knows about the Talent.'

'I have a cousin . . .' said Livie, trailing off.

Good. It had just become a little easier.

'Think of the Castle', said Rue, 'like a Life building. A Life building only exists in Life, right? Well, the Castle is like that. It exists somewhere, somehow – but maybe not in a way we conventionally understand. When you go there, you know that you're not in a place that behaves like normal places. It's filled with rooms. Rooms that show you your past. You could go

285

into a room and it could be from your childhood, and you see your own memories unfold before you. Or you could go into another room and it shows you . . . it shows you the future. A future you, an older you, doing something you never remember doing before. And this place is endless, endlessly amazing. You could wander it for days, only days don't pass there the way they do in the real world. You could get lost in it. Think of all the incredible things you could see.

But you can't. Because there's something else in the Castle with you. They live there. It's their home, the in-between place of all realities. And they are enormous. And they are terrifying. And what they like absolutely best of all is eating you.'

She saw White's outline twitch in the corner of her eye. He had closed his eyes for a moment, and his face had that strange sharp, shadowed outline when someone felt sick. Cho was looking at him curiously.

'So you run. You have to avoid them, but it's like they can smell you and they just keep coming after you. But it's okay because you can leave the Castle if you want, and they can't. You can wake up. But what if someone wanted to *open* the Castle?'

'What does that mean?' said Livie, who looked enthralled, as if Rue were telling a particularly good story.

'I don't really know,' said Rue, honestly. 'All I know is that it lets them out into the real world. She wouldn't tell me much more. Just that there were hardly any humans left. That it was awful.'

'Who wouldn't tell you?' said Cho.

Here was the really tricky part.

'A girl from the future,' said Rue. She tried to make it sound as bland as possible, as if she were talking about some girl they all knew. In a sense, she was. But she couldn't tell them who the girl was, not yet. She just couldn't. In this airy, bright room, with the sleek trappings of technology all around them. In this kind of world, it sounded like a silly fairy tale.

'Oh,' said Cho, amused. 'Right.'

Livie tutted at her. 'Hush.'

'You're not saying you believe this, are you?' Cho rolled her eyes.

Rue watched them anxiously. It was falling down, so soon.

'Think of it like this,' she cut in. 'When I first learned of World, I thought it was magical. No, listen, Cho. Listen to exactly what I'm saying. I couldn't understand food units, or Life, or implants. I still don't, not really. But in the beginning all I saw was a magic box that gave me food from nothing. When I first went into Life, I saw walls come alive, and things so real I swore I could touch them, even though they're *not* real. They're just trickery projected into my brain. But I didn't know that. If you don't know how something works, if it's beyond you, you'll call it magic. D'you see?

'I think the Castle is like that. I think the Talented are like that. They're beyond our understanding right now. So all we can see is magic. But if we knew more, we'd just call it clever technology. We'd look at a Talented's make-up . . . the things, the things they're made from . . .' She faltered and looked desperately at White.

'Genetics,' he said.

'Genetics. We'd look at them and point to a spot and say "there". That's what makes someone Talented. And then everyone would know, and it wouldn't look like magic any more.'

'Yes, all right,' said Cho. 'I mean, I'm not saying I . . . But I understand what you mean. Just keep going.'

'So,' Rue continued, feeling a small surge of relief. 'This is where it gets to the part you might have trouble with.' She forced herself to look directly at White.

'Tell me.'

'You've met her before, the girl from the future. It's the girl who looks like a ghost.'

His face cleared, and for a moment he looked shocked.

'Yes,' he said, fast.

'Let me just get this all out. In the future, in her future, she says that you stay friends with Wren.'

She couldn't help it – she watched his eyes for a reaction. It was there – a flash – and then it was gone. Pain, or something. Anger.

'You and he are great friends,' Rue said. 'And you both want to open the Castle. I don't know why. Maybe you know, though.'

He was silent.

'Maybe you don't know what will happen, not really. But when you open it, that's it. That's the turning point. Everything goes wrong from there. And she's trying to stop it from ever going wrong.'

Silence. All eyes were on White.

'How?' he said.

'She separated you. She said that only you and he together were strong enough to open the Castle.'

'Separated us how?' he said urgently.

Rue knew what he was feeling. She knew because she'd felt it herself.

My life might not be my own. My mistakes might not be my own.

'She helped Wren leave Angle Tar,' she said. 'She changed the past to stop the future.'

'So . . . it worked,' said Cho. 'Rue, you're away from this Wren guy now. And so are you, Jacob. So you're separated.'

'As long as you never try to open the Castle together,' Livie put in.

White's face dropped. 'That will never happen. Never.' For a moment he looked ugly with anger. Then it faded. An uncomfortable silence followed.

Rue took a deep breath. Get it out.

'It's not enough,' she said into the quiet.

They looked at her.

'She said the future hasn't changed. The Castle is still open. So we haven't stopped it.'

'So it's someone else.'

'No,' said Rue. 'White and Wren are the only two Talented powerful enough to open it.'

'What if there's another one you don't know about?'

'If there is,' said Rue, 'we're screwed. So let's say there's not. Let's say –'

'It's Wren,' said White abruptly.

Rue looked at him, and he glanced back at her.

'It might be,' she said. 'If he somehow finds a way to do it on his own.'

'We can't take the chance. We have to find him.'

'And talk to him,' Rue replied, firm. 'Just talk. We have to tell him all this. We'll change his mind.'

'You don't know him like I do. He wants to change the world. He'll do anything to get what he wants.'

'I know him better now,' said Rue quietly.

White stared at the floor, his jaw tight.

Cho cleared her throat. 'Look. This is a great story, but, you know, time travel? It's been disproven countless times. None of what you're talking about is possible.'

'Possible?' said White. 'Let's by all means talk about what's possible. What are the current Life theories on teleportation? Or dream spying? What do they say about this, Cho?'

And he disappeared.

Rue sighed.

White reappeared crouched next to Livie, who gave a whole body flinch and a breathless, strangled squeal.

Cho was on her feet. 'Don't do that!' she shouted. 'Don't show off just because I'm sceptical about time travel, okay? One bloody impossible thing at a time, please!'

'White,' said Rue, her voice quiet. The effect was immediate, she was surprised to see. He looked at her, and his body relaxed.

'Just listen,' she said to Cho, who was still prickling. 'We just need your help, that's all. You don't have to believe in it. I'm not asking you to believe. But we can't do what we want to do on our own. We need you.'

'For what?' said Cho.

'We need to get to Wren. And we need to do it without anyone getting caught.'

Rue locked eyes with her, pleading.

For your brother, she thought. *I know you love him as much as you hate him.*

'We can help you,' said Livie. She was still clutching her chest, and she looked shaken. But her eyes danced.

'We can help.'

CHAPTER 28

ANGLE TAR

FRITH

'What's the matter?' said Fernie.

Frith bit into the apple she'd given him from her own tree in the back garden. The juice ran down his throat, sweet and clear-tasting.

'Nothing,' he said, when he'd finished chewing. He had begun to learn that if Fernie wanted the answer to something, she merely waited until you gave it to her – which you inevitably did, even if you thought you'd successfully avoided it.

'You young types have no patience,' she groused, flying around the kitchen. She was hardly ever still, either, so when she was, and her focus was on you, it was unnerving. 'Memories are tricksy things.'

'It's not that,' said Frith, though it partly was. He was trying not to stuff the entire apple down his throat at once. The food was so good here. He had a feeling that he'd never cared about food too much in his before-life. It certainly seemed to be making an impression on him now he had time, nothing but time, to enjoy it.

'Then what?' said Fernie. She wiped her hands on a dish rag, watching him.

Might as well take it out and show her. She probably already knew about it. It was that kind of village. Mail, from the Capital, with the university seal on it, and for him, the exciting, tragic stranger with memory loss? He supposed everyone knew. So he fished it out of his coat pocket and waved it towards her.

'I ain't going to read it,' she said. 'It's your business. Tell me what you want to tell me out of it.'

Frith shrugged, placing it on the kitchen table. 'From them,' he said simply. 'Ordering me back to Capital. I've had enough time to sort it all out, apparently. So back to the doctors I go. Back to my old life.'

'Is that so bad?' she said, and he glanced at her sharply. 'P'raps you should give 'em a chance. They are doctors, after all.'

'You were my key.'

'Did you think coming here would just unlock it all?'

'Why else would I remember your name, Penhallow, and the riverbank, so clearly?'

Fernie pressed her lips together. 'It's not only me that had that name, is it?'

Frith was silent. She'd told him the bare bones of what had happened between him and Oaker, her son. She'd said it in careful tones, as if telling him might break something open, and suddenly the old him would come rearing out of his current shell, alive and snarling.

But nothing. The behaviour she'd described embarrassed him, but not much more. He couldn't remember it, so couldn't connect himself to it. The young him had sounded like an insufferable sod.

'Well,' he said. 'We tried telling me about that. And him. But it didn't work.' He regarded her. 'We've tried a lot of things.'

'And we'll keep trying,' said Fernie, firmly.

Frith merely raised a brow, cynical.

He still had holes inside him, gaping black wells that were now beginning to fill with new material, new life. There was precious little memory material to rebuild himself from, so he was using what was around him. And he was starting to feel like more than a shadow. It was a good feeling. He wasn't ready to let go of it.

'While you're draping yerself miserably over my chairs, you could do a bit of work for me,' said Fernie.

Frith faked a put-upon look. The entire time he'd been here, in between treatments, she'd never let him rest. He was up on the roof, fixing a broken tile or two. Mending the chicken house where something had tried to get in and tangled up the wire meshing. Digging over her vegetable garden in preparation for spring planting. A hundred little things that it just hadn't occurred to him needed to happen when you owned your own things and weren't, as she put it, swaddled by servants your entire life.

She'd mocked him severely when he'd said that he had no idea how to bake bread, and sent him off to Til the baker one evening to learn. Three of the old salts from The Four Cocks who liked to occupy the downstairs bar of an evening had taken him out at the crack of dawn last weekend to go fishing in the river. Their Bretagnine accents were so thick he could barely understand them, but that was all right because they didn't talk much. He'd caught three trout, and the men had clapped him on the back and announced to the world at The Four Cocks that evening that he was 'not bad for a poshie', which seemed to be high praise indeed. He'd got drunk with Til that night, who turned out to be a surprisingly sharp and funny sort when he let go.

It was all Fernie. He knew it. It was her ham-fisted and painfully obvious way of drawing him in slowly, tangling him up in her web like a benevolent spider, filling the emptiness until he began to forget the shape of it. What was irritating him the most was that at times he'd caught himself enjoying it.

'I've got a visitor coming,' said Fernie. 'The spare room needs cleaning out.'

Frith sighed. 'Cleaning? Oh, joyful day. My absolute favourite.'

She raised a brow. 'Get on it, and mebbe I'll make you a cake.'

'I only clean for the lemon one. All others pale in comparison.'

'Done.'

He stood, stretching out his back. 'Who's coming?'

'Oh, just a family member,' she said vaguely. 'I ain't seen him in a while.'

'Does this family member have a name?'

'His name's Jason.'

She had a funny cast to her voice as she said it. He wondered what it meant. Was this Jason a bit of a black sheep? He supposed he would soon find out.

He whiled away the afternoon sweeping and scrubbing. He was aware that his contemporaries back in Capital would be horrified at how he was spending his days. He knew he should be, too. There was no intellectual fulfilment, no changing of the world. There was just the application of his body to repetitious movements while his mind did nothing much. Maybe he was supposed to feel anxious about how time slipped out from under him while he did nothing of use with it. But he couldn't. It ran away from him, a river of seconds and minutes and hours, and he sat on its banks and watched it go.

It was well into the evening when Fernie's visitor turned up. Frith heard the front door open. He'd been stretched out on the plump little couch in what he would call the parlour but Fernie referred to dismissively as the 'sitting-about room'. She had a decent collection of books for a country woman – they weren't cheap, and some of them had rather odd bindings. His favourite was a weighty tome on the history of Bretagnine, which he had to prop open on a table to read, holding the thick-coated pages down flat with both hands.

Frith looked up from a particularly fascinating section on the noble art of deliberately wrecking ships on the coastal line to plunder their cargo – not practised any more, of course – and wondered if he should go and say hello.

He heard a man's voice in the hallway.

He gave them another twenty minutes and then decided that politeness would no longer stand for it. Marking his place carefully with the book's velvet tassel, he got up and made his way to the kitchen.

They both looked up from their seats at the table. There was a strange tension in the air – perhaps he'd been right earlier, and this Jason was a bit of a troublemaker. Fernie's expression was grave. Jason was surprisingly dressed in city fashion, with his chestnut hair cut in the latest style to rest curling on top of his collar. Perhaps he came from a well-to-do part of the family.

He was also alarmingly handsome. He had something gently exotic about him, around his dark eyes and high cheekbones.

Frith stopped short, waiting for Fernie to introduce him. But she sat silent, looking at Jason. The man stood, hesitated, shifted on his feet.

He was nervous. Which was odd.

Frith bowed to him. It seemed a silly thing to do in Fernie's kitchen – bowing was considered hilariously formal out here, as he'd found out to his cost on first arriving. But from one rich man to another, he thought.

The silence stretched on.

Frith gave a small smile. 'My apologies,' he said. 'I didn't mean to intrude. But I thought it ruder not to come and introduce myself.'

Jason's eyes were flickering over him, raking him from head to toe. 'You were right,' he said at last. 'His line is . . . shattered. It's all over the place. Although it's started to solidify again recently.'

'Well, that's good news at least,' Fernie commented, sounding pleased. 'I thought if we couldn't bring it back, we'd at least try to start repairing it.'

'Excuse me?' said Frith.

Jason canted his head. 'My apologies,' he said. 'I was talking about your head line. Have you told him about head lines?'

'No,' said Fernie.

'Well, why not?' Jason said, impatience creeping into his voice. 'You have to explain things to him, at least.'

'Everything in its own time.'

'Gods, Mother, I wondered how soon you'd get your favourite phrase out. I had a secret bet with myself, and I bet about two hours. It's been twenty minutes. *Twenty minutes.*' He sounded triumphant.

'Then you lost your bet, din't you?' said Fernie.

Jason raised his eyes heavenwards.

'Sorry,' said Frith. 'This is your son? You never told me you had more than one.'

Fernie clasped her hands together in her lap. She looked young, suddenly – young and uncertain.

'I didn't,' she conceded. 'Because I only ever had one son. This is him.'

The nervousness had crept back into Jason's body. He stood stiff and fidgety, watching Frith.

'The one that died?' said Frith. His voice was sharp. What kind of new, ridiculous treatment was this? Shock therapy?

'The one that died,' said Fernie. 'Only he didn't. He moved up North and took a new name. That was his choice. We thought it best to let people think he'd died.'

'And why on earth would you do that?'

Fernie exchanged a glance with Jason.

Jason clasped his hands behind his back. He gave a short, panting kind of sigh. And then he disappeared.

Frith stared at the air where he'd been.

It wasn't like he didn't know about that. The Talent trick.

297

It was just that the room had started to tilt on him, which was odd.

His memories were coming back.

It was the most curious sensation he'd ever felt. They sluiced through his veins, trickling into the fibres of himself. There was a rolling heaviness in his head, as if the memories had weight and he was full of their soup.

He remembered that day with Oaker at the riverbank. He remembered the exact moment when he had vanished, the golden hair on his arms curiously stiff in the hot sunlight. He remembered what he did afterwards in the village square.

He remembered meeting what he knew was a Talented girl in his university military history class, a few years later. Pretending to like her so he could get close and confirm it. Seska, her name had been. She'd thought, towards the end, that they might marry.

He'd had Oaker in his mind the day he'd gone to the Spymaster and pitched the Talented programme to him. And he remembered recruiting the first student for it.

Some things were still missing. The recent past was especially murky. There was something about a stone room, and a boy with long, black hair.

But it all seemed to be coming back. Whether he wanted it to or not.

He wasn't alone. He felt it in his shoulders.

'I'm fairly sure I'm not usually the fainting type,' he said to the wall.

'It was the shock of the memories coming back, I expect,'

came Jason's quiet voice. 'I can already see fewer holes in your head line.'

Frith was silent.

Jason cleared his throat. 'You seem angry.'

'Well, I *was* told you were dead, Oaker.' Frith turned and sat up slowly. His head pounded.

Jason was hunched on the dressing chair a few feet away. He held up a hand. 'I go by Jason now, please. I haven't been Oaker for a long time.'

'As you wish.'

'Did you care?'

Frith glanced at him. 'What?'

'Did you care?' said Jason. 'When you heard I was dead.'

'I don't know how to answer that. What do you want me to say?'

'The truth. That's all.'

'The truth is that I don't remember how I felt. I don't remember feeling anything.'

Jason was silent.

Frith watched his profile. 'Why did you want to be dead?' he said.

But he got no reply.

'I suppose the silence means that it was because of me.'

'You set up the Talented programme. It's your project, your life. Everyone knows how obsessed you are with the Talent.' Jason paused. 'And I know I was the catalyst.'

'Are you really trying to tell me that because you're Talented, you decided I was *so* dangerous that it was best for you to die?'

'You'd have come back for me, as soon as you had the power to.

299

Mama didn't want that for me. *I* did, though. I was a stupid brat. And I hated you for what you'd done. You made life unbearable for me down here, did you know that? Everyone whispering about me everywhere I went. People wouldn't serve me in shops any more. Filthy looks. I lost all my friends. Do you understand what that's like, in a place like this? Your life is over.'

'Then I apologise,' said Frith, stiffly. 'That's what you want, isn't it?'

And is that all you want? Or do you want to punish me?

Jason just smiled. 'It's really strange to see you like this. You're as open as the sky. You've never been like that before. I can read people so easily. It's part of my Talent. I can see their head lines, their pasts. Sometimes what they're thinking about.' He caught Frith's stare. 'Oh yes. Just sometimes. Are you beginning to see how valuable I would have been to you? What kind of a life would I have had if we'd kept my name alive? Even if I'd moved out of Kernow, you'd have found me eventually, with the resources you have. So the name had to die. I had to die.'

'You look like you did all right,' said Frith. 'You look well-off.'

'I'm doing fine. Being able to read people comes in very handy when you're in a strange city and you desperately need a job. It served me well.'

Frith shrugged. He felt Jason's eyes on him. 'So there's a history between us.'

'How do you mean?'

'You say you know me. Very well, it sounds like. I realise I may not have all my memories back quite yet, but as far as I'm aware, we met once, for a summer, when we were both just

300

past childhood. I find it hard to believe that you know me so well from just that.'

'I . . .' he hesitated. 'All right, so I followed you.'

'You . . . what?'

Jason looked at the wall, the ceiling. He tapped his foot. 'Um,' he said. 'I followed your career, I meant.'

'You're starting to make me very nervous, *Jason*,' Frith said, putting delicate emphasis on the name.

'Well, at least we're on equal ground, then. You've made me nervous my entire life. Just thinking about you makes me feel sick.'

Frith was shocked into silence.

Jason picked at the material of his trousers. 'I work in government,' he said. 'Not anywhere near your department. We nearly met, several times, actually. I always avoided it. I just thought you'd take one look at me and know who I really was. You have . . . a pretty incredible reputation. Most people think you're some charming titled fop with a contrived government project to keep you out of harm's way. And maybe you've encouraged that thinking. But I've met one or two people who know you better. They're afraid of you. I could see it in their head lines when I asked about you.'

Frith felt a chill deep inside him. What kind of person had he been, before the memory loss? Fear was power. It was good to have power over people, he supposed. But it was also empty. What had he filled that emptiness with?

'You don't seem happy about that,' said Jason, softer.

His hackles rose. 'Did you expect me to rejoice at finding out you've been mining people for information on me? Keeping *watch* on me? And what exactly were you intending to do, the whole time you were skulking around my life?'

Jason paled.

Frith swung his legs off the bed. 'You don't know me. How can you? I don't even know myself. I'm nothing. I'm a shadow of who I used to be.'

'That's not true,' Jason said. Frith could see his hands gripping the sides of the chair. The knuckles were white. Was he really so afraid? It seemed ridiculous, and extraordinary. 'It's not. Here, now, you're real. You're more whole than you ever were before.'

'Because you're right here,' said Frith, his voice cold, 'talking to me in the most vulnerable state I've ever been in. You said that you never even spoke to me before in Capital. Of course I seem more real.' He stood. 'Thank you very much. Thank you for coming here and ripping what little life I had left to shreds. I suppose this is revenge for what was done to you. Well, congratulations, consider yourself revenged. I'm leaving. If I catch sight of you anywhere near me in Capital, I'll use some of the awe-inspiring power I apparently have at my disposal and get you thrown in prison for some arbitrary reason I'll think of on the journey back. Stalking, perhaps?'

Jason stood. 'Wait –'

Frith pushed past and opened the bedroom door. He walked into the kitchen and up to Fernie, who was at the table wearily grinding powder in a little bowl.

'I trusted you,' said Frith. He was pleased to note that his voice did not tremble. 'I put myself in your hands.'

'I never asked you to,' she said. 'You came to me. This is my way of helping. If you don't like it, you know what you can do.'

Frith stared at her.

Fernie put down the pestle she was holding. 'Trust goes both ways, Frith. I just gave you my son's biggest secret – his real identity – you, the one person we were trying to protect him from most. D'you know how hard that was? I'm trusting *you*. Do you see?'

'I don't want your trust!' he shouted. 'I just want to be left alone!'

Frith turned, finding Jason behind him, his black eyes wary.

He walked out. He walked out and through the front door and into the night.

Behind him he heard Fernie say, 'Let him go.'

CHAPTER 29

WORLD

WHITE

'Wren's in a medical hall,' said Cho.

She had spent the last few hours lying on a couch in the social room, locked away in HI-Life, carefully mining, probing, investigating for news of Wren. She was sat in front of them all now, sipping water. HI-Life, she claimed, always dehydrated her.

'A medical hall? What's happened? What's wrong with him?' Rue turned her head.

'The hall records don't say, which is weird. But I hacked a trainee nurse's ID, so maybe she doesn't have access to that kind of information remotely. It can't be too bad, whatever it is; he's not in an isolation unit or anything. It sounded like a regular room.'

'Where is it?' said White.

'It's right across the other side of the city. We can get you there, but I've no idea how you're going to get in by yourselves. I can't even give you fake IDs since neither of you have implants.'

'We'll do it somehow.'

'No, you won't. You haven't the first clue. What if you get stopped? Won't it look a bit funny that there are two people with no Life signals wandering around?'

White swallowed a sigh. He had missed his sister, but he had not missed their constant scratching at each other.

'What do you suggest, then?' he said.

'Livie and I come in with you. We'll hack the IDs of a couple of nurses who work there. Trainees, so it won't look weird that we're so young.'

'And they have to be off-shift,' Livie put in. 'Otherwise it'll be suspicious, two of each person in the same place.'

'It'll be more suspicious if they're in the building when they shouldn't be,' Cho argued back. 'At least if there's two at the same time, even if it gets noticed while we're still there, they'll just think it's a signal glitch or something. Security will get an alert if their shift patterns don't match, though.'

White watched her. She had grown up so fast. In some ways she was still the bouncy yo-yo of a girl he remembered, passionate and irritable, quick to every emotion. She'd always shown an amazing aptitude for Life, but he'd never dreamed just how much. That was her Talent.

Okay, so she used it for hacking. She led a dangerous life. He could shout at her for that. He could snap and snarl, but he wasn't exactly blameless himself, was he? He'd shown her the way to rebel.

'All right,' he said. 'You'll have to come with us.'

Cho was smirking at him.

'Admit it,' she said.

'Admit what?'

'You need me because I'm cleverer than you.'

'You child.'

'Admit it or I won't help you.'

'Fine. You're cleverer than me. Happy?'

Cho gave him another little smirk.

'When do we go?' said Rue, absently. She was staring out of the window.

Livie answered. 'Tonight. It's a social night, so there'll be loads of people out on the streets, going to each other's houses. It won't look weird to be out walking for such a long time.'

'That means you have to dress up,' said Cho. 'It has to look convincing.'

White blinked. He'd got used to his demure version of Capital fashion. Attempting the insane vomitous rainbow mix people seemed to be wearing in World right now was more than he could handle.

'I have nothing to wear,' he said.

'I'll go shopping for you now. You're still the same size, right?' said Cho, as she jacked in.

'You can't get something for tonight, it's too soon.'

Livie laughed. 'Oh, you *have* been away.'

'Some Life shops do two-hour delivery now,' Cho said absently. Her gaze was far away. '*This* shirt is amazing.'

'If you get me anything ridiculous, I will refuse to wear it,' said White, but her grin only deepened. 'We're supposed to be inconspicuous. This is not a joke, Cho.'

'Calm down, I'll get you a classy shirt.'

'Rue, you can borrow something of mine,' Livie said.

Rue turned her head and smiled. 'Thanks.'

She went back to staring out of the window. White found himself watching her uneasily. Being here with her now felt different to the dreams they'd been sharing. It was more complicated, less obvious. They knew each other, and yet they didn't. Parts of her were still a complete mystery. The Talent was their common language, but it was almost like she'd begun to speak a different dialect of it to him.

Livie had jacked in, too, and began to argue with Cho over shirts and IDs and the quickest route to the medical hall. White let their tinkling voices divide them from him like a wall as he went over to Rue and sat next to her.

She didn't turn around. Simply bent her head and leaned it gently on his shoulder. His heart leapt. It was such a little thing, but she did it so unthinkingly, as if they always did this, as if they were just that intimate with each other that she could lean her head down and his shoulder would be there.

'Are you all right?' he said quietly.

She didn't reply.

He waited, giving her space.

'This whole thing is insane,' she said, finally. 'Is that what it is? Has the Talent finally made me lose my mind?'

'Mine too, then,' White replied. He hesitated, then took a piece of her hair between his fingers. It was thick and wavy, a kaleidoscope of chestnuts and brassy browns. 'I've been to the Castle. I've seen those things.'

'So we're all mad.'

'Maybe. Does that make it feel any less real?'

'No.'

Now, while they were talking about it. While things were still calm.

'Do you know who the Ghost Girl is?' he said.

Her head shifted on his shoulder, but she was silent.

'You don't have to tell me if you don't want to.'

'I don't want to keep things from you,' she said. 'I don't.'

'Is it important that I know? Will it affect what we need to do?'

'I don't know yet.'

'Then when you know, you'll tell me.'

A pause.

Then a little 'Okay'.

'Try to look happy,' Cho hissed. 'And a bit less like you're going to a torture chamber or something. We're supposed to be out partying.'

They'd been walking the streets for forty minutes straight, and the closer they got to the medical hall, the more annoying Cho had become. It was her way of dealing with nerves, he supposed.

She and Livie had bought nurses' uniforms from Life that afternoon. There was nowhere to change along the way – everything was so ridiculously open here, airy nothingness stretching out everywhere – so they had already donned them and pretended that they were going to a fancy-dress party.

He knew he was too prickly around Cho. That he pushed her away and stopped her trying to be involved. She thought it was because he didn't trust her abilities, that he still saw her as a child. Somehow he couldn't find the words to explain that he was trying to protect her. She'd never had to go through what he had had to go through.

She'd never been in prison.

And never would be, he promised himself silently. Not now he was here to do something about it.

The medical hall loomed large as they turned the corner. It was so flat and strange-looking. He would never, ever again see it how it was supposed to be seen, in Life. He would never see a World city the way it should be – a riot of colour and art, beautiful and funny and with stupid human scribblings everywhere you looked.

It hit him, suddenly, and he felt his throat constrict. He hadn't missed it before this – not really, not since the first few weeks of living in Angle Tar. It had drained from him, the need for Life, as he'd adjusted. He'd only thought of it occasionally, in an abstract way, because it had stopped mattering.

Here, it mattered.

'Let's go in the back way,' said Cho. 'None of the staff would use the front door.'

'What if there are guards?' Rue muttered.

Cho scoffed. 'It's a medical hall, not an army base.' But her mouth was set in a tense line.

Cho and White walked together, while Rue and Livie dropped behind. It would look better if each of the 'nurses' took in a single implantless individual, rather than them crowding in a more obvious group.

'You okay?' said Livie in a low voice. She had a stiffness to her now that they were alone. Rue understood. It wasn't every day you found yourself breaking the law for some stranger who believed she was trying to save the world from monsters.

You don't know all of it, she thought. *I said I'd tell the truth, but I didn't tell about White.*

She had a horrible idea that the Ghost Girl wouldn't care so much about the rest of the world if she got White back. That if faced with a choice, she'd choose the one over the millions. She sounded like she'd had a good life, at least until the Castle was opened. No silly running away to World. A relationship with White. A *relationship.* The word made her feel strange. They'd been happy together. Why else would she risk everything to come back to the past and try to make it so that he never died?

Maybe happiness made you more selfish, then. Because you'd never had to live without the things you wanted, so when they were taken away, all you could think about was getting them back. Maybe everyone needed a little strife in their lives.

Because when it came to it, if Rue had to choose right now, she didn't know whether she could let many people die if it meant that White would live. Wasn't that the wrong thing to do? The *selfish* thing?

She watched the back of him as he walked. Living, breathing him, here with her. Looking at her the way the dream version of him had, not the way she remembered him in Angle Tar. Or maybe he'd always been like that, and had never felt like he could express it before. Maybe she'd given him courage. It was nice to think that.

310

The back doors of the medical hall opened and two doctors came out, talking together. One brayed laughter. They were off-shift, their steps springy. Maybe they were going straight to a party. They didn't even glance around as White and Cho disappeared inside. One was talking about a little girl, his daughter, as he passed them. She was beginning to talk properly, forming real sentences. His face was animated. He couldn't believe it.

Real people, thought Rue. *It's so much easier to pass judgement on everyone when you don't let yourself see real people.*

It wasn't so bad here. It had some weird ideas, but didn't every place where humans were? If you fitted in here you probably thought it was the best place in the world, and that people like Cho and White, who didn't fit in, were insane. It had been the same in Angle Tar. Even Fernie had never been treated the same as everyone else. There was a satisfaction to that, if you were the sort of person who thought yourself better or more interesting than the rest of the world. But it was also lonely.

No wonder they all moved around, trying desperately to find a place that felt right. That felt like home. People could feel like home, too, if you found the right ones.

She felt a shiver as she passed inside. Cho and White were up ahead, talking together, looking perfectly natural. Then they stopped in front of a door blocking the way.

'Hang back a second,' murmured Livie. 'Pretend you're looking at something in Life.'

Rue glanced at her, baffled. She was glazed over.

Up ahead, White and Cho had moved off. The door closed behind them.

'It's an implant scan,' said Livie. 'The door won't open unless it reads a registered staff implant. There don't seem to be any cameras, though, so we should be fine.'

'How do you know all that?'

'Cho just sent me a message.'

They came to the door. Livie stood right in front of it, patient. There was a tiny grey panel on top of the door, but nothing else.

The door clicked open, and Rue slipped in behind Livie as it swung shut.

It was busier this side. They started to walk. She felt like everyone was staring at them. She had no idea if they were. Surely they'd notice that neither Livie nor Rue worked here?

Livie turned her head to Rue, her mouth hanging open in mock outrage. 'That is *so* typical of him. What did you say?'

Rue gaped at her.

'What did you say?' Livie prompted.

'When?'

'When he *said* that to you!'

'Um.'

'I would have killed him,' Livie rattled on relentlessly. 'What a sot.'

It finally dawned on Rue what she was doing. She shrugged. 'He is a bit. But I still like him, you know.'

In this way, with their fake IDs and their fake conversation, they moved further into the building.

'Wren's registered to the room down the next corridor,' Cho said. 'What now?'

They were huddled together in a tiny cleaner's cupboard,

surrounded by sleek, portable Hot 'n' Dry machines and disinfectant hoses.

'We stick to the plan. I go in first,' said Rue. 'He might . . . He might react badly if White is there, too. We still don't know what's wrong with him. I mean, can he even move?'

'The records still don't say.' Cho shrugged, uneasy. But it was too late to back out now, wasn't it?

Gods, Rue. Why don't you ever think? What if he can't even talk? What if he's really badly hurt? This is so stupid. This is the stupidest thing you've ever done, and now you've dragged other people into it, too. You're a child playing grown-up.

Rue closed her eyes for a moment, willing the voice away. When she opened them, Cho was looking at her anxiously.

'Don't worry,' Rue said. 'If we can't talk to him, then we'll just have to Jump him out of there.'

Cho blinked. 'You can do that?'

'White can. He's the only one strong enough to pull Wren into a Jump if he . . . if he doesn't want to come. Or he can't come. That leaves you two to get back on your own, though.'

'Oh, don't worry about that,' said Livie cheerfully. 'We'll be fine.'

Cho nodded. 'It'll be easier without you.'

Rue looked at White. 'Are you ready?' she said.

'Yes,' he said simply. His black eyes held hers for a moment, and they assessed each other.

Rue opened the cupboard door and slipped out into the corridor.

'Livie?' said Rue over her shoulder.

'Right behind you.'

Room Sapovene, Wren's room, was just down there on the left. Cho had told her that all the rooms here were named after famous poets. It seemed an odd thing to do in a medical hall.

Before hesitation could take hold and start screaming at her *what are you doing this is all going to go wrong*, Rue opened the door to Wren's room.

The first things she saw were machines. The second things she saw were tubes. And buried on a bed in the middle of it all, a prone figure, its head turned away. The room was otherwise empty.

Rue stepped forward.

'Threya take us,' she whispered.

She felt Livie come in behind her and close the door. Under the musical hum of machinery, there was a rattling, susurrant something. She crept closer and realised what it was. His breathing.

'Wren?' she called. 'Can you hear me?'

He didn't stir. His skin was pale and clammy-looking, hair in twisted wet strands across the pillow.

'He's hooked up to loads of shit,' said Livie, prowling around the machines. 'There's no way he's even awake.'

'Can we get all this stuff off him?' Rue said, starting to feel frantic. This was so much worse than she'd thought it would be. He had needles in him. How the hell were they supposed to Jump him with all these machines attached? What if he needed the machines to survive?

'I'm not a doctor, I have no idea.'

They looked at each other.

'*Help.*'

Rue's heart stopped briefly. Wren had his eyes open, half

lidded as if he was struggling to keep awake. He was looking straight at her.

'*Help.*' His voice was barely there. His eyes went to the drip inserted into his arm. Then they went back to her face.

Then they closed again, and she heard his painful, laboured breathing.

'Oh gods,' Rue breathed. 'They're keeping him here.'

'What?'

'They're drugging him. So he can't Jump, perhaps. Maybe he did something, tried to escape. I don't know.'

'They can do that?' Livie sounded astonished.

'They did it to White when he was in prison.'

'He was in *prison?*'

'Wren,' Rue said, urgent. 'Can you hear me?'

But he didn't stir.

Rue turned to Livie. 'We have to get these things out of him. The drug things.'

'Drips.'

'Drips. How?'

'They're just taps, I think,' said Livie, cautiously. 'Hang on.'

Rue waited, trying to keep calm.

'Okay. I took a picture and uploaded it to search on. They're definitely just taps, so you should be able to . . .' She moved as she talked, her eyes focused in Life. 'Like a valve. Okay.' Her fingers hovered over the tube coming out of his arm.

Don't hurt him. Grad knows he's a prick, but just . . . don't hurt him.

Livie gently grasped the tubing and worked at a connected joint. It came loose with a clipped little sound and she fiddled.

315

'Okay, yes. It's easy, you just disconnect it and close the little valve thing.' She moved to the other arm and began to work on it. A moment later and it came free.

Livie turned, triumphant. 'What do you want to do?'

Rue stood for a moment. He was unattached now, but still unconscious and drug-addled. Would a Jump be okay?

'Send a message to Cho and tell her to get White in here,' she said.

Livie blinked once, slowly. 'It's done.'

'Well, this is interesting,' said a new voice.

Rue spun.

Greta's face was on the wall.

'So you've decided to skulk back, have you? Good, because I was about to put out a search for you, and that would have been expensive.'

Rue was silent. Her heart hammered. Every nerve ending screamed RUN. But she couldn't.

On the wall screen, Greta's face tilted. 'Good job I have an alert on his implant, really. His levels just changed. What did you do?'

'I haven't done anything.'

'Still a terrible liar, I see. Let's get a doctor in here to check, shall we? I should have kept some security in here, but I honestly didn't think anyone would care about him, apart from his girlfriend Sabine.' She paused. 'You just missed her, by the way. She's quite distraught.'

'What lies did you tell her?'

'I told her the truth, Rue. He's in a coma. It's his own bloody fault. He overdosed.'

'Overdosed?'

'Are you a parrot? Yes. Sabine found him on his bedroom floor. He's been taking too many drugs.'

'That's a lie,' said Rue. 'You're keeping him here. You're keeping him drugged so he can't Jump.'

She heard the door open. She saw Greta's eyes widen.

White came up beside Rue. 'I think there are people heading this way,' he said softly in her ear.

It was decision time. They had to go. They had to get everyone out of here. But all Rue could see was Greta's face as she gazed at White.

You. Stupid. Stupid. Girl.

What had Wren told her? What had she begun to suspect herself? This whole thing was about getting White back, wasn't it? And she'd brought him straight to Greta. The only thing missing was the gift wrap.

It was all going so wrong, so fast.

The door opened again. In came Cho, backwards, and with her came three security guards, followed by a technician who slipped in quietly behind them. The guards spread out into the room. One blocked the door. He was heavy, solid. No one was taking him down.

'Miss Hammond?' he said, his voice curiously high and polite.

'Thank you for coming so quickly. A few questions and then I need you to take them downstairs to the police, who should be arriving soon.'

Rue's heart sank, sick with misery.

'And, Dr Brein, can you please check the patient's levels? They dropped a moment ago and I want to know why.'

The doctor frowned and moved to the bed.

'Okay,' said Greta. 'Since you're not going anywhere for the moment, would you mind telling me what you're doing here?'

'Not going anywhere?' said White. 'We can Jump right now.'

'But your sister can't. Are you really going to leave her? And her friend?'

White was silent with shock. Rue could see it on his face – who was this woman and how the hell did she know so much about him?

'It's fine,' said Cho. 'Jacob, it's fine. Go. Take Rue and go. Livie and I will be fine.'

'No.'

Cho spat an oath. 'Just go, would you?'

White wavered. He couldn't think. Neither could Rue. They saw it in each other's eyes. Neither of them had any idea what to do.

And it was in that moment that Wren saved them all.

'Um,' came a voice from the bed. Dr Brein, who had been in the middle of re-attaching the drips, was backing away.

Wren had sat up.

Everything dropped and went sideways, as if she was going to faint.

'White . . .' Rue whispered. 'Something's wrong.'

'I feel it, too.' His voice was ragged.

Rue looked up. Cho and Livie were standing together near the door, staring at them.

Are you okay? mouthed Cho.

Greta sighed, massaging her forehead as if she were just unutterably weary.

'Doctor,' she said. 'Please sort this out, will you?'

'Um, you don't *understand*,' said the doctor. His eyes were very, very round. 'He shouldn't be moving. The drips were only disconnected minutes ago. There's no possible way. No one can do that.'

Wren was gazing around the room as if he'd never seen it before.

'What are you talking about?' said Greta. 'Just inject him again, then.'

'Except he should be in a coma right now,' the doctor snapped. 'Any more and I'm risking heart failure.'

'What is this?' said Wren. He looked down, as if surprised by his own mouth. 'Where,' he said, enunciating clearly. '*Where* is this?'

Dizzy. The room was trying to turn on her. Rue fought it.

'Wren,' she said. Wren looked at her.

'Where is this?' he repeated.

'The real world,' said Rue. She wasn't even sure why she said it.

Wren smiled.

'Needed a body,' he said. 'Needed a body to get out. Got a body.'

'Well, he's clearly still drugged, he can't even talk sense,' said Greta. 'And he's clearly not in a bloody coma, is he? So just do it.'

The doctor put out a hand. 'Wren?' he said, his voice pitched to a careful level. 'I need you to lie back down now, okay?'

Wren looked at him.

And then disappeared.

319

Greta sighed, and her mouth opened, but she never got further than that because Wren reappeared standing behind the doctor and snapped his neck.

There was a wet little cracking noise.

He disappeared.

He reappeared behind one of the guards, who didn't even feel it coming. Wren reached out with his slender arms and snapped his neck.

Rue felt White grab hold of her.

'We need to get out of here,' he said desperately.

'Oh gods, oh gods,' Rue whispered, breathless. 'It's too late.'

Wren reappeared behind the second guard and tussled with him briefly. The guard went down.

There was no sound from the wall screen. Rue couldn't tear her eyes away from the third guard, the one in front of the door.

'Run,' she begged him. 'Please. Please.'

The guard was standing, a statue of shock. His eyes were on the bodies of his colleagues. 'What?' he said. That was all he seemed capable of.

Wren reappeared in front of him. The guard reacted instinctively, flailing out a meaty arm and punching him in the chest. Wren should have gone down. He should have been floored. But instead his body folded around the fist, and he staggered back. Then he came forward again and started to struggle with the guard. They danced across the room.

'We have to go,' said White. 'Cho, come on!'

But Cho was rooted to the spot. Livie was the same. They looked like all the colour and the life had been leeched from them and they'd forgotten how to move.

'What's he doing? What's he doing?' said Livie, her voice wavering with hysteria.

White started to move towards them both. Behind him, the guard went down, crashing into the bed and falling still.

And then Wren appeared in front of Cho.

'No!' White roared, pushing her back and standing in the way.

Rue knew she was moving, and there hadn't even been time to think about it – she was just moving. Because maybe this was the moment. It had taken her by surprise. She didn't think she'd have to save him if he never opened the Castle. She had already saved him, hadn't she?

But there was no saving him now. He couldn't Jump with Cho – he'd kill her. And he couldn't leave her to die.

So *he* would die. They'd all die.

Is it really going to happen like this?

But Wren hadn't moved. He ducked his head oddly, like a chicken.

'Vessel,' he said.

He disappeared.

He reappeared in front of Greta's screen. Her face was still there, slack with shock.

'Fucking *bitch*,' he said. He raised his hands and tore the screen off the wall. Rue was astonished to see that it was as thin as paper. Wren shredded it in two, and then dropped the pieces.

He disappeared.

After a while, it looked like he wasn't coming back. The dizziness had gone – that was how she knew for sure. Everything came back in a rush – the painful bright and hard edges of the real.

'They're dead, aren't they?' Cho was saying. 'They're dead. He killed them. They're dead, right? They look dead.'

'We have to leave,' said Rue, trying not to cry. 'We have to go right now. We have to walk out of here like nothing's happened.'

'Rue,' came a voice.

Gods. It was Greta.

Rue edged over to the other side of the bed. She could see the doctor's body out of the corner of her eye.

The ripped sheets of wall screen lay curling on the floor. They were dark. But Greta's voice still sounded from a thin panel attached to the bottom of one half.

'There are police outside the building,' she said. 'You won't get far, I promise you.'

Rue lost control. 'Did you just see that?' she shouted, her voice cracking and peeling at the edges. 'Did you *see* it? Did you see what it did?'

A pause.

'I saw.'

'We have to stop it!'

'I'll find him,' came Greta's voice. But she sounded uncertain. She sounded bewildered. It was horrible to hear.

'No, you won't,' said White. 'We're the only ones who can find it now.'

'Don't be ridiculous.'

'Ridiculous? It can teleport faster than you can react. It can do things Wren could never do. Did you hear it call me a vessel? That's what they do. They can't come here unless they can find a vessel. A body. They're non-corporeal, they must be.' White's voice had grown fast and urgent. He was trying

322

to cope, trying to stay on top of his fear by puzzling it out. 'They use the Talented as vessels to come to the real places. To leave the Castle.'

'You're telling me that Wren is no longer Wren. What is he supposed to be now?' Greta said.

'Something else. Something . . .' Rue bent over. She suddenly felt sick. Violently, awfully sick. It didn't come.

'You'll never find it on your own,' said White. 'You need us to track it down.'

'Work with me, then.'

'No.'

It was Greta's turn to snap. 'You don't have a choice! Or are you going to leave here without your sister?'

'You can't detain me,' said Cho. Rue was gratified to hear some of the old fire back in her voice. 'I haven't done anything wrong. None of us has.'

Greta laughed. 'You really want to go there? It would be the easiest thing in the world to have you arrested, Cho. Do you know how thick my file is on you? Did you think you could have secret meetings and hang around with Technophobes and display an astonishing proficiency for hacking without *someone* taking notice?'

'So you'll arrest her anyway,' said White. 'It sounds like you have enough evidence to do it. In which case it doesn't matter what I do, does it? Come on, Rue, let's go.'

'Wait.'

Greta paused. She sounded tired.

She doesn't know how to deal with this, Rue realised. *She doesn't know what to do.*

'Propose your terms,' she said. 'Come on, hurry up before I change my mind.'

'You let us go,' said White. 'All four of us. We walk out of here. You send Cho a Life message if you need to talk to us. We're going to go and clean up your mess.'

'*My* mess?'

White's whole body was stiff. He was angry.

Very, very angry.

Rue felt her fear trickle back into her, filling her up.

'Yes,' said White. 'Your mess. Wren didn't open the Castle on his own. He *couldn't*. So you did something, didn't you? Something to accelerate his Talent. You just couldn't stop fucking tinkering, could you? Always picking us apart, trying to know. Trying to control. And due to the fact that I've mentioned it twice now and you haven't even blinked, I'm guessing you know all about the Castle. And that means you know what's inside Wren's body. What you helped let loose.'

Silence from the wall panel.

'Fine,' said Greta. 'You can leave. But if you want to disappear on me, Jacob, please remember that I can have your sister picked up any time I like. And if you would rather she didn't go to prison, then when this is finished, you'll come back.'

'I understand.'

'I'm sure you do. I'll be in touch. Let's see who finds Wren first.'

'This isn't a game,' said Rue, disgusted.

'No, it isn't,' said Greta, and her voice had regained its hard edge. 'Wait for the police. They'll take you home.'

Silence.

* * *

It all went past in a blur.

The police came. Everyone came. Greta instructed. Her security clearance was obviously sky high – everyone obeyed her without question.

There was no panic. There should have been panic. People milled, talking, ordering, organising. The four of them were taken into the corridor and made to sit on the chairs there. Questions were asked. Rue couldn't even remember what was said. How much had she told them? The woman questioning her kept giving her careful eyes, the kind of eyes you made when you thought the person in front of you was brittle, breakable. Crazy, or traumatised, or maybe both.

It was loose inside Wren. It was loose in the world. It could be anywhere.

Questions crowded in her head, blotting out everything around her. What was it doing? What did it want?

How?

How?

How had it happened?

The sound of a snapping neck kept echoing in her head.

Eventually, they were taken outside and bundled into a police transport. It should have been exciting – Rue had never ridden in such a thing before. The vehicle hummed along, whipping the grey scenery past her window. All four of them huddled into the back together.

She hadn't even noticed how silent they all were until Livie spoke. Her voice was hoarse, like she'd been talking, or crying, a lot. Probably both.

'Can you all do that? What he did?'

'No,' said White. 'He was being pushed to the extreme. The thing inside him. Pushing his strength. I'd be surprised if it could keep that up. It's still got to work inside a body, after all. Bodies have limits.'

'You're talking as if . . . as if he wasn't a he. That was a human being. That was a guy. Your friend. Your friend, you said.'

It was *friend* that did it. It was too much. Rue burst into tears. Great, painful tears that squeezed out of her eyes like rocks and hurt her chest.

Wren, she wailed in her head.

'I'm sorry,' she heard Livie say, astonished. 'I didn't mean to . . .'

'He's . . . dead . . . isn't he?' she managed, in between hiccuping sobs. 'We can't . . . get him back. It . . . killed him.'

White didn't reply. She looked up. She didn't want anyone seeing her with these horrible scrunched-up eyes, this red face – especially not White. But she had to know if he thought so too. If he thought so too, then it was true.

Her heart quailed. White had bowed his head, and his eyes were hidden from her. She could see tears slipping down his nose.

He nodded. He couldn't trust himself to speak.

I'm sorry. I'm sorry, Wren. I shouldn't have run away. I should have stayed and made you tell me everything you thought, everything inside you that made you look at the world and want to punish it like that. I should have tried. I left you all alone.

As soon as she thought it, she knew it was true. And she knew that White was thinking the same thing.

'I thought you hated him,' said Cho, in a cautious, frightened murmur. Rue wondered if she'd ever seen her brother cry before.

'I failed him,' White muttered. His voice was tight, wavery.

'We failed him,' Rue said.

White held out his hand, head still bowed. Rue took it in hers, and they rode the rest of the journey in silence.

CHAPTER 30

ANGLE TAR

FRITH

It was too late to turn back. Jason had heard him approach, feet snapping over twigs.

His head turned, showing Frith his profile, hair curls shifting against his collar. The sky was moody, but the clouds hadn't broken. Not yet.

Frith paused.

The riverbank looked different every time he came back here. It was less familiar, too. The picture he'd carried in his head of a riverbank from years ago had faded, replaced by the shifting nature of the real version, the smell and sight and sound of it.

'I thought maybe you'd gone back to Capital already,' said Jason, over his shoulder.

It had been two days since the night he'd stormed out of Fernie's cottage. No one had come for him. He'd sat in the inn, brooding, picking over the ceaseless flow of memories that now trickled into his head. Writing letters of his return to the Spymaster, and then throwing them away, unsent. Eating alone. He'd packed all his belongings up, twice nearly sending for a carriage to take him to the train station.

He didn't quite know what stopped him. Only that he couldn't let go of this place. Nor could he let go of the curiosity that was Jason. Not quite yet. He needed to know what Jason wanted from him. There had to be an agenda there. Everyone had an agenda.

Frith hadn't really expected for him just to be there at the riverbank. A part of him had hoped, perhaps.

Yet here he was.

Frith approached, stepping carefully down to where Jason sat with his arms on his knees and settling a few feet away.

'How long have you been here?' he said.

Jason shrugged. 'Since yesterday morning. I stayed until it started to get dark. Then I came back this morning, just after breakfast. Until now.'

'Why on earth would you do that?'

'I made you wait for me here, for hours, once. It seemed only fitting that I wait for you.'

What an insanely illogical thing to do. It made his heart kick.

'This isn't a poem, Jason,' said Frith.

'I know. It's not as neat. You might still leave.'

What was he doing? Why was he so raw all the time, pushing his soul forward in Frith's face as if to say, 'here, read me'?

Frith threw his hands up. 'I don't understand what you want from me.'

'I just . . . I just want to help you.'

'Why? *Why?* I made you pretend you were dead. But instead of staying away and having whatever kind of life you wanted, you come to Capital. You deliberately pursue a career that brings you within my line of sight. Why?'

Jason didn't answer. He was infuriating.

They sat in silence for a moment. The sound of the river came back to Frith. For some reason he couldn't fathom, the noise put him on edge. He felt danger, but a quiet danger that he didn't know how to fight.

'How are the memories?' said Jason, suddenly.

Frith rubbed his face. He'd barely slept last night. 'Still coming. With or without my consent.'

'What are you so afraid of?'

Frith's first instinct was to lie, but he fought against it. Had that always been his first instinct? Who was the real him?

'That I'll be who I used to be,' he said. 'And I have no control over that.'

'That's just not possible.'

'So you've met someone in my situation before?' said Frith, drily.

'Do you really believe that you're simply the sum of what you remember?'

Frith looked out across the water. 'Yes,' he said. 'How can you not be? Experiences make a person. Take those experiences away and you're left with just a shell. I know this. I've *been* this.'

'Well, you just said it yourself – experiences shape you. So now you're getting your memories back, you'd be those . . . *plus* what you are now. You'll be a different person to before, Frith.'

330

It was a really odd sensation to hear his name on Jason's tongue. That Bretagnine accent he'd obviously tried so hard to shed . . . and it sounded like he'd succeeded until coming back here. Surrounded by the trappings of his old life, it came out every so often, soft and rounded. Old lives were hard to shake.

But not impossible, maybe.

'Shall I tell you what I saw in your head line that first night?' Jason said, stealing a glance at him. He had a serious look on his face. Frith still had no idea what a head line was, but he shrugged acquiescence.

'I saw a big hole where I used to be. And smaller holes, dotted throughout. Any connection to me, or to Talent, I think. It was all wiped, like a chain reaction that started off with the memory of that day, here, between us.'

'Can you see what happened to me to cause it?'

'No. I only see the absence. If you don't remember, I can't see it. But you may, in time. Or you may not. Trauma does funny things to people.'

Frith sighed, releasing a weight he hadn't realised he'd been holding. Maybe it would come back in the dead of some awful night, springing into him fully formed. He had no idea whether he really wanted to know what had happened.

'It was a giant hole,' said Jason. 'Where I used to be in your head line. It really surprised me when I first saw it.'

'Why?'

'I thought you'd forgotten all about me. That I was just some dim, distant childhood memory you were barely even conscious of. But apparently not.'

Frith looked away. His heart thrummed.

331

'If you could see my head line,' said Jason, staring out across the river, 'you'd see a big weight around that memory. And you'd see my life arranged around it, everything pulled towards it. I didn't want it to be like that at first. I just wanted to forget you. But I couldn't. So then I thought I'd find you again, as an adult, just have a look. And maybe that would remove all the mystery, the way I'd built you up in my head. I'd see you as just some man, and then I could dismiss you, and everything would be fine.'

Frith stared at the grass as hard as he could. The problem with Jason was that he kept telling Frith things that he both did and didn't want to hear. It was like being pulled apart.

Jason picked up a little stone and turned it over in his hands. His skin had a pale gold cast to it, fingers long and nimble.

'But it wasn't fine,' he said. 'I found out how powerful you were. Still. I found out that you'd become obsessed with Talented. I wondered if it was anything to do with me. I just . . . See, I think we're linked, whether we like it or not. I started something that day, here. And now I have to finish it. For both our sakes.'

'What does that mean, Jason?' said Frith, wary.

Jason looked away. 'You don't trust me,' he said.

'I don't trust any Talented. Anyone with that much power is inherently mistrustful.'

'Then we're equal again. By your logic I should be at least as mistrustful of you.'

Fernie's words flashed into Frith's mind: 'I just gave you my son's biggest secret. I'm trusting *you*.'

'Perhaps you should be,' he said, looking squarely into Jason's face. 'If there's one thing I understand about myself now, it's that I'm not a nice person, Jason. I never have been.'

He expected Jason to respond with optimism. Something tedious like, 'Oh, you are, you just don't know it yet.'

But instead Jason replied, simply, 'Neither am I.'

Frith felt a chill walk down his spine.

It was not altogether unpleasant.

And then the latest in a long line of 'odd things that Jason does' happened, because he saw Jason's eyes flick down to his mouth.

They stopped there too long.

Then Jason looked away, across the river.

'Neither am I,' he repeated, as if to himself. 'Come on.' He stood, brushing his trousers off.

'Where?'

'I'm hungry. It's time for lunch.'

Frith watched him walk away. There was a choice now. There was always a choice. Which one was the right one?

'Are you coming?' said Jason, as he turned amid the trees.

Frith didn't think. He got up and followed.

CHAPTER 31

WORLD

WHITE

'Um. Sorry to interrupt. But I think you'd better come and see the news.'

Cho was hovering in the doorway. She had become muted over the last day or so – they all had. But with Cho there was another reason. He caught her watching his interaction with Rue sometimes, a curious look on her face like she couldn't quite believe what she was seeing.

Rue was curled next to him, asleep. Her head was too heavy on his shoulder now, but he hadn't wanted to move her.

'What's wrong?' he said in a whisper.

'Just come and see.'

He disentangled himself from Rue as gently as he could. She stirred but didn't wake. He moved out of the room and closed the door.

'Is she asleep?' said Cho.

'Yes.'

'I mean . . . she's not . . . gone somewhere, has she?'

'No, just asleep. It's too dangerous for anyone to go to the Castle right now. It might be overrun. I just don't know.'

'Oh. I always freak when I see her asleep. She does it a lot.'

They made their way downstairs and into the social room. A screen, similar to Greta's in the medical hall, had been stuck up on one wall like a poster.

'Aren't they ridiculously expensive?' said White, in surprise.

'Um, Livie's rich. I don't know whether you've noticed her house.' Cho fiddled with the screen. 'No one really needs them, anyway – they're just for being a show-off. But, you know, without your implant I can't share anything with you. That's a really weird feeling, by the way, like you suddenly stopped being able to speak a language, or something.'

'I know.'

'Is it . . .?' She hesitated. 'Is it, you know . . . weird, not having an implant?'

'It is here. In Angle Tar I got used to being without Life. Here it's like being partially deaf and blind.'

'I think about it sometimes,' she said. 'A lot, actually. I know I'm a hypocrite, you know. With what I do. Preaching about how awful Life is but still massively connected. But the truth is, most hackers are the biggest addicts there are. I don't know if I can live without it. I wouldn't feel like me any more.'

White shifted, swallowed. He wasn't sure what she wanted from him.

'It's hard,' he offered. 'But it's possible.'

Cho shrugged, like it didn't really matter one way or the other, even though they both knew it did.

'Are you going to tell me what's happening?' he prompted, trying to be gentle.

'Hang on, hang on, I'm trying to show you. I just need to connect the screen to my account . . . Okay.'

She stepped back.

The screen lit up. It showed an aggregator feed, pulling in images and text and video based on a search subject. Cho had inputted the search term 'arrests/teleporting/dreamers'.

White felt a coldness squeeze his chest.

He scanned the feed. There were photos of people being arrested, looking dazed. One had a sedative dart sticking out of him – still the weapon of choice for the police, it seemed. Fast, effective, more humane than bullets. There was a jerky video someone had taken with their implant recorder; the voice on the video shouting a string of curses as they watched a friend led into the back of a transport vehicle.

'They're rounding up Dreamers,' said Cho. 'Sorry, you say Talented, don't you?'

'Based on *what evidence*?'

'Based on the fact that you're all religious loons with ties to terrorists, and they can do what they like with that, remember? Also . . .' she hesitated.

'Tell me.'

'Look, I never know how truthful this kind of thing is, but apparently, over the last couple of days, there've been a few cases of Talented suddenly attacking people – even their own families. Um. Disappearing into thin air. And then, you know, reappearing. So they started arresting them. I think now they're kind of pre-empting, arresting any Talented they know about, just in case.'

White put his head in his hands. So fast. So unbelievably fast. Wren had opened a crack, and now it was turning into a flood. More monsters had escaped, possessing the Talented, using them as their vessels, riding around in them like cars. How much havoc would they wreak? How many deaths would they cause?

He thought they'd have more time. They needed more time. They hadn't even talked about how they would go about finding the monster inside Wren's body. He hadn't counted on having to find more than one.

He felt so small, suddenly, like the world was spinning out of control and all he could do was sit in the middle of it all like a frightened child.

'I have to do something,' he said, eventually. 'I have to . . . I have to stop this, somehow. *Somehow.*' He laughed, the sound a little too wild for his liking.

'Jacob.'

'What?'

'Are you . . . Is this going to happen to you? I mean, it's the Talented this is happening to, not anyone else.' She jerked a thumb at the screen. She was scared angry. 'I mean, I really don't want you being possessed or something, you know?'

White opened his mouth, but nothing came out.

They needed the Talented, didn't they? That was why the Wren thing had called him a vessel. That was why it hadn't killed him. The Talented had the right sort of minds to be taken over. They were already displaced, half in other worlds. Untethered. It'd be so much easier to take over a mind like that than a mind rooted in reality.

He'd thought of the Talented as weapons – the only ones who could protect the weak from the horrors waiting patiently in the dark spaces for their chance. But the truth was so much worse. *They* were the weak. *They* were the problem.

If you got rid of all the Talented, you solved the problem.

'Then we have to go back to the Castle,' said Rue. She was awake and raring after they had filled her in. White had been afraid it would dispirit her. If anything, she was jiggling, impatient.

'No,' he said. 'No. It's too dangerous.'

'How else are we going to find them? We can't just roam around spotting Talented and then . . . what? Kill them?'

'Of course not,' he said. 'We'll leave that to the police.'

'They can't even slightly get away with murder right now, Jacob,' said Cho, impatient. 'They're just locking them up. We're not completely fascist here, you know.'

'Anyway, they have the right idea,' said Rue.

White swallowed a reply. They did have the right idea, and that was what galled him the most.

'They're cleaning up this end as best they can. But they can't stop it at the source, can they? That's up to us. And we have to do it before there's none of us left.'

White stared at his hands, trying to think. 'All right,' he said reluctantly. 'But what do we do once we get there? I remember how it is there, Rue. Do you think you could face one of those things and not die? Do we even know how to kill them? We have no idea how . . . how he managed to open the Castle. So how do we close it?'

Rue chewed on her lip for a moment. She needed to stop that. It did something to him that completely broke his concentration.

'I've been thinking about that a lot,' she said. 'It's a question of perspective.'

'Explain.'

'Well, when we go to the Castle, it's just like another Talent dream to us, right? We visit it with our minds. All your lessons, all the training you did with us, it was about controlling our minds. Controlling where we wanted to go, and then controlling what we did when we got there. You know. "Move forward." "Look around." "What do you see?"'

'Mind spying.'

'Yes. And I always thought of mind spying more like "awake dreaming". Well, you can take that control from awake dreaming into your sleep dreams, can't you? I've done it loads of times before.'

He stared at her. She was constantly, overwhelmingly, the most surprising person he'd ever met. Just when he thought he had a handle on her, she threw him again.

'You're talking about lucid dreaming,' he said.

'What the hell is that?' Cho was frowning.

'It's when you can control what happens in a dream,' said Rue. 'If you're having a nightmare, for example, and you manage to stop whatever it is chasing you. Or you turn it into a butterfly or something. Or you think, "I want to wake up now." And then you do.'

'Oh, *that*. Even I can do that. Well . . . I've only done it once or twice, maybe.'

'Well,' said Rue. 'That's what Talented do all the time.'

'Jack,' muttered Cho. 'No wonder you're all so weird.'

'That's how I pull people into my dreams, I think. I mean . . .' She glanced at White. 'That's how I pulled you in. I wanted to see you, so I made it happen. That's how all Talented works, isn't it? Maybe we just have more . . . lucid dreaming ability than everyone else. Our minds detach themselves, and they go exploring, and when we learn to control where we go and what we do, well – that's lucid dreaming, except we do it when we're awake.

'Well, why can't we lucid dream in the Castle? It's the same thing. Just because we're afraid of it, doesn't mean we can't control it. So when we're there, couldn't we just try to control what happens? Couldn't we think, "I want to close the Castle?"'

White shook his head. 'No. No. It doesn't seem possible. It can't be that easy. I don't think anyone has that power.'

'I think you do,' said Rue, quietly. 'You're the best in the world at it.'

But I don't know what I'm doing! he screamed in his head. *I can't save everyone! I can't do that!*

Rue reached out and touched his face. Cho looked away, uncomfortable.

'We work together,' she said firmly, as if she could read his mind. 'And we won't be alone. The more Talented we have there, the better. We'll be stronger.'

White looked into her eyes. Then he dropped his gaze. She seemed to reach inside him and he felt open, wide open.

'Who do you propose taking with us?' he said.

Rue leaned back.

'Some people we both know.'

She talked.

She really had thought it through. While he'd been busy tying himself up in knots over everything he'd failed at, over Wren, she'd come up with it all. He had no faith at all that any of it would work. Neither did she. But it was better than doing nothing. It was better to try than to hide away and hope someone else took care of it. It was courage. He could feel it leaking from her to him.

At some point, Livie wandered into the room. She and Cho left, and then came back with food. He couldn't remember the last time he'd been so hungry. Did hope bring appetite back? They thrashed arguments back and forth. They made lists.

It felt good. It felt insane, and ridiculous. It didn't feel real.

'Cho,' said White, when it was all laid out. His whole head felt heavy – they'd been at it for over two hours. 'We need you again.'

It was the right thing to say. She was like him – she hated feeling powerless. She wanted to *do*.

'Just as long as I don't have to go anywhere near that Hammond bitch,' she said.

White wanted to reach out and touch her somehow. Touch her shoulder, or lift the spike of hair she always had dangling in her eyes and tuck it back. But they had never been that way.

'Not this time,' he replied.

Cho took Livie's hand, grasping it tight. 'What do you need?'

* * *

341

It had taken two days to arrange everything.

In the meantime, the news got worse. Rue stopped looking it up. They all did. Greta seemed to be holding up her end for now – there were no visits from the police, despite the fact that she must know exactly where they all were.

Everything was in place for tonight.

It had gone too far to back out now. If this didn't work, if more people died, it was all on her. Rue felt sick, as if her fear were rotting inside her, poisoning her blood and her mind.

Livie's guest bathroom had a steam function. Rue filled the room with it until it choked her. She sat in it until her clothes stuck to her in moist folds, and then she stripped. She was hot. Her skin was hot. Her head was hot. But she still felt cold.

'Rue?' came a voice outside the room. 'Rue!'

White opened the door.

She looked up as the steam was sucked away, billowing past his lean figure.

He didn't say, *oh gods, sorry*, or even *Rue, you're totally naked*. He just stood there, looking at her. She liked that. Maybe he finally knew that she was his, and that he didn't need to apologise for it.

'The temperature alarm was going off,' he said. 'You've got it on too high.'

She just gazed up at him, sat on the floor with her knees hugged to her chest.

'I can't get warm,' she said.

'It's horrible in here.'

She didn't reply.

'Are you all right?'

The concern in his voice broke her. He was supposed to be cold and unfeeling. What was wrong with him? More to the point, what was wrong with *her*? This was a life she had in front of her, a living breathing person. You couldn't play around with that.

'White,' she said, her voice sharp and jagged. 'What are we doing? *What are we doing?*'

He crossed to her and crouched. He slid his arms around her, and then sat down awkwardly, folding himself around her hunched figure.

'We're no one,' she said against his chest. She could feel his heart beating. It was too meaty for her, that reminder of the blood that was pushed around his system in rhythmic pumps, the muscle and bone that caged it. She hated hearing his heart beat. What if it stopped?

'We're not no one,' he said into her hair.

'We are. We're just these stupid kids. Why would anyone listen to us? I wouldn't listen to us.'

'You wouldn't listen to anyone.'

Her laugh came out more like a sob.

'They're all coming,' he said, quietly.

'Because of you.'

'Because of what they believe in.'

'What's that?'

He was silent for a moment.

'I don't know,' he said. 'I just thought it sounded good.'

She kicked her shoulder into his. 'Idiot.'

She settled. She felt warmer already, against him.

'They're afraid,' White continued, his chin resting gently on the top of her head. 'It's happening to the Talented in Angle Tar, too. Then I come back and tell them there might be a way to stop it all.'

'We could get them all killed.'

'They'll die anyway, Rue. We will, too, if we don't close it.'

Her heart plummeted.

'What if we're wrong? What if it's all . . . one big dream? One mass illusion?'

'You know it's not. You just want it to be because that's easier than dealing with reality. But it's time for reality now.' He paused. 'You showed me that.'

She shifted and he spread his arms, releasing her. She pulled herself up and knelt before him, carefully. She saw his eyes move down to her chest.

'This is real,' she said.

White looked like a startled rabbit.

'Yes, it is,' he replied. His cool voice had a funny little catch to it. She knew that catch.

'Dream me, or real me?' said Rue.

He knew what she meant. 'Real you. A thousand times over.'

'Dream me was easier.'

'Dreams are always easier.'

Her heart was racing, hammering, joyful and terrified. Everything around them was darker somehow, shadowed out. There was only him, and where she was making this go.

'We have time,' she offered. 'Before you have to go and start fetching people.'

He was silent. His eyes moved back up to hers.

'Now?' he said. 'Like this?'

'When else?'

Her message hit home. His mouth thinned. Maybe tomorrow would be too late.

'Door lock,' he said.

The bathroom door slid closed and clicked.

Rue gasped. 'I didn't know they did that,' she said accusingly. 'No one ever told me.'

'Rue.'

She looked at him. He was leaning back against the wall, his legs still flanking her. Gods, he was lovely. So awkward and so magical and lovely.

There weren't any more words left. Slowly, delicately, her fingers trembling just once, she reached down and began to undo his belt.

CHAPTER 32

WORLD

RUE

'Come on,' said Cho quietly. 'Let's go in.'

'Give me a second.'

'The longer you leave it, the harder it's going to be.'

Rue crossed her arms. The sickness was back, roiling inside her, telling her that she did not know what she was doing. She was not a leader.

I can't do this.

'Hey,' said Cho, touching her hesitantly on the shoulder. 'I have some advice for you.'

'Go on, then.'

'Don't let them see your fear. If they think you're uncertain, they'll lose it. It'll all fall apart.'

'Great.'

'No, listen. You have to act a little cocky, a little bossy.

Basically, you know . . . just be yourself.'

Rue shot her a glance.

Cho held up her hands. 'The truth hurts, right?' she said with a shadow of a grin. 'But in this case it'll help you. Remember cocky, bossy you? The one who burst into my bedroom and demanded that I help her? The one who shouted at me in the safety hall? The difficult girl from old Angle Tar who cut her own path. Be her.'

Rue breathed out.

Easy. Pretend you're fearless and totally, utterly in the right. This is all going to work.

How do people do this?

'Come on,' said Cho, taking her arm and dragging her towards the social-room door. 'No more time for thinking.'

But the door opened before Cho could touch it, and Livie slipped out. A slice of humming noise slipped out with her before it slid closed again.

Livie looked shell-shocked. 'They just keep turning up out of thin air. Out of nothing he steps, holding someone's hand, pulling them out of nothing too behind him. He's been at it for hours. I think that's everyone now. He said it was. I hope so, because there's bloody loads of them in there.'

Rue had frozen on the word 'loads'. 'How many?' she said.

Livie opened the door. 'See for yourself.'

The noise rolled over her. Rue peeked inside the room.

'Oh *gods*,' she said in Angle Tarain.

White had been really quite busy.

He'd spent the last two days Jumping back and forth to Angle Tar, visiting every Talented he knew and asking them for their help. She'd expected him to persuade a handful at most; Lea, maybe Lufe, plus a couple of his students that she'd never met. It was an insane kind of request.

She had underestimated how frightened they all were.

'How many?' she said to Cho.

'Twenty-three.' Cho had a freakish ability with numbers.

They were clumped into little groups, talking. Some of them were as old as Fernie. She stopped, doubt flooding her mind. What would they think when they saw her?

A girl had peeled off from her cluster and was coming towards Rue at speed. It was Lea. In her wake trailed Lufe, Marches and Tulsent. She couldn't believe it. They were all here.

Lea stopped in front of her.

'Hi again,' she said.

'You . . . You came.'

'You said,' Lea replied, looking nervous. 'You said that you might need us. So I got everyone ready. We were waiting around for you to come back. Then Mussyer White shows up in Red House last night and he tells us everything.'

Mussyer White, thought Rue, fighting a grin.

'He says we're to come to World, and that he'll come back and get us, lead us in a Jump. I was fine,' Lea said proudly. 'But Marches threw up when he got here.'

'I did *not*,' protested Marches. 'I retired to the bathroom to acclimatise to the situation.'

'I heard you retching!'

They began to argue. Rue's gaze landed on Lufe. He gave her a small smile. He looked tired, and so much older than before.

'No one in Angle Tar knows how to handle what's going

348

on,' he said. 'I trust us more than I trust them. We've got to try, haven't we?'

'I missed you,' blurted Rue. She looked at Tulsent, who blushed and glanced at the far wall. He'd got taller since she'd been away. 'I missed you all, and I'm sorry I left.'

'Oh, shut up,' said Lea. 'All of that's past. What happens now?'

'Rue will explain,' said White. He had come up behind the group. His accent twanged in Angle Tarain. She'd almost forgotten how he used to sound.

'Not by myself, I won't,' she retorted.

He gave her a serious look. 'You will not be by yourself. Ever again.'

She saw Lea nudge Lufe.

Still as subtle as a hammer, she thought drily.

Her heart had swollen with them here. She already felt better.

'This is all I could find,' said White. 'There are more but they were not on campus.'

Rue scanned the crowd.

'What about Frith?' she said.

'Frith's still away,' Lea replied. 'No one's told us where, as usual. I don't think he's supposed to be back for weeks.'

Rue tried not to let her disappointment show. He wasn't Talented, but just him being here would have made her feel more courageous. But then, maybe it was better that it was only Talented here. He wouldn't have believed them about the Castle, and everything that was at stake.

'We should begin,' White said to her, quietly. 'We must explain everything, so there can be no misunderstanding. So they can make a choice.'

So they did.

It took a while, but between them both, they laid it all out. Then the questions began.

'You're saying that you can get us all to this Castle? All of us?' said someone. It was a woman Rue didn't recognise, heavy set.

Remember, Rue. Cocky. Certain.

'Yes,' she said. 'I've practised before with a group, and it's easy.'

She didn't mention that the group had consisted of just Cho, White and Livie. Perversely, it seemed to be easier if she was physically close to the people she was trying to pull in. They'd slept in Livie's ridiculously huge bedroom together a couple of nights ago, and she'd done it easily, taking them all to an empty room in the Castle for a few seconds before pushing them out again.

'It's a shared dream,' she went on, raising her voice. 'I pull you all into my dream of the Castle. Then we close it.'

'You still haven't told us *how* we close it.'

This was the troubling bit. Because neither of them had any idea.

'I think we must *make* it closed,' said White. There were puzzled looks. He glanced at Rue.

'Put your hand up if you've had a dream before where you could control what happened in it,' she said. 'What they call . . .' she fumbled for the best translation of the word, '. . . lucid dreaming.'

After a moment, every hand went up.

'I thought that was normal for us,' said Lea. 'A sign of the Talent.'

White nodded. 'It is a question on the Talented recruitment test in Angle Tar.'

'Now please put your hand up if you've been to the Castle,' Rue continued.

Far fewer. Less than half. But more than she'd dared to think of.

'And when you were in the Castle,' she said, 'could you control anything that happened?'

No hand went up.

Play your card.

'Well,' she said. 'I can. So that means you can, too.'

Or at least, I think I can.

Murmurings. The beast of the crowd shifted before her, its ears pricked.

'And we need you – all of you – to help us.'

'What about the things that have already got through? The ones that are here, right now, causing mayhem?' said a greying man at the front. He was Mussyer Joan, the Angle Tarain Minister for Transport ('Andrew, please,' he'd said, when White had introduced him).

'That is for the authorities to deal with,' said White. There was a snort of derision from the back. It sounded like Cho.

To anyone else, this whole plan would have sounded ridiculous. Not for the first time, Rue felt a kinship with her Talented. Not one of them looked like they didn't believe. They simply accepted. They'd been simply accepting the extraordinary their whole lives. Their minds were made for it.

In the end, no one backed out. There were some dubious looks, and there were many, many more questions. But no one backed out, not even the older Talented. Mussyer Joan was government, authority, and even he looked at White like it was natural that they follow him.

What was even more terrifying was that some of them were starting to look at her that way.

It had begun.

The entire group was lying or sitting as comfortably as they could on the floor. Their hands clutched two little pills each. The lights were set to dark. Livie had dragged every cushion, pillow, blanket and sheet from the house and had made a giant nest of sorts in the middle of the social room. Twenty-six people made an intimate kind of space. The sound of so much soft breathing was driving Rue to distraction.

'Lie down,' said White, next to her. They had reverted back to speaking in World between them. The people closest were giving them strange looks.

'I can't. It's not working.'

'You took enough sleepers to down a man twice your size. You can't have any more. You have to go first. We won't take ours until you're asleep and we can be as sure as possible that you're dreaming in the Castle. Try to relax.'

She laughed. Everything was starting to feel slow and thick, like the world was made of syrup, but somehow adrenaline was still keeping her upright. Everyone was trying not to watch, but she felt eyes on her, a constant stream of eyes. Waiting.

'Come here,' said White, finally. Rue looked at him. He held a hand out. 'Lie down on me.'

'You want to do this in front of everyone?'

'They already know.'

'You told them all?' said Rue, astonished.

White looked away. His posture was stiff and uncomfortable.

'No,' he said. 'They can see it. The way I look at you. The way I am around you. All right? I can tell they see it. They stare at the both of us.'

'Because we're the freaks standing up in front of them telling them we can save them all,' Rue muttered.

'Everyone is a freak here,' he said. His arm was still out. She turned reluctantly, leaning her back into it, and he pulled her against him.

Better already. His heat, the side of his body solid against hers. A soft sound in her ears as people murmured to each other.

Her heart slowed.

'White,' she said, her eyes closed. Her voice sounded thick.

'Yes,' he said above her.

'Good luck to us.'

She thought he said something back, but couldn't be sure.

She was gone to the dark now, where it was waiting, always waiting for the moment it could suck her in.

I want the Castle, she said firmly to the dark. *Give me the Castle.*

And then there was light.

She arrived in the corner of a dusty little room, bare of anything much.

Nothing felt different. You would never know the Castle was bleeding.

Don't look around. Don't listen out for them. It's all fine.
This will work.

There was no point in giving them time to take their sleeping pills. Time didn't work that way here. So skin furring, heart trembling, Rue clenched her fists, closed her eyes and pictured them. The whole room. Each Talented in that room, sitting or lying. They were all holding hands or touching somehow. That made it easier, too. A physical connection that they could latch onto. Maybe you always had to have a bit of the real in there. It helped to make the dreams more alive.

White's face came first into her mind. He would start it off. He'd get them there. His hand had been clutching Lea's when she'd gone to sleep. Lea would make sure Lufe came with her, and Lufe was holding tightly onto Marches, who'd had his arm protectively around Tulsent's angular shoulders. Tulsent had locked hands with someone he didn't know – a woman who had introduced herself as Hester and who worked as a clerk for an Angle Tarain government minister. It had touched Rue oddly to see it. Hester had someone else's hand. And so on around them all.

Rue thought about them all there, waiting. Their heads were tipped up to her. White was looking at her steadily. A snapshot her mind could work on. She coaxed it into life.

Surprisingly, Lea came first. No spangly noises or sounds of popping air – she just appeared. In a rush, five more followed. And then more. White was last.

They crowded into the small room, silent and shivering like frightened rabbits.

'What now?' said someone. 'Gods, I'd forgotten how awful it is here.'

'We have to find the opening first,' said White. He glanced at

Rue, and she nodded. She wondered briefly if the Ghost Girl was around somewhere, before cautiously opening the door of their little room and looking about. The hallway beyond was deserted.

'Come on,' she said. The stone outside was cold against her bare feet. Why did she always have bare feet here? Her toes left prints in the dust. She felt the group shuffling out behind her.

Lead, girl. They look to you.

Fernie's voice in her head. No-nonsense Fernie. Rue wished she were here instead. She'd have all the monsters rounded up in a trice, talking at them sternly until they repented of their horrible devouring ways.

Rue grinned, and felt a little better.

White came up beside her as they walked. She heard a few whispers between people behind them, the shuffling of their feet.

'Are you all right?' he said quietly.

'Fine. I just need to find the stupid opening. I don't even really know what I'm looking for.'

'You need to bring it to you, like in a lucid dream. Like we used to practise in lessons. Concentration, remember? Let everything else go.'

'Bloody teacher,' Rue muttered. She felt his hand touch hers, briefly.

They passed into a corridor with a low ceiling that hovered barely a foot above her. The carpet was a bright blue, the exact shade of cornflowers.

'I'm banging my head, here,' Marches said behind her. 'What is this crazy place?'

'The main corridor in my old village school,' said Rue.

Marches was silent.

How long they walked seemed immaterial. There was no time reference. Rue was waning. The effort of concentrating pressed on her, a hot weight. Where was it?

Bring it to me.

Bring me to the opening.

Give it me, damn you. Give it up.

She hesitated in front of a small wooden door. The bottom slats had been eaten away, rotting or gnawed by rats.

'Through here ... maybe,' she said. It drew her to it, but she wasn't sure why. The best thing to rely on here was instinct, and they could be wandering around for days. So she opened the door.

Beyond was a throne room.

'Jesus,' said someone, as the group crowded in behind her.

It was vast, the roof sky-high above them. A fluttering of wings drew her eyes up. Birds peeked from rafters, lit by shafts of sunlight from roof windows. Tapestries lined the walls, stretching on forever, dark and faded. Their end of the room was raised, stone steps leading up to a grim-looking throne made of black wood, with black jewels running in rows up its back and nail-studded armrests. The top of the throne curved over, as if shading the occupant from the glare of the sun or the drumming of rain.

'Emmon save us,' said Andrew, his face slack with wonder.

'Don't be invoking the dream god in a place like this,' Hester murmured. 'This is probably his castle, and all. Maybe that's even his throne.'

Rue felt the beauty of that idea tug at her. It was easy to believe in gods here. Easy to believe that dreams were better than anything the real could give you.

'There's a *feast*,' someone said, and a few people stepped forward. A long table ran the length of the entire room, longer than anything Rue had ever imagined before, stopping a few feet before the raised throne. Underneath it was a rough-looking black carpet. There were no chairs, which was odd, but that soon left her mind because the table itself was packed with food.

She moved closer.

There were bowls, long trestle dishes, serving platters; their surfaces winking with tiny black mosaic tiles. Each was loaded with fat pastry wraps, round balls in sticky-looking sauce, sliced wedges of terrine, plump fruit, browned meat legs, shredded flower salads.

'That stuff looks amazing,' said Marches.

'Don't touch it!'

They all looked around at White, who was still stood near the door. 'Don't,' he said. Rue saw then that her hand was half outstretched, fingers skirting close to a gleaming bunch of grapes. She hadn't even realised she'd begun to move.

'Why not?' Lufe replied.

'He's right,' said Rue, snatching her hand back. 'It's Castle food. We've no idea what it might do.'

'I haven't eaten since yesterday,' said a woman called, Rue thought, Mervaine.

'We need to keep going,' Rue replied. She moved back from the table.

Then two things happened at once. She saw Mervaine reach

357

for a leg of meat, picking the joint bone up in her fingers. Then someone gasped. It was the kind of gasp that froze you – the strangled, horrible grawping noise of pure shock.

'It's not a carpet,' said White, still by the door, his voice choked.

'What?'

'It's not a carpet. Get away from it, now!'

Lea gave a high, breathless scream.

The black carpet under the table was moving, growing. It began to disintegrate before Rue's eyes. For what felt like the longest time as it roiled towards her feet, she couldn't understand what she was seeing. Then it clicked.

Bugs.

Thousands and thousands of them. Some of them as big as her thumb, with shiny, fat carapaces. They scuttled, spilling outwards, their bodies rocking rapidly. Their backs moved, splitting open. A few took flight. Then more. But by that time, Rue was running back to the door.

Shouts and pounding. Someone smacked into her from behind and she almost fell. Everyone was running. Everyone was vanishing. The floor had turned black with curved insect backs. Something buzzed past her ear and she flinched, her hands coming up automatically. There was a doorway. Someone called her name. Something landed on her shoulder. She screamed and knocked it off without even looking around. There was one in her hair; it tugged at her scalp as it landed, tangling itself up. Another tried to land on her mouth, legs buffeting against her bottom lip. She smacked at it. It fell away.

Rue ran through the doorway and then turned. The door

had closed behind her. There was no black carpet here, and they hadn't followed. She flipped her head over and shook her hair violently, unable to bear combing through it with her fingers. Eventually, the bug fell out heavily onto the floor. Its back split, about to fly, fly right at her, down her throat.

No. No, I can't. I don't have shoes on.

You have to, Fernie's voice said in her head. It was the voice she used in emergencies – calm but tight, cracking like a whip. *It's trying to get inside you. Do it now!*

So she did.

She brought her heel down on its back and it cracked under her weight. Her throat convulsed and she thought for one moment that she might be sick, right then.

But she wasn't. She lifted her foot. It was definitely dead. She scraped her heel frantically against the floor, rubbing and rubbing.

It wasn't until after all this that she looked up and realised she was completely alone. She hurried back to the door she'd come through, hesitating before opening it.

What if those bugs are still behind it? They'll come arrowing through in a giant swarm and eat you alive.

Don't, Rue, DON'T.

But she had to find the others.

She put her ear to the door. It was quiet. She opened it up a crack.

The throne room had disappeared, and a corridor she'd never seen before stretched away from her. It was deserted.

She was alone.

Rue turned, despairing.

The room she'd run into was a handsomely sized parlour, decorated with elegant caramel-coloured furniture – the kind of room that wouldn't have looked out of place in a well-to-do Angle Tarain house. Except for one small difference.

This room had a giant hole in the floor.

Rue stared. If she had moved back from the doorway just a few more steps, she would have fallen into it. The carpet was torn into tufted strings around the edges, revealing stone slabs underneath that sloped into the murky darkness. The hole itself was bigger than her old bedroom in Red House, and impenetrably black.

The little dresser closest to her was full of pictures on springy little silver stands. Rue moved closer to look.

Every single picture was of Wren.

There were his silver eyes and his lithe body, and in this one he was laughing, and in that one he had a fathomless expression, his gaze far away. There were some more of a boy Rue didn't recognise, a softer-featured boy with sandy hair, whom she supposed must have been Wren before he went to World. And some of him as a chunky child, shorts and knee socks, his baby teeth on display in a grin.

This was it, wasn't it?

She looked around the room. This was the opening that Wren had made in the Castle. She wondered if it was a room from his past, a room he'd grown up in, perhaps. It had him all over it, as if he'd somehow left his life behind, imprinted on the walls.

She'd found it.

Her eyes slid back to the hole as she edged around the room. It was like a giant had punched his fist through the floor. If she jumped into it, where would she go? Would she find herself back in the real, in her own body?

Close it, Rue. Quickly, before anything else finds you.

How?

Your lucid dreaming. Make it closed. Force it closed.

The door she had come through was almost opposite her now. She knelt carefully, her knees inches from the sloping edge of the hole. She put her hands down, running the frayed carpet through her fingers. Maybe if she just imagined it whole?

She closed her eyes, hands on the ground, and pictured the room as it should be in her head. Normal. Quiet. The kind of room only used when company came round. She saw the carpet, unblemished. A rug on top, maybe, and a small table for laying tea and cakes on. People in chairs, talking and rustling. Someone pouring the tea.

But then the rug started to bow in the middle. The table wobbled and fell, plates and cups flying. The hole was sucking everything into it.

Start again. Imagine it without the hole. Normal and perfect and just a room.

She tried three more times. But every time the hole appeared in her mind.

Rue opened her eyes and gave a little shriek of frustration. She wasn't sure she could do this by herself. She had to find the others. But if she left this room, what were the chances she'd get back to it? It would shift on her again, she was sure of it. It seemed like the Castle was playing with them.

As she stood and turned back towards the door she had come through, there came an echoing clicking noise from the hole.

Rue glanced towards it.

Something was inside.

Her heart began to thrum in her chest. There was something inside the hole and it was coming for her. It could *smell* her.

'Rue!' said a voice.

Rue looked up, startled. A figure had come through the door and slammed it closed behind her.

It was Cho.

Oh gods. White is going to kill me.

'No. No! Why are you here? How are you here? I didn't mean to pull you here! You're not even supposed to be asleep!'

Cho had a cool, determined set to her mouth. 'You didn't think I was going to be a coward and stay behind, did you?'

Rue gaped. 'How . . .?'

'I took sleeping pills. I waited until everyone else was asleep, and then I took them, too. To be honest, I didn't think it would work without you consciously pulling me here. I guess you're more powerful than you thought –' Cho stopped, staring at the hole. 'What the jack is that?'

'Oh gods,' Rue whispered. 'You complete idiot.'

Cho's feet were so close to the edge. Rue tried to think through the panic that clawed at her, shredding her control to ribbons. She had to keep Cho close – Cho would never, ever get out of here without a Talented. She didn't know how. Which meant that Rue had to protect her from whatever was in that hole, because here, Cho had no weapons.

'I came to help, actually,' said Cho. She was trying for bold and irritated, but she was afraid. Her voice was thin and strange. 'I mean, I know I'm not Talented, but I can still help.

I've had lucid dreams before, haven't I? Where's White?'

'Cho,' said Rue, striving to sound calm. 'Listen to me. You have to leave the room now. I'll be right behind you.'

'There's a door behind *you*,' said Cho. 'Let's go out that way.'

Rue clenched her fists by her sides. There was the clicking again. It was louder.

'Cho, please,' she said. 'I can't leave this room, but you have to. Don't come in any further.'

'I'm not going back that way,' she said. 'Rue, I can't. There was . . .' She swallowed. 'There was this . . . *thing* in that room back there. I can't. I'll just come round to you.'

'Stop!' said Rue, holding both her hands up. 'I'm not joking! Stay where you are!'

But Cho had begun to move.

The clicking was louder. And suddenly, she seemed to hear it. She looked down towards the hole, her hair sliding against her chin.

'What is that?' she said.

'Please! I told you to go! I told you not to come in!'

Cho knew what was coming. She could feel it, finally, like Rue could – it weighed down on them, pressing them to the spot.

Run! Rue's mind screamed at her. She felt her legs twitch in response.

Not without Cho! she snapped back.

It was scrabbling up the hole. Cho was rooted to the spot, her mouth open.

And then Rue felt the last piece of doubt inside her snap in two, because all at once she knew she'd dreamed this before. Just like the nightmare she'd had about Wren, just like the life bomb attack she'd dreamed back in Angle Tar, she'd seen this already, weeks ago, before she'd ever even met Cho. How had the dream ended? How, how, *think*.

From the thick dark it came, a leg wider than her body, one, then two, as it heaved itself up the sides of the hole. It would eat Cho and then it would break Rue. It would break her and take over her body in the real and it would have a really good time. That was all it wanted. A really good time. Kill and eat. The real was so much better than the Castle. The Castle was a cage; a horrible, boring cage. It wanted out. They all did.

Cho was frozen in place as it clambered out, ten times, fifteen times her size, fat body suspended in the middle of a network of legs.

Rue didn't think, she just did. She threw her hands out and screamed with everything she had.

'STOP!'

The effect was alarming. The creature reared, then choked back as if it were being strangled from behind. A front leg passed within an inch of Cho's face.

Cho was breathing heavily, her cheeks streaked with panic tears.

'Cho,' said Rue urgently. She didn't dare lower her arms or take her eyes away from the creature's trembling body. 'Get over here.'

Cho moaned.

'Cho!' she snapped. 'Get your irritating behind over here right now. Move, move, move!'

Slowly, Cho inched along the wall. The creature seemed to follow her progress, but it didn't reach for her. Its legs shivered, bracing it against the sides of the hole. Rue felt her body

364

grow thick and trembling with the effort. This was leeching
something out of her. She didn't know what it was, but it was
probably important.

Oh well. Time enough to worry about that later.

'You can control them,' said Cho as she reached Rue, her
voice thin with hysteria. 'You can *control them*.'

It had always felt like no one could possibly have power
here. That the monsters had all the power. But it wasn't true,
was it? The Castle was hers as much as theirs. It was *her* dream.
It held *her* rooms, her history, her past and her future. All you
had to do was realise the power you had in your own mind.

The leg closest to them twitched. It was fighting her. It had
power, too.

'Not for long,' she whispered, her voice trembling. 'And
when I lose it, it's going to eat us.'

'Then let's fucking go!'

'I can't, Cho. This is the room. This . . . the hole . . . it's the
opening Wren made. We have to close it. We can't go anywhere.'

She felt Cho open the door behind them – a gust of freezing
air stirred her hair. 'Where's everyone else?' said Cho.

'I have no idea.'

'Shit. Shit. Okay. Don't worry.'

Rue felt the beginnings of hysterical laughter try to push
its way out of her.

'Don't . . . worry?' she said. She couldn't seem to talk
normally any more. It was all slowing, slowing. 'Look . . . at it.'

'I'm trying not to, actually! Okay. Stay there! I'll be right
back. I'll keep the door open! No. I can't leave you!'

'Go, you . . . idiot!'

'Okay, okay! I'm keeping the door open. I'll come right back. I'll find them!'

And then Cho was gone.

Rue closed her eyes. She felt like sinking to her knees. Sinking into sleep. It would be so easy to just let it all go. Not to have to feel any more, or try or think or care. No more anythings. It would be wonderful.

Yes, said Fernie's reasonable voice in her head. *But you'd be dead, Rue, my love. Don't you want to see the world, still? Did you think you'd seen it all already?*

Her heart flared, afire with curiosity. That was right.

Gods, what had she been thinking?

'I don't want to die, *actually*,' she spat. It felt good to copy Cho. It almost felt like she could be as brave as her, if she wanted. 'So you just stay there like a good little monster.' Her arms locked with renewed strength. The creature scrabbled on the ground, pinned.

Someone, Rue thought. But her thought was so weak and small. No one would hear her. No one would come. *White. Please. Come find me. Somehow.*

They were supposed to be here by now. They were supposed to be right here, right at the end of it all when she had nothing left to give. Because here it was.

But they weren't. She was alone.

So she kept going.

Just one more minute, she thought. Her whole body was sobbing. Her face was sopping with tears. *Just one more minute, and then I'll give up. But I can't give up until they're here.*

It was so long.

It was so, so long.

This was what heroes did, wasn't it? They hung on so that the day could be saved. But hanging on felt like dying, very slowly, and not in a heroic way at all.

The creature scrabbled. Rue realised she was lying on her stomach on the floor, arms outstretched. She had no idea when it had happened. She had no idea of anything any more. All she had, all she could be, was the word STOP. If she lost that word, it was over. Her mind formed the word in a thousand different ways, the letters made of stars, of shells, of those tiny colour beads in Dam's shop, of the scarves that Lea wore, draped artfully into STOP, and now it was leaves, and now it was graffiti across a building in neon pink letters ten feet high, and still she was dying.

It mattered. It all mattered. How could she have ever thought otherwise?

Then someone was skidding to her side and someone else was gripping her hands and pulling her up, and it was Lea, and Lea was covered in blood.

Then there were more piling into the room, the sudden sound of them an awful, beautiful cacophony in her shredded mind, like lemon juice on a cut.

A man was shouting something that sounded like orders.

'Rue,' said a breathless voice in her ear. 'They're here. You can let go. Jacob has it, Rue. He's got it pinned.'

But she didn't know how, because all she had become was STOP and there was nothing more to her than that.

'Cho, you're going back with her,' said a voice. His voice. Her White.

'No! I'm staying, I'm helping!'

Instead of getting angry, White's voice grew closer and softer.

'Cho, look at her. You're going back now, and you're going to look after her. You're going to make sure she's fine and alive until the rest of us get back. Do you understand? No one else is going to die. I will not let that happen.'

Else? Rue tried to say. *What do you mean? Who else? Tell me!* But she wasn't sure anything had come out.

'I can't.' Cho's voice broke. 'Not again. I can't just let you go away again.'

'I'm not going anywhere. Please, Cho. Please look after her.'

Cho groaned. Somehow, even through the fear in her voice, it still sounded comical. 'Jacob, *don't* tell me you're in love with her. You're such an idiot.'

'Just take her hand.'

Rue felt an arm slide around her back.

'Don't die, okay?' Cho, angry.

'I won't,' said White.

And then Rue felt a push. Soft at first, and then insistent. White was pushing her back to the real.

Darkness.

Then light. Painful light.

'Rue? Oh crap.'

Someone was hauling at her.

'Rue, say something!'

She coughed. Her mouth was on fire. Her head was acid concrete. Her body howled.

'Throat hurts,' she croaked.

'Yeah,' said Cho's voice, relieved. 'You threw up a lot.'

'In my sleep?'

'Yeah, it's pretty disgusting. It's a good thing he put you on your side.'

Rue's gaze fell on the clean white walls of Livie's social room.

'We left them all behind.'

'White made us leave, actually,' said Cho. 'Your fault.'

'Oh. Sorry for saving your life, then.'

'You probably will be.'

Rue sat up, using Cho's arms as support. Her head rolled, pounded.

'How do you feel?'

'Like I'd rather be unconscious.'

'Are you going to be sick again?'

Rue considered. 'No.'

'Do you want to go to a medical hall?'

'No! We can't just leave them! Ow.' Her whole body throbbed alarmingly.

'Okay, okay.'

'Cho,' said Rue. 'It isn't closed, is it?'

'They can do it. Jacob was there, loads of them were there. They can do it.'

'Were they all okay? Were they . . . was anyone missing?'

A pause. Then a reluctant, 'I don't know.'

Rue closed her eyes.

Cho was lying.

White was forced down to one knee.

Enough. Enough of this. His hatred became a knifepoint, a skewer. The creature shuddered. White stabbed with his mind.

Rue's face flashed before him and he stabbed again. Wren's face. He stabbed, and then twisted.

The creature screamed, a horrible keening sound.

And then it disappeared.

He heard gasps around the room. The group were all backed up, flat against the wall, ranged around the hole, watching with wide, stricken eyes. The legs had gone. The bulky body had gone. The hole was empty.

'Go,' said White, his eyes searching for the creature. It couldn't have died. Nothing was that easy. 'Close the hole.'

'Now, now, NOW!' Lufe shouted. The group scrambled. They each sat or crouched as close to the hole's edge as they dared. 'Link hands.'

Then Wren appeared. Out of thin air he stepped, feet away.

He turned his head towards the hole, and sniffed. His gleaming silver eyes moved back to White.

'Oh you,' he said, with a wicked grin. 'Now tell me you haven't missed me, and I'll call you a liar.'

White looked him up and down. He felt his control falter, just a little bit.

It was the monster that had killed Wren. It must be. But ... no. That one was out in the world now, wasn't it, in Wren's body? So it was a different one, trying on Wren's shape to toy with him. It wasn't Wren.

Wren was dead.

'You're not him,' he managed.

'No? Why not?'

'Whatever you're doing, it won't work.'

'Shall I tell you something only Wren would know?'

370

said the monster before him.

Don't look around. They can't help you.

They need you to help them.

'I'm not listening,' said White.

Wren's face twisted, a sudden whipcrack of temper. 'You don't have a choice. Because I'm here and you can't go anywhere. So you'll listen to me now, like you never listened to me before.'

'I listened.'

'You *pretended* to listen while you planned to steal my girlfriend and screw my life up.'

It was bait and he took it and he couldn't help it.

'I never stole your girlfriend, you paranoid idiot! We were friends! We were friends, and then you tried to kill me!'

'You betrayed me,' Wren shouted. His hurt and his pain were a physical weight on the room. 'After you, nothing went right any more. I came to World and all they did was use me. I tried to have a life, but it's all gone wrong. It's all gone so wrong.'

Wren's face was crumpled. White felt himself heave in response.

'This whole mess is your fault,' said Wren, throwing a hand out to the hole beside them. 'Did you know that?'

'No. No, it's not.'

'Do you even care? Do you even care that I'm dead?'

But White couldn't reply. Because it was too soon, and too much, and he knew it was his fault. He *knew* it.

'White!' Lufe called, his voice wavering with alarm. 'White, it's not real! It's not him! Jesus, wake up!'

He woke up.

Wren was inches away from him, a hand outstretched.

White scrambled back, snapping his mind back to focus.

'Stay away from me,' he said.

Wren jerked to a stop.

And changed into Rue.

'You're not her,' said White. He felt his anger spike. How dare it use her against him. That was what it wanted. To make him angry, careless, lose concentration so it could break free of his grip.

He could not let any more die.

His mind sharpened to a point once more and he pinned the creature with it. Rue cried out and sank to her knees. He felt himself shrivel, just a little.

It's not Rue.

She looked up at him. 'I'm sorry,' she whispered.

Behind White, the group swayed.

They had become one animal, shifting together, feeding off each other and pushing it all into the darkness before them. They were closing the hole.

He had to be the distraction. He had to give them time.

'I'm so sorry, White,' Rue said again, her liquid eyes turned up to his. 'I had sex with Wren. I loved him. I'm sorry. He was just so nice to me, when you weren't. He liked me back.'

He wanted to be sick. He wanted to scream at the horrible thing until his throat burned.

He didn't.

He had often dreamed of that face. Now it was his to touch. Now he had the right. He would hold onto that. Whatever it said, he would remember the way Rue had looked at him in the bathroom, in the *real*.

372

'You're not her,' he said simply. 'And I don't care what she did with Wren. That's over now.'

'Because he's dead,' Rue wept.

White flinched, but held.

Rue grunted, and turned into his mother.

She squatted, her bulbous frame wobbling wetly against the stone.

White felt his whole body flush with fury. It was trying to embarrass him. It was showing all his secrets. It knew how he guarded his secrets. How pitiful and crushed a little boy he was inside.

'I don't blame you for leaving, Jacob,' said his mother, kindly. 'I know you found it hard to be in the same room as me. I know you could barely look at me. You thought I was disgusting. It's okay. I understand that.'

I never thought you were disgusting, he wanted to say. *Never. You're my mother.*

But that wasn't the truth.

'I'm sorry,' he said. 'I did think you were disgusting, and I carry that guilt around all the time. I hated having to go into your room and see you lying there. I hated you a lot. I was never sure how to love you. I abandoned you because I'm a coward. Is that what you want to hear?' His voice was rising. 'I'm a coward! And now everyone knows! Bring them all out! Who are you going to be next? Cho? The girl I tried to kiss in school and who told everyone I was a rapist, you know, for a joke? Be Frith. No one knows what I did to him, yet, do they? Go on. I fucking *dare* you.'

He stared the monster down. 'I have nothing left to hide.'

His mother was looking at him, expressionless. For a moment he thought he'd beaten it. Whatever it brought out, he could deal with it. He'd imagined the worst and said it out loud. He'd taken its power away.

But then it stood up. Its hair grew long and dark, its nose thin. The body was willowy, now, wrapped in black. It pursed its lips and watched him.

White felt a freezing trickle of fear down his spine.

'No one really knows you quite like *you* do,' it said. And it smiled his smile, with his lips.

Was his face really that thin? Did he always have such a smackably aloof expression on it?

Did he really go through life like that?

His copy held its hands up. 'I'm not going to spill all your secrets, if that's what you're worried about.' It shrugged. 'I just want to talk.'

He tried to gather himself. Tried to pin it harder with his mind. But this time it didn't flinch, or cry.

'I want to talk about the times I sat in my bedroom, alone,' it said. 'Times when I couldn't look at the news feeds any more because they were making me sick. The shitty things people kept doing to each other turned my stomach. The people in charge were all the same, promising everyone everything until they got into power, and then doing whatever served them best. No one, *no one* gives a fuck about anyone else until they have to experience poverty, or illness, or injustice for themselves. Because the world is full of selfishness, and everyone is walking around half dead, just killing time until time kills them.

'I hated myself most of all, because I was one of them as

much as anyone. I wanted to *do* something about the things I felt, but I never did. All I've ever done is run away. Hide. Feel sorry for myself. I've always been alone, because I hate people, and I can't let them in because I think I'm better than everyone – of course I am, I'm different. I *think*, I *question*, I have a power that they don't have.

'But at the same time I know, I know I'm not better than anyone else. So I don't deserve anyone's attention. In fact, I despise people who like me, because that means they're weak. Only weak people like people like me.'

White felt himself slide. Like the hole had grown bigger and was beckoning him in. The other him was close. Very close now.

'Rue, she'll leave me,' it said, softly. 'Because it won't take long for her to realise that there's nothing inside worth having. I'm just a collection of weaknesses and hate. I've done nothing good in the world. But I could change things, if I would just have the courage. The people who change things have courage. They take extraordinary leaps. They have to make the hard choices because being good *is* hard. Being unselfish, and thinking of the good of the world, *is* hard. If it were easy, everyone would be doing it. It's meant to feel wrong. It's meant to feel like it'll break you in two if you do it. But you have to do it. This one thing that will give your life meaning. Let us in, and we'll change the world with you. You'll look back at this moment in time and wonder why you ever hesitated. Let me inside you, White.'

He felt something brush close to his forehead. It had stretched out a hand.

It was too late to say no.

Maybe it was easier to just stand there and let it happen.

Then Cho flashed in his mind. Scornful, fiery Cho, who knew her weaknesses and went ahead anyway, everything on display. She was the most courageous person he knew.

She'd be so disappointed with him right now.

With a horrible groan, White wrenched himself away. It was like trying to move in thick, cloying syrup. He fought and fought, pulling back until he thought his whole body would snap.

The other White reared up, startled.

For a moment, he thought he had it. Then he saw his copy's face twist, and the hands lunge forward. If it couldn't use him to get out of the Castle, it would eat.

He had no time to be afraid. He just lashed out. He punched with his fist and his mind, wild and unfocused but with so much fury he could choke on it. He hacked it all up and made it into a weapon and he punched.

The copy didn't even scream. It just staggered back, clawing at itself.

Then it melted into the floor. He watched it shrivel, folding inwards like burning paper, curling and furling until there was nothing left. He made sure there was nothing left, and when he was sure, he let go.

The room tilted. For a horrible moment, White thought he was going to faint; or maybe wake up and find himself back in the real. But then it faded, and he was left crouched on the floor next to the hole.

He had never, ever felt so utterly exhausted.

But it wasn't over yet.

He lifted his face to the group.

The hole was still there, but he could feel them pushing at it with their combined strength, willing it back to a smooth floor. He didn't want them to be here any longer than necessary. More monsters could come. It was the last thing he felt like doing, but he dragged himself to the group, and sat on the edge of the hole next to Lufe.

You've done enough! said a voice inside, angry. *Why the hell are you giving more?*

Because I can, he told it. *Because it's needed. So shut up.*

White hesitated. He'd never thought that touching could amplify their power like this. That had been Rue's idea again; always thinking differently to him. He reached out and took Lufe's unresisting hand, feeling the warm palm against his own.

The group flowed into him at once, pulsing and alive. It was like a hot shower, skinny dipping in a lake at midnight, shoving your burned finger into snow. He was part of the group now, and they were part of him. He could feel them. But he wasn't much of a he any more – he was a them.

It was wonderful. It was terrifying.

With White they were stronger. It took time, but not any time they could tell. There was none of that kind of time here. And together, they felt it when it happened.

Somehow, he'd thought that maybe the stone would grow out from the hole's frayed edges, carpet knitting itself back together before their eyes, but there was no pleasing logic to it. The hole was still there. And then it was not. It was as if there'd never been a hole in the first place. This was the new reality they had created, cancelling out the old one.

They could remake their realities as they saw fit. That was a Dreamer. And it didn't matter if the reality existed in only one place, like the Castle, or the inside of their heads. Real was as real as you let it be. You had to work to make the reality you wanted.

This was the lesson he had finally learned.

They woke.

There was no more group mind, now that they were back in the real. It was a strange sensation, like his hair had suddenly been shaved off. They were all supposed to be there, brushing against him.

Rue and Cho were waiting for them. Both had been crying. Rue smelled and looked awful. White didn't care. He doubted he looked any better. She was alive, and that was what mattered.

But others were not.

Five had died in the Castle, before they had got to the hole. Five he couldn't save.

Peater, Sam and Justin – three junior clerks White had taught last summer, young men who had grown up together and loved each other like brothers. They even worked for the same stockbroker company in Capital. Had. Had worked. One of them was married with a little baby. They had died together in the throne room.

Hester. She'd given him such grief in their first lesson. Prickly and bossy, and very naturally Talented. She never smiled. She'd smiled at him, once, when he'd told her how good she was. He hadn't even seen what had happened to her, but Lufe had found her in another room.

Marches.

Marches was dead. Lea had been with him when it happened.

White pressed his fingers hard to his eyes to stop himself from crying. Tears were no use right now. They were just no use at all.

In the real they looked peaceful. Each had blood that had trickled out of their noses and half dried onto their skin, but that was the only obvious mark of what had happened. He wasn't responsible for them. He knew that. He would go on knowing it in the dark hours when they came back for him, memory ghosts to add to his collection. They would help him remember pain.

In the here and now, their bodies had to be dealt with. It was a very practical thing, death. There was just no time to fall apart. The group Jumped each body back to Angle Tar. Lea insisted on helping to take Marches, but then dissolved into furious sobs when she touched his body. Lufe moved her gently out of the way and took him, Tulsent helping. Both looked completely broken.

They took all five bodies to Red House and laid them out next to the hearth. They placed the hand of one in the hand of the next, so they were together.

Andrew said he would take care of it. He would wake the right ministers, the right people. It would all be dealt with properly. There would be questions, but they would handle it. The others crowded to him like lost sheep. White was grateful. He had been playacting at leader too long, and he never, ever wanted to do it again.

'You can't stay,' Andrew said to him, firmly. They stood

apart from the rest. Rue had her arms around Lea, and they were talking together in jagged whispers. 'They're still looking for you.'

'I will not leave you all with this mess here,' White said. He would start taking on the responsibility of the choices he had made. No more running away.

'They'll lock you up, White. They think you did something to Frith and then bolted.'

White looked at him. 'I did.'

Andrew sighed. 'Then I don't think I can help you.'

White nodded. 'You have done more than enough. You risked your life for us.'

'For everyone,' said Andrew. 'I believe that. I didn't at first, I confess. But I saw . . . I saw things in that place I never even . . . but it's over now. Isn't it?' The last was said with an anxious tone.

It was too soon to be a cynic.

'It is over,' said White.

He caught Rue's eye from across the room.

She watched him. He watched her.

CHAPTER 33

ANGLE TAR

FRITH

'I brought you something.'

Frith laid the package down onto the kitchen table.

Fernie wrinkled her nose. 'Trout?'

'Fresh this morning. I caught them myself.'

'Well. Mebbe I'll make a pie, then.' Fernie looked up at him. 'You'll stay for dinner, course.'

'Of course.'

She had been writing painstakingly in a little leather-bound notebook. He'd never seen it before.

'It's my tricks,' she said, without looking up. 'All the bits of the craft I've picked up over the years.' She gave a little laugh. 'I 'ave to write it all down, my memory's awful.'

'That makes two of us,' Frith said, lightly.

He thought he'd disguised it.

But then she said, 'Something on your mind?'

Here we go, then.

Frith sat opposite her. 'I got another letter,' he said.

'They sending people to drag you back?'

'Something's happening to the Talented.'

Fernie looked up at him. But damn her, she didn't look surprised or even curious, even though it was clear she'd caught the serious tone in his voice.

She put her pen down and sat back.

'The letter is from the Spymaster. He doesn't really describe it very well,' Frith continued. 'He says there have been some incidents on campus. A suicide. Two attempted murders. Five more bodies found laid out in Red House, cause of death unknown. They're all Talented – the suicide, the would-be murderers, the other deaths. He's being pressured to do something about the rest of the Talented. Doing something, in this case, is rounding them up and putting them in what they charmingly call a "secure facility for their own protection".'

Fernie merely nodded. 'And you need to go back.'

'I need to go back.' The thought wrenched his guts. But it was time to face the wreckage of his old life. 'I need to go back and see if I still have a career.' He gave a little laugh.

'Will you be in trouble?'

'There will be questions. And I'll probably be put in charge of the task force to round the Talented up.'

'A loyalty test.'

She was sharp.

'Quite,' he replied. 'To prove I'm not on their side. To even prove I'm not the instigator of all this.'

'They can't think that.'

Frith sighed. 'They can, and they will. You have to know how it is there. They can barely acknowledge the Talent exists, never mind understand how it works. Some of them view Talented as akin to performing monkeys rather than people.'

Frith leaned forward.

He had to do this while he still had the courage.

'I want to take Jason back with me,' he said.

A yawning pit of silence.

He tried to fill it up. 'I can't protect him here. People will get sent after him. I won't be able to stop that. But at least in Capital I can keep him close.'

'All right,' said Fernie.

It burst out of him. 'What?'

Fernie shrugged. 'I ain't his keeper. He's a grown man, he can make his own decisions. Have you asked him?'

Frith struggled for control. 'Not yet.'

'He'll say yes.'

'Why do you think so?'

Fernie smiled.

She knows, said an anxious voice in his head.

What does she know? he snapped back. *There's nothing going on between Jason and me.*

Fernie was staring at the tabletop. 'Sounds like you've got all your memories back, then.'

'There are still gaps. But yes. Over the last few days, they've been coming back.'

'Feeling your old self again?'

He caught the barb in her voice.

'I honestly don't know,' he said. 'I don't remember how I felt before.'

'You're not the same, you know.'

'So you both keep telling me. But perhaps I am.'

'Oh-ho, you think so? There would have been a time, young man, when you wouldn't have even asked me about going back with Jason. You'd have just taken him.'

'I'm not sure I like your phrasing.'

Fernie laughed, a pleased smile on her face. 'Good.' She turned her face to the window, seemingly watching the sky.

Frith folded his arms, nettled. 'There's one memory I've recently reacquired that I'd like to discuss with you, if you don't mind.'

Her mouth thinned. 'Go on, then,' she said.

'It's more a collection of memories about a person. He called himself White.'

She was still watching the sky.

'I'm not sure, but I think he might be responsible for my memory loss,' Frith persisted. 'He's Talented. Shockingly Talented. And he has a very distinctive face.'

Fernie gave a tiny little sigh.

'I say that because when I started to remember him, he reminded me very strongly of someone else.'

Silence.

'Different hair, of course. And skin tone. But the eyes, and the face.' He watched Fernie, but she didn't turn her head. 'I wasn't the only reason you wanted Jason hidden away, was I?'

Silence.

'I thought I was confused,' he said. 'Perhaps I'd somehow

muddied the memory with Jason's face. But I can see now that I wasn't.'

Fernie was studying a wheeling flock of birds.

Frith leaned forward. He wanted to shake her. 'What the hell is going on? Why does Jason share features with White? Are they brothers?'

'Let it go.'

Frith shook his head, impatient. 'Fernie –'

Fernie shot him a look. 'Please. It don't matter. Just forget it.'

'Do you understand what you're saying?'

'I can't tell you, so you just won't know. Can't you be content with what you do know?'

Frith spread his hands, trying to make light. 'You're telling me to just not pursue the truth? How does one do that?'

Fernie slammed the table with the side of her hand.

Frith watched her in silence.

'Damn you and your truth,' she said. She didn't seem angry so much as upset.

'Look,' said Frith. 'I apologise. I'll let it go. All right?'

'Yes, but the trouble is you won't, see? It'll keep gnawing at you and you'll find some other way to it. Mebbe you'll even ask Jason, and then what am I to do? I've no choice.'

'I won't ask him about it, then.'

Fernie sighed. 'You're still a good liar, Frith, but you ain't fooling me over this. You're the type that needs to know. The worst part of it all is that I want to tell you.'

Frith watched her carefully.

'Just remember I said no,' Fernie said. 'Will you do that for me? 'Cos once you know, there's no going back.'

Good god, how bad can it be? thought Frith.

But he held his tongue, waiting for her to find a way in.

Fernie plaited her fingers together, running one thumb over the other. 'You don't know the real reason I decided to help you, not really. It weren't because you got to me – although you did. It was because I already knew that you and Jason end up together. That you're happy. That he's happy with you.'

Frith swallowed the impulse to laugh disbelievingly, or protest against her insinuation. She was scrutinising him as she spoke.

'When we met for the very first time,' she said, 'it was right here in this village. No, not when you were a kiddie. When *I* was. You recruited me. I looked up to you. I thought you were the prize horse, Frith, my dear. Then I left Angle Tar.

'The next time we saw each other, I was a bit older, and you were different. More . . . open. I didn't know what had happened to you, and I didn't ask. And then I met Jason. You brought him to our house a few times. Mine and White's house, I should say. 'Course, I didn't realise who Jason really was until much, much later.' She smiled at the memory. 'But this was when I loved you. You and me and White and Jason, we worked together for a while, as equals.

'Then we didn't meet again for some time. I had my life. I saw the world. Things changed. And a while later, I ended up alone, with a baby – my baby. White's baby boy. I just wanted to go back to a simpler life, see. I wanted to go back to a time where everything felt safe and clear.

'So I decided to leave my present, and I travelled back to the past. Took some doing, let me tell you, but I did it. And

386

the next time we met, down here in the village, I was older and had a son, but you were *younger*. I'd only ever known you as a man, a man I loved like a da'. To see you as this young thing, barely started out in life, it was confusing. And that was where it got hard for me. Because this bit was a part of your past you never told me about when I knew you as a man, so I had no idea what was coming next. I had no idea you were going to ruin my son's life. I didn't know you were capable of that. D'you see? It was the first time I saw your flaws. Even though you'd grow up to be the Frith I knew, I couldn't see past what you were right then.

'The problem is that I know you out of sequence, Frith. It's tricky, living back in the past, while knowing all the things I know. I met my own son before he was even born. That sort of thing can really addle you, if you let it. Best not to let it, really. I just try to focus on the here and now. That's all you can do without going mad.'

She subsided.

Frith rocked back on his chair. He managed to stop himself from laughing – just. 'What are you trying to say? You travel through time?'

'I just did it the once,' Fernie replied, patiently.

'I see.'

'You think I've lost my mind. S'all right, so did Jason when I first told 'im.'

'You told him all that?'

She fixed him with a stare. 'Course I did. You think I'd keep something like that from my own son?'

'You told him about his father?'

'I asked him if he wanted to know who it is. He said no. I didn't tell him that he ends up meeting White, but I think he knows. He's got an uncanny way with the future himself, that boy. I s'pose he got that from me. But I remember when I was younger, and we saw Jason with you, he did act odd around White. You're right – they got the same eyes, the same face shape. We made a joke of it at the time, but Jason took it a bit serious. You didn't think it was too funny, either, as I recall.'

'Stop. Stop. This is just a mess of . . . I'm trying, Fernie. I'm trying to understand.' Frith massaged his forehead. 'So what you're telling me is that you're Vela Rue.'

Fernie watched him.

'And that we first met when I recruited you not that long ago.'

'It's a lot longer to me. Decades and decades.'

'Okay. And that later, when you were an adult, you and White spent time with Jason and me. You met your own son when he was, what . . .? Older than you were at the time.'

She shrugged.

'And that . . .' Frith battled on. 'At some point after that, you went back to the past – this village in the past – to live out the rest of your life.'

She traced a knot in the tabletop with a finger.

He kept his annoyance in check. How could she believe such an insane version of her life? He tried to reason it out with her. 'What you're saying, it's just not possible. You're saying that you're Rue, but there's also the Rue *I* know, the younger Rue, out there in World right now. At the same time.'

'Seems like it, don't it?'

'But you were her mistress. You *lived* together. Do you expect me to believe that it's possible the same person from different times could just . . . do that?'

'I don't expect you to believe nothing. It just is. I can't tell you how it works.'

He couldn't help it. He laughed. 'This is . . . very confusing.'

'Just you try to see it from my way,' said Fernie. 'You'll lose your marbles. I don't bother keeping track any more. I used to. I had diff'rent timelines written down, diff'rent memories, so I could work out which bits of my life were happening at what points to the Rue you know. But it's too hard. And I learned to just let it be.

'All I can say is that everything that's happening right now – Rue runnin' off with you, and then to World; the Talented being possessed, and everything that happens after – it's already happened to me. I was the Rue living with my hedgewitch mistress, and then recruited by you. I was the Rue who went to Capital and met White. Ran away to World, lived with Wren. Tried to stop the Castle from being opened.

'But I've *also* been the Rue who was there when Wren and White opened the Castle, and then paid the price. The Rue, the one called the Ghost Girl, who went back through the Castle and recruited *you*. Who changed the past to stop her future.'

Frith felt his blood, his life, draining from him.

The Castle. The Ghost Girl.

How could she know about that?

Had he told her, under the truth drug? But that was impossible – he'd only known about it himself a couple of days ago, once his memories had started to return.

'I don't remember Ghost Girl Rue's life too good any more,'

Fernie mused. 'Funny thing about that – once you change the past, you forget the one you had before it. Reality heals itself and deletes your memories. I know I was her because I wrote it all down. I knew I'd forget, see. But I've only one past I remember properly now.

'It just all got too complicated. And all I wanted was for it to be over so I could be with White. So I could make a life. And we did, after we closed the Castle. We had a life.' She grinned. 'It was a good one.'

Frith tried to speak, but nothing came out.

Because, perhaps, a tiny part of him was beginning to believe her.

'Then, well . . . to tell you the truth, I missed home. Things changed. Angle Tar changed – for the better, I think.' She nodded to him. 'You helped in that, or rather you will. But I was alone by that point, and I'd just got so tired of all the adventuring. I'd seen all I wanted to see. And I thought and thought about it, and I kept coming back to this place, the way it'd been when I was a girl. It was the simplest place in the world. I understood it. I missed it. And I just wanted to bring my son up in it. That's all I wanted – to settle down and be forgot. I couldn't be forgot in the world we'd created. You'll see, in the future, what happens to the Talented. The best thing for everyone was if I just disappeared. So I did.'

She took a breath. He saw the tremble in her shoulders, and realised. This was hard for her.

'I found out how to come all the way back to the past,' she said. 'You can do it through the Castle. You can do most anything through the Castle. That's why it's such an attractive place. Such a dangerous place. I swore I'd never use the Castle again after that. D'you know, that was part of the problem? We weaken the walls when we're in the Castle – the Talented. After a while, it starts to bleed into reality. It makes it so much easier for them to get loose.'

He didn't need to ask what 'they' referred to. He remembered those things now. Oh yes.

'What . . . happened to White? Jason's father?' he said.

'That ain't your business.'

Frith was silent.

She caught his expression. 'I know,' she said, mildly. 'It's a lot to take in. Trust me, I know.'

'Why take on . . . *yourself* . . . as an apprentice? Wasn't that dangerous? Didn't she recognise you? Didn't anybody?'

Fernie tutted. 'I came back here before she was even born. It wasn't like she'd see me and think, *Ooh, that fat old witch looks just like I might in forty years' time*. People don't think like that. *You* know people. I was a bit nervy, though. I had my face reshaped a touch before I made the journey, and my eyes changed, just in case. They used to be brown.'

Frith studied her eyes. They were a sharp blue.

'I took on a new name and said I came from a village on the southern coast. Well, no one moves around a lot here, and no one was going to check that sort of thing. And time moved on, and you came and went, and then Oaker moved up North, changed his name to Jason. And I was all alone again. And then it got closer to the year, and then the month, and then the day where I remembered being picked for hedgewitching. And I just couldn't help it. I just wanted to see her, Frith. I promised myself I wouldn't meddle. I'd meddled with the future enough and I swore I'd never do it again. So I thought, *Well, I could take her on*. Try to steer her straight, you know? Make sure she was loved. Looked after. She never had no real parents to do that. I remember how troublesome I was as a kid. I s'pose I just wanted to look after myself.'

Her voice cut strangely, and Frith realised with a sharp stab of surprise that she was trying not to cry.

'It was selfish, I know,' she said, after a moment. 'I am a selfish creature. But I try not to be. That's why I'll let Jason go with you. I'll let it all go and be content with the life I've made.'

Her eyes were wet with tears, and she wiped them away crossly.

Frith took her hand and she looked at him in surprise. Her skin was warm, rough and calloused. 'This is, genuinely,' he said, 'the most fucked-up thing I've ever heard.'

She laughed a cracked little laugh.

'S'okay,' she said. 'Really. You'll understand, soon enough. It'll come to you. Just mind you don't go telling anyone else about it. I never did with Rue.'

'So you spent all that time around Rue and never told her the future?'

'It ain't fair to do that,' she said. 'Can you imagine, if you knew what was to happen to you? How would you act? Wouldn't you be wondering the whole time if it was really you doing it, or if you were just doing it 'cos you knew that was what you were *supposed* to do?'

'I understand the logic. But what if you knew something about the future that could change someone's life? How do you justify keeping what you know to yourself?'

'I broke that rule more than once,' said Fernie. 'And all I can say is, it's more trouble than it's worth.'

'So when I meet White again like you say I will, I'm just supposed to not tell him about Jason? I just don't tell him that he's standing in front of his own son? How do you make decisions for people's lives like that?'

'Because the alternative is cruel. Why *would* you tell him? What good would it do?'

'He should know his son.'

'Should he? Should you burden him with that? And then you'll have to tell him it's because he never gets to see his son in the future. And then, of course, he'll want to know *why* he never gets to see his son in the future. And even if you say nothing, he'll know. 'Cos the only things that would stop him from seeing his own son grow up are bad things. So now you've ruined his life, because he'll be obsessed with the bad thing that's going to happen. Every day it'll be on his mind – is *this* the day the bad thing happens? The question'll eat at him 'til there's nothing left. And he won't never again live in the present. What kind of a life is that that you've given him now?'

Frith was silent.

Fernie touched his arm gently. 'All you can do is live like you don't know what's going to happen. Like I said, it's the only way to stop yourself going mad. Take it from someone who's lived more than enough lives in more than enough times – live in the now, Frith, dear. You only get one life. Make it count. Every day, make it count.'

He didn't know what to think. Not yet.

'What now?' he said.

Fernie leaned back. 'Now you get yourself and Jason back up to Capital. Try and sort out the mess going on up there.'

'I don't suppose you'll tell me whether I succeed.'

Fernie snorted. 'I ain't telling you another blessed thing.'

The train rattled comfortably.

Frith watched the Bretagnine landscape slide away from him. The sky was brooding above it, spitting thin rain onto the windows, smearing his view. It was such an ordinary sight.

'What are you thinking about?' said Jason. He was sat opposite Frith in their carriage. From the outside, they were two gentlemen of business, making their way back to the city. But if anyone were inside the carriage with them, would they be able to sense the tension in the air?

'I'm sorry, I'm rather distracted,' said Frith, at last.

To say the least.

He had tried to understand Fernie's story. The kind of person it took to do the things she claimed to have done. The idea that when he'd come to recruit Rue all those months ago, he'd been sat there at that kitchen table looking at the same person in two bodies; that he had persuaded the old Rue to give up the young one to him. Though he now no longer believed he'd persuaded her at all. She'd let Rue go because she knew that was what had to happen. Because it had already happened to her.

So he'd met Rue three times in three different guises. First as a witch who frightened him with her power, then as a ghost bringing him the fear of the future, and finally as a young girl, full of promise. Everywhere he turned, his memories led to her, or to her son.

394

He was her creature.

He wanted to believe that it didn't make sense.

'She told you, didn't she?' said Jason, breaking into his thoughts.

Frith looked at him. His face was serious.

'Told me what?'

Jason looked away. 'About my father. All of that.'

Jesus.

'You believe her.'

'Of course,' said Jason. 'But don't feel bad about not believing. I didn't at first, until she showed me the Castle. Just once. It's easy to believe, once you've been there.'

Frith didn't want to agree with that. But it was. That place was still coming back to him, but he remembered how it was there. What it could do.

Jason's shoulders were stiff. His fingers curled around his mouth as he propped his chin up and stared out of the window. 'They will circle each other in time. The old Rue and the young Rue. A forever dance, a never-ending loop of a girl. I think it's incredible. But she's paid a lot for it. I can see why she doesn't want anything more to do with it.'

'It's an amazing power,' Frith said, watching Jason. 'I'm not sure you understand what people would do to get hold of it. Of her.'

'I think I understand very well.' Jason's black eyes flickered onto Frith's face and rested there, making his heart beat faster. 'And I think she must believe in the man that you are, that you become, to give you access to that power and trust that you won't try to use it.'

Frith willed himself to hold Jason's gaze. 'If there's one thing I've learned, it's that I can't make that woman do anything she doesn't want to do.'

Jason laughed. 'It's about time someone else shouldered that burden with me. She's impossible.' His expression changed, clouding.

'We'll come back to see her,' said Frith. 'As often as you like.'

He'd let himself open up there, just a little. The 'we' implied so much that he could not now take back.

Jason looked at him, and smiled.

Trust did not come easily to someone like him. He suspected the same of Jason. He couldn't know for certain what this thing was between them, but it seemed like it could be the beginning of something, if he took the risk. He'd never been one to gamble before.

Today he felt like rolling the dice.

CHAPTER 34

WORLD

GRETA

'What's this all about, Snearing?' said Haramanga. He was head of the Talented task force in the Hispanic Federation, and Greta had never liked him. Too much of a questioner. 'The Castle didn't call this meeting.'

'No,' Alasdair replied. 'I did.'

Mutterings around the table.

'We need to talk about what has been going on recently. And what we're all going to do about it.'

Snearing launched into his speech. Greta watched approvingly. She'd coached him on it, and he was doing well. There were barely any interruptions.

After that, it only took an hour or so to thrash it out between them all. Alasdair had been worried that they would need some convincing. Greta had known better. No one had the smallest clue how to handle the Talented so far, and no one had thought beyond trying to harness their powers – officially, at least. Unofficially, they would all have contingency plans in place in case of failure, and they probably resembled hers.

History would see her – see them all – differently. History would see the sacrifice they made – the few to save the many. That was the difference between good, courageous people and good but weak people. Good, courageous people made the hard choices so the weak people didn't have to. And often it was the good but weak people who turned on them for it afterwards.

But in the privacy of their own minds, some of those good, weak people would be breathing a sigh of relief.

In the end, they took a vote on it. A few of the softer members around the table needed the reassurance of a complete commitment, not one dissenting voice.

'Where's Angle Tar?' said Derger. 'Frith. We need his vote, don't we?'

'Unfortunately, Frith has become indisposed,' said Alasdair. 'And Angle Tar have not managed to produce a replacement in time for this meeting. So I think we can say that their vote doesn't count this time.'

'Oh, you must be heartbroken,' said Derger, blithely. 'But we need to make sure that this plan is nevertheless carried through in Angle Tar as well, Snearing.'

'Don't worry, I'm in contact with their – what do they call it? – Spymaster.'

A few small chuckles at the quaint translation.

'He has already agreed, in principle,' said Alasdair. 'He took our advice and began incarcerating the Talented as soon as the trouble started. He'll do as he's told.'

The table seemed satisfied.

As the chat around them grew, Greta briefly touched Alasdair's arm. 'You did well,' she said, in a soft voice.

Alasdair sighed. This whole thing had aged him. He was a good man, but he worried too much. 'It feels . . . drastic. Hasn't the problem stopped now?'

And, irritatingly, he needed a lot of reassurance.

'It's . . . lessened,' Greta said. 'Certainly. But we have to think forward. It will happen again. We have to make sure it doesn't. We'll keep a few Talented, to carry on investigations. There's one in particular I'm trying to recover. If we have him, we'll be years ahead of everyone else here. We're making strides with the genetics team – they think it's only a matter of time before we isolate a set of Talented genes. And then . . . replication, perhaps. The possibilities are quite revolutionary.' She paused. 'But in the wrong hands, Alasdair . . . in the hands of these Talented *children*, people who can't be controlled, can't be reasoned with . . . the risk is just too great. This recent situation was very nearly a disaster, a worldwide crisis. The threat must be eliminated.'

Alasdair massaged his brow. 'It makes sense.'

Greta squeezed his arm.

Saving the world, one problem at a time.

She pitied people who had no such meaning in their lives.

CHAPTER 35

ANGLE TAR

WHITE

'Someone to see you,' said a voice outside the door.

White looked up.

Another round with the Spymaster, perhaps. There had been a tacit agreement between them when they'd first met, a few days ago – the Spymaster knew no conventional prison could hold White, and that he had therefore chosen to stay where he was. And White knew that the situation could be much worse – he could be stuffed with drugs and tortured to keep him there. So he stayed by choice instead.

They weren't telling him what was going on in the outside world, and they would not let any of the Talented come to see him. He wondered what they were afraid of. That didn't stop Rue pulling him to her through her dreams at night, of course. But they didn't know that.

It was, all things considered, a decently comfortable room for a prison. He got the feeling he was in quarters reserved for the rich criminals.

The door to his room opened.

He looked up, and in walked the last person he had ever expected.

White buried his head in his hands.

'Well, you're obviously ecstatic to see me,' came the familiar voice.

The door shut, locking the both of them in together.

You don't have to be afraid of him any more, said a voice in his head. *You beat him. You won. You can leave any time you like.*

That only works if I want to spend the rest of my life on the run, he replied silently.

The voice had nothing for that.

'White,' Frith's voice commanded. 'Look at me, at least.'

There was nothing he could say or do to make it okay, so he raised his head.

Frith stood before him. It hadn't even been that long since they'd last seen each other, but something was off.

Trees, whispering in the wind. Frith's face contorted into a scream of rage.

Frith broke his gaze, and laughed. 'Are you surprised?'

'No.'

'No?'

'It's you, Frith. You always find a way.'

Frith seemed disturbed by that assessment. What was his game?

'Do you want to know what happened to me?' he said, after

a moment. He was practically shifting on the spot. Nerves? He appeared to notice what he was doing, and sat himself down.

White watched him. Frith seemed to take his silence as assent.

'You took half my memories with you,' he said. 'I've been living as a ghost these last few weeks.' He hesitated. 'I still don't . . . I still don't quite remember what you did. But you did something. Didn't you?'

'Do you want a confession from me?' said White.

Frith stared at the wall.

'No,' he said, at last. 'Because I want to make something very clear to you. I understand why you did what you did to me. But my memories are . . . fractured now, I suppose. I don't remember them the same way I used to. Things are different.'

White held up a hand. Things *were* different, and enough was enough. He was not the White who had danced around Frith, playing his games. He could not be that White any more.

'Frith,' he said. 'What are you going to do with me? Am I to be executed?'

'Jesus, White,' Frith breathed out, leaning back. Some of the stinging tension seemed to leave his shoulders. 'No.'

'Then what is my punishment?'

'You won't be punished.' His voice was quiet. He was still staring at the wall.

'Then what?'

'Then nothing, White. Then nothing. I'm not pressing charges against you. In fact, I've actively campaigned for your release.'

White felt the sickness begin, in the pit of his belly. It tried to climb up the sides of him, but he swallowed it back down.

402

He'd faced all his fear. He'd faced it and he'd beaten it. He needed to remember that from now on.

'Why would you do that?' he said. 'So you can find a way to revenge yourself on me in the future?'

Frith's face flushed. 'No, no. Listen to me. I'm trying to *apologise to you.*'

The words hung in the air, fat and strange.

'I'm sorry. For all of it.' Frith's voice became a flat, hard line. 'That's all I can give you.'

White was mute.

Frith sighed. 'Please say something.'

'I do not understand what you want.'

'I want to move on.'

White looked at him, finally unable to hide his surprise.

'I want to forget everything that ever happened between us,' said Frith, his voice just a little bit uneven. 'I wish that the memories you took from me hadn't come back. It was . . . bliss, for a short while. To be released from myself. I miss it. But I can't afford to mope around. Things have happened. Things I need your help with.'

He paused.

'You'll be released,' he said. 'Free to go back to World, if you like. Or anywhere else, far away from me. I won't follow. I won't chase. But if you want a life here . . .'

He left it dangling, tantalising.

'I've been told . . .' Frith stopped. 'That is, I believe you and I are going to be working together in the future. I do believe that, now. But it can only happen if you accept my apology. If you can accept me.'

403

The last was said blandly, but that couldn't disguise the wealth of fear behind it.

Frith was very afraid that he'd say no.

Rue looked up as the door opened. The room was comfortably abuzz. After their time together in the Castle, the Talented tended to hang around each other now, as if they couldn't quite let go. Andrew was often at Red House, even though he had no business being there, and his ministerial duties meant that he could only visit late in the evenings. Rue had taken her old room again, and Lea and Lufe had taken theirs, though she suspected they shared Lufe's.

As White came into Red House's study, the noise dipped for a moment, and then swung back up into the rafters with exclamations of surprise.

'They let you out?'

'White, you're back!'

'What happened?'

Rue remained where she was, curled up on a couch, watching. Her heart gave a lazy, delighted kick at the sight of him. White's eyes found her, but he glanced away again almost immediately.

Andrew was in front of him, looking serious. 'White?' he said. 'Have they dropped the charges?'

'They have,' White confirmed.

The room broke into whoops.

'I will be staying in Angle Tar,' he said, amidst the noise. The group quietened. 'I wish to stay here.'

'I'm very glad to hear that,' said Andrew. He clapped White on the shoulder, looked awkward for a moment, then stepped away.

'What happens next?' said Lufe.

White paused. 'The Castle is closed, and no more . . . creatures can escape,' he said. 'But I have made a promise that we will help to find any still remaining in our world.' He glanced again at Rue. 'Wren . . . the one that killed Wren, the one we saw in the medical hall, is dead. World confirmed it this morning. He was captured somewhere in Ifranland.'

'Thank gods,' said Lea.

Rue wasn't quite sure what she felt. A cold kind of happiness. Regret. Pain, like a needle in her.

'Yes. But we must find any others that managed to get out also.'

'Then we will.' It was Tulsent. He was hunched up by the fire. His voice was thin but determined. He wanted revenge for Marches – it was all over him.

Rue waited until the lull had ebbed and White had been congratulated enough. He approached, but she stood before he reached her. He seemed cautious.

'I saw Frith,' he said, in World. 'He came to visit.'

Rue examined his face curiously. Something had happened. 'Is he angry with you for leaving to find me?' she said.

'No.' White groped for words. 'No, he was the one who got me out of prison.'

'Oh good,' Rue replied, surprised. 'Well, apparently I'm pardoned too, so he *has* been busy.'

'Really?' Somehow White seemed more shocked by this than anything else. 'You can stay? *Frith* said you can stay?'

'I can stay.'

White seemed to sink into reverie, staring off into nothing. 'What is it?' said Rue.

'There are some complications. Andrew told me they've

created a new task force to systematically question any known Talented and assess their threat level to the general populace.' He paused. 'Frith is head of this task force.'

'But he's on our side.'

'Frith has never been on anyone's side but his own.'

Rue canted her head. 'One day,' she said, 'you're going to have to tell me what happened between you and Frith. Because something did.'

He swallowed. 'One day I will,' he said, quietly. 'For now, just know that I find it hard to trust him.'

'All right. But he's letting me stay. And you. What does that mean?'

'That he needs us for something. I think . . . I think he wants to fight World.'

'Fight?' said Rue, startled.

White lowered his voice. 'The task force directive came from World, handed to the Spymaster himself. They're rounding up the Talented all across World to do who knows what to them. Not just assessing them for potential threat – locking them away without cause. Maybe even executing them. Frith thinks the same thing will start happening here, unless we fight it.'

Rue felt her insides harden. 'Then we will,' she said. 'We have to prove the good we can do, not just the bad.'

White looked troubled. 'They'll never trust us, Rue. They're right not to. Look at what happened. Look at what we unleashed. The deaths we caused.'

'Look at the potential you have,' said a quiet voice behind White.

Frith was stood off to one side, his hands behind his back, watching them both. How had he come into the room without anyone

406

noticing? More to the point, how had he heard their conversation from over there? *He must have the ears of a bat*, thought Rue.

It had been a long time since she'd seen him last, and maybe her memory was faulty, but he seemed different. Unsettled. Which was odd, because Rue had never thought him the kind of person who could ever be unsettled.

'Rue is correct,' he said. 'We will prove what a force for good you can be.'

'Everyone hates us,' White said. He had a tense set to his mouth.

'Public opinion is rather embarrassingly easy to sway,' Frith replied mildly. Rue ran her eyes over him. She'd forgotten how lithe he was, like a dancer. A man you didn't notice until he let himself be noticed. For the first time, Rue began to really sense the power he had. You would not want to make an enemy of him.

She started to feel very glad that she was on his side.

'I will not let us be used,' White forced out. 'Never again.'

'Agreed.'

'If I sense manipulation in any way, we disappear.'

'As you have already proved you can.'

Rue watched them both. This seemed to be White's battle. She would not interfere.

Frith cleared his throat. 'What I said to you earlier still stands. I wish to put the past behind us. If you think you can do the same, then we can begin. There is a lot of work to be done, and I would rather have you – all of you –' he swept his hand out to the room, 'at my side. Please. Please think about it.'

He turned, and began to walk away.

White opened his mouth, hesitated.

'I am thinking about it,' he said, finally.

Frith stopped, and turned on the spot. He seemed happy, and relieved.

'Thank you,' he said, simply.

Then Frith swivelled to Rue and gave her the strangest look she'd ever had in her life. He seemed as if he were searching for something.

'It's good to have you back, Rue,' he said, at last. 'I look forward to working together.'

'So do I,' Rue replied, a little taken aback.

He smiled, bowed and walked off. They watched him close the door to the study quietly behind him.

'That was a funny look,' said Rue, musingly.

'He's a funny man,' White replied, and then sighed. 'What have I done?'

'The right thing.'

He glanced at her. 'Do you really believe that?'

Rue gave him her firmest look. 'I do. We have to work together. It's the only way.'

White ran his hands over his face. The plait of his hair swayed as he sank onto a chair. Rue sat beside him, and they looked out across the room together, at their Talented. Their friends.

'What about Cho?' said Rue, after a moment.

'She left me a letter. Cho's not coming here.'

Rue felt her whole body heave with disappointment. But how could she have ever thought otherwise? Cho was not this place. This place was not Cho.

'But she can't stay in World, with Greta after her,' she said as gently as she could. He was ever painfully aware what he had done to his sister.

'No. They've gone to China – her and Livie. They left only a day or two after we did. It seems there are hackers everywhere – they have friends over there, helping them out.' He paused. 'They'll be all right, she thinks. She sounded excited about it, if I'm honest. She blotted half her words on the paper.'

'They have Life in China,' said Rue, beginning to understand.

'Apparently what they have is much more sophisticated than Life. She could barely contain her glee.'

Rue smiled. It sounded sort of perfect for Cho. But she would miss her.

'We could visit them, right?' she said.

'I've never been to China.' He looked a little defeated.

Rue scoffed. 'White. We've both done things you never even knew were possible in the last few weeks. How's a piddly little problem like that going to stand in your way?'

He looked at her strangely. The group murmured and laughed around them. Gaslight flickered up the walls.

'What?' said Rue, unnerved.

'I need you,' said White simply.

Her breath caught.

'Me too,' she said. 'You make everything better. You make everything more alive.'

She reached out and took his hand. His fingers curled around hers. But still there was something in him that held back.

'Aren't you afraid?' he said, at last.

'Of what?'

'Of not knowing what will happen between us?'

Rue shrugged.

'Let's find out,' she said.

EPILOGUE

ANGLE TAR

RUE

The meadow is still today, as if waiting for something to happen.

Old Stumpy juts into the sky, alone. The young of the village are in morning lessons – he won't see action until dusk. The grass stirs in the autumn breeze and the trees whisper to themselves. They like gossip as much as the villagers.

Near the forest line, the air pops gently, and a woman steps out of nothing. The breeze hits her, stirring her short hair, which floats above her ears in a wispy cut that will cause comment amongst the women later on. Her eyes are a piercing blue and she hugs a sling to her chest protectively. The baby inside it niggles and she hushes it, gently jiggling the underside of the sling until it quiets.

At her feet is a travelling bag, stuffed to the seams. She bends down and hoists it onto her shoulder.

She should stand and look at it all. She should suck down the air, the smell, those particular things that spark her memory. But there will be time enough for that later on. For now, she's exhausted, and the baby will need feeding soon.

She sets off walking until she arrives at the square. It's a decent mid-morning crowd and she catches some stares as she stalks past. She did her best before coming but her clothes are just a little off, her hair too weird.

It isn't until she passes the bakery and the smell catches her that she feels herself swell as if she might burst. She's close to crying, and that won't do. It's been so long since she's been here. Years and years to her, even though to the village she isn't even born yet.

She makes her way into The Four Cocks and straight up to the barman. His name is Pendrew, Pendrew John. But she shouldn't know that, so she gives him the smile of a stranger.

'All right, Dam?' says John, with the easy manner of a Tregenna man and the curious eye of a local. 'Can I help you?'

'I'd like a room, please,' she says. 'For a couple of nights, mebbe, until I can find something more permanent.' The accent comes back to her easily.

'Wanting to stay, is it? Werl, there ain't much around at the moment, but I should ask at Beads in the morning, the shop along the square a bit. The Dam there, she'll know more 'n me.'

'Thank you.'

John eyes her baby. 'Alone, is it?'

'Yeh.' She watches him file that away for future gossip.

'How do you call yourself, then?'

She hesitates for just a fraction. This is the moment she could choose differently, if she wanted.

But she doesn't.

She can't.

'Penhallow,' she says. 'But no Dams or nothing for me, thanks. You can just call me Fernie.'

'And what do you do, then?'

'I'm a hedgewitch.'

John's face changes. Perhaps she sees a little bit of suspicion, a little bit of respect unfurl there.

'Ah, right,' he says. 'Welcome to the village, then, Fernie.'

Rue smiles.